PRAISE FOR THE WORKS OF JILL BARNETT

"A ray of summer sunshine...."
— *Publishers Weekly — STARRED REVIEW*

"Barnett has a wicked way with a one-liner and she makes the romance sizzle."
— *Detroit Free Press*

"A charming romance from the Queen of Love and Laughter."
— *Romantic Times*

"Powerfully poignant and memorable.... An unprecedented six stars!"
— *Affaire de Coeur*

To Pat, reader extraordinaire,

MY SOMETHING WONDERFUL

My sincerest thanks for your help. The book is better because of you.

JILL BARNETT

Best,
Jill Barnett

MY SOMETHING WONDERFUL
Copyright © 2017 by Jill Barnett All rights reserved.

ISBN-10: 0-9831804-6-6
ISBN-13: 978-0-9831804-6-3

Cover design by Dar Albert
Interior formatting by Author E.M.S.

This is a work of fiction. All characters and events portrayed in this novel are a product of the author's imagination or are used fictitiously.

No part of this book may be reproduced in any form or by any electronic or mechanical means, including information storage and retrieval systems, without written permission from the author, except for the use of brief quotations in a book review.

Published in the United States of America.

To those wonderful readers of mine who waited so long for another historical romance, I'm back in the saddle. Let's enjoy the ride.

Sisters of Scotland Series

by Jill Barnett

At a time when kings fought for the right to rule, some won, some lost, and the women who loved them paid the price....

Book One
My Something Wonderful
Glenna's story
August 2017

Book Two
Caitrin's story
Spring 2018

Book Three
Innes' story
Early 2019

ALSO BY JILL BARNETT

Bewitching
Dreaming
Wonderful
Wild
Wicked
Imagine
Carried Away
Just A Kiss Away
The Heart's Haven
Sentimental Journey
The Days of Summer
Bridge To Happiness
A Knight in Tarnished Armor
Saving Grace
Fool Me Once Anthology 1
Daniel and the Angel
Eleanor's Hero

MY SOMETHING WONDERFUL

BOOK ONE

SCOTLAND

PROLOGUE

A woman's screams pierced the air, echoing high in the silent canopy of ancient trees. Dawn was on the cusp of the horizon, light barely beginning to turn the edges of the eastern sky the color of larkspur. Morning mist on the damp ground was still and opaque and hid the wild wolves prowling toward a fringe of thickets in the small glade, where a large striped tent flew the pennant of the royal house of Scotland, and two guardsmen, faithful knights handpicked for their duty, stood watch to protect their lord's lady.

Inside, a frightened handmaiden tried to comfort her breeding mistress with wintergreen leaves to soothe her bitten lips and a wet cloth on her sweaty brow, but her hands shook as the midwife bent down near the foot of the bed, her hand on a knife at her belt, ready to cut the babes from their mother. The labor had been long and the poor young queen was exhausted, her belly huge—the biggest the midwife said she had ever seen.

Though royal blood ran in the queen's veins, her womb was like every other woman's; it twisted and contorted with excruciating childbed pains the men of the church claimed were a woman's punishment, Eve's legacy for leading Adam astray.

The handmaiden pressed a cloth to the queen's brow. Surely her beloved mistress did nothing to deserve this. Could God truly be this horribly cruel?

In her delirium, the queen had first called for and then cursed her beloved husband for giving her not one child to bear but two. He was in the valley below the Forest of Glengarran, on a wide plain thundering with warriors and their battlecries as the grass beneath their mounts turned red with spilt blood. There he met and fought the men who had betrayed him, and the enemies who would destroy his kingdom and steal his bloodright to rule the land.

Inside the tent, the queen's urge to push was overpowering and came in hard, fast waves of pain that wracked her sapped and bulging body. She screamed again and bore down until her whole body shook, desperate to expel the babies, then she collapsed on the bed. "Take them." Her voice was weak and waning. "The pain is too much. Take the babes… I cannot do this…"

The midwife pulled the knife from her belt, and the handmaiden panicked and held up her hand. "Nay! Stop! Wait." She was crying when she lifted up her limp and sweaty mistress from the bed. "Bear down, milady. You can do this. Please. Bear down!"

And the babes came, the first girl born as peaceful and quiet as the dawn, the other born red-faced and squalling loudly, her small fists in the air as she came into such an ominous and bloodthirsty world. The pale, weak queen looked down at her babes and in a waning but tender voice named the firstborn Glenna and the other Caitrin, the beginnings of joy in her expression, then she frowned and moaned weakly, "Holy Mary Mother of God…. The pain is here again." She looked at the midwife, panic in her expression, then her eyes rolled back in her head and blood gushed like a river from between her quivering legs. In a matter of moments the life bled out of her and she was gone.

The pair of women stood silent over the bed, where death had come in a mere blink of an eye and the air felt strangely empty. The two infants lay in their dead mother's arms, one still crying and the other quiet and sweet, unaware of what had happened. The handmaiden made the sign of the cross and knelt down, rosary beads hanging from her chain belt clenched in her hand as she fixed solely on her need to pray for her mistress.

Curiously, the midwife stared at the dead woman's belly. "God's teeth! Her belly is moving..."

The maid did not respond and was still kneeling on the floor, chanting her prayer with her head resting on the edge of the bed.

"There's another child!" the midwife shouted. "Get up! Get up off of the ground and help me, lass! If you need to pray over those beads of yours, pray for this last bairn." She cut the last infant, another girl, from the woman's belly and wiped the mucus from her small, blue face, before she held babe up and shook her. Then she spotted the child's withered foot. She looked down at the infant and said sadly, "Better if she does not breathe, when her life would be so ill-fated and filled with nothing but unhappiness. No man would ever have her."

And the baby cried out.

The handmaiden who had loved her mistress became angry and took the poor wee child from the bitter midwife before her wicked prophesies spoken over such a small and innocent babe would curse the child. The babe had the palest fringes of silver hair, like the queen's, whose hair had caught and shone in both the sun and moonlight.

She cleaned the child and wrapped her in swaddling to hide her feet. Under the wrapping, she slipped a sprig of mistletoe for healing and luck, and some wintergreen to keep her safe. Cradling her in her arms, rocking, she stared down into the perfect face of an angel. "She is beautiful, like her mother. You are wrong, old woman. That she lives is the true miracle. This child is the strongest. God does not curse her; God watches her." The handmaiden faced the midwife and made the sign of the cross.

"Before the Lord, I say she will be called Innes, and she lives for no mere man."

The earl of Sutherland rode into the woods, his charger's hooves quiet on the damp earth. In the valley behind him, the battle still raged onward, but inside the stillness of the thick woods, the lack of sound was strange and portentous, not peaceful. He had lived most of his life as a warrior, so he sat straighter in his saddle, an action that was instinctive; silence usually meant an ambush or death. The air was heavy and moist, and felt slow with no ringing echo of sword clanging against sword, no screams of men and horses, the sounds that had been all around him for the past hours.

The moment he came into the clearing, he judged the news was not good. Blood and death was a scent all too familiar to his senses. He dismounted heavily, his sword hilt clanking against his chainmail. The battle had taken its toll on his body, weapons had nicked his mail and his leg muscles felt heavy as granite.

The queen's guards, valued knights to both her and the king, walked toward him. Sir Hume Gordon nodded toward the tent. "The queen is dead, my lord." His voice was rough with emotion, and the other knight, Sir Balin of Dundee, made the sign of the cross.

Whatever Sutherland thought and felt at the news he concealed, a skill acquired and honed from years of dealing with enemies and traitors. He said nothing as he strode to the tent, threw back the flap, and entered. The queen lay on the bed, covered with a velvet blanket the color of sapphires, her eyes closed, and her face carried the unmistakable chalk of death.

He turned to Jonat, the queen's devoted young maid, whom too many men had coveted but with her ties to the queen, none had yet won. She had hair the color of the flames of a bonfire, braided and pulled back from her high and regal brow. 'Twas a shame that with her mistress' death the maid would not live to see another sunrise.

Her arms were filled with the two infants, one crying fitfully, tiny pink hands knotted and flailing in the air, and she pulled the babe a little tighter to her chest.

"Where's the midwife?" he asked looking around him.

"Gone, my lord. She ran off not long after the last babe was born."

The midwife was no fool. She must have known she, too, would be silenced. He could smell the steely odor of blood and jerked back the blanket covering the queen. Her belly was butchered. "The midwife did this?"

"There was another babe, and the queen was already dead. To save the child, she cut it from her womb." Jonat stepped back with the infants, away from him, and to his utter dismay he saw a third child in a wicker pannier on the ground.

He stared at the infant and groaned with disbelief. "There are three?"

"Aye, my lord. All daughters."

He had first thought the other child she spoke of was the second babe in her arms. Now what? His liege's carefully thought out plan made provisions for two babes. "Hand me the infants, and you bring the other." She placed the babes in his arms, and the squalling one stopped crying, which made him pause. Her face was red and heated, wrinkled like an apple dried in the sun, but he saw she was a true Canmore, crowned with a thick crop of her father's black hair and considering all the bawling noise she made, perhaps she had his temper as well. The other looked exactly like the caterwauler, same dark hair, but she was calmly asleep, her fist in her pink mouth.

His orders had been clear: he'd ridden away from the battlefield, left his sovereign, friend, and overlord, the man he'd sworn on his honor to protect, in order to execute the royal plan and make certain the queen and newborn babes would be safe.

He glanced from the children to the queen's body and realized he did not want to stay inside the tent any longer, so he carried the infants outside with the maid Jonat at his heels. "Your time to serve has come," he said to the two knights, who gathered their mounts and joined him. To Jonat he said, "I need the birth order. Which is the eldest?"

"She is the quiet one, my lord, wrapped in the crimson coverlet the queen stitched herself with black rooks and borders of white roses and golden braid. My lady named her Glenna, my lord." Jonat pointed to the sleeping babe draped in soft, silken cloth the color of rubies and cradled in his left arm.

"Gordon," he said to the largest knight, who mounted and took the firstborn child from him. "Godspeed." Sir Hume had his orders and was to ride west, to a place far away from the machinations of men of power, and where the child called Glenna would be raised in secret, protected and innocent. Sutherland watched him ride away.

Immediately the babe in Sutherland's arms—the Canmore she-warrior—began to cry again. Face flaming, she clenched her fists, and some mad part of him wondered if she realized what was happening.

"She is called Caitrin, the second born," Jonat told him.

Sutherland looked down at her and touched her chin with a finger. She stopped crying, looking up at him with moist eyes as dark as a night sky. Her fine coverlet was like that of her elder sister's, made of silken velvet in the deepest purple with a circle of red roses stitched around a graceful, long-necked white swan wearing a golden collar.

Sir Balin moved his mount forward, but Sutherland held up his free hand, unable to pull his gaze away from the infant in his arms. "Wait. You, maid. Give Sir Balin the last babe."

Jonat took the pale-haired bairn from the wicker basket, swaddled in sackcloth and handed her to Sir Balin, saying, "She is the youngest and is called Innes." The knight tucked the infant into his doublet and pulled his heavy fur lined cloak around to protect her from the cold bits of ice that had just begun to fall.

"You have your orders. God be with you," Sutherland said briskly, and Sir Balin of Dundee rode off toward the east with the babe called Innes. After he disappeared through the stand of birchwood and rowan, Sutherland turned, knowing he still had to take care of silencing the queen's maid.

Jonat looked at him for a long moment. Her gaze went to his hand on his sword hilt, and she shook her head, fear making her skin paler, her hands in front of her as she backed away. "Nay, do not, my lord. I pray... My lady warned me, before, but I did not believe her death would also bring on my own. Please. I beg for mercy."

Sutherland took a step, and she turned and ran across the clearing like a frightened doe. Her brown velvet coat caught on the thickets and she pulled at it, crying hysterically, until it tore off the shoulders of her gown, jeweled pins flying, and sobbing, she stumbled into the darkness of the forest trees. The sky high above grew black and ominous, and a white veil of snow began to fall.

The moment he took off after the handmaiden, the babe in his arms began to squall again, so he pulled the infant under his coat, shielding her from the freezing weather. But he stopped at the edge of the clearing when he heard the sound of snarling wolves in the depths of the woods beyond. Lovely Jonat stood little chance of survival. Could be the wolves had her scent now. To chase and catch her, he must leave the babe alone in the clearing, where she would be prime bait.

The wolves and weather made his decision for him. He needed to burn the tent and the queen's body with it. Nothing could be left behind. Babe still in his arms, he built a pyre over the queen's body, with the tent and its meager belongings, and he torched it, standing by his mount while the flames burned hot enough to melt the falling snow, which made the fire sizzle and snap.

The child still cried. "Quiet now, little one," he said, unable to believe what he was going to do. He was sworn by his name to the child's father, and on his honor he would do whatever he needed to keep the infant safe.

Her squalls changed to whimpers, pitiful and somehow tied to a weak part of him he had thought was lost, a sweetness he had ever only felt for his younger brother, who had died in the late fall. He held the child closer.

When there was nothing recognizable left in the blackened remains, Sutherland knelt with a quick prayer for his lord's lady, before he mounted and rode off toward his lands in the north, newborn babe once again squalling in his arms. He viciously cursed to the Heavens over his chosen fealty, while in his mind he planned the fable he would spread about her birth.

The island sat like a sleeping camel on the Western horizon, surrounded by a great, roiling winter sea the color of blue granite. The wind was icy, cold and could be brutal along the coast, but the snow had stopped hours before, when he had hired a wet nurse to serve the needs of the infant tucked deeply inside his cloak.

Sir Hume Gordon was coming home, home to his two young sons, the youngest born while he was away, home to a future that was peaceful. No more calls to war. The only duty left him was to protect the child of his liege lord, his king, a man he had known since before William was crowned king, before the king had fallen in love with the angelic daughter of a great Northern overlord and the worst plague of treachery and war ignited the land.

He turned to the wet nurse and said, "We will cross the Firth, then it is only a half day's ride."

"We should stop soon. To feed your daughter, sir. She will be hungry."

His daughter.

"There will be time before the ship sails," he told her.

And the lie began.

Nothing comes fairer to light than what's been long hidden.

— *Scottish Proverb*

ONE

The Western Isles

Under the glare of an extreme sun, Glenna Gordon ran across the island moors toward the brutal cliffs of the coast, her wild black hair as free as the seabirds wheeling in the cloudless blue sky beyond. A great brown beastie of a dog the size of a pony loped by her side, leaving only to romp and bark at the queeping plovers flushed out from the heath. Even in summer, such overly hot weather was rare; its warmth and intensity had burned away whatever morning dew spotted the wild pansies on the heath, and the barbaric heat of the previous day had turned clusters of weeds dry enough to crack beneath her feet.

During this time of year, only a few hours of darkness befell the island and the night before had been short, the air still as stone, and warm. And so the promise of another eternal summer day, one of scorched air and sweaty skin, sent her half a day's walk to the coast. Down into the cove below the cliffs, the air was cool. Land ended there and the great wide sea began, and went on and outward to the very edges of the world.

Clusters of black and white puffins bobbed on the water beyond the surf, and seals lay in brown lumps upon the coastal rocks, barking and squalling at nothing but the air and sea. Her dog raced ahead of her through the shallow water, so she pulled off her wooden shoes, tossed them on a rock, and chased after him along the golden crescent of damp sand, where blue-green saltwater foamed and the tide pulled at her bare ankles.

"Fergus! Fetch!" Glenna called to the hound, and walking out toward deeper water, she threw a rope of knobby kelp. He barked and dove at it, his head popping up out of the water, kelp rope between his grinning teeth. She laughed at him before a wave knocked her under and she came up spitting saltwater and searching for her footing.

A piece of bleached wood drifted past on swell. She tossed it high in the air for him. The two of them played with the stick for a long time, stopping to paddle together in the calmer sea between waves, until they both were cool and breathing hard. She trudged through the water with the strong tide pulling at her clothes, before stopping in the sand to pull up her tunic and tighten the rope drawstring on her sodden peasant trouse.

On the northern edge of the cove, the huge granite rocks were warm from the bright sunshine, and she climbed atop a flat one without a seal stretched out on it, and lay back, hand over her eyes. A nearby seal barked, but didn't deign to move when Fergus jumped up next to her, circling twice before he hunkered down for a nap, shaggy wet chin resting on his enormous paws. Soon she drifted off.

What woke her she could not say, but Fergus' head shot up with her and he growled lowly. A horse and rider came around the far southern end the cove, where there was a small, less rocky trail from the far cliffs down to the sea.

"Come, Fergus! Quickly! Down!" Glenna rolled over and went down behind the rock, climbing back and around so she was hidden between the seals.

Who was this man?

She and her brothers lived on the midwestern edges of the

island, far, far from the only village to the east. Even the Norse on the northernmost tip of the island stayed clear, so beaten and gaunt was the terrain here. There was no value to the land or what little grew on it; they lived in complete isolation, which her brothers claimed was what their battle-weary father had wanted, to be hidden at the end of land where no one would call him to war or had a reason to come within even a half day's ride.

She had no weapon. Her belt with its knife lay next to her bed in the cottage. A fool's mistake. Slowly she eased up between a group of seals to keep her eye on the stranger, then quickly shoved Fergus' head down when he decided to follow her lead.

"Stay down," she whispered to him, and he whimpered and put his snout on his paws, clearly unhappy with her.

As the man rode closer along the edge of the water, she could easily see his rank as a noble warrior dressed for protection in a padded jack gambeson of leather and mail covered his legs. He rode with no troop of men, and she glanced up at the cliffs to see if there were others above, but there was no one. She looked back at him. A shield emblazoned with a rampant golden lion on an azure field hung down from his pommel and soon the sun caught the glint of his sword and she spotted several large stones the size of crabapples inlaid along the scabbard strapped to his hips. His wealth was evident; his horse was one of the finest animals she had ever seen, head high, perfect arch of the neck, black mane and tail flowing. And she watched, somewhat lost in the beauty of the two them; the horse and man cut an exquisitely handsome figure through the wet sand, sea spraying up behind them and turning into rainbows in the glare of bright sunshine.

He dismounted, tossing the reins over his saddle and stood at the edge of the water, looking out to the sea, his hands resting on his narrow hips, and she wondered what he was thinking and why he was in this singular and lonely place. Within moments he had unbuckled his sword and tossed it in the sand, pulled off his boots, jack, mail and linen, until he stood there beautifully and quite wondrously naked, a golden image walking into the water, almost like some Norse idol come to life; the man was pure gold from the thick head of hair ending at his wide shoulders to every inch of skin she could see. For just the barest of moments, the sun caught and glinted off a gold cross he wore on a chain around his neck and she smiled—perhaps he was her gift from God.

He dove under a wave that would have taken her down, his head coming up behind the swell like one of the seals and he swam across the water, riding in on the waves and swimming back out again, his arms making powerful strokes that seemed to cut easily through the pull of the sea.

Glenna eyed the horse, then the man, who was swimming even farther out to the larger swells beyond. She leaned against the rock with one hand as she slipped on her wooden shoes one at a time. "Bare-assed fool," she muttered. "To go frolicking in the sea while that fine, fine animal stands there…sorely abandoned." She sighed, as did someone who had little choice in what they were about to do, and made her way over to the lovely horse, Fergus trailing behind her as she began to speak to the black in a low and melodic voice.

The animal's ears went up and twitched, but she easily took the reins, stroking his head. "There…there, my sweet and lovely thing." She began to hum softly and saw trust soften his eyes.

She slowly led the horse in a half-circle so the beast stood in front of the man's clothes, hiding her from his view, before she pulled the lion shield from the saddle; it dropped heavily into the sand, then she lifted the solid sword and its scabbard from the sand with both hands and a grunt, and hooked it over the pommel, quickly flinging his lighter clothing, leather gambeson, and lastly his weighty mail onto the horse.

"God's blood! You, there! Stand back from that horse!" Sir Golden Himself was swimming back toward shore.

'Twas a shame, really, about the golden cross. She was certain it would fetch a good penny.

"Get away, I say! That horse will trample you before he will let you touch him! Back away, you!" A wave washed over him and he came up from behind it, standing in the water, his wet skin gleaming jewel-like in the bright sunshine, his hair slicked back and his face red and angry as he strode waist-deep through the strong pull of the tide.

Poor fool, she thought. He was not moving quite swiftly enough. She gripped the horse, her foot in the stirrup, and mounted, leaning over to stroke the black's arched neck. "You won't hurt me, sweet lad. Will you?" Reins in her hands, she looked back at the man, so huge and trying to power his way to shore through seawater, ebb tide, and the next waves.

"What are you doing?" He bellowed so loudly his voice echoed in the cliff caverns and birds flew into the sky.

Glenna wheeled the horse around. "Me, good sir? Why, I'm stealing your lovely sword—nice jewels—" she patted the scabbard meaningfully, "also your clothes," she added, as the black sidestepped in the sea foam that curled on the sand and around his hooves. "Fret not, for I will leave you your most precious jewels," she said pointedly. "And your shield to protect them."

"Get off that horse!"

"This horse? I think not. But I thank you for him!" She gave the poor man a final wave and took off down the beach on that powerful black beast with his hooves pounding in the hard wet sand, riding like the wind away from the golden fool, Fergus loping along behind, and her sweet, wicked laughter echoing back in the warm air.

Some half a day's distance away from the cove, solidly built into the downside of a grassy slope, was a stone cottage with a sod roof that blended in with the terrain, and inside the main room stood a long wooden trestle table with a scarred top. The open shutters on the window alcoves let in air and plenty of light from a lingering sun still shining past evening.

Glenna pushed the sword across the trestle table toward her eldest brother, Alastair, who was closely studying the scabbard jewels, while her younger brother, Elgin, rummaged through the man's belongings.

"These are emeralds and rubies," Alastair said to her, testing the hilt and holding up the great sword." And the largest stone in the center is a sapphire, which would be considered rare at half its size." He stood and moved across the small room, swinging the sword at imaginary opponents. For a time, their father had begun to train Al in the arts of war, but for Sir Hume Gordon, whose wife had died just after he came home from war, death came suddenly and had robbed her eldest brother of any dreams of fostering toward knighthood.

"Look here." Elgin said. "Manna from Heaven." He set five plump bags of sterling on the table, a silver meat knife with a gold filigree handle circled with rubies and a matching rare, two-pronged fork. There was a small handwritten parchment book with tooled leather covers tied together with silk braid in azure blue and gold, a wine chalice with an ebony inlay and a stem shaped into a rampant golden lion, a signet ring again with the lion, and a rolled sheaf of papers marked with an important looking wax seal.

Only Alastair could read and write, and he often shook his head many times as he tried to decipher some document or letter, so Glenna thought he could not actually comprehend all the words he tried to read. But he had been only ten and two when their father died, and Elgin was barely nine, and she but four.

Alone they had buried their father, and for as long as she could remember life had been just the three of them.

Alastair picked up the papers and screwed up his face as he concentrated. It was a long time before he looked up. "These papers are assurance for safe passage."

"His passage was not safe with Glenna." Elgin laughed.

"Not when you turn your back for barely a moment," Alastair added.

"What about these clothes?" she asked, unrolling and laying out the heavily-padded, leather gambeson. "Can we sell them?"

"I cannot believe you took the poor man's clothes," Alastair said, trying to look serious but she could see he was having trouble. Her brothers could never scold her or even stay angry with her for long.

"Twas not the first time," Glenna said easily. "And these clothes are anything but poor." She took a roasted capon leg from a platter in front of them and bit into it, chewing as she added, "He left them beside his poor horse. Seems only proper that someone should relieve him of them, particularly when he seemed to care not a whit for any of it."

Alastair shook his head. "Glenna… Glenna…What am I to do with you?"

"Did not Hercules say to the waggoner, 'the gods help those who help themselves?'" She shrugged, picking clean a small bone. "I merely consider myself an apt student of Hercules—I helped myself. In truth, I doubted we could sell his shield, so I chose to leave it behind. The fool is lucky to have it."

"Not when the man's shield is what identifies him." Elgin couldn't seem to stop laughing; he had always been the cheeriest of them. "Can you see him? Bare-assed as the day he was born, making his way home with naught but a shield, one that tells the world exactly who he is."

"Ah…but from what wee, wee bit I saw," Glenna said

pointedly. "The man didn't have much to cover. His shield was more than large enough. Were I to really think on it, I believe his gold ring could do the trick." She tossed the bone away.

Her brothers laughed out loud and she tried not to smile at her lie, but when Elgin, with tears of laughter in his eyes, snorted like a pig she lost her composure and giggled, the image of Sir Golden Himself with nothing but his emblazoned shield to hide behind was more humorous than even she could pretend to ignore. "You should have seen him, plodding through the water to catch me—truly, the man was a knight on a lost crusade."

Elgin slipped on the gambeson, which hung off his shoulders, down over his hands, and the leather hem drooped near his knees. He trudged slowly around the room like a jester mocking the knight in the water in a sing-song voice, "Bring back my horse! Bring back my horse! You cursed thief!" He stopped suddenly and straightened, one hand in the air. "Know, lass, you must ransom my clothes, for I shall pay a fortune—five bags of silver and all my worldly possessions—to protect my poor ballocks—"

"Poor wee ballocks," Glenna cut in.

"I stand corrected," Elgin said, pausing before he flung his arms out to his sides. "To protect my poor *wee* ballocks from the hot sun burning them to the color of embers if I am forced to walk bare-assed over the countryside."

For the next few minutes they made jests about the man, and then Alastair stood and stretched. "I should feed the horses."

"Sit," Glenna said, pulling an apple from a bowl and slipping it into her pocket. "I will go. I want to check on the black." Her dog was standing at the door, tail wagging, tongue hanging out of his big mouth. "Nay Fergus. Stay." He whimpered and lay back down by the hearth, nose on his paws. She walked outside and paused.

To the west, the sun was finally beginning to trail down the sky, and the distant horizon was turning deep violet and gold.

The narrow path she followed snaked over a hillock and down to where stables, like the stone cottage, were built into the slope and a wide wooden pen adjacent to the byre contained all the horses when they weren't feeding or in their stalls.

Their father had bred and raised horses and sold them far away on the mainland, until the day he was thrown from a frightened gray in the paddock and killed. Her brothers Alastair and Elgin continued to raise both prime Gordon horseflesh and Glenna. So she grew up around horses, beasts ten times her size, yet she held no fear of them. Her gift: there was no horse yet she could not sweet talk and ride.

Glenna opened the gate to the outside paddock and crossed to draw water from the stable well, pouring it into the wooden water troughs, before she refilled the feed, waving the flies away from her face. She spoke to each of the animals as she searched the stalls for the hayfork, then turned quickly when she felt someone watching her.

From the last stall, the dark doe eyes of the black watched her. He whinnied and shook his regal head as she moved closer. "You are a great beauty," she said quietly, stroking him as she pulled out the apple and let him nibble it from her palm.

"Look how gently you eat from my hand. You are no wild one, sweetness." And she ran her hand along his coat. The curry brushes hung from hooks on the wall, so she took one and stepped inside the stall. "You are too fine a beast for a fool of a man," she told him easily, brushing his glossy coat and humming. Soon words came from her mouth like honey, her voice lilting in the stable as she sang:

> There once was a golden knight,
> Who could not foresee his plight.
> Across the heath-covered moors he rode,
> Gallant, brave and so very bold,

> Down he went to the sweet sea cove.
> Abandoning his horse, in the water he dove,
> The water was so very cool,
> But the man was a fool…

Humming, she rounded the horse, brushing his coat, and the man came out of the shadows more swiftly than a snake striking, taking her from behind by twisting her hair around his fist. His bare arm pinned her hard against his warm, damp skin. He released her hair and leaned close to her ear. "Now who is the fool?" he hissed angrily and slowly pressed the prongs of a hayfork deeper into her neck.

TWO

He had the thieving witch right where he wanted her. But angry as he was, he forced himself to remember she was the reason he was there. She began to scream and bite and kick, so he set the fork aside, shifted his grip on her and ripped the sleeve from her tunic. Were he less angry, the panic in her eyes would have stopped him, and he might have eased her mind. Clearly she thought he intended to ravish her. But he was in a foul mood, walking naked for too long in the hot sun, so he let her think the worst. She needed to be frightened and to understand who was in power after that escapade in the cove. He gagged her with the torn sleeve, grabbed the hayfork again, and with her squalling under his arm, he carried her outside.

Halfway back to the cottage he pulled her head back and checked the gag. She wiggled and kicked, but was still pinned to his side, and he swatted her for good measure as well as vengeance. But she retaliated by pinching him blue and viciously twisting his skin. "God's legs, woman," he muttered and shook off her hand, then he struggled, tossing her this way and that like a sack of turnips until her arms were pinned at her sides and she was safely pinned back under his arm.

The element of surprise was in his favor. He crossed over the rolling hill and was soon outside the cottage, with her still fighting him. In one swift motion he kicked in the cottage door, standing in the open doorway, the woman now clamped to his chest and the hayfork against her pale throat. He was angry as hell and naked as the day he was born — he and his 'poor wee ballocks.'

"Do not move if you value her life," he warned the two young men who were frozen in their seats. The dog rose up from the hearth, growling and baring his long teeth. "Hold back the hound." He pointed the hayfork toward the dog, and the girl cried out behind gag and tried to fight him. He tightened his arm around her.

"Fergus! Down!" One of the men said, and the dog obeyed, but stayed with ears perked and eyes sharp.

"Where is Sir Hume Gordon?"

There was a heartbeat of uncanny silence and the man who had called off the hound darted his gaze to the girl, who was still as a rock.

Lyall waited, before he said in a calm, deadly voice, "You move your hand under the table again and you will be dead and bound for hell before you can think to move again."

"Our father is dead," the other one said quickly. "I am Elgin Gordon. He is Alastair, the eldest. You are holding our sister, Glenna.

"I know well who she is. She is the reason I've come to the godforsaken ends of the earth. I am Baron Montrose of Rossie, the king's vassal, here to provide protection and safe passage for her. And she is no more your sister than I am."

He heard her gasp, but did not look away. The flicker in the elder Gordon's expression and the slight fall of his shoulders told Lyall all he needed to know. Alastair Gordon knew exactly who she was. "You may cease with your lie," Lyall told him. "I've come by order of the king."

Glenna was still as a rock.

"What lie? Alastair? Surely Glenna is our sister," Elgin said, looking back and forth between them.

"Montrose speaks the truth," Alastair told his brother, then ran a hand through his hair and shook his head dejectedly, looking at Glenna with worry in his eyes. "I beg you let her go, my lord."

"First, hand me my sword." Lyall leaned the hayfork against the wall but did not release his hold on it.

Alastair stood and reached for the scabbard.

"Wait!" Elgin grabbed his arm.

"He will not harm her." Alastair handed Lyall the weapon and turned back to his brother. "God's eyes, El, give the *Baron* Montrose his clothes."

The emphasis Alastair Gordon made on the word baron was obvious to all. Lyall watched Elgin shed the leather jack so quickly it was almost comical.

The younger brother gathered the rest of Lyall's stolen clothing and dropped them at his feet before backing away two steps. "Now you will let her go, my lord," Elgin said protectively, trying to stand taller. Still, he would only come to Lyall's shoulder.

Lyall released her and she scrambled away, but did not seek her 'brothers.' She backed away from them all, looking unsure and frightened, like a wounded and cornered animal. He chose not to feel anything for her. Any wounds to her mind and heart made by the truth were not his problem. She would have found out she was no Gordon at some point.

He dressed quickly and moved to the table. After a day of walking too many uncomfortable miles across the moors and through the bracken, the sun burning his skin and briars piercing his bare feet, he was in no mood for talk. He was starved, so he downed a half-full mug of ale, refilled it from a ewer, and helped himself to the meat and bread. When his belly was close to full, he turned, watching her as he sopped his last morsel of bread in the ale. She said nothing. Her eyes occasionally followed his motion, though her expression stayed stubbornly blank. Only once did he see her composure crack—she had angrily pushed her brothers away, then turned her back on them when they tried to talk to her.

Those two nitwits had so brainlessly included her in their thievery band, especially horse-thievery, which was punished by hanging. Would that have not made a great and welcoming tale for all and sundry, particularly for the returning king when he once again set foot on Scots' soil? 'Greetings, Sire, your eldest daughter was hanged by the neck for stealing horses, among other things.'

Their plunder was on every thick shelf and cranny in the room, stacks, sacks and large chests, all filled with what could only be the results of their thievery, much of what he could see was organized by type of item: the quivers and arrows in one corner, next to assorted daggers and knives, maces and swords, though none of the weapons as fine as his.

Hanging from the walls were copperware and leather-bound clusters of iron torches and candle holders, door and cabinet hinges, door locks, iron baskets and fire tongs, branding rods, pots and pans and kettle stands. Two long brass horns, a lute, drums, mouth organs and a harpsichord leaned against wall near the interior doors. Leather goods, shoes and boots, bolts of woolen cloth, bags, satchels and small wooden chests with sturdy locks stood in a precise line on wall shelves, beside a whole row of locked spice boxes that looked as though they were plucked right from a village fair display. He had caught the scents of cardamom and nutmeg the moment he'd first stepped into the room. Beneath those spice tins were salt barrels, sacks of peppercorns, and heavy jugs of vinegar, along with burlap sacks bulging with apples, and turnips, onions and other root vegetables.

The back rooms of the stable had been much the same, with neat rows of saddles and bridles, barrels of oil and bags of feed. As a lad he remembered walking across the castle courtyard to the kitchens, where the cook and the kitchen lackeys had, by order of his own mother, neatly arranged all the foodstuffs, wines, ale barrels, and salted meats in regimented lines along the shelves and in the cellars. He suspected Glenna with her woman's mind knew the exact placement of every single stolen item.

He poured another mug of ale and said, "You should pack your belongings, lass. We leave in the morning."

"Where?"

"The order is from the king."

"What king?" she laughed.

"William of Scotland."

"Ah…the exiled king who lives in England with his close friend Henry. He is not my king. Has he stepped a foot on Scottish soil in my lifetime? Nay, he has not."

"Glenna," Alastair Gordon said with a warning.

The look she gave him would have melted ice. She faced Lyall. "I have not agreed to go with you."

"The choice is not yours," Lyall told her. "The king has so ordered it."

She stepped closer, hands on her hips, her head high. "And why should I obey a king who has not been in the land for years, and who I have never seen or known? This king of yours is nothing but a fable to me."

"Glenna!" Alastair said.

She spun toward Gordon, walking over to stand but a foot away. "Do not speak to me like the older brother you feigned to be. You lied to me. Every day of my life you have lied to me. You made me believe I was safe and loved and bonded to you by our blood." Tears ran freely down her face and her voice was shaky.

"I have loved you like a sister, blood bond or no blood bond, and because I love you, I warn you. Even women are hanged when they speak as you have just spoken about the king," Alastair told her.

"They hang women, too, for horse-thievery," Lyall cut in harshly. "Anyone who steals merely a walnut can lose a hand, whether the thief be a woman, a man, or a child. The axeman cares not. She might curse you for lying to her, and that is between the two of you, but I expect the king would dole out his own punishment for involving her in a life of thievery. Look at all this. Both of you are idiots to involve her in your larceny. What were you thinking?" He pointed a finger at Alastair. "If you knew the truth, Gordon, then you also knew your father swore to protect her. I assume it was you who sent news of her over the years. Someone has been communicating. There were letters signed by Sir Hume and stamped with his own ring."

"Alastair has my fath—" Glenna seemed to choke on her words. "—*his* father's ring. And I will speak however I may about the king, for his exiled ears are not even in his own land and haven't been for too many years to count. What good is a king who runs from his land?"

"You are unskilled in the lessons of politics. The king is no coward, but merely a man caught in the turmoil of power, a destiny brought on him only by his birth name. I do not expect you, woman, to understand the vagaries, the glories or the demons that drive men, kings or traitors," Lyall said darkly.

"I care naught about the king," Glenna said with a wave of her hand. "However there is no question, none at all, about who in this room is the traitor." She glared at Alastair, who hung his head and couldn't look at her, and for a brief moment Lyall almost felt sorry for him. Alastair Gordon held all the appearances of a man broken by guilt and hurt.

"I will go with you, my lord," she continued. "Only because I will not stay a full day longer in this house where I do not belong. But know this. I care nothing for the king or his royal proclamations."

"I would suggest you find a way to care very much what the

king wants and proclaims, Glenna Canmore, because he is your father."

Glenna lay curled in a ball on her straw mattress, the truth throbbing through her head. Snippets of thoughts, mostly fears, kept her from sleeping. Sir Golden Himself, Baron Montrose, lay in a heap across the door. Light from the fire outlined his still form. Had he chosen to sleep there to keep her from running away? No. There were the wooden shutters she could easily crawl through. And, too, she understood Montrose was not the fool she had called him. He slept so quietly she wondered if he was asleep at all.

From across the room where her brothers lay on their pallets, she could hear their off-pitched snoring, and she cursed Alastair again for his duplicity, and because he could sleep so easily when she could not.

To be angry with him was safer than thinking about the truth—who she actually was, which seemed impossible—and how the knowledge shook her deep into her bones. Her father was the king? Nay, she shook her head and tears spilled down her cheeks. She was frightened, more frightened than she wanted to admit to anyone. She knew nothing of ladies and manors, castles and kings, only the tales Alastair told her as a child, and what did he know? Royal women must have servants and silks, and whole armies to protect them, while she grew up pitching hay and shoveling horse manure…and stealing.

She could ride a horse like the wind, but she did not use a needle or thread and would not know what to do with either. The only gown she owned she had to steal, only to put it on and find it was too big and too long, so she cut the hem with a dagger, and now the gown was shorter on one side than the other and the cloth was fraying badly.

How could her horse skills ever mean even a whit to a king? The king would take one look at her in her peasant's rags or jagged gown and have her banished, particularly once he saw how poorly skilled she was and that she was so terribly untaught.

What king would tolerate a thief for a daughter? Or he could lock her up in a tower. He was the king. She shuddered at the images that came to her mind: the executioner's platform, the axeman's stone. She closed her eyes tightly and her hands tightened into numb fists.

Perhaps he would do even worse than lock her away.

At that thought she lost control and sobbed into her hands, her knees to her chest. It took a will of iron for her to stop shaking. Her breath caught and she felt like she was dying inside. Her destiny was done. She could bring nothing but shame to her father, to his name and to the whole court, when her finest qualities were the ability to pick a pocket and steal a horse.

Her silly tears wouldn't change tomorrow. Tears wouldn't bring back yesterday, when her name was Glenna Gordon and she was happy with her brothers. Crying like a ninny accomplished little more than making her eyes burn and her nose run. She wiped her face and sat up, pushing open the window shutters above the bed.

Outside, there was a clear night sky, darkness being so rare in midsummer and so fleeting, just a few hours of starlight. The only sky she knew was this one—great and unending over the one small stretch of land that had always been home to her. The moors and the sea, the horses she loved and cared for, her brothers with whom she had felt safe and loved…

Now she would have to face all the unknowns—of place and people, an unknown journey with a stranger. Even her own identity was a mystery. There was nothing she could hold onto that was true and familiar. She had no idea how to grieve for what she had lost, because the truth was: her life as she knew it was not hers.

The next morn, Lyall checked to make certain all his belongings were in place, in particular, his money. Though he had left a bag of silver with the Gordons, he wouldn't put it past those two pilferers to make a switch. He hooked a plump skin of water to his saddle pouch, and turned as Glenna readied to mount a big, spirited bay Elgin had brought up from the paddock. Lyall studied the horse appreciatively. "Tell me now if there is a chance I am going to be chased from here to Kingdom Come by the true owner of that horse of yours."

"You have nothing to fear, Montrose," Glenna said haughtily, using the title like a seasoned noble. "I was there when she was foaled, and since I have fed and trained her. No one else. Skye is mine."

"That is well, then. Our journey will be long and I do not relish outrunning a hangman's noose," he said. He was jesting, but she did not respond or even look at him. He laughed softly.

She looked up at him. "What is so amusing?"

"Skye, Glenna? Your mount has a name?" He laughed heartily and then thought of his sister, who as a child would have named all the fleas on his dog.

"Why is naming a horse amusing? What call you that one, on which sits your arse? Horse?" Now she was laughing. "Better yet…arse carrier."

His eyes narrowed. "He is my horse, a fine animal, but nothing more."

"Then you should have left me be and let me keep him, if he matters so little to you that you cannot give him a name."

"There is no need for me to name my horse."

"Perhaps," she said sweetly. "Had you given him a name by which to call him, I might not have stolen him so easily...my lord." She reached the other side of the saddle and slung a small bow and a quiver of arrows from the saddle.

"What is that?" Lyall stared at the weapon.

"My bow and arrows."

"You will have no need of weapons, woman."

She faced him. "How do you know?"

"You believe you can save us from attack with those?" Lyall laughed. A broadsword would cut her down before she had notched an arrow.

"I do not ride without them."

"I do not ride with them."

They exchanged the same look, then Lyall said, "Fine. Give them to me." He held out his hand. "I will not ride with an armed woman. Should we meet with trouble, you might shoot me while you're trying to notch that thing."

"You know nothing—"

"Give them to me." He would argue no more with her, for it was like trying to beat down a drawbridge with his head.

She rolled her eyes and handed them to him. "Here, then, my lord. I wouldn't want you to fear for your life because of an armed woman."

That was when he'd had enough of her mouth. He broke the bow in half and all the arrows, then tossed it aside, ignoring her gasp. "Now there will be no reason to argue any longer."

The look she gave him could have caused a fire. He cared naught but sat there staring back at her until she shook her head and looked away, clearly angry.

A bee buzzed 'round his head and he swatted at it, but it landed on his neck and stung him. He cursed and slapped a hand on it, pulling it and the stinger from his skin. He was scowling down at the dead insect when she said with a half laugh, "No doubt lured by your sweet manner, my lord."

She checked the rolled bundle she had tied to her horse, and her leather satchel bags then ran her hands down the horse's legs and examined the hooves, before she adjusted the bridle again. This was the third time. She was stalling.

"Come now. We can waste no more time dawdling," he told her sharply. "You should bid farewell to your brothers. They are waiting."

"I would if I had brothers." Glenna adjusted the bridle for the fourth time.

He understood pride, and its fall. Watching her, listening to her words and manner, made him vastly aware there was more of her father's blood in her than she knew, more between them than merely her great likeness to the man. One thing no one could change was who had sired them. Blood was blood. He knew that all too well.

"Glenna." There was true pain in Elgin's voice as he moved closer "I knew nothing of any of this. I beg you, do not hold me to blame."

Lyall could see by the forced set of her shoulders she was battling her own bitterness. Silence fell over them and she stood still. She closed her eyes briefly, and then spun around. "Oh, El...." She threw her arms around him and sobbed into his neck.

Elgin patted her back gently. "You must forgive poor Alastair. He loves you well, as do I. Know this, Glenna, you will always be my own sister." He spoke fiercely and with great heart.

Alastair stood back and away, listening, looking awkward, but clearly afraid to come closer lest she reject him. Her words must have cut him deeply. Certainly Lyall had felt the lash of a woman's tongue before, and knew well how guilt could eat at a man long after the words, and even the woman who had spoken them, had died.

Glenna released her tight hold on Elgin and stepped back. He handed her his wide brimmed hat. "Here. Tuck up your braid and travel safe."

She wrapped the long, thick braid of black hair around her head and plopped the hat on, grinning up at Elgin Gordon. He tied the strings under her chin and smiled back at her. She looked like a lad and Lyall wondered how many times she had done this; it looked to be a ritual between the two of them. She grabbed Elgin's hand and kissed it, her expression soft for barely a heartbeat, then she let go and cast a glance at Alastair.

Her chin went up. Everything about her screamed *Traitor!*

Yet Alastair bravely closed the distance between them. "Here." He held a small package wrapped in plain cloth.

"What is this," Glenna asked. "I want no parting gifts from you."

"It is not a gift. I had forgotten about it until this morn. This is yours. When father brought you home, you were wrapped in this infant coverlet. He told me your mother made it, and you were to have it someday."

She took the parcel, then turned away to put it in her pack.

"For me also, Glenna, you will forever be my sister." He reached out to her as if to touch her cheek, then caught himself. The two of them stared at each other, looking for answers. Alastair glanced away, as if searching for courage to say the words. When he turned back he said, "I will treasure all those years we had, and never will I forget the way you looked up to me. I will always, in my heart, be your elder brother. I will never forget when you were small and you sat in my lap every night begging me for another tale, another ancient fable. Remember this. I was naught but a green lad back then. Raising you and El alone…that was what made me into a man."

Her face fell slightly and her dark, almost black eyes grew moist. She straightened and held her head even higher.

"Those stories I told you at night were not true, either, but you thrived with the knowing of them, and I thrived from the telling. I care naught about the lies I had to tell you or what I did. I care only that I hurt you. But know this, too, that you are alive and well and going home now. To protect your destiny was the task my father left me, and I did the best I could for you with so little knowledge of how I was supposed to go about it. I do love you dearly, my sister, and shall miss you every morn and every night until I die."

Glenna did not look away from him, nor did she give him the burning, bitter glare from the night before. However there was great sadness and disappointment in her and Lyall thought he caught the glimmer of moisture in her dark eyes. She mounted astride the bay, settling into her seat, reins in hand, before she turned to him and said simply, "Goodbye, Alastair."

From what Lyall had seen that morning, those were the first words she had spoken to Alastair Gordon since she had cried openly the night before and called him a traitor. This time her words were not spoken in anger or with coldness.

She edged her mount over to Lyall's side. "Fergus! Come!"

The hound trotted over from where he was sitting quietly with her brothers and he circled and plopped down next to her and her horse, waiting. Lyall looked at the dog in horror.

"I am ready, my lord."

"The hound will stay."

Her look was brittle.

"We will be riding hard," he told her sternly. "I won't have that hound hold us up."

She laughed with little humor. "Fergus? I assure you he can keep up, my lord."

The dog sat there, tongue lolling out, looking at him with a human look no dog should wear. He had been but a lad the last time a dog had looked at him like that. What happened long ago had naught to do with now, with her dog, or even with his choices. Somehow he knew Glenna was going to fight him more than he would like. His hands tightened on the reins. He did not want to bend to her will so soon.

"I do not go without him," she said again, clearly understanding her power quickly.

Yes…she was the daughter of a king.

He did not speak but gave her a sharp nod and took the lead as they rode off together across the grassy knolls, Fergus loping easily alongside her. He rode without looking back, expecting her to learn to stay up with him, but was aware of the sound of her mount's hooves. She rode alongside him. His mount took the hillside with vigor; they rode higher and farther, until he reached the very top of the rise.

"Montrose!" she called out. "Wait."

He swore silently. He knew it. Already the dog was trouble. He reined in and turned, expecting to see the dog lagging behind. The dog was sitting next to him, grinning like a jester who had just performed his best trick. For one moment he wondered if the dog could juggle, too.

But Glenna had turned her mount around to face the half-hidden cottage well below, and the dark and distant figures of two young men left standing there.

They had not moved.

She stood in her stirrups and waved vigorously, looking like the child she must have once been. He was captivated, watching her. So he waited, arm resting on the pommel, giving her as much of a farewell as she needed, and wondering if she even knew she was smiling.

He knew the power of a woman's smile, he had a mother and sister who also understood a woman's power over a man, and he reminded himself he was in no position to relinquish anything to a woman. He had a single goal. He had a mission to complete. That was all. That was enough.

When she was done, she settled into the saddle and waited expectantly. The dog barked anxiously, ready to run. Lyall studied Glenna for some sign of female weakness, for the suggestion of tears or the tension of her strong pride, the things that would mask what she was feeling. After a long moment she cast a glance at him under the wide flat brim of her hat, her chin up. He had the insane thought that he would hear the king's deep and commanding voice spill from her lips, so alike did they wear that same dark and imperious look.

"Come now," she said mockingly. "For a man in such a hurry, Baron, you certainly dawdle for long, wasted moments."

His own words thrown back at him.

Before he could speak, she turned her horse and took off down the other side, hound loping coltishly at her side.

Lyall stared at her narrow back and laughed aloud, riding after them, heading eastward, aware the journey ahead of him would be far from dull.

THREE

The wind carried the salty taste of the sea over the moorlands, and coastal birds with wide wingspans and mournful calls scavenged in spiraling circles in the clear sunshine. All around her spread mound after rolling mound of heather, the same color as the edges of an early morning sunrise. One never understood the gloriousness of a place until you had to leave it. She could never come back here, and perhaps that made her look all around her with different eyes, eyes needing to memorize all she saw, because if the day came when she could not picture this in her mind's eye, then she would have no past behind her, and all the years she had lived before would be worthless. She would be nothing. She would have nothing…not even a memory.

Fergus romped some distance away from her, his long gangly legs sending dust and pieces of purple heather into the air. He frolicked and barked at it, as if the heather were bees and flies coming to get him. Glenna had to laugh at him, at his silliness, like that of a tomfool she had once watched at a Michelmas fair. Fergus brought her great joy and she felt some sense of peace in that, if for only a moment.

As long as Fergus was there, she was not completely alone in the world.

The last fortnight of summer on the island was always filled with color and sunshine. For those few gay and glorious weeks, the view from the rise above their cottage had always been that of the rich waves of heather upon the rugged land, soft color brightened against the broad blue of the unending skies and her island landscape of huge granite cliffs and sloping rises of dark gray rock.

But this wasn't her island any longer. That she was leaving now, when she most loved the place, was even more bittersweet. Thoughts of home, and El and Alastair made her feel more lonely. Her mood grew heavy and she wished the storms would come; they were always the first warning that summer was coming to an end. 'Twould make the leaving easier to swallow. Sadness seemed to grow in her the more they rode eastward, but she did not want to feel anything and stubbornly steeled herself against the weaknesses of her heart and memories that were not hers to own. They belonged to the girl who had brothers.

There was no Gordon blood in her veins and she could not be a sister only because she longed to be, only because she believed the lies told to her for years, or because she longed to go back to yesterday, before one encounter and a few words changed everything and she discovered she was alone in a world full of strangers.

Her skin began to prick and she shifted uneasily in the saddle. Montrose was watching her. His cool blue gaze was not easy to ignore, so she steeled herself to appear as if she were not, deep inside, merely a roiling, boiling cauldron of weakness and doubt.

Al and El were forever grousing about her stubborn pride, claiming it came naturally to her. Pride was her close friend, and gave her strength when the stakes were high.

She considered these stakes high; she refused to let Montrose see any frailty in her.

In truth, she did not know what to think of him, her lark in the cove the day before aside. The vision of him in the sea, a golden sea lion riding under the waves, came unbidden to her mind's eye, and she felt a strange warmth as her blood sped through her. She had the sudden urge to ride as far away from him as possible.

Who was this man whose tone was often gruff and harsh? When he looked at her, he did so not in anger or disgust, at least not since that moment outside the cottage when she had kicked and bitten him. He was understandably angry then, and angrier still when he was naked in the stable. His body had shaken with it. She had thought he would kill her.

Instead he did worse. He killed the person she thought she was. But since then, he seemed different, as if he understood she'd had her fill of pain, and truthfully, she might have thought his words were gentle had El or Al spoken them. She wondered if that were the truth or only that her judgment was so flawed that she believed it to be the truth. She had no faith in anything any longer since she could not even trust her own judgment.

A quick glance at Montrose told her nothing. He only seemed to want to ride, something she supposed was best. She couldn't outrun her own thoughts, and could not run and hide on the island. No one seemed to question that she would go willingly to meet her fate in the hands of a powerful, commanding father who knew her naught. Fools.... Her only choice had been clear—to wait until the odds of getting away were in her favor. And she needed more than the knives she'd hidden. She needed her bow and arrows.

She glanced at him again. The silence had stretched out between them. If she couldn't put him in his place, then she wasn't going to talk to him. Questions drifted through her head. Why had he come now? Fate was a cruel and bitter enemy. What was it about this particular time in her life that she was to be plucked out of the northernmost isles? Why him? Who was Baron Montrose to her father. What kind of man was her father?

A coward, she thought bitterly. Her hands closed tightly over her reins and Skye balked at the bit. Glenna eased up and took a long breath. She knew the tales of the great house of Canmore, merely some of the many stories told to her over the years by Alastair, a fact that made her immediately question the accuracy of what she had been told.

Montrose claimed she was a Canmore. The name was mythic and didn't seem to fit her. All had heard of the infamous Canmore king, who as a young man came across a maiden in the North Woods, fallen from her horse, injured and unable to walk, frightened and alone.

With her long silver-hair in hand-thick braids that reached her knees, skin like freshly drawn milk and eyes the color of the deepest sky, she was to the king, a Northern light, an angel fallen from Heaven. He carried her to his great white horse and, within the protection of his solid arms, he fearlessly rode without escort into his enemy's fortress, the winter home of the great North prince, risking everything he was to take her safely home.

Oh, Glenna thought, if that were only true....

Their love was inscribed upon their hearts from the moment they met, the kind of romance and heartache in epic legends. In time, the great Norse Prince knew he would lose his beloved daughter if he did not agree to give her to the young king, who wanted the hand of no other.

So they wed in peace and happiness and joy, their love open and there for all to see. And for a short time, there was no war in the land. No more raids. No more plunder. Most understood that the Norse raids had finally ended with a blood bond treaty and the marriage of two great bloodlines. Yet that peace only opened the door to another war, more insidious, because many in his own country hated the gallant and brave young king, hated him for his fairness and intelligence, while some hated him for his success, for his passion, and others hated him even more for choosing his queen from the North.

Glenna could never think of the story and not wonder at that kind of legendary, epic love. For her lifetime, the king lived in exile after a group of power hungry men had contested his sovereign right to rule and had risen up with the aid of King Henry of England and defeated the young king. His beloved queen had died in childbed, along with the infant.

Glenna's heart stopped. Was she that child? Could it be true? She closed her eyes. The world was full of lies.

A dead infant that in fact was raised as someone else?

How could it be? Was that enchanting, Nordic, prince's daughter truly her mother? She looked as unlike a Nordic royalty as a ruby did to a lump of coal. Her black hair and black eyes bespoke nothing of the coloring of the Norse. But, she thought, perhaps they were pure Canmore...

That romantic tale was of people Glenna knew little about. She could not hope for a legendary love. Thieves did not fall in love. Eventually thieves died by a rope to the neck, or bled to death from having their hands chopped off, or rotted in a dank, rat-filled prison. She could steal a gown, a spirited horse, she could steal a fat purse and a spice box—boxes—but she had no hope of ever stealing a gallant heart.

Her belly growled like a wolf and she pressed her hand to it. She did not want Montrose to hear. 'Twould be all she needed to make her humiliation complete. This morning, she had been in such a rush to make all the men in her life as miserable as she was, that she'd forgotten to break fast or even to pack some food.

She took a deep breath, willed herself to swallow the air, and then stared out at the southern horizon, where there would be no farms to stop and purchase food, no fisherman's cottage with herring drying in the sun. Ahead was only the stony wilderness where no man could even scratch the surface with the sharpest spade, and not even the heath could grow through acres of bare, brindled stone, which formed in sheets and boulders, covered only near the streams with some green lichen from the moistness of the water. There was nothing to eat but her own hunger.

Off in the distance, the blue sea blended into the sky so she could not even see where one ended and one began and to the southwest was the distant hump of Bjorn's Isle, morning mist still surrounding its coastal edges. Then, riding over the arch of a hillside stood a pair of red deer, grazing until they looked up and stood startled and motionless, staring, before loping off to the streams fanning downward through a trail of rocks towards the steep slopes at the sea cliffs.

Her belly called out again and for a brief moment a platter of plump, juicy venison swam before her eyes, surrounded by savory browned onions and turnips.

Over another golden mound that reminded her of freshly baked bread they rode, and her mind filled with dandelion honey dripping from a honey comb and running like liquid amber over that warm bread....

Their direction led down toward a gathering of rocks that looked like plums or roasted chestnuts or perhaps gooseberries and she thought she might die with the need to chew on something other than her lip.

Without a word, Montrose reined and dismounted.

She almost ran over him, and pulled back hard on the reins. Skye reared immediately and only Glenna's consummate horse skills kept her mounted.

Montrose swore and reached for the reins.

But Glenna pulled Skye away, glaring at him. "Some warning you were going to stop would have been helpful." She cast him a withering look, then turned back to find Fergus, who came loping down from the hillock, tongue lolling, and he ran past them to toward the stream.

"I am used to traveling alone."

She supposed that was the closest thing Montrose had for an apology.

"There is water over there for our mounts and your hound." He came over to her, his hands heading near her waist.

She jerked the reins and pulled back from him. "I've ridden horses for as long as I can remember, my lord. I need no help getting down and will do so when I am ready." She had a purpose; she stayed in the saddle because she could look down at him.

Pointedly silent, he studied her through narrowed eyes that probably longed to chop her head off, or perhaps cut out her tongue. She understood she had made him angry, which was her point, but she wondered why she had the sudden urge to apologize. Bah! She was changing already and becoming someone she didn't know.

Immediately she sat taller in the saddle and her smile melted into a thin line. "I have questions for you. Who are you to my father?"

He looked at her as if she were a flea he'd plucked from his shirt.

She wished she had fleas…she might eat them.

"Dismount Glenna." Was all he said.

"You did not answer my question."

"The animals need water and to rest. So do you."

"I can take care of myself. I do not need a man to tell me when to stop, when to dismount, when to water my horse. My bro—Al and El learned that lesson many times. You would do well to learn that." Her belly tightened again, and began to gurgle and churn, so she closed her eyes briefly, willing her hunger and anger and hurt to go away.

Look how well she had taken care of herself. She was a fool whose pride was more important than remembering to pack some food.

Silent, Montrose did not move. Standing there looking all too powerful dressed in padded leather, heavy hose and his powerful legs in tall books, she had to look away because of what looking at him did to her. Fergus was romping in the stream, barking and splashing water. Her mouth was dry, her head growing light. She sighed heavily and dismounted. Pride be damned, water would fill her grumbling belly. And there was the fact that her pride would be sorely damaged if she swooned into a dead faint in front of him.

She did as he asked and took her horse to the stream, but only because that is what she would have done. Montrose followed her. Ignoring him, she pushed back her hat, knelt down and cupped her hand to drink.

"I have a water skin."

Wiping her mouth, she turned and looked up at him standing over her, all noble baron who was used to telling everyone what to do. "And you are welcome to use it, my lord." Then she continued to drink from the cool stream until she was full and washed the dust of the land from her face, which felt sticky with sweat and grime, then wiped it dry with the hem of her tunic. She sat back on her heels; she was full of water but still famished, and stared listlessly at the cool clear water skipping over rocks bright with green lichen and pooling below where it reflected blue from the cloudless sky overhead. She wished it were soup.

Pea stock flavored with salt pork.

A river of bean pottage.

Something thick and hearty to fill her gut.

Bread. Oh sweet Lord…she would give her heart away for a loaf of bread.

At that perfect moment her belly betrayed her and growled loudly. Her vision swam and she pressed her fist into it.

Montrose turned, swore under his breath and pulled her to her feet. "You should have told me you needed to stop."

"I did not need to stop," she said quietly, stumbling along behind him, before she plopped down bonelessly on a flat rock that was shaped like a pie. "I need to eat."

He pulled a cloth from his bags knelt down next to her, unfolding the cloth to show her the bread (from God's ears to her mouth) and a fat wedge of white cheese. "Here, Glenna. Eat."

No more pride. She took the cloth, ignoring the soft look she saw in his eyes,—so blue they too reflected the sky—and tried not to devour the food whole. "If you had not destroyed my bow and arrows we could have meat."

"I imagine that meat would be my liver roasting on a spit."

He was not wrong.

Sitting crosswise, she watched him as she ate. Fergus was wet and sloppy and trotted back and forth between them, then shook himself all over a scowling Montrose. Glenna looked away to hide her laughter. The dog settled beside her and she gave him a piece of cheese.

"You reward him for his behavior?" Montrose was refilling his skin, squatting down at the water's edge, his shoulders wide enough to block her view.

"I feed him. He is hungry, too. Would you have me starve the animals?"

He merely shook his head at her and went on as he had been. His light hair hung to his shoulders and was beginning to curl at the ends. She noticed he did not wear his gold signet ring on his tanned hand. She had tried the ring on as she rode home from the cove yesterday and it was heavy and big. Two of her small fingers could have almost fit into the ring.

He stood with the ease of a lion and she concentrated on her food and gave Fergus more cheese, then watched him from the corner of her eye. He took an apple from his pouch and sat down on a rock near her and used a small knife to cut off a piece, then paused and handed it to her.

She glanced down at the food in her lap and realized she and her dog had eaten over half of it. He must be hungry, too, she thought. A warm flush of shame surprised her, so she concentrated on folding up the cloth.

"Glenna."

She looked up sharply. Her name on his lips sounded oddly foreign and strange. Not like the sour notes of a horn or a lute, but low and it was almost as if she felt his voice all the way to her toes.

Before her was his outstretched hand, his thumb pressed on his knife and holding the apple slice toward her. "Take it," he said.

She did, then held out the cloth to him with a quiet, "Thank you."

"You finish it."

"Nay. I've had my fill." She leaned forward and set the cloth of food on his knees. Leaning back on her elbows, she stretched out, crossed her feet at the ankles and popped the wedge of apple in her mouth and began talking whilst she chewed. "You eat. The truth is, Montrose, I don't need you swooning halfway to wherever it is we are headed. You are huge and I don't believe I could lift you. Why I believe merely your hard head alone would be enough to break my poor, wee back." She paused, then added pointedly, "My lord."

He laughed loud and long and hearty and something warm ran through her at the sound. Amusement changed his face, brightened a kind and sweet gleam in his blue eyes and revealed the sudden dimples in his hard cheeks. She found herself smiling back at him.

Montrose was a beautiful man. She had not forgotten the image of him by the sea, the one that was burned into her memory only to return unbidden and plague her too often for her own comfort. That was merely yesterday?

Perhaps he dominated her thoughts because he was only

something new and different. Of late, her life had been mundane and uneventful, having spent most of the late spring and summer on the mainland, where they stolen their fill and had taken more than enough to trade for a long time.

His profile was strong, his nose long and noble, but she saw now as he laughed, that his mouth was wide, his teeth all there, white as the sun-bleached shells on the beach and perfectly aligned, not gaping like fence posts or crossed all over each other like a stack of firewood.

There had been a time when she'd had to pull one of Alastair's teeth after it festered, and last year Elgin lost a front tooth in a hard fall from training a horse. Her own teeth were crooked on the bottom, too close together and food often caught in them. She wondered now if there was bread or cheese stuck in them and quickly stopped smiling.

"You asked who I am to your father. You said you had questions." His voice was quiet, kinder, and she thought they might have reached a new kind of truce. He chewed on a morsel of cheese he had wrapped inside some bread.

Her mind raced. She might need to change tactic. Test the waters so to speak. She needed to find the way to gain his trust. When the time and place came for her to run, she would be best served if he was caught completely unaware. "Yes. I asked because I do not know you or know of you, and here we are together." She sat up and leaned forward. "You claim you have a duty to the king." She paused. "It would give me some comfort to know what I am facing."

He finished the apple and sheathed the knife away before he spoke. "My father fought with yours, they were close friends, but he is dead." The look in his eyes went suddenly distant. "Our family has long been sworn to yours by oath and by blood. My mother, through her own stepmother, was a distant cousin to your father, as was my wife."

"Your wife is my cousin?"

"Was," he said pointedly. "She's dead." His flat words carried not a lick of emotion and he casually tossed Fergus a crust of bread. He did not look at her, but seemed elsewhere.

There was more there he could not hide, even by not looking at her. What would be in his eyes if she were to look into them now? She wondered if Montrose and his wife had a great and legendary love as did her mother and father. Was his coolness hiding a deep loss? Certainly 'twould explain why he was silent and gruff—she paused in thought—not that any of that mattered to her. Wounded or not, the man's heart—if he had one—was none of her concern. "So it is for your family's honor and deep ties to mine that you come to the very ends of the earth to bring the king's lost daughter home," she said curtly, using his own words. "Wherever home is. Tell me where my home is when my father happens to be a king who has been exiled for seventeen years?"

"There are many royal holdings," he said.

"And you Baron Montrose. Do you have many holdings?"

"Castle Rossie, home to the barony, is on the River Esk."

"Is that where you are taking me?"

"Nay." His voice was gruff again.

She waited, but he didn't elaborate. "Where then?" she asked finally.

"To a safe place," was all the lunkheaded oaf would say. He started to eat the last bit of cheese, but looked down at Fergus, who had slowly slithered closer to him and away from her. But then she had no food…the traitor.

Montrose eyed Fergus for a moment, then tossed him the cheese. He stood. "Come. The horses are rested and I need us to be in Steering before the tide can delay us for a day.

Steering. God's bones! She said nothing but closed her eyes and followed him, trusting she could think of something to save her before they arrived there.

They rode on the beginnings of a rough road that started from the standing stones near Callenish, and by late in the day they came near the outer rim of the only coastal hamlet on southern ends of the isle, where they passed by some crofters stacking cut squares of dried peat into carts for the coming winter months, and where the air smelled of fresh soil and firesmoke. Glenna knew the road went through the center of Steering, and wound directly through the traveling market which was there for a sennight in late summer. If she were fortunate, the market would already have packed up and be gone until next year.

The closer they came, the more her hands began to turn clammy and she grew uneasy. Luck was not with her. She could see the colorful tents of the summer market, their bright flags waving in the sea wind. Sweat began to drip from her brow. Her hands tightened on the reins and Skye side-stepped. She looked down at her dog. He was as much of a liability as she was.

"Fergus. Heed!" she whispered harshly, panic racing through her. She pulled her hat down lower, then edged her horse to the left side of Montrose, hoping his size and horse would shield her. She should have cut her hair off and ridden hatless. She should have found a way to get Montrose to ride around the village. She should have, should have, should have…

He was a baron, and one who would not pass unnoticed through a village on the mainland, let alone such a nobleman on remote island village. His presence demanded attention, this man whose fat purse would appeal greatly to every single one of the vendors. Sneaking past them? Ha! 'Twas like trying to hide the sun.

They were but a short distance from the market stalls. Her heart sped. She looked in the opposite direction and kept Skye even with his great black horse, and then the first call came. "My lord!" said the ironmonger. "Lanterns and candleholders. Kettles and pots! Only the finest wares!"

"Fresh pies, my lord!"

"Wool from Flanders!"

"Spices, my lord!" The familiar voice was loud as a fishwife.

Oh no... Glenna closed her eyes.

"Fresh hare and marten furs!"

A moment later a horrific shriek made Glenna wince and hunch down.

"You!" The spice merchant's wife was looking at her and she screamed again, grabbing and shaking her husband's arm. "'Tis him! Look! The thieving bugger! There he is! Stop him!" The woman moved from the stall faster than Glenna thought possible. Leaning low, Glenna kicked her heels into Skye and took off. She did not look back, but from the corner of her eye, she could see the barest bit of Fergus's head; he was staying with her, right at her side.

"Thief! Thief! Thief!" came the incessant shrieking.

Montrose's cursing sounded like a battle cry and echoed from behind her.

Her heart pounded in cadence with Skye's hooves. From over her shoulder she saw his horse rear, and a moment later he was thundering after her, his face frighteningly intense.

A sudden cacophony of voices was shouting "Stop! Thief!" The market was utter chaos, as a motley contingent of merchants pursued her, brandishing counting sticks and long knives, brands and candle snuffers, and the spice wife was leading them all, running after her and waving a hatchet. Villagers followed and the crowd grew.

'Twas common practice to cut off the hand of a thief. And horse thieves had been hung from the nearest tree. Island law was unto itself, with no resident lord to oversee, and few questions were asked. Not that she had any answers.

Chills ran down Glenna's spine. All were still after her.

Ahead of her, where the road narrowed next to a smithy, a

drover struggled with a lumbering hay cart, the cart horse balking.

Think fast.

Montrose was closing in.

"Stay with me Fergus!" She snapped her fingers at him and he barked. She smiled. "Good dog."

The cart was stopped now, blocking most of the path. She did not slow, but sped past so close her leg brushed the cart.

As she passed the drayage horse, she snapped her fingers and Fergus barked at her command, spooking the cart horse and sending it rearing into air. Fergus loped safely past.

More of Montrose's curses filled the air as the cart spilled over with a loud crack and blocked his path. Hay went everywhere, and the noise suddenly became like a battlefield.

In the chaos, a spark from the smithy's fire caught the hay. Smoke billowed upward. There was a shout—a warning of fire—then a heartbeat later, the whole thing flamed up like a bonfire on solstice.

Ahead of her were the long docks and the end of the road. Wharvesmen were unloading crates from a ship onto a cart and others were rolling barrels of pickled fish down the plankway up to the wharf.

There was no way she could keep riding. At a haphazard row of stone cottages, she went left and past a back lane near the cooper, flanked with huge empty ale barrels, and sped across a stone path that turned and led down to the docks.

In the distance behind her, the noise and shouts were fading, so she slowed Skye to a walk and easily doubled back around to the lane, where ahead of her, like an answer to a paternoster, stood the open doors of the stable behind a dockside tavern. She rode straight inside and dismounted before her horse had barely halted. Quickly shoving the bay and Fergus in a stall together, she muttered her thanks and ran back to close and lock down the stable doors, leaning against them, her heart pounding in her ears.

Now what?

Hay flew everywhere, a cloud of flying straw, and as it settled, Lyall saw the hayrack and horse blocked the whole road. Swearing, he had no choice but to rein in. Beyond the cart he could see Glenna, bent low over her horse, glancing back over her shoulder and riding as if the hounds of hell were after her, her own hellhound, all legs and fur and tail, at her side.

The colorful group of angry merchants was coming fast toward him, shouting en masse, weapons raised, a mob of curious villagers trailing at their heels. He knew they were not after him. To keep her safe, he had no choice but to keep them away from her. Lyall turned his mount, raised in his stirrups and took a stand, pulling the sword from its sheath. It felt strangely odd and unfamiliar in his hand.

A sword was a sword, he told himself and instinct overtook him. He shouted a battle cry, "*A Robertson!*" Realized what he had said and wanted to swallow his words. This was not a battle. He cursed himself for an idiot and brandishing the sword he cried out. "Halt! All of you! Cease!"

The mob stopped immediately, eyes wide, murmuring. A few of the merchants taking up the rear took one look at his raised sword and turned and ran. A merchant in the forefront, the ironmonger, looked uneasy, before his eyes grew suddenly wide and he dropped his fire iron and frantically began to point. "My lord!"

Someone shouted, "Fire!"

"Behind you!"

There was a loud whoosh! A blast of heat hit him in the back, and his horse reared. He was suddenly falling through the air—intensely hot air—and bright flames flared all around him. The strong and sudden smell of smoke filled his nose and lungs, and he hit the ground hard, landing flat on his back. His head shot with jabs of sharp pain. Impact sent the air from his chest. Word would not come; they were lodged in his throat. He could not speak or move, could only stare upward, rendered frozen on the ground, the world spinning around him in images as foggy as if he had drunk too much wine.

Time too moved slowly, too, and the edges of his sight turned white and began to fade. He could not breathe and pain slithered in waves down through his whole body. His sword in his hand was heavy and warm and the metal was growing hotter and hotter. It was burning his hand. Why could he only lay there?

Burning ash swirled into his line of vision. He blinked his eyes. Red fire and flames licked all around him. Like before. So much like before… The air was burning, scorching and sweltering hot. Almost as if he were being cooked alive.

No! No! his mind screamed. He was coming back to his own hell. Something burned his eyes and he almost cried out, gasping for breath and he felt his lungs finally fill, but the air was choked with smoke. "Malcolm," he murmured as his brother's face swam before him. Then blackness descended, and he saw and heard nothing more.

FOUR

Fifteen years earlier

Lyall was barely ten that day when he sought escape from the dark moods of home and fell asleep in the deep woods, cradled against the thick, sinewy trunk and sprawling roots of an ancient river tree. Between those roots was his favorite fishing perch and next to an outcrop of flat rocks where a narrow, clear and swift running section of the River Tay cut through the dense forest to the south of Dunkelden Castle.

Above him, through gaps in the crown of dark and lacy yew leaves, the sun grew warm and bright and speckled over the ground like the skin on the sweetest trout. He opened his eyes then yawned. His hound Atholl lay next to him, the wolfhound snoring, snout resting on his lap.

Before Lyall could move, a bee buzzed near his nose, so he stayed perfectly still. The bee lit on his hand, which was resting on his ribs, and Lyall held his breath. Someone once warned him if he held still, a bee would never sting him, but instead it would realize he was not sweet clover and fly away.

The bee sat as still as he did, wings down, tail up, then it dropped and stung him. He yelped and jumped up, dancing around and shaking his hand with the stinger in his skin. Atholl awoke and frowning up at him as if he were mad. He pulled the stinger out and stuck his hand in the cold river water. "Hold still," he muttered. "And a bee won't sting you."

When his hand stopped burning he pulled it from the river. Atholl sat waiting, watching him from familiar trusting brown eyes while his thick tail began to thump on the damp ground. Lyall stood, gathering his things. "Come, you worthless hound," he said with affection, rubbing his pet's ears before he bent and picked up a sack full of freshly caught trout and tied it to his belt. "We are late."

Looking up, he studied the sun moving across a wedge of blue sky, which told him they had been gone from home too long. "Mother will be worried. Come, else she will send Malcolm to prod me home with the sole of his boot and he was in a foul mood this morn. If he has to spend his time searching for me, then he will be angry and blustery and refuse to play draughts with me."

Atholl sat at Lyall's feet, head cocked and listening. "You know how Malcolm's anger swells and then he's as impossible to live with as the English." He laughed out loud, because he was jesting, preparing his sharp words for nightly bantering with his older brother. The truth was he worshipped Malcolm, who would be ten and three and was not all that much older. In less than a fortnight, Malcolm was due to leave Perthshire and Dunkelden for Angus, to Castle Rossie, where he would be fostered. The agreement had been drawn and sealed before their father was killed—the reason why home was uncomfortable and why their mother hovered around them all too closely of late and sometimes looked as if she was in a place far, far away from the rest of them. Without their father, Mother was not the same woman and added to her fretfulness was the fact that too soon her first born son would be leaving.

After their father's body was brought home and buried in the small lime washed chapel at Dunkelden, Malcolm wandered the whole castle with his hands in fists because he did not want to leave and fought with everyone who would listen and even those who did not. Still he lost his frantic bid; all said Malcolm must do what his father wanted and foster with Ramsey. His brother was repeatedly reminded of the honor and respect of following their father's wishes. Now that Ewane Robertson, the great warrior and friend of the king, was dead, the agreement he'd struck for Malcolm was even more important.

That same night of the death of their father and under the light of a full moon, Malcolm had dragged Lyall up to the tower parapet, pricked his hand with a knife, and made him blood-swear to protect their mother and sister in his absence.

Lyall understood that his brother would be gone all too soon. His heart grew heavy and he slowed his steps, thinking about his father's wishes. He, the younger, did not know what his father had wanted from him, other than to grow into a man of honor. He did not like to think of his father, who had always talked to him as if he were not too young to understand, and who oft times rested his strong hand comfortably on Lyall's shoulder as he spoke to him and told him of the world in which they lived and about the kinds of men who inhabited it.

Those moments when he forgot his resolve and thought too long about his father, his grief came back hard and strong. He would not shame himself and weep again like he had done when they buried his father's body deep in the bowels of the small family chapel. Someday he, too, would be a great knight; he would be like the men his father spoke of, the proud and the good, and knights did not cry. He stomped faster through the woods, the mulchy leaves soft beneath his heavy boots, Atholl panting faithfully at his side.

Once Malcolm was fostered at Rossie, everything would change. He did not know what he would do when he was left at Dunkelden with naught but his flea of a sister, who shadowed him almost everywhere and drove him away this very day with her pestering, and his mother, who would coddle him and watch over him like a babe and want to know his every move.

He kicked a stone. How would he practice his bow? Who knew when he could get away to go fishing again? Now he could spy a trout and pierce it with a single draw of an arrow. His hard won skills would grow slow if he were stuck to the sides and shadows of his womenfolk.

Soon he was running, Atholl at his heels, as he played a war game and wove and spun and leapt his way home through stands of larch and pine, running faster and dodging as if they were each his enemies coming at him with lance and sword, shield and mace. His feet were quick, he knew, but not as quick as his brother's. He swore to himself he would practice his footwork. When Malcolm came home at Yuletide, Lyall vowed he would be the faster.

With his free hand outstretched, he moved swiftly toward an old and infamous yew tree, his fingers grazing the ancient wood as he passed. Some said the old tree with its huge, clawing roots had been planted by Druids to mark a sacred well. He did not know of sacred wells, but he knew as surely as the sun rose each morn, that if he passed by the yew and touched its trunk, he would catch as many fish as he needed, which always pleased his mother. And served to irritate his older brother, who couldn't catch any fish at all. His brother could spend from dawn to dusk at the stream or at the loch and would come up with nothing. Malcolm accepted his inability, though it frustrated him, especially when fish seemed to land in Lyall's hands. Malcolm swore that if a stream full of leaping salmon were swimming right toward him he would come up with empty hands.

Their sister Mairi said the best way for Malcolm to catch a fish was for someone to throw one at him.

Lyall proudly patted his day's work—a sack full of fat, speckled river trout, but froze when he heard the sudden loud crack of a branch behind him. Atholl barked. Nerves suddenly raw, Lyall's heart beat loudly in his ears.

"Ach!" Came a worried cry. And a familiar voice.

He turned slowly, angrily, and planted his hands on his hips and looked up.

His sister's feet and plump legs dangled from the huge yew tree above him.

"Mairi!" He shouted at her. She was sitting on a high branch but he could not see her face. "When will you cease following me? Come Atholl." He started to stomp away.

"Lyall! Wait!" She swung down lower, holding the branch by her hands as she hung from the tree. "Stop! Please!"

He heard the panic in her voice.

"Stop, Lyall!"

Was she crying? He moved back to her, concerned. "What is it?"

Her face was pale and she was truly frightened. He reached up and lifted her down.

"Malcolm told me to hide here. To wait for you." She clung to him, clutching his tunic in her tight fists and burying her face against his chest. "Oh, Lyall. They are attacking Dunkelden."

"What?"

"Look there!" She pointed into the air, where above the tall trees a dark cloud of smoke billowed into the blue sky.

"Who?"

"I do not know, but they say Papa was a traitor and those men hung the traitor's flag on the gates. They said that he died a traitor's death and he betrayed the king."

"Our father was no traitor," he said fiercely. "Where's Malcolm? And Mother?"

"Malcolm took me out through the back caves and made me swear to wait here in the tree for you. He went back to get mama. But, Lyall, that was a long, long time ago." She began to sob.

"There, Mairi. Stop crying. We need to be brave."

"I'm afraid."

"Come," he said easily, but feeling as frightened as she. He knew his father would be shamed if his youngest son showed fear to his sister, who he was so recently sworn to protect and not scare witless. He took a deep breath. "Stay close. I am here to protect you. That's why Malcolm brought you here to wait for me." He took her hand and moved more stealthily through the woods, his dog at his side. He wanted to run, he wanted to see what was happening, he wanted to try to help his brother, but sense told him to protect his sister and move cautiously. Glancing down at her, he took some bit of comfort in the fact that she had stopped crying.

Dunkelden was of motte and bailey construction, the bailey serving as the heart of the timber castle. For protection, a water ditch and spiked-wood curtain palisade encircled its raised motte, and the deep woods of Dunkelden surrounded the rear half and stood some distance away to the east and south. The back two caves had been dug at his father's command and led out toward the east with the escape plan that one could run the few yards of open land into good cover within the dense woodland forest, which was how Malcolm had escaped with their sister.

Their father had made them practice the route repeatedly. Once, when Malcolm had asked why they needed escape caves if they were all under protection of the king, his father told them he took no pledge of protection or fealty for granted. He said that to trust was a gift you could give, one which you might not receive in return and only a fool, a dead fool, would believe otherwise. "Be aware. You must be prepared to save your own neck, my sons, and not to depend upon someone else to save it for you."

Those words held even more meaning now that their father was gone. Why and who would do this? Who would falsely accuse their father—a great and loyal friend of the king—of betraying him, a man he loved as a brother? Lyall moved onward, his heart pounding in his chest and sweat beading on his brow, acutely aware Malcolm had not returned with their mother. Not a good sign.

Although still some distance away, as they neared the edges for the forest, he would stop, every few feet and listen sharply. But he did not hear the chaos he expected, and only once did he hear the distant thunder of horses. He turned to his sister. "Stay here. You sit. Atholl will stay with you." He knelt down in front of her and took her small hands in his. "Do not be afraid. I will come back. Do not follow me. Do not move. You stay here. You must swear to me." He untied the sack of fish and let it drop to the ground.

"I swear on my eyes," she said solemnly, and he knew not then the irony in her words.

"Atholl. Stay," he commanded. His dog sat next to Mairi, so he left them without looking back and crawled through a berry thicket, his bow catching on the branches but he was afraid to be too much in the open this close to the castle. He carefully threaded his way through another copse of trees, and edged toward the rim of the woods, moving from trunk to tree trunk, using them as shields.

He came down a small rise and over a rock outcrop where he could finally see the whole scene. Motionless in horror, he sagged against a tree, staring at something he could never imagine, before his knees gave out and he sank to the ground on his hands and knees. His breath was coming so fast he became light-headed. He crawled to the edge of a rocky rise and stared at the unbelievable scene below.

All was afire. The watch towers were gone. The drawbridge spanning the ditch was down and abandoned. No guard, none of his father's men, though since his death many had gone back to their own families at his mother's urging.

Flames flared from the high palisade built of huge, dense logs close to four times the height of a man. The logs had been carved to sharp points and stood as the first defenses past the ditch and surrounded the whole of the motte, there to protect the inner buildings. The roof and upper parapet of the tall wooden hall was burning, and what structures hadn't burned nearly to the ground inside the bailey were pluming up into the air in bright and deadly flames, sending huge clouds of black smoke into the air. He saw a few of the servants leaving the castle and running down the road, their arms filled with chickens and geese or other supplies.

On the west side of the hall was his brother running down the outside stairs of the burning building, pulling along their mother, her familiar dark green hooded cloak floating behind her as they ran. They reached the third story landing and Lyall watched in horror as her cloak caught fire, the flames fanning out behind her and creeping up her clothing. He shouted but they could not hear him.

Without thinking he leapt to his feet and jumped down to the soft ground below the rocks, pausing only to catch his balance, and then he ran as if the Devil were after him, toward the edge of the forest directly across from the castle cave. He looked quickly then burst out into the open and leapt into the ditch, where he hit hard and rolled down, his arm tangled in his bow and his quiver dug into his back. The stench of pitch and the oil used to burn down the wood wall was all around him. He scrambled up the side, clawing at the dirt and rocks and mud with his hands, ash swirling about him and smoke stinging his eyes.

Once inside the dank cave, he slowed down, his breath coming in pants and his chest tight from the harsh pitch. It was dark and growing darker with each step, until there was almost no light left from the small opening now far behind him. The air was smoky and his eyes teared. He reached the wooden ladder by rote and touch, and thought then of their father's constant demands that they practice escape every fortnight, which he and Malcolm resented, tedious as it was to them, but now proved worthy beyond all possible thought.

The ladder rungs ended at a wooden trap door and he stopped and listened closely, then pushed it open a crack and scouted the back cellar doors of the ale room, the building closest to the main hall. He swiftly pulled himself up and out and closed the trap, then scrambled to the wall and moved stealthily to the arched door, which stood open, smoke billowing inside and flames just beginning to burn dangerously through the overhead rafters. He had expected to meet Malcolm and his mother by now, on their way to the caves.

Where were they? He shot out of the door and to the shadows on south wall of the hall, edging toward the corner where the outside stairs ended. He heard a pitiful sobbing. It came not from 'round the corner, but from the burning stables.

Inside was an inferno, the stalls all open and empty, the stock gone, flames licking up the walls. His mother lay atop a sprawled form, his brother's blue tunic sleeve showing beneath her and her cloak hood half-covering her head. The other half of the hood and some of the cloak was burned away; she was crying hysterically.

"Mother! Malcolm?"

She looked up, his beautiful mother. Half of her face was red and blistered, her eyes tearing and red and swollen. "Lyall!"

"Who did this?"

"They are gone. The cowards threatened all at the castle, then lit their fires and left. Come. Quickly! Help me. Help your brother." She reached out blindly toward him. "I cannot see clearly. My skin is burning and there is ash in my eyes. Malcolm lies here and he speaks not. Help me waken him." Her hands were on his brother's chest. "He wanted to help me and thought 'twould be quicker to ride with me to seek help for my injuries. He tried to mount your father's horse and was thrown."

The horse was nowhere to be seen.

"He has not spoken or come awake since he fell. Please son, help him. I dared not leave him." Her voice caught and she was crying again. "Lyall. I cannot hear his breath."

Lyall stared at Malcolm and took a long deep and shuddering breath. He could tell by the angle of his brother's neck he was dead. Around his broken neck, but lying in the dark muck of the stable was the precious golden cross Malcolm always wore, a gift from their father, who was given it by his father, passed from oldest son to oldest son for generations.

"Come, Mother," he said gently and set his hand on her shoulder. "Where is everyone? The guards? The servants?"

"They all left. Ran for their lives after it was clear why those men came. Some tried to stay, but I told them to leave or they would be named traitors themselves. They dared not rise up against them. They came in the name of the king Lyall...your father has been accused of betraying the crown, and they hung the flag of treason at the gate, and then with torches and oil burned everything. But it is not possible, what they say." She shook her head. "It is not. Ewane would never betray the king's trust."

The fire raged around them and a burning truss fell hard to the ground behind her, sparks flying upward and over them. His mother gasped and flinched, cowering on the stable floor. Hot ash flicked up into the air and spat painfully into his eyes. He groaned and wiped them, blinking. He knew he had to get her out of the building before all the rafters fell in. "Come. We must get out of here."

"Not without Malcolm. Please. Take him first."

"No one can save him. Not now."

The wail that came from his mother was the worst sound he had ever heard.

"Mother, Mama...Please. Come. We must get out of here," he said quietly, and he managed to lead her weeping form outside and across to the castle well, where he rested her hand on the rocks. "This is the well. Stay here. I will go back for Malcolm."

She clung to his hand, still crying. "Who is this God? This God who takes all that I love?"

Oh Father, why hast Thou forsaken me? The words echoed in his head and he could not answer her, so he just pulled his hand away. What God? He thought angrily. He dropped his bow and quiver to the ground.

Two deep breaths and he ran back inside, arms up and fighting the ash and pieces of burning wood that came at him. Hot wind from the fire howled around him, and his eyes burned and teared. He grabbed his brother's arms and dragged him out of the stable just before it all collapsed.

Outside, Lyall fell backwards to the ground, choking and coughing. His eyes felt gritty and his breath was shallow and uneven. Malcolm lay dead where he had dragged him, barely a foot away. The fire crackled and spit around him and he heard the crash of another building collapse. But worst yet was the sound of his mother's pitiful crying.

Around him, his whole world melted into the flames. He stood and led his mother into the woods and farther still. He took Mairi and his mother all the way to the stream, where he used cool water to soothe her burns. He told them he would return, exacting a promise from Mairi to stay put, and assured them they would be safe with Atholl sitting between them. Then he left.

As he passed by the old yew tree, he did not touch the trunk again. The ability to believe in anything, especially foolish things such as luck and wishes and sacred places had left him.

Lyall walked back to Dunkelden without thought or care, out of the cover of the woods and out into the open. He walked to the front entrance and over the bridge, but paused when his eye caught a muddy scrap of yellow that lay in the ditch. He hopped down and picked it up—the traitor's flag, a banner of yellow with a red 'S' for the serpent from the Garden of Eden painted over his father's emblem. He climbed back up to the bridge with the flag in his fist and forward through the burned out gates and the cinders of the guardhouse.

Nothing stood before him but blackened ruins, buildings collapsed, and smoldering fires, the burnt remains of chickens and caged hares that were not taken by the servants. The upper floors of the hall were naught but a huge skein of wood and were still smoldering.

There was no one left in the place but him. Not a chicken, a cow, a lamb or a dove in their mother's cote, even the rats that had oft times been in the cave had fled. His was the only heart that beat in the midst of what once was theirs.

Gone, too, were the men who had done this. The servants, the animals…at least the ones that weren't dead and burnt. He let the banner fall from his numb fingers…the loneliest boy in the world, standing in what felt like hell, with everything he had known as safe now destroyed and burning down around him.

He had two choices: he too could melt under the weight of it all, crumple into a ball and sob himself silly like a wee child. Since his legs were quivering and his blood was racing 'twould have been all too easy. Or he could choose the path he knew his father and brother would have chosen. His age and years were only sums—numbers that had naught to do with anything. His choices and actions were all that mattered. When faced with the choice of cowardice, to just run, run away to anywhere as fast as his legs would carry him, he could not; his true heart could not go there. His father was no traitor, and he vowed he would prove it so, and his brother's life had been uselessly ended. Malcolm would be avenged. Someone had lied, and those lies had set all of this in motion.

Moments later he dragged his brother's limp and broken body toward the smoldering ruins of the chapel and searched the bailey until he found a shovel in the embers of a shed near the stables. The handle was hot, and he used his tunic to pick it up and then dropped it into a nearby trough where it singed and spat when it hit water as if it were just cast by the smithy. Soon he was back standing amidst the black ash and waning smoke next to Malcolm's lifeless body and the flat carved stone marking their father's crypt. Lyall wiped his eyes and began to dig.

It was a long time before he placed the last rock on a stack of stones where Malcolm lay. Exhausted, he fell to his knees beside the graves, his brother's golden cross in his hand, his face heavenward, his arms outward and his head thrown back, and he swore in his brother's name, in his father's name, he would right the wrongs done this day to the house of Robertson.

He picked up his bow and quiver and left; he never looked back, but walked slowly, deliberately. What he carried in his heart was heavy on him. What he carried in his soul and memory affected him through every inch of his blood and bone, down to the very meat of him, and he thought then that he understood the man who carried his own cross to Golgotha.

By the time he joined his mother and sister in the woods, his sister was sitting against the tree as he had been earlier that day, her head nodding forward, looking exhausted. He knew she was frightened. Today she had seen too much of life. He picked up the sack of fish, tying it to his belt as he studied his mother. Her clothing was burned, her face red and swollen, one cheek puckered with burned and blackened skin, one of her eyes unseeing, one hand holding the damp cloth he had torn from their clothing. She sat on a rock by the cool water of the stream as serene as if she were not scarred and half-blinded and mourning. Her lack of emotion said how truly broken she was.

His need for vengeance overcame him in almost uncontrollable waves. His body felt thick with anger. It ran hotly through his blood, firing the need in him to want to kill the men who did this.

Keeping his control and his sanity was not easy, but he needed to be able to see his mother and sister who needed him, not the red heat of revenge.

He knelt down by his sister. "Mairi come. Climb onto my back. I will carry you." He shifted her small, exhausted body, bow and quiver, and stood with her on his back. The silk of her fine hair brushed his face as she laid her sleepy head on his shoulder. Her shallow breaths quivered in her chest and her silent tears dripped onto his sore, fire-scorched neck.

That almost broke him; his own throat choked suddenly with the urge to cry, but he clearly understood his duty and walked over to stand by his mother.

She reached out for him and touched thin air, her good eye spilling with tears and the other naught but a blank stare in the burnt and puckered skin on one side of her once-breathtakingly beautiful face. "Lyall?"

"I am here," he said.

She turned to look at him from her good eye. "Where's Mairi."

"She is asleep. I have her here on my back. See?" He turned. "Take my hand. 'Tis time to go." He helped her to her feet and together they slowly walked away.

FIVE

Glenna opened the weathered stable door barely enough for her to see down the narrow back lane, which was empty. The smell of smoke and the sound of distant voices carried back to her. Before she could close the door, the black suddenly came trotting 'round the corner and down the back alley. He was riderless.

Montrose?

Oh God... She moved swiftly, throwing open the stable door and running down the shadowy lane toward his horse, which was skittish and looked as if he would bolt if there had been any sign of open road.

Cooing and talking softly, she approached him, watching his ears flicker and his eyes dart to hers, then she easily grasped the reins. "Come, my laddie," she said to him. "Come..." In a half run, she led the horse back to the stable. Montrose was in trouble. If she went to help him, the mob would recognize and overtake her.

Her thoughts sped toward some kind of plan, and a moment later she pulled off her hat, unbraiding her hair as she walked with determined steps toward the stall and Skye. Inside her satchel was the package Alastair had given her and she touched it before she moved past it to take out the stolen gown, the only one she owned; this was her only chance. Surely the spicewife would be the only person to recognize it. She had filched it a long three summers before. She changed her shoes, from peasant boots to an expertly tanned and tooled pair of costly red leather lambskin shoes only a noblewoman could afford. She had stolen them near Invergowrie and knew they would show from the jagged edges of the gown as proof of what she was about to claim. But they were too big and slipped when she walked. She ran her fingers through her long hair, wavy and full after its tight braiding, and felt the relief from her scalp from no tight braids. She took a deep breath and glanced out the doors.

She did not dare abandon him when she needed him to get off the island so she could escape safely. Neither a woman nor a lad traveling alone was safe to ferry across the sound. Both El and Al made her swear on her life she would never try to do so.

So she told herself, she needed Montrose for her own safety.

Minutes later, black hair flowing down over her shoulders and back, his signet ring in one fist and her knee up near the pommel and she precariously rode the black back down the lane, praying for balance and courage as she headed for the main road, hoping she could pull off the guise.

What she saw ahead of her did little to ease her nerves. A crowd hovered to either side of Montrose, who was splayed unmoving on the ground and from the looks of the dirt trail, had been dragged over to the side of the road. A group of men were passing buckets of sea water to put out the hay fire and the burning cart. Smoke was everywhere and she could feel it burn her chest.

"Get away from him!" Glenna commanded, waving smoke away, and she rode straight into the middle of the mob. The crowd parted slightly. Montrose was almost unrecognizable. His skin was not burned or charred away—Glenna had unfortunately seen a burned man once and it was horrifically unforgettable—yet his whole face was black with ash and smoke, his clothing singed or burnt where it was covered with chips of ash and pieces of burnt hay. Even his golden hair was ash grey. There was a deep red-blue welt in the crucifix shape of a sword hilt across the skin of his palm, which lay limply next to his fallen weapon. He was so still her heart stopped.

Then he moaned loudly, which gave her great hope, and she released a breath she had not known she had been holding.

"'Tis my gown! I stitched it myself! Look at her! She is wearing my gown!"

Glenna turned and rode directly up to the spicewife, mere a hand's breadth away from the stubborn woman, her chin high so she could look down at the woman when she waved an arm and said, "What is this? You worry over some measly piece of cloth and naught for the life of my lord, Baron Montrose." She paused meaningfully before adding, "You do not know that all you in Steering have grievously harmed the emissary of Himself the king."

The woman stepped back, her eyes narrowed in disbelief, silent but looking pointedly at Glenna's gown and then up to her face. She opened her mouth to speak, but the woman's husband, pulled her back again none too gently, speaking harshly in her ear. That Glenna had implied the whole village was responsible for Montrose's condition was threat enough.

She turned and closed the small distance to Montrose, the crowd stepping away from the black as she eased him forward, and she stopped and dismounted. Montrose lay still as stone. She knelt down, searching for a sign of movement in his chest, a sign he was breathing, but she saw none. "My lord?"

Nothing. Panic raced through her. She leaned over him, her hair shielding them and pooling on his ash covered chest. "Montrose!" she whispered harshly into his black rimmed ear. "Can you hear me? *Montrose!*"

He groaned again and his words were lost and sounded deep and raspy as a wolf's growl. She relaxed somewhat. The man was not dead. The sound made her wonder if his throat was burned, and that perhaps he was gravely injured. Her chest tightened and she touched his jaw and whispered, "I'm sorry."

She turned to the men hovering around them. "Help him. Please."

They looked at her dumbfounded, standing there as useless as ears on a stone.

"I am the Lady Montrose," she lied easily and held out his signet ring as proof. "You must help my lord husband."

Suddenly the men began to move swiftly, giving her helpful words of kindness. The smithy and his laddie rushed back carrying a long wooden door, and four of the men lifted the baron onto it.

"Where can we take him?" She asked, looking up and down the crowded village road. "Is there an herbwife? There must be someone who can help me."

"You! Laddie!" the smithy said to his young apprentice with a gentle swipe at his head. "Go fetch Old Gladdys."

Someone gasped. The smithy ignored them and turned back to her. "We shall take him to the tavern, milady. The old woman will come and help ye care for him."

A fearful muttering spread back over the crowd, "Old Gladdys? The witch? Not her, surely…."

Glenna faced the smith. "Why are they wary?"

"The old woman ferried across from the mainland one day," he explained.

"'Twas the day of the summer solstice," someone else said in the dire tone of a Greek chorus.

The smithy looked at Glenna, shaking his head with exasperation. "She is naught but an old crone claiming healing powers. Some are suspicious. A few call her a witch because of her potions and strange Welsh ways, and she herself claims to be some kind of Druid, as if they still exist." He laughed at the idea.

An older woman standing nearby crossed herself and mumbled something dark about witches and witchcraft existing beyond time.

"For as many who believe she is a witch, or question her sense and words," the smithy continued, "there are twice as many who have been saved by her potions and will argue she is truly an angel."

"Aye, milady," said another woman, elbowing her way to the front of the crowd. "Old Gladdys saved my husband when he was injured from a scythe and his arm festered."

"She saved my babe!" said another.

"And my daughter in childbed."

"I care not what she is called," Glenna said. "Only that she is skilled."

"Take solace, milady. She has yet to send a single soul to his grave."

"Although looking at her could surely do the trick," a young man said and some of the crowd laughed. "Hers is not the face of an angel."

But the men were already lifting the board with Montrose to their shoulders and moving slowly and carefully toward the tavern. Glenna turned to follow, but a rough hand on her arm stopped her. The spice woman would not let things be.

"I would advise you to take your hand away, spicewife," Glenna said imperiously, and she faced the woman once again. Then she glanced over her shoulder where the men were carrying Montrose and realized the woman's husband was one of the men helping him.

Her gaze met the woman's briefly, and then she turned to the black's saddle and reached into Montrose's bags. With a handful of silver, enough to buy more fine gowns than she could ever imagine, she pressed the coins into the woman's rough hands and then held them tightly in her own. "I say to you that my young brother gave me this gown as a gift. What say you, spice seller?"

The woman slightly opened her hands and glanced down, her reaction first shock as the coins caught the sunlight and shone in her palm like fish skin, then she looked up at Glenna and smiled as brightly as the sun when she said, "I say your brother has a fine eye, milady."

Inside the Steering alehouse, the men carrying Montrose set him down atop two oak tavern tables shoved together and stood around arguing over what should be done first, all of them talking to Glenna at once. The scent of stale ale made her belly wallow and her head was spinning. She was greatly worried. Montrose was still out.

The whole of the village, curious and noisy, looked to be shoving their way into the small room to see the great lord felled and almost burnt to death in the middle of Steering. A tavern maid set down a tray with some pieces of linen, a wooden bowl, and a ewer of water on the table next to him. The girl called Glenna milady, so she was feeling less fearful of discovery and more afraid of what she would do if Montrose didn't awaken.

While all were discussing remedies and cures encompassing everything from a poultice of mustard, goose blood, and cow spittle to a tisane of St John's Wort, Glenna wrung out the cloth in the cool water and laid it on his filthy brow, thinking she should pour the water over his head like she did when El got drunk last year and fell off his horse and wouldn't awaken. If that did not bring Montrose 'round, at least it would clean his face, she thought with humor as black as his sooty skin.

From the doorway came a strange and sudden murmuring, and the crowd parted slightly as a small old woman elbowed and twisted her way through the thick throng of people gathering in the small back room of the tavern. She wore a long, dark woolen tunic, the side panels embroidered with colorful images of suns and crescent moons, animal-like figures in odd positions. A huge cat-like creature standing on hind legs and reaching upward toward a large silver moon was stitched entirely of a silvery thread. The tunic was belted to her thin waist with a hammered metal girdle that had strange and ancient looking markings engraved into it. In her right hand she carried a long willow staff strung with small brightly-colored, cloth herb bags, one with cattails sticking out of it. A long bladder pipe also hung down from the bend in the staff.

"Where is he? This nobleman who was hurt," she was saying, her voice clear and as melodic as harp music, a sharp contrast to her hair and face. Using her staff, she shoved a young farmer aside and chided him for not moving swiftly enough.

"Old Gladdys," she heard some of them whisper as the woman passed them.

"Stop yer gabbling and get ye out of my path. Is not a great lord all but dying?"

Glenna supposed if there were a Druid witch alive at that time she would have looked like Gladdys. The Welsh woman had wild and curly white hair, a face weathered by the sun (and perhaps the wind, a strong wind…a storm…a raging storm) skin like spotted sausage and the sharp black eyes and a nose like a beak of a peregrine falcon. As El would have said, 'she has a cheese-face, one that could curdle milk.'

But then Glenna had noticed oft times men were all about the look and shape of a woman and cared not a whit for her mind, and even less for her tongue. Her brothers were no different. She preferred to believe that perhaps Gladdys might have been a handsome woman in her youth, which looked to be a long, long time ago.

Gladdys glanced down at Montrose, put her thin, knobby hand on his throat for a moment, then looked away. She unhooked her bladder pipe and blew a loud, discordant note that quieted the voices in the room and said, "Stand back ye!" Then she began to hum and twirl, spinning in a circle, her long white hair the color of morning mist flying outward as she turned, her arms out, the staff almost swiping at the heads of some of the crowd, who backed quickly away. Her humming quickly changed into a chant:

> "Eena, meena, mona, mite,
> Basca, tora, hora, bite
> Hugga, bucca, bau ,
> Eggs, butter, cheese, bread,
> Stick, stock, stone dead.
> O-u-t! Out!"

Within heartbeats the room had nearly cleared, most running from the old woman like their hair was afire. Even the believers' eyes grew wide and they scurried away. Only two merchants and the smithy remained.

"Need ye help with your lord, milady?" the smithy said kindly. "We will stay."

Glenna declined. "There is no need for you to stay. My thanks to you, all of you. My lord will be grateful," she added as she pressed a piece of silver into each of their hands, and they shuffled to the door.

"If ye need help, send someone." And the smithy left, but not before he glanced at Gladdys, then shook his head muttering about her tossing wood on the fire of fools.

With the room empty but for Montrose and the two of them, the old woman grew silent and slowly stopped spinning. For merely a heartbeat, Glenna thought that Gladdys could see her for who she was, and wasn't, saw into her past and her future, saw her weaknesses and even her escape plan. It was unsettling to have someone look at you as if they could see not only what you hid from the world, but also see inside to the darkest corners of your heart and your head.

The old woman tapped her staff three times and stared at Glenna from sharp and knowing black eyes. It took a trickster to know one.

"That was curious display," Glenna said to her, skepticism in her tone and waving her hand casually at the old woman's performance. "Tell me. What exactly does your chant heal?"

The old woman eyed her for a long moment, and then she smiled quite evilly and winked when she said, "An overcrowded room."

Glenna laughed. But Gladdys was looking at her no more and instead had turned to Montrose. She leaned low over him and used the cloth to clean around his eyes and some of the soot from his face. At the sight of the old woman's frown, Glenna smile fell away and she stepped closer. "He will wake up."

Gladdys looked at her. "Ye be the *wife*?"

"Aye," Glenna lied, trying to look down her nose as if daring the old woman to doubt her word.

"Hmrph," was all Gladdys said, a word that carried a load of doubt, and she turned back to Montrose and slid open each of his eyelids with her thumb and peered closely into his eyes. "His eyes be red and swollen from the ash." She lifted his head from the board and felt around underneath. "And he has a knot the size of me fist on the back of his head."

She pulled her hand away and began to clean his face and brow and 'round his closed eyes. As Glenna hovered closer, Gladdys waved her away and said in an irritated tone, "Go and make yerself useful. There, see?" She pointed to her staff leaning against a chair. "Bring me that brown bag, and the green one." She used her unusually long-fingered hands to squeeze and press gently downward on his chest, and he moaned again.

Glenna stopped, worried.

"Bring me the bags! He's not dying. 'Tis but his ribs, and why his breathing is so shallow he looks dead. Most likely he cracked one or two rib bones. Go fetch a bowl and spoon from the maid, and another ewer of water. Go, go...."

Glenna spent the next few minutes scurrying back and forth and doing exactly as Gladdys demanded, even when she asked her to send someone for a cup of sea water from the nearby sound. She made a poultice and used linen to tightly bind it to his chest.

The old woman mixed the sea water with some powders from the bags, opened his lids and spooned the concoction into his eyes, then waited, counting in Welsh, "*Un, dau, tri, pedwar...deg,*" before she put more liquid in again. The ritual continued a few more times then she set down the bowl and spoon and stood back, watching him closely as if she were waiting for something.

After a few tense moments she laughed out loud and pointed at him. "There 'tis. See? The poultice and bindings are good. His breathing is becoming deeper."

Glenna studied the deeper rise and fall of his chest, watched the golden cross around his neck move as he inhaled deeper than before, and she felt her own relief. He took another deep breath and the cross on the chain fell to the side, revealing a bright red mark near his throat. Like the sword imprint on his palm, this was a burn mark from the cross, which must have grown too hot from the heat of the fire. He'll have a scar, she thought.

He murmured something she did not hear.

"Look there," Gladdys said with a slight cackle. "He's calling for his mum."

"There's no shame in calling for one's mother," Glenna defended quickly, her gaze meeting the woman's.

"If ye had one," Gladdys said sharply.

"Aye." Glenna's voice drifted off. "If you have one." She looked away.

Gladdys placed her hand on her shoulder and said kindly, "Fret ye not, girl. Trust old Gladdys. All will be well, but it will take some time for ye." Then she picked up the pitcher and stuck her finger in it, stared at her finger glistening from the water, then looked inside the ewer for a moment. She looked up. "I believe 'tis cold enough," she said and dumped the water on his head.

Lyall reared up, coughing and choking. Eyes wide open but seeing only blurred light and shadow. He drew a large breath of air and pain shot from his chest like an arrow down through his body, and he groaned loudly, bent double, and a blasphemous curse left his lips. His ribs had been broken many times at tourneys and at the tilt field. The pain was all too familiar. His eyes teared from it, which did not help; they felt full of sand, and he shook his head...his wet head...and his hair slapped and stuck to his cheek. Disoriented, he instinctively reached for his weapon, but his sword belt was gone. He squinted at the smaller blurred figures, women, standing nearby.

The brittle stench of smoke and burnt wood, a smell and taste from his youth he would never forget, was lodged in his nose and on his dry tongue. Light-headed, he raised his hand to his brow, which was hurting, then slid it to the back of his neck, where the skin felt sore, as if burned by the hot sun. What was this? He was a man, not a lad of ten. Where in the bloody hell was he?

A gentle hand touched him, followed by the shadow of a woman, her hair long and flowing brushed against his arm. "You are in Steering, my lord. In a tavern. You were thrown from your horse."

All came flooding back to him. "Glenna?"

"Aye."

"Yer wife," a woman with a musical voice said.

"My what?" Lyall swung his legs over the side and tried to stand. The room swam and he gripped the table till his knuckles felt white.

"My lord, husband," Glenna said quickly, taking his hand in hers and nearly squeezing all the blood from it. Her other hand pushed hard on his shoulder. "Lie back down, my love," she said through gritted teeth. "You hit your head and your sense is meandering. Fret not. I am here with you."

He followed her lead, stayed silent and let her push him back down, curious to see how this played out. His sight was still off and he was weaponless. "Where is my sword? Bring it to me."

"You must rest," she insisted, starting to turn away.

He grabbed her by the hand and pulled her down close enough to whisper in her ear, "Afraid I might use it on you...wife?"

"No more afraid than you were of my bow and arrows. You need no weapon," she hissed back at him. "There is no one here now but the healer. You are safe."

"That I am lying here on my back and half blinded is proof I am not safe with you nearby," he said.

"Step back, milady," said the melodic voice. A strange, full-haired shadow of light and dark loomed over him. "Let me put more mixture into his eyes."

He released Glenna's wrist and she scurried back away. "My eyes? What mixture?" he asked the shadow.

"To wash away the ash and soot and soothe your poor eyes."

"The hay cart fire," he said flatly, remembering, and he eased back down and let the healer minister her medicine.

" 'Twill clear your vision, my lord."

So he blinked and let her add more.

"Can you see yet?"

"Soon. Try again," he said encouraging her as she added more liquid to his eyes. It was working. She repeated the process and each time he blinked his vision became clearer, then slowly the shadow above him took sharp form.

His first reaction was to flinch but to do so would have insulted her. Out of appreciation for the old woman's help, he returned her gaze kindly. He sat up again.

"You can see clearly?" Glenna came nearer.

"Aye...wife. As clearly as the day we were wed," he said wryly and watched her flush. "Ah, one of my favorite memories. Surely you, too, remember it well."

"Aye," she agreed, eyeing him suspiciously.

He snatched her hand and pulled her closer, slipping his arm around her waist and resting his hand low on her soft and rounded buttocks. "Tell our tale to the miracle healer here. I'm certain she would find our great romance vastly interesting...a tale for the bards."

Her eyes narrowed dangerously, and he merely smiled and rubbed circles over and over on her backside. She looked ready to bolt, so he gripped her more tightly. In turn, she cleared her throat loudly and pressed her elbow near his sore ribs and he winced and grabbed her elbow in a tight grip.

She would pay for that, he thought. She tried to edge away a step, but he pulled her back, slapping her buttocks harder. "Stay close, my sweet and tell the tale."

"It was in the spring," Glenna began.

"Winter, sweetings," he corrected. "After the first snow. Surely you recall as do I, as if it was yesterday, not but barely two years—"

"Six month hence," she volunteered at the same time, and she hurriedly said, "Two years and six months."

"The winter air was clear and brisk."

" 'Twas spring," she said pointedly. "Look, Montrose. Do you wish for me to tell the tale or not? Remember, my love," she said sweetly, "that you have been recently knocked silly in the head, which would not have happened if I had my bow and arrows."

"But not even a blow to the head could make me forget meeting you."

"Most likely because your head is so hard," she said under her breath.

"On with you, wife. Tell the tale."

"I do not think so. Since you do not know the time of year we met, it is certain you are still too feeble-minded from your ordeal. You should rest now," she said, patting his hand overly hard. "One would hate to find you exerted yourself and then turned into a simpleton."

"It would take more than a conk on the noggin for me to forget that day...you vixen." He held her to his side in an iron grip. "She was like a cat in heat, so hungry she was for a good man. I carried the scratches on my back for weeks." He brushed her chin with his knuckle. "Close your mouth, love, else 'twill catch flies."

"It is you, my lord *husband*," she said quietly, "who is made of the same stuff that attracts the flies."

"Aye. Sweet as honey," he said loud and merrily. "That surely is our love. Sweet. Sweet. Sweet." He nuzzled her ear. "I could lick you all over."

She gasped and stepped away.

He gave an exaggerated sigh. "I see that our great romance is not to be told of on this day. Therefore I apologize, madam. I believe my *wife* has grown suddenly modest."

The old woman turned and reached for her staff, but not before she gave him a quick wink. Lyall shifted, looking around the room, and he spotted his saddlebags in the corner along with Glenna's belongings. He noticed then the great hound was not at her side and wondered where it was. Slowly he stood and felt the solidness of ground with relief, his legs firmly planted and his head did not swim, his sight clear, perhaps, surprisingly, clearer than before the hay fire.

A few minutes later he handed some silver to the healer. "You have my gratitude, old woman."

"I am Gladdys," she said, giving him a penetrating and long and silent look, before she turned to leave. "And I can only heal a hairsbreadth of what has passed."

His mood, light from all that foolishness with Glenna, waned quickly, and he grew quiet and pensive from the old woman's knowing look.

She paused in the doorway and faced them both, tapping her staff three times, until Glenna, too, had turned around and was paying attention.

"This room still be over-crowded," she said directly to Glenna. "Deceit weighs heavily in the air."

He stared long and hard at the woman. What was she about?

"Know ye, girl," she continued. "I have no chant to fix what problems plague ye in the here and now."

Lyall could see Glenna's unhappy reaction—her pale skin and tight lips and jaw. She did not like what she'd heard.

The woman's wise dark gaze moved to him. "Nor can I mend yer troubles, my lord. Ye will find that prize which ye seek and all that goes with it…that which foolish men believe they want, what drives them to do what they will. But understand and trust me when I say to ye both…there are far too many lies inside this room." And she left them alone.

The room grew heavy with their silence and the strange and unsettling truth in the old woman's words.

After another tense moment Glenna turned around and laughed bitterly. "Foolish woman and her predictions. Druid? Bah! Lies? Aye, there are too many lies. After yesterday, I've had my fill of lies." She marched toward the doorway. "I'm going to the stables. I need to check on the animals." And she closed the doors without looking back.

He did not try to stop her, but what Gladdys had said cut to the quick...not about lies, but about truths, and soon he, too, got up and left.

SIX

'Twas late when Lyall returned to the tavern, the closest thing to an inn in the small coastal village on the southeastern side of the island. Their preplanned traveling route had been in place, secure before he ever ventured out on this secret deed, one which could turn out to be his biggest folly. Though their destination was to the south, he had chosen Steering for a reason, not knowing then the truth about the Gordons' thieving trade over the past years, something that put a chink in all those well-made, well-mulled over plans.

While the southern side of the isle had a port and shorter crossing, they would land on the northeastern edges of Skye, part of Leod lands, and Leod had strong ties to the King of Mann. The more who knew what was afoot, the higher the risk for failure, so the decision was made to take Glenna over the longer route. The most trouble would come from the unpredictable. Who knew how many victims of the Gordons' antics he had yet to face…and buy off?

Lyall sought out the tavern master and made arrangements for hot food and sleeping pallets. Early the next morn, they would take the first ship to ferry them across the Minch and back to the mainland. He'd paid a handsome sum for the speediest ship of the two available, one with a large sail, a sleek bow, and the strongest oarsmen. But what had cost him most dearly was the ransom he'd paid to the sellers of the merchant fair, where his marks bought recompense and promised peace for all goods Glenna and the thieving Gordons had stolen...and probably some for goods never stolen, considering the final sum he'd paid for their vows of silence.

From all the yammering and many tales that filled his aching ears, the threesome had been robbing them blind for a long time. His wealth—which was hard won through tourneys and the hiring out of his sword arm—could not buy back his family's lands, he thought bitterly, but it bought silence in Steering.

The back room of the alehouse was empty when he returned, but the shutters were tightly closed and a tended fire cast amber light as it burned in the rock pit in the center of the room, where a smoke hole in the roof pulled the firesmoke up and out. He grabbed a lantern and went in search of Glenna in the stables. His intention was to care for his horse and then drag her back to the tavern.

The air was overly warm, heat from the livestock, which made the odor of horse sweat, manure, and hay even more pungent. In the closest stall, her bay mare had been curried down and fed, while his own horse, also curried, was eating comfortably from a feed trough half-filled with fresh oats.

Glenna was nowhere to be seen. He turned to leave, wondering where the hell she had gone, when he heard a thumping against the wooden boards, coming from a back stall.

Inside was her lop-eared hound, looking at him like a simpleton, adoring and more beggar than dog. The hound's mouth hung open, tongue lolling as if he were grinning and his tail drummed excitedly against the stall.

Curled next to him on a bed of straw lay his owner. She was sound asleep, her head resting on a silken piece of crimson velvet trimmed in gold braid, the tail of black rook showing under her cheek. Her ragged-tailed gown had drawn up to reveal a shapely leg, calf, knee, and thigh, as milk white as the unblemished skin of her face. The image of her naked, that pale skin like fresh snow, came racing into his mind's eye.

Hand resting on the post of the stall, Lyall couldn't move for a moment and took in the beauty before him. Her long black hair was as dark as midnight against her skin and spread about her shoulders, curling like thick Shetland wool. Standing and looking at her like that, there was no denying her lineage; she was the daughter of the king, a treasure hidden from the world, and his own salvation.

Oh, that he could pull this off. He looked away from her and rubbed the back of his neck, then found himself drawn to her again. At first glance, one would think she looked like a waif from the streets of Edinburgh with her jagged-hemmed gown that hung wrong, lying there asleep in a bed a straw, her head resting on what was clearly an expensive piece of embroidery. One of the overly large red leather shoes was half off her foot revealing a fine-boned ankle.

Red shoes. He shook his head again and felt a smile touch his lips. He shoved away from the post and knelt down in the straw, his hand reaching out to her. But the hound trotted over to nudge against his palm, and so he scratched the dog's floppy ears.

"Glenna...Wake up, sweetheart," he said quietly, then realized what he called her and wanted to swallow his foolish words. He looked at the dog, who was staring at him expectantly. The hound was most likely starved. "Fortunate for me that she sleeps like a boulder," he said to the dog and paused. "Two days with her and I've gone mad...I am having a conversation with her dog," he said, aware more than ever that he had been knocked hard in the head that day.

He scooped her up into his arms and winced when a sharp pain shot through his ribs. He paused, then crossed the short distance to the stable doors. "Come, dog!" he said sharply, refusing to call it by some foolish name. The beast loped happily after him. He kicked the doors closed harder than was necessary and turned toward the tavern backdoor.

She moaned softly and wiggled closer, her cheek against his shoulder, the velvet cloth spilling over his arm, her mouth soft and the color of a ripe berry and her lips parted. Her long hair fell down like black silk and brushed against his thigh as he walked. His reaction did not please him.

Inside the tavern's backroom, he lay her down on a straw pallet in the corner. Heat seemed to surround him, and he felt singed. He quickly put some distance between them and slumped miserably into a chair, his ribs sending biting pain through his upper body. He stretched his long legs out in front of him and drank copiously from a goblet of wine, ignoring her, glowering at everything, even the barmaid who brought them oatbread, butter, and some bean pottage.

Earlier the tavern lass had made it clear he was welcome to her bed in the loft above the ale room. He tossed her a coin and watched her sway out of the room. She paused at the door, faced him, apparently unaffected by his foul mood and ignoring Glenna's existence, and she smiled fetchingly. "If you change yer mind, my lord, ye know where I be."

He turned away to look at the sleeping form in the corner, rubbing his mouth with his hand, elbow resting on the chair arm. Here, when his body could use a good romp and swift tumbling, he could not bring himself to go to the wench whose soft, full body promised satisfaction and whose exotic, sloe-eyed stare told him she wanted him inside her. He closed his eyes, ignored his ribs and finished off the wine.

Hell's teeth...half the village thought Glenna was his wife—a fact that would not stop many men of his ilk from seeking comfort wherever offered. No one in Steering knew the truth...except that old Welsh witch who knew all too much.

His gaze wandered back to Glenna; he did not need a woman so badly he would insult her, even if their marriage was a lie. He drove a hand through his hair, then rubbed his tight neck. Her public claim and his agreement would have amounted to a handfast, and a binding public betrothal. Luckily for him Glenna was not the Lady Montrose. Half the village thought Glenna was his wife. The real Lady Montrose was not dead, but alive and more than likely happily sitting before her embroidery stanchion in the tower room at Rossie.

Deception had its advantages.

Handfast marriage was supposed to be a convenience, and existed here in a land whose breadth and wild extremities made marriage ceremonies convenient only when there was a clergy nearby. Men of God were readily available to the wealthy nobility (the Church and a man's coin were seldom far apart from each other). Silver and gold bought absolution and penance, bought ceremonies of baptism, funeral, and marriage.

But for the people of villages, of the manors and castles where their lords were often gone to war—to crusade, diplomacy, or forced by their oaths of honor and fealty into eight months service to their liege, the laws of handfasting made marriage possible without waiting for months and even years for a priest to happen by. A public declaration of husband and wife by a man and woman was a binding handfast betrothal, and if the handfast was consummated, the marriage was legal.

Consummation... He took a drink of wine. The lust he was feeling be damned to Hell—at least that was what he mentally chanted over and over when his gaze repeatedly wandered to the corner where she slept, her bare legs uncovered again and calling to him. He shifted uncomfortably in his seat, refilled his goblet and drank deeply, telling himself he controlled his body, not the other way 'round. But the truth was: he was living in his own hell, where the flames were licking at his feet...and between his legs.

He recognized the danger before him, but knew, too, that if he wanted her, he could have her. A young man on the tourney circuit learned more than the techniques of war. Seduction was as much a weapon as his finely-forged sword, and as a careless youth he had used that power merely because he could, or to fill time and satisfy his own curiosity—a desire to learn the extent of man's power over a woman—how far could he go? He learned he could go as far as he wanted.

But he was no longer a callow youth whose lust guided his actions, who plunged his sword recklessly into his prey—he had lived that lesson—and his ego was not such that he needed to tick off another conquest. The consequences were too high a price and he had waited a long, long time for Dunkeldon.

The half full wine ewer sat in front of him, and he refilled his cup. His desire and drive to regain what was taken from them was what consumed him—an obsession that was behind every single piece of silver or gold he'd earned, and behind the choices he now made. He drained the goblet and set it down hard on the table, wiping his mouth with his other hand. The girl did not matter. She was merely a means to an end.

"Get up!"

Glenna awoke from the prod of Montrose's boot tip. Disoriented, she opened her eyes. The wooden wall was just inches away from her nose. She had to turn over to face him and winced.

He stood over her, his face hard and shadowed; he held a bright yellow torchlight that flickered over his taut features.

She threw her arm over her eyes and groaned.

"God's eyes, woman! Cover yourself!"

What was wrong with him? She kicked and wiggled her gown

down over her bare legs. He grunted something and turned away, so she closed her eyes. Just a little more sleep...

"Get. Up," he said impatiently. "The ship sails with the early tide." He paused, then bellowed. "Glenna!"

Lord, but the man was loud. She took a long-suffering breath and sat up, shoving the hair out of her face and frowning up at the intensity she saw in his gaze. "Why are you so angry?"

"'Tis late."

"But it is still dark."

"Change back into these." He tossed her peasant clothes at her. "We have no time for arguments."

"I was not arguing. I was pointing out a simple fact."

"We have no time for idle chatter." He spun around and walked to the door that led to the stables. "Come dog!"

Fergus loped over to his side—the traitor—and a minute later the door closed with a resounding thud. The urge to throw her shoe at it was overwhelming, but she cherished those red shoes and would never risk damaging them. Although... Had he still been standing there barking at her—Montrose not Fergus—she might have risked her shoe for the joy of watching it bounce off his hard head.

She paused and picked up the infant coverlet, touching almost reverently the stitches that formed the intricate designs. *Her mother made this for her.* She bit her lip against the silly tears she felt rising. She swiftly wrapped it up and tucked it away before Montrose came back in bellowing for her to hurry. She dressed, carefully sliding into her peasant boots—the red shoes had rubbed blisters on her toes—and she braided her hair, muttering a litany of new names for him, "My lord Judas..." No, that was her dog. "My lord Thickskull. My lord Goathead. My lord Lackwit." All had a certain satisfying ring to them.

When he came back through the door, Fergus at his side, she was ready to leave and stood there hugging her satchel tightly to her chest, stubbornly determined to remain silent. Apparently he still was angry because he was glaring at everything. He bent down and picked up her hat, shoved it down on her head and said, "Cover your cursed hair."

Silent, she twisted her braid up under the hat and tied the strings under her chin. Like some lackey she followed him outside, where their mounts were waiting. They led their mounts toward the docks with him lecturing her about acting like a lad—apparently there was time for idle chatter—before he went moodily quiet. From then on he spoke no more, except to warn her to stay clear of everyone and to keep 'that hat on.'

"According to my brothers, my lord, even a lad is unsafe from some men aboard the ships, so I don't see why keeping my hat on matters."

"Just do as I asked," he said through gritted teeth, tightening his grip on her arm and half dragging her along.

"Odd that I heard no question…only a command."

He said her name as if it were a curse word.

Fine! Do as he arrogantly demanded, she thought miserably and was about to say so until she caught a glimpse of his face. Clearly he wanted to fling her into the sea and be done with her. At the gangplank, he released her and stood stewing as she led Skye up the wooden ramp, then he began barking directions at her and warnings that were completely unnecessary, since Skye moved swiftly and easily onboard. Montrose followed with his horse, which balked and pulled at his bit and gave him some trouble. She smiled, then echoed his warnings, which earned her a cold look that said he had no sense of humor.

On the captain's orders, poor Fergus was stowed on the dark belly of the mid-deck with the horses and cargo, above the oar deck. After she removed Skye's saddle and secured her belongings by Montrose's packs, she paused, then turned toward the ladder, but Fergus gave her that big-eyed lonely look. She started to walk away from him, head high. "Do not look to me for pity, you traitorous hound. Turn your lamenting looks upon your new master, my lord Thickskull, Goathead, Lackwit Montrose."

Fergus whimpered pitifully.

So Glenna ran back and rubbed Fergus on his big shaggy ears and under his chin. "You are an ungrateful whelp."

His eyes wide and contrite, he licked her hand lovingly.

"I'll come back later," she promised, just as Montrose stuck his head down the hold, a bright lantern hanging from his fist—the man had a penchant for blinding her—and he blustered at her to come up.

"Did you not hear me?" He half-yelled.

Blinding her, apparently, was second only to his penchant for shouting at her....

The sun was not yet up and already her head ached from all his bellowing. Did the man not understand the concept of honeyed words?

"Are you deaf?"

She stopped. Her brother El would have turned and run like the Devil himself was at his back from the look she gave Montrose, but he appeared completely unaffected. The more he browbeat her, the more she felt the intense need to try to spite him.

She took her sweet time, moving as slowly as she could without being overly obvious, then she stopped, wincing. "Oh! There is a stone in my shoe." She removed her shoe, shaking it, searching inside and taking her sweet time.

Eyes narrowed, he pinned her with a hard look that told her steam was ready to come out his ears. In a serious and deadly calm voice he said, "You would be well-served to move more swiftly."

"With a stone in my shoe, my lord, 'tis difficult to move at all much less more swiftly," she said sweetly and then pretended to drop her shoe. "Oh!" She bent to pick it up and leaned against a beam for balance while she took her sweet time slipping it back on and tieing the strings.

His eyes were closed and his lips were moving as if he were praying...or counting.

"Oh. Wait," she said. "How the devil did that happen?" She sighed hugely. "Look at this." She pulled on a hat string. "My hat strings have come loose. How fortunate for me I caught it. We wouldn't want my hat to fall off and reveal my cursed hair." She fumbled for a moment, then another, and another before she set about retying them...as swiftly as an ancient blind woman.

'Twas quite enjoyable when she was finished to look up and see his jaw clenched that tightly. She resisted the urge to whistle a jaunty melody as she sauntered over to the ladder leading above-deck. She paused at the base, hand on the ladder rails and then sweetly smiled up at him.

He was counting.

She was trying not to laugh. A cursed eye for an eye.... A cursed tooth for a tooth....

The wind picked up shortly after dawn, and the oarsmen kicked the locks and pulled in their oars. Square sails caught the breath of wind and billowed and snapped, sending the ship cutting through the water and out into the open firth, where the waters eventually grew as wild as the skies above, and became stormy and gray...the same color, Lyall realized, as Glenna's skin.

For most of the day the ship rolled over the growing sea, and she clung to the railing near the aft, hanging there limply, and soon her pallor was no longer gray, but greenish, as if she had eaten grass. She lay with her cheek pressed to the side of the ship, her arm flung over her head.

He placed his hand on her shoulder.

She opened her eyes and stared dully at his boots. "If you have come to bellow at me again, do not...please...just kill me and put me out of my misery."

She looked miserable. He thought to help and tried to give her some water, but she groaned, held up her hand, and told him to leave her be.

When he offered her an oatcake a while later, she muttered curse words he had never heard come from a woman.

The waters grew, waves sloshing over the deck, sending the ship lurching over the waves, and he was worried about her. He waited longer than he was comfortable before he approached her again and told her she should be under the canvas shelter where she was safe.

She answered him by spilling the contents of her belly at his feet, so he went to wash his boots. The crew appeared too busy to notice her, or if they did, they chose to ignore her. But Lyall stayed within sight of her, his hand on his weapon.

Overhead the clouds grew thick and thundering, and in time, blocked out everything. The only light he could see came from crackling flashes of lightning and he could not say what the time of day. The wind came on strong and wild; it began to howl like wolves and the ship pitched and rocked as the sea slapped against it.

The sky grew blacker, as did the sea, and the some of the crew scurried to take down the sail before the wind sent them keeling over. He could hear the oar master shouting commands on the oar deck. Whenever the ship rolled over a swell, the oars cut through the water in desperate rhythm to steady the course.

Though Glenna clung to the side and continued to beg him to leave her be, Lyall stood solidly behind her, worried she was no longer safe there, weak as she looked; the waters were growing into a tempest, buffeting the ship over the roiling sea.

The clouds swooped down ominously dark and low. Rain began to spit down on the decks; the swells grew higher, and a wave washed dangerously over the decks as the sharply-arched prow of the ship plummeted down the backside of the steepest wave yet.

As they plunged down the next swell and the next, Lyall saw the oars come up on the starboard side and the ship listed sharply. Men began shouting and one of the crew was the first to lash himself to the mast. Lyall tightly pinned Glenna to the strake of the ship with his whole body, his ribs protesting. Her head lolled back, her hat still on but sodden, her braid tumbled out, and she looked up at him as if she wanted someone to throw her overboard.

He took a deep breath and swept her up into his arms, planning to take her to safety despite her stubbornness, despite the pain.

She grabbed a handful of his hair in her fist and yanked hard. "No! Please…do not move. Do not move," she moaned and her hand went to her mouth just as a wave swept over the side and sent them both crashing to the deck and sliding down as the ship listed.

Water went up his nose and in his eyes. He lost his hold on her, pain stabbed through his chest and the deck seemed to sway and rock and slip.

He heard her scream his name.

"Glenna!" he called out but the sound was swallowed by the storm.

Panic hit him. By luck or by God, he grabbed a handful of her wet tunic and gripped the ballast stone with his other arm as another wave washed over them. If he had not broken his ribs before, if he did not know that pain, he was not certain he could have saved her. The ship righted and he clung hard to her clothes. She coughed and spat. He held fast, saltwater stinging his eyes, then he felt her move, crawling onto him, her arms clinging to his thigh.

"Montrose." Her voice was waterlogged, panicked.

He hauled her up to his chest with one hand and sheer determination and held her fast. "Wrap your legs around my waist, your arms around my neck. Hang on tightly." He crawled over the square stone, then pulled them upright, his feet slipping on the slick deck, but he gripped a line overhead and held them steady. Before the next wave washed the deck, he made a run for the hold, slipping and sliding the last short distance.

The wooden hatch was closed and he gripped the iron hatch ring just before the ship's motion sent them down onto the deck boards. He lay over her, protecting her with his whole body as the vessel moved straight up the side of a wave and more water sluiced over and past them, before the ship pitched downward again and hit the floor of a wave so hard he heard her grunt from the impact and pain from his ribs almost blinded him.

He took two deep breaths, then quickly got to his knees, jerked open the hold, shoved her down and slammed it shut just as another wave came and sent him tumbling across the deck. He hit hard against the side of the ship. His ribs sent piercing pain down his whole body. The air left his lungs.

Suddenly the water was lifting him, up and up. He reached out blindly and grasped a rope, pulling himself hand over hand until he hit the knot at an iron line cleat and held on with everything he had.

Below decks the oarsmen still rowed, their master shouting, his voice distant in the sound of the wind and sloshing sea, almost as if they were on another ship. Soaked, Lyall's clothing kept weighing him down. He tried to pull off his gambeson, but it was stuck on a shoulder, tugging, pulling him with the next wave. The ironwork inside of it was impossible to cut with his knife, so he hacked at the leather seam, the blade slicing into arm and he felt the instant sting of saltwater.

The hatch flew open with a loud thud, and Glenna's head, black hair wet, straggling and loose, came up through. "Montrose!" she screamed.

He realized she was going to climb out and try to come to him. "Nay! Stay there! Close the hatch!"

But she only looked at him with such a look of fierce determination that he knew what she was going to do. Foolishly, she braced her hands on the edge of the hold and started to pull herself up and out.

He had one chance, a break between waves and pitches of the storm, and he shoved off from the side of the ship, sliding, almost swimming across the deck toward her. His hands closed over the edge of the hatch. Then she was pulling him down head-first, her fists tugging on his sodden undertunic as he fell down into the hold.

Water rushed in and over them, a nearby lantern hissed and the tallow candle went out, but other lanterns with candles as thick as his forearm rocked and flickered from iron hooks on the mid beams. Somehow she managed to slam the hatch closed. Standing on the ladder, she turned toward him. "Montrose?"

Unable to move, he lay flat on his back on the wet boards, the air driven from his chest, as if he had been thrown from a horse. He could hear the panic cries of the horses back in the aft deck, hear their hooves stomping on the boards. He tried to move but the edges of his vision began to darken. He was going to black out. Panic swelled in him as he watched the world fade…

Lastly, limned inside his last circle of vision was Glenna, hair like a tangle of black seaweed, leaning closely over him. Her frightened eyes searched his face.

A moment later her small fist jabbed him hard in the belly.

He gasped, sucked in a breath, and air, sweet, wet air, filled his chest… His ribs protested and pain like a lance down his right side. Starry bright light swam before his damp eyes. When the shadows of pain disappeared, he was breathing again, shallow breaths, because his ribs were still so battered that he dared not take even half of a deep breath.

She grabbed his shirt and shook him. "Montrose? Montrose! *Montrose!*"

"I hear you," he said, then winced. "Stop shaking me, woman." She let go and he slowly pulled himself upright, wincing, head down for a moment, his arms resting on his raised knees. His search for more breath was not a simple one.

When he felt he could speak, he met her worried gaze with a dark look. "That was a most foolish thing to do."

"To hit you in the belly? I think not. You can breathe again."

"No. Not your fist in my belly. I thank you for that. 'Twas folly for you to open that hatch."

The ship pitched again and she fell into him. He pulled her against him and she did not fight him; she settled into his side as easily as if she were grateful for his presence. They did not speak, and he wondered if her thoughts were where his were: what might have been? Was she wondering like he was how long he would have withstood the tormented seas.

Below deck the oarsman still shouted his commands. The oars slapped at the water, and a man screamed out that his strake had broken. There was a ruckus. The horses were skittish; he could hear the thuds of their hooves shifting on the boards, and Glenna's hound got up and padded over to them.

The realization of how close they had come to dying hit him, and he thought of Robert Grey, Mairi's husband who had drowned last winter in a shipwreck. What would his death in the same manner have done to his sister? Lyall closed his eyes and took a deep breath.

Glenna shifted and placed her arm around the dog, who laid his big hairy head on her lap and put one paw on Lyall's leg. The boat rocked again, hard, lurching as if it was ready to pitch over, and she looked above them, at the thick wooden rafters that creaked and moaned dangerously, sounding to Lyall as if even the ribs of the ship were about to crack.

"You may call my actions folly, Montrose, but I do not," Glenna said to him. "We are most likely going to die in the middle of the strait." She looked up at him, her face unreadable. "Call me a fool, but I shall feel better if we die together."

He closed his eyes and rested his chin on her damp head, aware that she had probably saved his life. He could feel the warmth from her small body and from the closeness of the furry hound and he could rest his tight jaw...a trick he used to keep his teeth from chattering. He felt his arm relax, holding her comfortably—this woman who had taken such a risk to save him, and his memory went back in years...to another time.

SEVEN

Fifteen years earlier

Lyall Robertson had ceased to be the boy who wandered all over the forest and played at war with the tall trees of Dunkelden Wood, the boy who had out-fished his older brother, and believed that if you touched a tree trunk you could change fate. Charred images of the utter and complete destruction of his great home, of that cowardly yellow flag, and the bitter image of his dead brother were burned deeply into the darkest recesses of his young mind and nothing, not even the slow healing of time could fade his memories or touch the bleakness in him, where accusations lie unchanged: he was the son of a traitor. He dared not ever let himself remember for long the boy he had once been. The past was done; it was unchangeable.

From the day he walked up to Castle Rossie frightened at the sight of that great stone edifice, so imposing compared to a timber fortress like Dunkelden, and secretly frightened, too, at what would happen once those inside saw the bedraggled family of the traitor Ewane Robertson standing at the gates. Rossie was intimidating in its size and strength, even its position, sprouting up like a stone giant, defensive and guarding a massive gorge with a long river cutting through it.

Castle Rossie was a good five times larger than Dunkelden; it assured all who looked at it of the wealth and strength and power of the man who had built it. Ramsey land ran for leagues around it, for all of Rossie, almost to the sea, for surely for as far as the eye could see one man's lands filled the horizon.

With his poor burned mother at his side and his little sister's hand in his own, Lyall hid his fear behind a façade of bravery far beyond his ten years and walked evenly and straight up to the gates. He had one goal.

Baron Montrose, Donnald Ramsey, was a long time friend of Sir Ewane Robertson, who had been cousin to Ramsey's dead wife. To Lyall's relief and surprise, there had been no question from the moment he rang the gate bell. Donnald Ramsey immediately took them in, gave his mother Beitris and sister Mairi chambers and told them with sincerity they were to think of Rossie as home.

The Lord Ramsey was to have fostered Malcolm, so within moments Lyall faced him and insisted the baron take him in Malcolm's place. But Ramsey refused, the look in his eyes kinder and more pitying than Lyall with all his wounded pride wanted to see at the time. He wanted to see belief in Montrose's eyes, belief their father was innocent and belief his only living son could be worth training.

"You are too young lad, too small yet." Ramsey said. "Perhaps in time, after you've grown some, we can find a place for you with the squires, for now, you can take your place with the castle pages." And he was dismissed.

A place for him...not the fostering Lyall wanted. He had heard his father's words often enough to understand there was honor among men, and Lyall knew because he was the son of the traitor Sir Ewane Robertson, few would agree to foster him. Most believed strongly in the tenet that bad blood begat bad blood. Ramsey was his only chance to learn the skills he would need to earn respect beyond the name he carried.

Every morn he was up with the sun and the crow of the cocks, seeking out Ramsey first thing, waiting outside his chamber door dressed in his azure page's tunic and with gold piping. He hounded the baron, asking him repeatedly to grant him the right to train despite his age, and every morn the baron said he was too small, or too young. Every negotiation Lyall tried failed. But he was unrelenting.

Almost as if he willed the very hand of God, Lyall grew taller and longer of leg over the next months, until he was nearly as tall as Malcolm had been. Still, he pleaded with the baron but the answer was always the same.

His mother had begged him to cease, lest Ramsey send them away because of all his pestering, and though many throughout the castle began to jest and laugh at him. "Lyall does not know his place," some said with malice, and Ramsey's knights and squires made him the brunt of their jests and tricks, teasing him incessantly. Sending him on fool's tasks and poking fun at him for doing what he was told, even taunting him into walking the wall when one of them found out he was not comfortable high above the ground. He did not let them know how frightened he had been, and once he was away from them raced away before they saw his fear revealed in the damp spot he felt shamefully spreading in his hose. Lyall did not care what jests they played on him. He cared only that he succeeded in getting what he wanted.

And while all at Rossie thought him foolish, rash, and harebrained, his sister Mairi did not.

'Twas the Easter season, Maundy Thursday to be exact, and dusk had fallen at the Castle Rossie, where the servants had earlier hurried to light the torches in the great hall and replace the dark evergreenery, the purple foxglove, fragrant rosemary, and colorful primroses left from the celebration of the sennight before. Most inside the hall were in a gay mood with that night's coming feast and celebration and anticipation of the addition of Morris dancers and an egg pacing. The past week had been all rain and mud and gloom, so the whole of the castle sorely needed some entertainment.

In the center of the longest trestle table set with bread trenchers and silver spoons stood a huge bowl filled to the brim with pace eggs—made by the women of the castle—each one different and decorated with flower and vegetable paints, with bits of cloth and ribbon fixed upon them and rows of small, sparkling disks of metal to match those in the hall. Hanging from an iron post high on the tallest wall was the Easter tradition: a huge golden disk to symbolize the sun, and on the opposite wall, near the stairs leading to the solar above, hung an equally bright silver moon. Plenty of wine and ale and cider made the rounds of the tables, along with large platters of roast lamb, tansy cake and honeyed fruits, and sugary dates from the east. As the meal wound down and all the pages came into the hall armed with lavers of warm, scented water and towels for washing, a musician strolled into the hall, trumpet to his lips, and he blew a long, heralding set of notes.

To the sudden sound stamping steps and jingling bells came twelve dancers in wooden clogs, dancing in a line into the hall, holly wreaths on their heads and ankle bands laden with tiny bells on their feet. They carried long straight canes hung with flowing scarves of every color. The room erupted with laughter and cheering, clapping and song.

Tabor drums, pipes, and cymbals followed the dancers with a raucous and lively tune. , The dancers formed patterns to reflect the sun's path across the sky, their feet pounding out elaborate steps that, long ago, were said to awaken the slumbering gods of the field. As the music grew louder, some dancers jumped high in the air so the grain would grow high and the flocks would multiply.

There was almost as much pounding at the trestle tables, fists on the table tops and feet on the floor in time to the drumbeats. Some knights broke into loud singing, songs of Noah's flood. As the wine overflowed, bawdy and bawdier versions of maids and ploughs and eventually the love songs made known to all and sundry by traveling bards and minstrels.

Lyall stood before Ramsey, laver in his hands as the baron washed and then used the towel draped over Lyall's arm. "Tomorrow I will be ten and one," he told the baron before he was finished wiping his hands. "I want to train as one of your body squires."

"What is this? You do not merely desire to be a squire any longer, lad? Now 'tis to be an even higher position as my body squire?" Ramsey laughed and shook his head. "You reach for the stars, lad." He leaned back in the great throne of a chair at the center of the table, the rich fur neck of his deep velvet robes surrounding his throat and wide shoulders as if he had a pet marten sleeping there. The look he gave Lyall was different than the kind one he usually wore and this one was not unkind, if one desired a mere pat upon the head.

The baron studied him for a seemingly unending moment, his hand rubbing his dark beard thoughtfully. "'Tis a courageous thing you desire, Lyall Robertson. To train to become a knight is a difficult task, and the trust of a body squire is a heavy load for a lad of even five and ten, which is why I tell you again and again that you are too young. Such a position takes a man with a brave heart to go through the trials of the difficult arts of war, to learn the skills and strength and quick mind of a knight. I know you have seen the skills and trials of which I speak. My men tell me when you are not following and pestering me, or attending your duties, you are out in the sidelines of the field, watching keenly."

"'Tis true," Lyall said without a lick of remorse in his voice.

"What makes you think you, barely a lad of ten and one, has the strength of mind, the strength of heart, and are brave enough to become a knight?" Ramsey asked with an edge to his voice.

Lyall's belly turned and he wanted to vomit up his supper. He had crossed the line for a traitor's son. And finally he had pushed the man too far. There before all, Baron Montrose was questioning his honor, he, the last son of the great traitor, Ewane Robertson, a man who was Ramsey's friend as well as the friend of the king.

"I shall tell you, my lord," came a familiar voice.

Lyall was startled and looked down to see that Mairi was standing by his side, not shy but firmly looking Ramsey, their benefactor, in the eyes.

"I know of no one who is more brave than my brother, my lord. I say to you this. Was he too young at ten to save my mother from the burning stables in Dunkelden? He did so without thought. Was he too young when he brought us here, my mother, her face and hand badly burned, and me so frightened, brought us all that way on foot from Dunkelden, walking for days and nights, his faith and kindness to us unflagging?"

Lyall was speechless, watching his sister so proudly defend him.

Mairi took a step closer to Ramsey and the whole hall had become silent. "Was he too young when he fed us with fish he caught and cooked himself, and when he found us shelter every night, sometimes in the woods where the wolves oft times circled our fire? Was Lyall too young when he bartered his own hard labor for the mule to carry mother when her legs gave out and exhaustion over took her, and for the bread and cheese that helped us survive?"

She glanced around the room. "To all of you, she said." 'Twas he not old and wise and strong enough, my dearest brother who all here laugh about and think is a fool—he who is called too young and too weak—yet who more times than not carried me on his back because I was the one who was too weak and too tired walk any farther. How he went about all of this when I know he was as exhausted and hurt and lost as we were, I do not know."

There were tears in her voice when she said, "'Twas Lyall who dragged my dead brother from the stables and buried him next our father. 'Twas he who sacrificed his hound to the wolves in the forest one night when the choice was the dog or me. I know no one, my lord," she said fervently, her hands in fists. "No one as brave as my brother. All this he did when he was too young, not at ten and one, but at only ten. My brother is no green lad. He lives far beyond his years and he is the most brave person I have ever known…and you, my lord, would be a fool not to make him one of your squires."

"Mairi!" Their mother cried out, standing. "You go too far, girl. Sit down and be quiet. You do not speak in such a way to your cousin, the baron, who supports and shelters you."

Mairi spun around, hands on her small hips and her chin jutting out. "If he did not support us, if he did not support me, then I know Lyall would! And my brother is not too young!" She stood there so fiercely, and she must have realized what she had done and said, that all were looking at her in horror. She covered her red face with her hands and suddenly broke down sobbing. "He is not too young… He is not!"

The utter silence continued in the hall, until it was pierced by the scraping sound of Ramsey's chair legs on the stone floor. Lyall heard his mother gasp pitifully. Her eyes met his, so fearful for Mairi, for all knew his sister had gone too far in her defense of him.

A quiet swell of murmurs came from around the tables, and from the dancers and musicians who had been standing so quietly behind him. Lyall quickly put himself between the baron and his sister as protection, before he took a quick glance at his mother as if to assure her 'I will not let anyone hurt Mairi.'

With his eyes and face he tried to say to her, *I will take the blow.* He stood taller than he felt inside, waiting for the baron to come closer and fully ready to be struck down before all and sundry. He told himself it was only a blow and the pain from a blow was swift and would go away.

Ramsey was a tall and powerful man, and his form blocked the flickering rush light and cast a dark shadow over Lyall.

He waited.

Then the baron was there before him, so close. Lyall looked up at him. "Stand aside, lad," he said in a voice that told Lyall naught of what the man intended.

"I will not." Lyall stepped back, his arms keeping Mairi close to his back. "You can punish me, but not my sister." He gave Ramsey a direct look. "Strike me, my lord."

Ramsey frowned, and then studied him again. "Odd isn't it that you never show me fear, lad, even when yours is the first annoyingly eager face I see every morn. You are my constant shadow and pester me worse than a fishwife, day in and day out you are there." Ramsey drove his hand through his thick dark hair, looked at Mairi and then at Lyall again. "Perhaps I should strike you."

Lyall did not move. "I would suggest that if you want to hit me, you do so on the practice field, my lord. Should you make me a squire, you will have the opportunity to beat me soundly every day."

Lyall's words registered and Ramsey burst out laughing, loud and hard, then he placed his hand on Lyall's shoulder exactly the way his father always had. Lyall looked up at him surprised.

"Are you saying lad that if I make you squire you will learn the skills so poorly that I will be able to beat you every day?"

Lyall began to stammer.

"Cease! Cease before you ruin the moment. I was jesting." Ramsey held up the towel in his other hand. "See this? I had no intention of hitting Mairi. She is a brave girl to stand up for you."

He could feel Mairi's head peek out from behind him.

Ramsey squatted down and handed her the towel. "Here, child. Dry your tears. You spoke well for your brother. What great loyalty you have shown this night. I did not know the whole of your story, nor of Lyall's brave actions. I am suitably impressed...with both of you," Ramsey said and he straightened and it was a long moment before he said, "Ewane would be proud."

It was the first time Lyall had heard his father's name from the baron. He closed his eyes, certain if he did not he would shame himself and ruin everything by crying.

"I will give you a sennight to learn to use a weapon proficiently. You will work every day, all day, until you are so skilled you will convince me that you are not too young to be my body squire."

He had done it! He had done it! Lyall picked up Mairi and twirled her, planting a big kiss on her flushed cheek. "Thank you," he told her.

"You are not too young, Lyall," she said fiercely, hugging him back.

A murmur went through the hall. It was unheard of for anyone to be made a squire at ten and one, and Ramsey's terms had sounded as if Lyall would be body squire, those who trained with and were closest to the baron.

Ramsey crossed his arms. "Tell me, lad, what weapon you choose."

"The bow." Lyall answered immediately.

Some knights laughed quietly among themselves, thinking he had just failed and showed himself as completely unqualified.

"Archery? What foolishness is this?" Ramsey frowned, looking angry for the first time. "Knights do not practice archery."

"But my lord," Lyall insisted. "That is all the more reason I should choose it. The Welsh use the bow with great success, oft times against us. When I am a squire, I will learn to use the sword and battle axe, to wrestle and fight hand to hand in combat, to ride and use the lance as well as my sword and other weapons. A bow and a quiver of arrows merely gives me one more weapon than most, perhaps the same weapon used by an future enemy. Have I made an error? Is there shame in using the bow?"

"Nay," Ramsey said. "'Twas not what I expected is all."

"You only said I must be proficient in a single sennight at the weapon I choose. You did not give me a choice of weapons from which I must choose."

Already Ramsey was shaking his head and chuckling, making it clear he knew he had been played. "You are sharp beyond your years, lad."

"Nay, but I am confident I can shoot an arrow most accurately seven days from now," he said without one bit of humility.

"Then archery it is," Ramsey said with a wave of his hand. "You have seven days. And Lyall...."

"Aye, my lord?"

"This week I do not want to see your face for even a single morn when I open my bedchamber door."

"You shall not, my lord. I swear," Lyall said, unable to hide the smile splitting his face and adding wickedly, "For there is no longer the need."

And laughter erupted from the great hall at Castle Rossie, and Donnald Ramsey's was the loudest. Lyall picked up the laver, and all but ran from the hall he was so excited.

Lyall winced as he slowly and carefully unwrapped the strip of linen he had wrapped on his left wrist early that morning. After six days of the constant, repetitive swipe of the bowstring, his wound was deep, the skin rubbed completely raw, and blood had dried on it so the cloth was stuck to his scabbed skin. He took a deep breath, gritted his teeth and jerked the cloth free, a loud cry escaped his lips, tears filled his eyes, and he swore under his breath, something inventive he'd heard one of the knights shout and for which he would need to confess and do penance.

Fresh blood came from the wound and he tried to stop the flow with the wadded up cloth, gave up and crossed to the laver and stuck his hand in the water, something he should have done before he tore off the cloth.

Someone knocked on the door of his small chamber, and the door cracked open. "Lyall?" His sister stuck her head inside.

"Come in, Mairi."

She was carrying a food tray and she kicked the door closed with her foot.

His pride made him glad she had not been there a moment before. He looked down at his wrist in the water bowl; it was still bleeding and turning the water red. His shoulder ached, his whole body ached and he was exhausted.

"What have you done?" She asked him, worried and setting a tray of food on his bed. "You have injured yourself the night before your trial?"

"I'll be fine," he said tightly, not wanting to be reminder of the test that awaited him in the morning.

She held out her hands. "Come here. Let me see."

" 'Tis nothing. Leave it be."

"I'll tell mama."

"Brat."

"Oaf."

"Pest."

"Turnipbrain." She crossed her arms stubbornly. "I shall not leave until you show me."

He gave up and pulled his hand from the bowl, blotted it dry and stuck out his arm. "There. See?" He craned his neck to try to see the food. The smell was making his belly rumble like thunder. "What's on the tray. I'm starved."

"You wouldn't be if you would stop practicing long enough to eat something. Mama bade me to bring this to you. Should I get her for your hand? She has some salve that will help."

Lyall held up a squat brown earthenware crock.

" 'Tis mama's salve jar!"

"Aye," Lyall said, applying the thick grease to his bloody wrist. "I helped myself."

She flopped down on the bed. "More like you didn't want her fussing over you."

"That too."

She lifted a cloth that covered the food tray. "Look here. There is mutton stew and a fresh trencher. Cider and some goat cheese. A piece of apple tart and strawberries," she said, popping one in her bow-shaped mouth, the juice turning the edges of her lips a deep red.

Lyall filled his mouth with warm stew and tore off a piece of bread and pointed at her with it. "If you do not wipe your mouth, Mama will box your ears for stealing my supper, especially those berries, which I'll wager you already gorged yourself on at the table."

Beitris had planted a large garden as she had at Dunkelden only at Rossie she dug it near the granary where the sun shone most of the day, and the small, sweet red strawberries were her first crop. She doled them out as if they were gold coin.

His sister's eyes grew big and she wiped her mouth clean with the back of her hand, then she stole another, making him laugh.

"Are you frightened, Lyall?"

"About tomorrow?" He shook his head. "Nay," he said with a laughing tone, one filled with bluster.

"Not even a small bit?"

He smiled at her. "Well...perhaps just a small wee tad."

She laughed.

"The truth is, I'm restless and on edge, but not because I am afraid I cannot do this, or of the outcome."

"I shall be there to cheer for you. She took out a small bit of blue cloth left from the bolt of her favorite gown and pressed it into his hand. "This is my favor for you, to bring you good fortune." She leaned over and kissed his cheek. "I am so glad you are my brother, Lyall."

"And I you, sprite," he said with emotion. "I will wear this so all can see. I would not have this chance were it not for you."

She shook her head. "That's not true. The baron would have given in. You were wearing him down. But when it sounded as if he were questioning your courage, then I could no longer keep quiet."

She jumped up as quickly as she had flopped down. "I am off to the solar, where I must listen to chatter and sew a new fur collar on my cloak. I was to have finished it yesterday." She ran to the door, then stopped. "You will do well tomorrow. Lyall. I know you will." Then she was gone, off like the water sprite he lovingly called her.

Lyall lay down on his bed, finishing another chunk of bread. His arms were so sore he could not cross them behind his head as he usually did. He lay there limply. There was not a part of him that did not ache, he thought, closing his eyes and he was soon sound asleep.

The call the cock crowing the next morn came all too quickly. Lyall had eaten the boiled egg his mother brought him, and they had talked for a few minutes, during which she tried to prepare him because of her worry. As he followed her out of his chamber, he wondered if she really was as comfortable here at Rossie as she seemed. She always wore a hood or a thick veil that covered the side of her scarred face, but still she knew it was unpleasant for others to look at and she often kept to the solar or her garden and most days did not eat her meals in the main hall for the looks of pity and curious stares. Her great beauty had been the talk of men and the song of troubadours. But more than vanity, her scars ran deeper than the skin, wounds of loss, of Ewane and Malcolm.

He kissed her on both cheeks because he had always kissed her so and refused to stop, even when she told him not to kiss her scarred and puckered skin. Today, as most days, he lifted her veil and placed a kiss upon her rippled cheek, before he came down to the practice field, just as the sun was just bringing on day.

Five times he had gone through his quiver of arrows at the quintain target before the house knights began to fill the area, curious, followed by the squires and his fellow pages, and soon it seemed the whole of the castle was there. On the left shoulder of his page's tunic he had pinned Mairi's favor and he wore his velvet cap to the side so the ribbons cascaded to one side and would not impede his aim, and he stood in the large dirt arena, awaiting Ramsey, refusing to show an inkling of his fear and nervousness.

"Lyall!" His sister stood with his mother, waving to him. His mother looked pale and he realized then he had not thought about what this trial had done to her.

Ramsey crossed the distance to stand by him. "You look ready."

"I am, my lord."

"I have created a series of trials for you, Lyall Robertson," Ramsey said to him in a loud voice so all could hear. "My men tell me that every day you have practiced on tree targets and the tilting dummy. The true test of war and weaponry is your strength or accuracy against an enemy, more often than not, your enemy will be a moving target."

Ramsey signaled to a pair of squires standing near the quintain. One carried a familiar pig bladder filled with sand, usually used for training the nimbleness and agility of the feet by requiring the squire to dash in, about, and around it. "The first of your trials shall be a moving target. Aonghas and Dughal will toss the bladder ball between them. You must hit it as it moves through the air." Ramsey raised his hand. "Ready yourself."

The crowd was still and quiet.

Lyall took his position, feet planted apart. He pulled an arrow from his quiver and notched it.

Ramsey lowered his hand, and the squires began tossing the bladder back and forth, arcing through the air and hitting their outstretched hand with a slap.

Before it had exchanged hands twice over, Lyall took swift aim....and shot.

The ball flew back and away and fell hard to the ground with a thud, the arrow true and protruding out and upwards from the ball.

The crowd shouted and clapped, and Lyall took his first real breath.

"Good, lad," Ramsey said and clapped him on his shoulder. Pain shot through his body and sliced down his bow arm. His muscles were filled with ague from over practice, and his shoulder was especially weak and sore from drawing back the bowstring constantly for so many days. He winced, slightly, but stood there steely and straight as a finely-honed sword,.

I dare not show a single sign of weakness.

Ramsey pulled an apple from the leather sache hanging his elaborately gilded belt and held it up for all to see. "We shall now test your accuracy on a smaller target."

Lyall readied himself, his eye on the center of the red fruit, the bowstring pulled back so taut it would have sliced off his ear were he were not careful.

Ramsey bent his knees and tossed the apple high into the air. His arrow shot true. The apple shattered, pieces of it flying about, and the crowd roared again. His sister was waving and shouting and jumping up and down, until his mother leaned down and said something and Mairi stilled, her eyes wide as she exchanged a worried look with Lyall. Lyall frowned. What had his mother said?

"And now you shall try an even smaller target, although this one shall be stationary." The baron held up a strawberry between his fingers. A hum of murmuring came from the crowd with some words clear like 'impossible' and 'his fingers' and 'never' and 'the poor boy…'.

"Wait!" Lyall's mother stepped forward. "'Tis my strawberry, my lord. I will hold it," she said firmly.

"Beitris, no," Ramsey said quickly, his voice protective.

"I have complete faith in my son's skills." She walked across the practice field with her head proudly in the air.

"You understand, Beitris, that if he misses, he takes your finger," Ramsey said while his expression tried to warn her when he added, "Let me do this."

"Why?" She looked at him and laughed as if to say what is another loss? She reached up and threw back her hood, her face completely uncovered, ignoring the murmurs in the crowd that quieted swiftly with a single harsh look from Ramsey.

His mother took the berry and faced the crowd. "What you do not understand, Donnald, is that my Lyall will not miss."

Lyall closed his eyes and felt his hands grow clammy and damp. He felt even more tension wrack his body. He dared not miss. He dared not….

His mother stood sideways as she held up the small red strawberry between her fingers, her head high, scarring exposed, her eyes staring straight ahead and her expression emotionless.

But Lyall knew she was far from unfeeling at that moment. She was a putting on a fine show.

He could not, would not fail her. He notched an arrow, took

two shallow breaths and his sharpest aim, eyeing the red strawberry, his eyes seeing nothing else, and then he released the bowstring with a snap!

There was a heartbeat of utter silence, then the thud of the arrow hitting and reverberating in the wooden fencing, the berry nothing more than red circle on the arrow tip.

Between the delicate fingers of Lady Beitris was no berry, only a small empty space and smudges of red berry juice.

The noise level became so loud that it sounded like that of a great tourney, but Lyall held up his hand and shouted," Wait! Wait! Stand back, mother, and count to ten." She did as he asked and did not look at him, did not question. She counted, "One…two…three…four…"

Gasps came loudly with each number. Faster than anyone had ever seen and in a way that would have seemed and sounded impossible, Lyall pulled, notched, and shot arrows from quiver to his bow so swiftly one could barely see each action. By the time his mother said "Ten," he had shot six arrows, one at a time, each one straight into and splitting the shaft of the one previous. It was a display of skill the likes of which no one had ever seen.

"These trials are over," Ramsey said clearly and with something Lyall thought might have been pride, but if not, surely it was honest respect he heard in the baron's voice.

The shouts and whistles and noise for all who were watching was unbelievably raucous and went on for a long, long while and even Lyall could not longer keep back his happiness. A huge, proud smile split his face. His mother joined him and he took her hand, knelt on one knee before her and kissed her hand gallantly.

Because of his sister and his mother, because of their faith in him, he was now guaranteed to be one step closer to winning his spurs…one step closer to giving respect to the name of Robertson. His battle was not done, but his side was winning.

When Lyall rose his mother hugged him with fervor, laughing and proud and he felt as though he held the world in the palm of his blistered hand. Ramsey raised his arm again to silence all.

He placed his hands on Lyall's shoulders and turned him to face the crowd. "This is Lyall Robertson, son of my friend, Sir Ewane, and as he has proved on this day, the finest archer I or any of you have ever seen. I present to you my newest body squire."

Thus began the learning years for Lyall at Castle Rossie. From the men at arms and knights, he learned hand to hand combat, to be quick and lithe on his feet, to feint, and to dodge to avoid his opponent's blade. Under the tutelage of great men of war came lessons in ability to ride like a warrior—to become one with his horse, to guide his mount with the pressure of his knees, so his hands were free to handle his weapons; in time, to wield his battle axe, war hammer, and heavy broadsword as if he were wielding his right arm, both on horseback and on foot. He learned to tilt, to charge with his war lance and unseat his opponent with unfailing speed and precision. He learned all a knight needed to learn, and true to form, he learned it swiftly, earning his spurs at ten and five. The only thing Lyall did not learn was how to forget.

EIGHT

The western coast of Scotland

Glenna stepped out onto the top deck of the ship and stretched her arms high in the cool morning air, yawning. All around her was the Minch, looking calm and like an unbelievably peaceful firth. The blue water was glistening like new coins in the high sunlight, as if the whole of frightening events of yesterday and the night before had been only a terrible dream.

She flexed her numb fingers. Sleep escaped her more most of the night. When she had finally slept, she felt as if she had been imprisoned in the hold forever, sitting there and hanging onto Montrose, wondering with each diving pitch of the storm when the ship would crack in half and they would all perish into the black depths of the sea.

She took a deep breath and rubbed her arms, which were marked with the thin red pattern of the rush mat used for sleeping pallets. Above her, the sails flapped unevenly with the wind now coming in soft sweet gusts, and she heard the splash of the oar wake, and the rocking, almost songlike rhythm of the oarsman's chant as the boat moved close to land and parallel to the coast. Against the eastern horizon the mainland was large, its shadowy grey-green hills now sharp enough to see the ragged tops of the trees, while the land's edges were still thinly shrouded by white morning mist floating just out of reach and ghostlike upon the water.

Montrose stood near the prow of the ship, his booted foot resting on a barrel tied to the ship's bow and he was holding a halyard with one hand. His hair blew back away in the sea breeze and his eyes were only for the skies and land ahead. He wore his sword belt and a pale blue tunic she thought looked the same color as his eyes. Dark blue woolen hose covered his long legs, and the silver hilt of a dagger showed from the top of his boot. She watched him with hungry eyes, his profile so hawk-like, strong—almost stubbornly so.

Standing there as he was, he looked as if he were defying the laws of nature, daring them to try to make him someone other exactly who he wanted to be. She'd seen his jaw grow tight and ridged when he was angry, and now unshaven, his beard had grown in dark, like his brows, looking like storm shadows on his jaw and neck. Her first impression of him had been so very different from the man she'd seen since.

Who was the golden one who so easily and carelessly dove through the waves in the sea?

The breadth of his shoulders, the thick, lean sinew of his thighs held her captive, led her mind to places where only dreams were made. That he was an impressive man was undeniable, and, were she in the market for one, he might have been a decent choice.

Clinging to him the night before made her feel safe, something she had thought she'd lost. She looked away, disliking the direction of her thoughts. Survival was what she needed to concentrate upon...not standing there ogling him like she would a honeyed comfit. She was wasting time, time she needed to be plotting how to get as far away from the man as possible. She turned swiftly, moving toward the stern, running away from him and her foolhardy thoughts.

However one thought led to another, and a few moments later she was almost brought to her knees by a new revelation. She reached out blindly and sat down hard on a ballast stone, white-knuckled and suddenly feeling pale.

What a fool she was... She had been frightened her father would lock her away or send her into exile? She was the daughter of the king...a pawn for men to use. Surely her father would marry her off to someone. When he saw she was nothing remotely royal, a worthless daughter, he would get rid of her quickly.

But a king would use the match to his best advantage... country and politics had to come first. Just the fact that she was raised in secret was proof enough of her value.

Oh God...she hung her head in her hands and for a moment, she wanted to heave over the side. Were she weak and a coward, she would have flung herself overboard. All the possibilities of her plight raced through her mind. She could be given—would be given—to some man as a prize, a reward for duty or a task well done. Her father could easily give her away in marriage to one of his enemies as a peace offering.

What else was her worth to him? She was little more than a roasted boar on a serving platter with an apple in her mouth. *Here, take my daughter.*

She could and probably would be sent far, far away, to the places she only heard of through Alastair's storytelling. To England? To Normandy? Germany? She shuddered. Did not the Germans bury their women alive as punishment?

"You... Lad."

Her father could send her off to the burning hot deserts of the east, where a husband had the right and duty to chop off his disobedient woman's head with a scimitar.

"Lad!"

The Norse! Visions filled her head...of men clad from head to toe in thick wolf fur and rough hides, who tied their women to their waists with ropes and dragged them to huts where they forced them into servitude as cooks and bed slaves.

She looked up, feeling terribly despondent.

"*Lad!*" Montrose shouted.

She faced him.

He was striding toward her, his hands in fists, his long legs eating up the distance between them. Some things did not change. She sighed with a bout of hopelessness. He was her own personal guard, sent by her father, and unbeknownst to all but her, he was leading her to a future she could not chance.

"Are you bloody deaf?" Montrose towered over her, huge fists on his hips. "Lad."

Oh, I forgot. I'm lad.

A heaviness that was almost too overwhelming swept over her. She could barely face what she believed lay ahead for her. She faced him instead, aware she'd like to forget she was the daughter of a king.

The Marram wharf at mid-morning was busy. They had come into port later than planned, having to travel northward along the coast after the storm blew the ship far south. Then they were forced to wait for a merchant cog to cast off from the end dock, many of them having sought safe moorage with the storm.

Lyall eased his temperamental mount down the gangplank, his hands firm on the lead, following Glenna and her horse and hound, both of whom happily trotted down from the ship in the blink of an eye. They waited on the edge of the wharf for him to conquer his horse, which was still riled and skittish from the storm. The truth was that for all the black's spirit, he was never good at crossings, rivers or seas. Standing and waiting below were Glenna and her hound.

Soon, no longer than it took their horses' hooves to cross the wharf boards, new clouds had begun to form high in the distant sky. Lyall wondered if they were an omen of more rain to come — or recompense for the deviled madness of his actions. He looked away and cursed. Now they would have to ride all that much harder and faster, and if another storm was coming, he would be hard-pressed to arrive as planned.

But as they wound their way on horseback, the crowd grew thicker on the narrow stone road by the wharves. Poor luck would have it that two ships besides theirs, along with several small local fishing boats, had come to dock that morning, so the town was bustling even before the drifts of morning fog had burned off.

A large English trade ship had anchored in the inlet, unable to unload yesterday, was now unloading supplies, and the hawkers' carts were set up by the docks. Blocking Lyall's immediate path was a cheese cart tilted sideways and filled to the brim with English cheese; its owner rushed to examine the damaged wheel, so they had little choice but to draw in their mounts and wait for the lumbering dray to turn. Nearby, fishwives sold savory smoked fish hung over their peat fires and fishmongers loaded their carts with ling and herring, haddock and cod from the small fishing boats offloading their morning catches.

Soon the hawking was loud and growing frantic. Lines formed around all the bright stalls fronted by servants from the local manors, who arrived with fat leather purses to pick the best catch for their lords' supper tables. His empty belly growled like a lion, and he knew Glenna must be even more hungry after puking for most the day before, so he dismounted and bought supplies, some smoked fish and fresh dark bread, turnips, apples and cheese along with a flagon of pressed cider.

He handed Glenna some smoked herring. "Here. Eat something." He drank deeply then gave her the cider.

She merely stared at his outstretched hand. From the look on her face, it was apparent her foul mood had not changed since the moment she woke.

"Why, my lord," she said, sarcastically. "How perfectly kind of you to ask so sweetly if I would care to break my fast."

He bit back the inklings of a smile. He supposed she had a point. "Take the food, lad." His voice was kinder.

She rolled her eyes and grabbed the smoked fish and cider.

After purring like a kitten against his side until the early hours of the morning, she had awakened in the hold with an attitude seemingly determined to give him trouble. Her seat in the saddle was spine-stiff, shoulders squared and back, her face shaded from her hat, pulled low now, like it could hide that Canmore pride he'd seen more than once. She looked exactly like what she was: the offspring of a king, even turned away from him as she was now. He imagined that were she not as starved as she was, she might have refused the food and called him something else altogether. Turnipbrain or clodpole or some other such female foolishness. Mairi must have called him every name imaginable over the years.

He tore off a piece of fish, and so they were both eating and going nowhere.

The longer they were at a standstill, the more the risk. They needed to ride, and ride soon and quickly.

They waited for the blasted cart, but the longer they were stuck there, the more likely someone might recognize him. On horseback, he was head and shoulders above much of the crowd. To hide in Marram, where some of the nearby nobles knew him was worrisome and one of the major reasons he traveled alone.

Had he sailed with Glenna in the evening as planned, they would have arrived in the evening, Mornings at the docks were hectic and crowded, and there was a stronger chance for him to be seen.

Time moved as if caught in mud. The sun was higher and the

approaching clouds began to fill the western skies, then to add coal to the fire, the cursed hound began to frolic, barking and running in circles around Glenna, restless after being stowed below for too long. Again Lyall was forced to calm his horse. To Glenna he said harshly, "Control that hellhound of yours!"

"Fergus!" She tossed some fish at the dog and it sat on his large haunches chomping with its big mouth and looking happy as a lark...unlike its owner, who glanced pointedly back at him, giving him a look that said she wanted the earth to open up and swallow him. She was like a flea in his hose. If her intent was to annoy him, it was working.

Women were his curse and his salvation. They were single beings with the most power over him and his conscience, and they were those who loved him most and who he had no choice but to disappoint.

He thought of Isobel, the beautiful and innocent daughter of Teàrlach de Hay, one of the most powerful and cunning men in the land. He had known he was walking into a snake pit, tying himself by marriage to the de Hay family, but in his rush to have all he desired, he gave little thought to his bride before they wed. Guilt washed over him, followed by a horrific image from the past. Marrying him had driven the fragile Isobel de Hay to her death.

His conscience spoke to him as clearly as if it actually had a voice. The idea that he was repeating his mistakes gnawed at him. Prior to his mission, he had not given much thought to Glenna, other than who she was: the king's secret daughter—more valuable than gold and his only means to Dunkeldon lands. He had valued her the same way he had valued Isobel.

He studied her for a moment, looking for frailty and seeing none. She was a thief, he had to remember that, and must have been trained to hide, sneak, and cover up any fears. Chances were high innate bravery and spirit were not what he saw in her, but instead schemes and deceit, as refined and honed as those who plotted treasons, kidnappings, and other betrayals.

Many men claimed women could be more deadly than any enemy, although the women in his life had great faith and belief and honest loyalty. He thought then of Mairi and what his sister would think of what he was doing.

He could feel his skin flush. She would chew his ears off, as would his mother. He looked back at Glenna, taking in her features, her stature. If she and Mairi were to have stood side by side, it would be like looking at a moonless night and a sunny day—both impenetrably strong.

She was an interesting mix—thief and royal daughter—no meek woman, simpering and wringing her hands and crying at the slightest dark look. Isobel.... He doubted Glenna Canmore would jump from a tower. More likely that she would man it.

A loud and piercing crack made him turn back to the wharf. Shouts and curses came from the cart seller, now stuck with a broken axle. The cheese cart upended and huge cheese wheels were spilling everywhere, some rolling down the small planked street and others headed for the water.

People were rushing after them, and the chaos was more than Lyall had patience for. He started to dismount and take over, but then there came the loud blast of a trumpet, heralding to all the imminent arrival of a nobleman with his troops. His gaze shot toward the southern end of the road.

In the distance, he saw the dust cloud of approaching horses, men-at-arms—and then to his dismay, he caught the flicker of a pennant. Swearing, he moved swiftly to hide his shield and turned his horse, sidling up to Glenna. "Turn around. We will go north and around all this madness. Come. Quickly."

Lyall all but trampled his way to the northern edges of Marram, earning shaking fists and curses from bold villagers and wharvesmen who gave not a fig for the powerful sword at his side.

When they were safely away from the edges of town and well out of sight of the wharves, he reined in, his mount side-stepping, uneasy and nervous and his own heart pounding like hoofbeats in his chest. His nerves were raw.

Ahead lay fields turned fallow after a recent harvest, then hill after rolling hill, some spotted with deep green copses of ancient oaks and rowan, and lacy birch just beginning to turn golden. Yet each hillock was a little higher than the last and led up to rings of surrounding jagged toothed fir forests to the north, from the middle of which stood a huge and majestic crag, bare and gray and looking like a wise old man's head. It dominated the northern horizon.

The safest and most obscure route was to the southeast, where all that stood before them were rolling green hills for as many leagues and as far as the eye could see…and the storm clouds, gaining size and heavy gray color and beginning to fill the southern skies with the promise of rain.

He nodded at her hound. "Can your dog keep up? The horses are biting at the bit for a good run."

"Perhaps, my lord, we should put your question to the test," Glenna said and kicked her horse forward, across the low rolling hills, her dog loping at her side and her sudden laughter carrying back to him on the brisk and waxing wind.

NINE

Glenna rode as swiftly as the fast approaching storm, across the wide expanse of rolling hills and staying a good five horse lengths ahead of him. 'Twas a gift to her, this race he had foolishly dared to start. She almost laughed at the irony—a test to see if he could catch her, if he and his black were faster than she and Skye, and whether Fergus could stay with her as long as Montrose and his horse could.

In other words: could she outride him? Could she escape now? If not now, then this was her mock escape. Surely she had run plenty of times before, Fergus at her side—any thief had close moments—although she was usually far away before anyone was the wiser…unless she was foolish enough to be stealing a spice wife's gown or take the horse right out from under a man. She had only done that once before Montrose, a serendipitous encounter with some earl's son who was so blindingly drunk it was barely horse-thievery at all.

Never had she been chased by anyone on a horse as strong and powerful as Montrose's. She leaned low and cast a quick glance over her shoulder.

He and the black were still well behind her.

Good. She kicked Skye, upping the speed, but then had to slow to jump a brook, landing easily on the other side, Fergus romping happily through the water behind her.

Her dog loved to run. She had almost laughed in Montrose's face when he asked if Fergus could keep up. Fergus could keep up, but she knew not for how long he could keep such a pace.

Dark clouds roiled in from the south, and the taste of rain was in the air. Ahead of her, she spotted a bird of prey—a hawk?—like a crucifix, wheeling in the sky, again and again, circling over its poor carrion. As she came closer, she saw it was not a hawk, but a golden eagle.

One quick glance back told her Montrose was hard on her tail. The wind whipped her hat back and then some of her hair flew from its braid. Perhaps the winds had brought her fortune and this was the moment she could escape.

I want to be free. I must escape. I must.

Escape to where? The silent voice in her head said plainly.

But just as swiftly as the thought had come to her, her mind flashed with the emotion that she cared not where, only that she managed to get far away and save herself. Alone now, only she could change her destiny.

She did not want to be the daughter of a king and did not ask to be. She did not want to be a pawn to be given in marriage to any man. Her choices were slim. She had to get away and hide. And for now, she cared not where that place was, only that she was safe and it was far away, perhaps as far away as England.

Ah! The perfect plan had escaped her! She had missed a perfect opportunity in Marram to stow on board that English ship. When given the choice: marriage—the choice of even facing her father—or running, she decided she would choose to walk all the way to London.

"Glenna!" His shout pierced the air.

She ignored him, a habit she was quickly honing to a fine art, helped by the fact that she knew Skye had more in her and Fergus was staying true. She used her heels again and Skye went faster, stretched her length in her run, her hooves eating up the ground and the distance. She could hear each whoosh of Skye's breath and her coat grew damp.

Montrose shouted her name again. His voice was loud, loud enough to call down the heavens, and sounded very angry. The race was his idea. Let him be furious, she thought recklessly.

If he and his mount are tiring, this is my moment.

Fear and some emotion she could not explain drove her on, pushing and pushing, past sanity and reason. Ahead of her was a wide copse of trees, wide enough she could take the chance and ride into them, perhaps losing him. She leaned lower and looked back over her left shoulder again.

Montrose was not behind her. She frowned. What?

To her utter shock, the devil was beside her, passing on her right, their horses almost neck to neck. The look in his eyes reflected the skies overhead when he leaned toward her then, another surprise, and before she could think what he was about, his arm snaked around her waist and he plucked her from the saddle as if she weighed no more than a sparrow, pulling her to him, pinned against his hard body, her buttocks planted sweetly between his powerful thighs.

Then he did not slow the horse, but rode even harder, as if anger drove him and his horse to push the limits of sanity. 'Twas madness, this. The speed of his horse seemed to grow faster, faster and felt harder than she had ever ridden in her life. The thundering of the black's most powerful hooves against the ground, pounding and pounding, and Montrose's hard, tense body against hers, and she who could do naught but cling to him or fall to a sure death. The ground passed by so swiftly it was a blur, like looking through fog. Fear gave her no choice but to wrap her arms around his neck and hang on for her very life, her heart pounding so loudly in her ears that she was certain she could not even hear him shout at her, exertion making his breath come hard and strong, like wind against her face, his spicy scent tinged with seasalt and smoke filling her nose and mouth with each panicked breath of air she took.

Truly frightened, she wanted to scream at him to slow down, to stop now. But her pride and fear stole her voice from her.

He finally began to slow the horse. She felt the tensing of his thighs and the black's well trained reaction. His arm tightened around her. "What the hell were you doing?"

Running away.

The horse slowed down to a trot. She had failed.

"That was foolish thing to do. Your antics made us ride the horses into the ground."

"You wanted a race," she said, but her voice sounded breathless and strange and more vulnerable than she cared to ever be with a man like him. Between them was only a startling and frightening moment, with his body so close to hers, his scent raw and the dampness in the air and on their bodies, the musk scent of his horse's sweat, his hot breath in her ear. She could feel the tensing of the muscles in his arm and knew he was strong enough to break her.

His face was but a hand's breadth away from her own. She looked up from his cruel mouth, from the thin line of his lips showing starkly from the dark beginnings of his beard, and into his eyes.

What she saw there made her heart race. Desire was not the reaction she wanted…in either of them. With all the arrogance and haughtiness she could muster, she added, "I merely gave you what you wanted."

His lips brushed against her cheek; his mouth was so close to hers.

I've gone too far, she thought…too late.

"What I wanted? I shall give you, sweet Glenna…" (There was nothing sweet about his voice or his meaning) "…exactly what you wanted." His hand moved so fast she did not know he had pulled off her hat until he tossed it aside.

She gasped in reaction.

His fist gripped her thick plaited braid already hanging heavily down her back, and she cried out, reaching for it as he spun it around his hand and held her tightly. His hard mouth swept down and closed powerfully over hers, possessing her in a way that shocked and weakened her, his tongue forcing its way inside, exploring, demanding, robbing everything from her he could steal and more.

The kiss was not all what Glenna had thought kisses were, soft sweet touches of the lips, like the touch of a butterfly, not this grinding, warring of tongues and even wilder warring of passions. Her blood rushed quickly to her head and made her light headed, made her skin and face flush so very hotly that she felt faint. She was melting…in her very core.

From somewhere in the back of her mind, she heard Fergus barking.

He pulled his mouth from hers. "Get away dog. Go! Lay down!"

Then his mouth was on hers again, softer this time but still greedy with hunger. He released his hold on her hair and cupped the back of her head. Some deep place between her legs ached and she moved closer to him, her chest against his, and she had to tighten her hold onto him lest she fall apart and break into a thousand pieces.

To feel powerless, swept away by feelings she never had and could not control was too much for her and she felt the swell of tears in her tight throat and the backs of her eyes. Then her traitorous body had completely forsaken her, squirming, needing with a sense of desperation to move against his, and reacting in all ways foreign to her. She was on fire, wanting a touch she had never had and not known she could want, between her legs, in a place where before now there had been nothing, not even a ripple of need.

Secretly, she had thought herself immune to romance, to a woman's need for a man, for his touch, and for coupling.

He was right. She did want this.

His lips left her mouth to slash hungrily across her cheek to her ear, and she moaned, wanting his kiss again, wanting the feel of tongue on hers, wanting his passion and his taste.

"You do want this. You want me," he said over and over as he kissed her and touched her whole body with his roving hands, her legs and arms, her breast and throat, hands that wickedly knew where she wanted his touch, lifting and turning her at one point, then he pulled her legs up to his waist, pressing her against the hard length of him, rocking her until her body melted and was answering his rhythm instinctively.

It took a moment before she realized he had pulled her tunic over her head and that was only because his words changed from soft caresses to curses at the cloth bindings he had demanded so passionately that she wear beneath.

In the next moment, she heard the sound of renting linen as he ripped free her breasts and pressed one upward, his head bent as he took it into his mouth, his tongue playing again. Desire so strong she cried out his name swept through her and she pressed her hips down on him, wanting more, needing more, so much more.

He slid down from the saddle, his arm clamping her against him and he carried her—feet dangling off the ground, him still suckling her—over to the trees and backed her against one with his knee and body. His mouth moved to her other breast and his hand finally lifted and cupped her possessively through the crotch in her trouse, one long finger rubbing the rough cloth between her legs. He did not stop, over and over, and she moaned, rising a little with each stroke. When her breath was out of control and her need almost too much to bear, he took her hand and pressed her palm to him. He taught her his need with his hand over hers, up and down, showing her what he wanted while his touch and the rough cloth took her higher and higher.

She was blinded by feeling, and though her eyes were open, she could not see anything and found she was capable of naught but a single sense: she could only feel, and she was flying, soaring like a hawk in the stormy skies, and her whole body raced and raced toward the heavens, feeling lighter and as if she were going so high she would shatter among the stars.

And she did.

Lyall was mad, completely, absolutely mad, insane, knocked senseless by the fall in Steering mad. Or he had somehow in the past three days turned into a formless being driven into idiocy by his cock. Her soft, sweet cry of ecstasy was like a bucket of cold water over him, and he tried to catch his shallow, panting breath, all the while staring painfully down at her awe—and passion—washed face, at her flushed skin bright with satisfaction from the upturned, sweet pink tips of her bared breasts to her glistening, kiss-swollen lips.

The sweet, salty, and smoky taste of her, the lingering taste of the sea on her skin and the smoked fish in her mouth was still on his tongue, driving him secretly insane and he wanted nothing more than to take her there against the tree. His lack of control scared him. His hands shook slightly when he stepped back away from the tree and eased her down until her feet were on solid ground.

Her eyes were the color of coal they were so dark, now rimmed in moisture and glowing from pleasure. The soft, sweet, unguarded way she looked at him then, with something akin to her heart in her eyes, touched him in a place where he was most vulnerable, a place he hid from all and told himself did not exist...could not exist, not ever again.

He turned his back to her, his brain hot and feeling as if his head was going to blow off.

She should hate him. He needed her to hate him. Eventually, she would hate him. That was inevitable.

He stepped farther away and drove his hand through his hair, frustrated and trying to find a way to fix what he had just done, find some way to change the bewitched look in her eyes.

At that moment the rain began to fall cool and wet against his own hot and flushed skin. He looked up at the dark sky, half expecting a lightning bolt to come down and drive clean through his black heart.

But there was only the rain dripping through the trees.

She stood there, unmoving, looking at him in a way that made his man's pride almost want to take her to pleasure again. He reached out and pulled her under the shelter of the trees, releasing her arm as quickly as if burned before he stepped back and away from her, putting a safer distance between them.

"Glenna," he said gently. "I should not have done that to you."

"Why?"

Frowning, he looked at her. He had not expected such a blunt question. "Why did I do it? The truth is that I wanted to punish you for disobeying me. I wanted to frighten you. The kiss was...natural. It came without thought or reason."

Her expression did not change.

"I cannot explain the way a man thinks, or acts when his blood boils. I can only say that what happened between us a few moment ago went much too far." He paused. "And I am sorry for that. 'Tis my doing. 'Tis my err."

She was quiet for a moment, before she laughed at him, which made little sense. He expected her to lash out at him, to call him the fiend he felt he was.

Where was the storm he expected from her?

God's teeth but the woman looked pleased. He began to pace.

"You are a foolish man," she said not unkindly and half laughing again. "Not *why* did you kiss me. Why are you begging for forgiveness?"

Begging? He stopped abruptly and faced her again. He was not begging, he thought in a puff of pride. He did not beg.

With one word she had put his manhood at stake. The silence between them drew out for a long time and the rain picked up, pounding on the ground beyond and starting to slip through the thick crowns of the wide and ancient trees.

Why would he expect her to act like other women, to be meek or practiced?

Why would he expect her to know of men and morals and the rules of courtly love?

She was truly innocent, — as innocent as a thief could be — he thought with irony — and had been raised outside of the world he knew and lived in — a world that taught him not to have faith in much of anything. Faith only made betrayal all that much easier and more devastating.

But Glenna had nothing to do with his past, but his guilt was not done eating at him. Perhaps he should have been begging.

Standing before him as she was, without fear or modesty, bare to her waist and facing him as if they were on equal ground was startling. Truth was: she was high on a hill and he was already deep in a dark pit. There was nothing equal about the two of them. Hell was his future. The day he found her, he had secured his damnation.

His gaze went to her breasts and his body tensed even more, his head ached. He could taste her... "Pull up your tunic!"

She was startled and frowned at him. "Why?" She stood there

so proudly naked, her shoulders back, hands on her hips, without a bit of modesty, and she strolled casually in front of him, then stopped barely a foot away and she looked right at him, her gaze narrowed when she said, "You do not like my breasts, my lord?"

"God's blood, Glenna, cover yourself!" Then he did the only thing he could do to save her innocence: he stalked away, walking deeper into the forest and away from her before he lost control and took her completely.

His whole body was on the verge of betraying him. There was the constant rhythmic crunch of leaves beneath his boots, and the crack of a twig sounded like thunder to his raw ears. He stepped over a felled log and moved even faster into the darkness of the trees, with long strides, his breath coming hard and harder. His hand was already inside his hose, moving and seeking the release he needed.

When he was well out of sight and hearing distance, he stood with his back to a tree and facing away from her, his jaw clenched and his teeth locked tight, head thrown back against the rough bark of a tree, and he closed his eyes closed until his seed spilt far away from her warm and submissive body. But in his mind's eye he saw her face as clearly as if she were carved on the back of his eyelids, and he imagined her beneath him, her soft pale skin the color of ivory, her lithe legs along his, him looking down into her face and those dark, dark eyes—the ones that had some kind of strange and powerful draw, like a lance that pierced straight through his heart.

TEN

Glenna stood watching the spot where Montrose disappeared into the woods. Above the thick crowns of the trees, dark clouds hovered over her. In the distance, they crawled over the low hills. The air grew thick, and misty, and suddenly cold. Rain slipped through the leaves and pelted her still flushed face. She closed her eyes and took a deep breath, then fixed her clothing and stalked over to pick up her hat, slapping it against her trouse to shake off the water. She crammed it on her head and moved toward the horses, both Skye and the black, abandoned and standing some distance away, completely forgotten in all that had just happened.

What had just happened? She wiped the rain from her face.

Something wonderful, she thought when she still had been light-headed and dreamy.

Until Montrose made her feel as if she should be ashamed. What she felt was not wonderful. Apparently, it was something terrible.

Surely their touches were not a sin...a thought she chewed over for a moment, before it struck her that some sins felt good, like cursing loudly.

To discover she was not who she thought she was: a young woman who could never feel a man in her heart, or joy between her legs like men did, was a huge revelation to her. Truthfully, when she had opened her eyes and looked up at him, it was all she could not to throw her arms around his neck and say, "Thank you!"

Lyall Robertson, the Baron Montrose, of all men had made her feel like a woman, and then crushingly apologized for his mistake.

Sadly her shoulders dropped, her heart sinking down to her toes. Try as she might she would never forget what she felt, her whole body and mind flying to the heavens, floating with the stars....

Tears choked her throat and stung her eyes, and she wiped them with her sleeve and told herself not to cry. He could not see her like this, though he had hurt her deeply, making her feel unclean and stupid for loving what they had done.

Her mind ran over things, searching for answers, and as she turned to walk back, she decided she might have a clue as to what he was doing in the woods, considering the size of the knot in his hose when he had stalked away...she did have two brothers. One quick look when he returned and she would know.

Once, when Elgin was ten and three, and she was still a brat, she had followed him down the stables, intending to pester him into letting her ride as she usually did, and instead, his furtive movements and secretive manner made her quickly duck into the next stall and quietly hide. But the sounds he was making were curious and odd and made her peek over at him. He sat in a corner holding himself, his hand moving till his seed was gone and he had grown small and lay limp and soft.

She wondered at what she had seen him do, and the memory of it had haunted her. For days she watched him curiously, some days thinking he could grow horns—because of something Alastair once said when he thought she wasn't within earshot. El seemed unchanged...no different...no horns. She understood what had happened—they did breed horses—but she had not understood why.

Finally, she could keep quiet no more, and in the middle of supper one night she plainly asked her brothers about what she had seen. Elgin stood so quickly he almost knocked the table over, sputtering at her, his face as red as the sunset, and then Alastair became angry—not at her, but at Elgin.

The two of them fought, almost to blows before, finally, frustrated, Alastair had sat down, running a hand through his long red hair, and he had gently told her how a man's body worked, using their horses and breeding as examples. When she asked him about what he had said once—that men could grow horns—he had laughed and explained it was not true, but merely an old tale. Then he explained to her the way he had always done about life and death and heaven and hell, about people and animals—he told her through stories—told her all he could about the sin of Onan, of a man growing horns, and the old Saxon prophesies of men going blind.

Until today, she had still not been able to completely piece together what she had seen in the stables with what Alastair had tried to explain to her about men and their bodies. She was not a man, and had no woman in their home to ask about her body. Women had fluxes. Men did not.

Naturally she assumed women's bodies were as different from men as their nether parts, and that women could never have the same reactions—that Alastair was talking about something only men could do and feel.

For most of her life there had been only Al, El and her, and they often thought in different ways, saw dilemmas from different sides of the paddock fence. She was convinced even more by her reaction to Montrose, that she did not understand men.

All the more reason for her to escape.

Her frustration and confusion did not leave her easily, nor did the sudden feelings of her heart. She gathered the loose reins of both their horses and tied the animals closer, under the same shelter of the trees where they could still munch on the grass and easily drink from a small brook. The rain had cooled them down, so Montrose could no longer bluster and be angry with her about 'riding the horses into the ground.'

Despite the rain, she walked back out into the open, her gaze searching the eastern horizon. But with the mist and low clouds, she could see little that would enable her to get her bearings, and she cursed herself for not learning more of the lay of the land when she and her brothers had plundered across the mainland.

Of course she knew well the long list of names of villages to avoid in Ross-shire and could recite them like a song: "Applecross, Dingwall, Suddy, Cromarty, Plockton, Garve, Kyle, Avoch, Knockbain, and Wester." She needed to stay as far away from them as she should have stayed from the Steering market fair.

Fergus lay at her feet, his nose resting on his paws, eyes closed. He was snoring. Lyall came striding out of the depths of the forest with his arms full of wood, which he dropped on the ground in front of her, knelt down, and built a small, warm fire. She watched him, laughing inside. No knot in his hose.

He glanced up at her from the fire. "What is so humorous?"

She turned away from him and muttered, "Nothing."

He pulled some food from his pack and handed it to her. "Eat something. We will rest the horses." He glanced at Fergus. "And your hound. Perhaps the storm will pass."

She laughed. "The storm that keeps following us?"

He seemed to smile to himself. "Aye." Sitting back he ate some fish and cheese.

She took one of the turnips and bit into it, chewing thoughtfully. She studied the horizon, where the clouds were almost black. She gestured with her turnip. "Looks as if the storm will not wane."

"Then we will have a long, cold ride ahead of us."

"Where are we going?"

"To Beauly Priory."

Her heart raced at the name. Beauly? Was not that near Dingwall? Would she be safe?

Her mind flashed with the image of a cruel sheriff wearing a deep green wool cloak pinned together with golden leaf brooches, a strap in his hand as he whipped a small frail boy bloody. Beauly Priory was most likely not in the center of any village, since the abbeys and monasteries were towns unto themselves. She decided not to press the issue. If she asked too many questions, he would have questions of his own. So she ate and kept quiet, occasionally watching him.

When it was time to depart, she unrolled the long woolen cloak from her pack and pinned it over the tunic with two leaf brooches she had stolen from a sheriff to distract him from beating a young peasant lad to death.

Montrose was already in the saddle. His look was impatient and thoughtful, as if his mind were leagues away. She repacked her bag precisely, putting each of her few items back in its place.

"I'd like to leave before winter."

She glared him. "Would you have me shove my belongings in every which way and then have to take three times as long to find what I'm searching for?"

"Mount your horse, Glenna," he said tiredly.

They rode all day in the rain, finding only a little shelter through woods and forests, and the longer they rode, the colder it became and the muddier. When they could, they rode over grass covered hills at a faster pace to avoid the mud. To the north stood tall granite crags, like massive gray guards of a gateway to another world. To the south gloomy green woods cloaked in clouds, some trees so massive and old they had sheltered Picts and Norse raiders. Streams rushed over rocks looking more like rivers than they must have merely a few days before.

Once again the storms brought an end to summer. Autumn was clearly there now and raining down upon her. She was wet from the top of her head to the tips of her toes, and despite the weather, the whole time she could think of nothing but what happened between them, of his touches, his taste and his mouth on hers…and his apology afterwards.

His continued silence annoyed her, especially after the saddle had pounded her so much even her backside was numb. Might as well annoy him. "I do not understand you, Montrose," she said finally.

"I do not understand myself," he replied, seeming to connect to what she was talking about without explanation.

"I am supposed to be ashamed over what passed between us?"

"The Devil's teeth woman! Can you not merely ride in silence?"

"I can ride without ever speaking, my lord. I choose not to do so solely because you want to avoid my questions. I'm disappointed, Montrose. I did not think you were a coward."

"I will not rise to your bait."

"What bait? I ask you one question and you are already angry at me? We are at war because you cannot answer a simple question."

"And that is where you are mistaken. 'Tis not a simple question."

"To me it is," she said quietly.

He slowed his mount and looked at her. She tried to hide her hurt by looking down at Fergus, who had wandered toward a large bush. "No!" she snapped her fingers. "Come."

Montrose said nothing for long moments and she decided it was time to give up.

"Surely you understand you are not supposed to be so cursed pleased about what happened between us." He sounded disgusted.

"No. I do not. But you can explain why."

"Why? Why? You keep asking why."

"And you become angrier. I am thinking I should keep asking until you answer me."

He turned in the saddle. "It is not my duty to defile the king's daughter!"

Her spine went rigid. "Oh, I see…" She said bitterly. "'Tis better to keep the daughter pure. Keep the royal virginity unsoiled, so it can be sold to the highest bidder or bartered to the first of my father's enemies to offer him peace. Me? Unsoiled?" She laughed without humor. "Why should it matter? I am destined to be a vessel for a man's use and pleasure. In truth, I am, by birth, naught but a man's whore."

"Glenna…" he said with a dark warning.

"What? I am to be married off, sold as the royal prize, and that is supposed to make me happy? Pardon me, my lord, if I do not dance about and shout with glee."

"You are a woman," he said so simply. "You will give your husband children, sons and daughters. Is that not a woman's desire, to be protected and cared for, to bring forth children from her body?"

There it was: a woman's entire life purpose in a single male thought. She laughed again. "Aye, Montrose," she said without hiding her contempt for situation. "I long so deeply in my heart to be a brood mare."

"You want an argument and I will not be lured into a game of words." He kicked the black faster up the next hill.

"*I* want an argument," she said indignantly, then glared at his back and followed, wishing she could ride off toward those tall gray crags and off into a world where her surname was not Canmore and there were no men around to pretend to love her, to protect and to guard her, or to use her.

So they did not speak of it again, and between them there was only silence and pouring rain. He rode and rode, onward for more leagues than she had ever ridden in such foul weather. Poor Fergus was drenched, mud on the long shaggy hair of his belly and sucking at his paws. He hung his head down and trudged gamely onward. The rain grew into splattering sheets of water and she was getting colder...she couldn't get any wetter.

Soon riding was difficult: it began to seem as if night would never come, but she followed, silent still, slogging along through rivers of water, soft muck and mud, the weather getting worse as the day grew to a close. When she thought she was going to give in and demand he stop, she looked to Fergus for courage, because her dog stayed the course, one paw in front of the other, not a whimper or a sound.

Rain sluiced off her hat and onto her hands. The reins were wet and she was becoming accustomed to the odor of wet horsehair every time she inhaled. She wondered at the man's endurance, and questioned her own, and his sanity. She had been wet for over two full days.

How much longer would they go? She watched Fergus stay at her side, plodding through the thickening mud, and finally couldn't let him slog on. "Montrose," she said, intending to rein in and pull the large hound up in front of her.

Montrose stopped. "Beauly Priory is over that hill," he said.

"I'm taking Fergus up with me."

He looked at her for a long, icy moment, then dismounted and picked up Fergus as if he weighed little and mounted with her wet dog in front of him.

The sky was dark and moonless and she could barely stop from shaking and could not respond her teeth were chattering so. She had almost fallen asleep in the saddle more times than she cared to count. Her hands were so cold she could not feel her fingers.

By the time they finally 'rounded the last hill, rang for entrance, and rode through the gates of the priory, her head pounded and she could barely see in front of her. Her teeth chattered no matter how hard she locked her jaw together, and she doubted her feet were still at the ends of her legs.

The horses clattered into the stone courtyard, where rivulets of water ran like small rivers down towards the southern walls. The thick oaken doors of the monastery opened almost immediately, sending warm yellow light spilling into the courtyard. She caught herself in mid-gasp. The light meant warmth.

Two young oblates rushed out to take the horses, followed by an older monk dressed in the black robes of his order and carrying a brightly burning reed torch, the shaven circle of his tonsure shining from the flickering torchlight.

"Hallo!"Montrose said.

"Who is there?"

"Lyall Robertson," he said. "The Baron Montrose requests shelter for the night!"

"Come! Come! I am Pater Bancho, the cellarer. Inside with you…the weather is foul."

Montrose dismounted with Fergus, who looked better than she felt.

"Come," Pater Bancho repeated and waved them toward the open doors as one of the oblates took Skye's reins and looked quizzically up at her with the sweet boyish features of an angel. He frowned, then cocked his head and stared at her.

Glenna smiled weakly, bent over to dismount and water poured off the wide brim of her hat and splattered onto his robes. Her hat slipped off; it fell forward before she could catch it and hit the ground. Her long braid tumbled out and hung down past her stirrup.

Montrose spun on his heel. With the light behind him she could not see his face, but she could only imagine the scowling look he wore and the vile curses that were going through his mind. Her disguise was lost.

The boy looked at her hair, then back to her face, apparently shocked at the realization she was a not a boy, and he gasped, "Milady?"

At that very moment, she did not give a fig. She slid down from the saddle, only to hit ground with a splash and have her knees start to give way. She reached out and gripped the saddle strap, and Montrose grabbed her by a fistful of her sodden clothes and kept her from hitting the ground.

Had she done so, surely she would have shamed herself and lain there broken and wet and burst into hysterical sobbing.

He leaned over and asked quietly, "Can you walk inside?"

"You may release my clothing, my lord," she said stiffly and pulled her shoulder away, knowing she spoke with false pride. She then ruined the entire effect of her words when she swayed and the warm golden light before her grew hazy and dark at the edges of her vision. "Oh no…" She raised her hand to her spinning head.

He muttered something she couldn't quite comprehend and swept her up into his arms as if she were made of nothing but goose feathers.

"I am able to walk," she said, though her arms linked around his neck then her body melted into his warmth. "I *am*," she insisted weakly, unable to stop the words because some small part of her needed to resist him at every turn.

"I'm sure you are able to try to walk," he said calmly. "And I will have to hold you up by the scruff of your clothing while you try so proudly to do so. Do you believe if you enter through that doorway in such a manner that your pride will stay unimpaired?"

Bugger! He made a good point, and she was too tired and cold to find the will or desire to argue with him over it. As Montrose carried her inside, she was vaguely aware that the old monk was rushing alongside. "Fergus!" she called out, worried about him and panicked he had been left behind. She hated that she sounded so pitiful.

"He is here. Do not fret. Come dog," Montrose said his voice sounding strangely thick.

"What is this, my lord?" the monk asked. "Is she ill?"

"My wife is exhausted," Montrose said. A half lie and a half truth. "We have traveled from Marram."

"Across all of Ross-shire in a single day?"

Montrose was scowling.

"You made her ride this far? In the storm?" Pater Bancho's tone said exactly what he thought...that Montrose was mad and cruel to attempt such a distance with a woman in tow.

Glenna cared not what either of them thought. She was sorely tired and her teeth would not stop chattering, although his big body was so close and warm. She wanted to crawl inside him.

The monk seemed to recover himself. "Quickly, my lord. Follow me...to the warming room."

With a huge effort she cracked open her eyes, because it felt almost as if Montrose was running. Images of the walls sped past her, iron candle pricks and flickering candles that seemed to cast dizzying shadows along the hall. He was running...fancy that, following the old monk who then opened a wide, creaking oak door and stepped aside, and she felt a thankful blast of warm air. She couldn't hear the groan of relief that gave her weaknesses away.

"Here. Come in," the old monk said. "There is the fire and more wood. In the corner are pallets for travelers. I will bring blankets and towels to dry yourselves before I go to the kitchen and fetch some food. Water is in the barrel in the corner. The kettle to warm it is near the hearth. 'Tis late here, my lord, well past Compline, and most have retired to their dorter and cells. I am on watch tonight."

"I had not planned to arrive this late," Montrose said in his deep voice, which sounded leagues away from her.

She was so very tired, yet the thought hit her that if he had not planned to arrive so late, that meant he had actually wanted to travel even more swiftly? She was too tired to voluntarily shudder, and her body seemed to be ready to shudder all on its own.

Luckily for him she was also too cold to speak or to argue or create some more havoc for him. The warmth in the dry room was so wonderful that she checked Fergus, lying by the fire, then closed her eyes, feeling the powerful edges of sleep come over her. There was no saddle to fall from. There was no longer the fear she would break her neck. There was no man riding in front of her as if his life depended upon staying on course. She needn't have to prove she was strong and could keep up…so she stopped fighting and let sweet, deep sleep take her away.

Lyall threw more wood on the fire, which flared and sparked, and the heat from it soon increased three-fold. He crossed over to where he had laid Glenna down, his boots squelching from the rain. She was sound asleep, yet still her teeth were slightly chattering, her lips discolored and grayish. Her skin that had been so flushed with pleasure earlier that day, looked almost dead with cold, and she lay curled in a protective ball, knees drawn up, as if she were trying to seek heat from her own body.

Calling himself every vile name he could conjure up, he dragged the pallet close to the hearth and unpinned her sodden cloak, removed her wet tunic and trouse. Her clothing was so wet it made puddles on the stone floor Her skin was blue, and he had to fight her arms—she kept hugging herself. So he peeled her arms away again and again, and he could not help but notice that her breasts—right there before his eyes—lay small and tight. Even the tips of them were bluish.

It was not desire that drove him now. 'Twas panic. He realized what he had done to her, again, he thought bitterly. All of his trespasses against her were in a single day.

And yet the worst of them is still to come.

He dared not go there and try to live with himself, so he took a linen towel from a stack of them warming by the hearth and rubbed it briskly over her cold, damp limbs. But thoughts of his sworn promises would not wane. He could justify his actions, all men did so, his mother claimed many times when she was sorely disappointed. 'Men can always justify their actions.'

But then he did not think women could ever understand a man's ties to land.

At that moment, Lyall felt trapped by the politics of kings and men; he did not like the plot he was involved in.

Dunkelden.... Dunkelden... Dunkelden...

Always in the back of his mind, the land was always there to remind him of what drove him. He continued to rub dry her whole body and then covered her with layers of rough woolen blankets, tucking them tightly around her.

For all his scheming and planning, he had not thought about how she would weather the road. Of course he was used to riding hard; knights were trained to withstand hardship, tiredness and hunger, along with the most extremes of weather, both hot and cold.

He'd even worn out her hound. Looking like a giant, soaking wet pile of freshly sheered lamb's wool, the poor dog lay sprawled out by the fire, as if his legs and body had given out at that very spot. The huge beast's eyes were closed. The hound wasn't dead; he was snoring.

The door swung open and Pater Bancho shuffled in carrying a tray of cold mutton, barley bread and honey, and cups filled with dark mead.

Fergus awakened to the smells, eyed the mutton on the tray, then grunted and went back to sleep.

"Do you need anything else, my lord?" Pater Bancho asked him.

"Nay," Lyall said and thanked him. "Here." He handed him

silver. "For your coffers," he said, paying with enough coin to be named a benefactor, and grateful that on this night they were the lone travelers in the public room.

The abbeys, monasteries, and small priories scattered across the shires took in travelers of all kind and pilgrims. They fed the hungry and healed the sick. They were safe havens, for even the worst of enemies were hesitant to jeopardize their hereafter journey. The power of the Church was great, and not only over men's souls.

Behind abbey walls and in the loft rooms and scriptoriums, the clerics and scribes put nib to parchment and wrote manuscripts and contracts, creating hand-scribed treaties and agreements into something more tangible than merely words between men, words which would often change over time and weak memory, and with whatever way the winds of the lands would blow. Not merely houses of God, of education and prayer, they were villages unto themselves, with workshops and store rooms, animals, cattle and barns, farms and grain fields, vegetable and herb gardens, orchards and even mills if built on a water source. Often they provided the only medicine and cures available to the nearby region.

A knight with his servant stopping at an abbey would have raised no questions. But a knight and his lady? Noble couples most often stayed with other landed nobility, those who owned the local manor houses. It was too late now. He could not go back and secure her hat to pass for a lad. It was what it was....

He moved the tray over near the pallet and knelt down by Glenna. "Wake up," he said quietly and touched her shoulder and said her name.

She did not respond. He shook her slightly but she slept on.

He used to awaken his sister this way: he took a finger and traced it down the bridge of her straight nose, and she wrinkled it. "Glenna, come now. Wake up, sweet..."

Nothing again.

He moved his fingertip along the soft sweet line of her lips, because he was powerless not to do so, and her mouth parted slightly. Only his sense and concern for her kept him from lowering his head to her open mouth and sipping at her sweet lips, tasting and drinking his fill of her.

"Glenna?"

"Sleep," she said in a half moan, then she sighed and merely pulled the blankets tighter around her chin. Her face was flushed now from the heat of the fire, looking as she had that morning when he had taken advantage of her.

He did not like that he had lost control, when the point had been to teach her who held the power. He sat back on the floor, his legs bent, resting his arms casually on his knees. Lying to himself did no good.

She called to him like the most dangerous of sirens—he, a man crashing into the deadly rocks. Try was he might, he could not control the powerful pull she had on him, the ebony fire he saw when he looked into her eyes, so black at times they held him captive, him unable to move for fear he would lose what passed between them in those few, oddly binding moments when he was reduced to nothing but a man starved for her, only for her.

What was it that drew him to her without thought or reason?

Whatever it was, it was there in her very coloring, the light and dark of her, as if by merely looking at her his heart was at war.

Her beauty was not the pale, angelic comeliness of Mairi, all silver and golden and light, but a stark, almost shocking—an untouchable loveliness. Forbidden to him, this beauty of the night at its darkest penultimate moment, and stormy, like the souls of lost men who had tried and failed to live down the name of traitor.

She opened her eyes then and the world fell completely silent. It was long time before she spoke, her voice like a whisper, her lips so pale and still tinged blue. "Fergus?"

"He is over there. Asleep by the fire. When he wakens I'll feed him. Do not worry. He is fine. I know I pushed you both too hard," he paused then, searching for something to say. "Glenna?"

"Sleep is good," she murmured.

"Aye, but you should eat something now. There is food here, meat, bread. And some mead."

"Food?" she said, closing her eyes again. "You eat." Her voice drifted off. "My throat and ears hurt. And I'm too tired…" Then she fell back to sleep.

Lyall, however, sat nearby, occasionally tossing wood upon the fire, watching and waiting and thinking. He did not fall asleep for a long, long time.

ELEVEN

Her screams woke him from a deep, hard sleep. Lyall leapt to his feet, crouched in an attack stance, ready, with his sword drawn, his eyes darting in all directions. But she lay sleeping. Other than the glow from the fire, the room was dark and he sensed, empty.

Her dog was sitting up and at her side, alert and growling lowly.

Sheathing his sword, he straightened. There was no one else was in the room. "Down, Fergus!" he said. But her dog's instant reaction confirmed he had not merely dreamed her screams.

With his free hand he grabbed an unlit rush torch from a nearby iron holder and stuck it in the embers of the banked fire, then moved across the room to where she lay. She was whimpering softly when he squatted down beside her. He cupped her face with his palm.

Her face was flamingly hot and feverish. Within a few moments she began to thrash, turning her head from side to side. He put a hand on her shoulder and said her name.

She opened her eyes and looked at him, unseeing. "Al? Applecross, Dingwall, Suddy, Cromarty, Plockton, Garve, Kyle, Avoch, Knockbain, and Wester! There, Alastair. See? I know them by heart. I swear I shall never show myself there again. I promise Al. I promise...." Her voice faded off.

Clearly she was delirious. Her brow was on fire to the touch. He rose and placed the torch in the wall, retrieved another towel and filled a wooden laver with water, then pressed the damp towel to her face and neck, trying to cool her down.

When one of the knights had been injured and then grew fevered after a winter tourney, they had bled him with cups and packed him in snow to freeze out his fever. The cure advice had come from a manservant from the East, who was attached to the great English knight Sabin Fitzwilliam. Both he and his manservant claimed Eastern medicine was most successful.

The fevered knight recovered in a single day.

There came a sudden but quiet knock on the door and it opened. Pater Bancho and three other monks came inside. One carried a sword, raised high, two were carrying cudgels and the other had a quarterstaff, their eyes darting and wide as new pages at a tourney.

And they knocked first? Lyall thought, looking at their weapons and shaking his head.

"You heard her screams." He drove his hand through his hair. "She woke me screaming. She's in a fever," he said flatly. "The ride was too hard on her today. I…"

"We were at Matins," Pater Bancho interrupted him. "Brother…fetch Pater Magoon. Hurry." He faced Lyall. "Pater Magoon is the barber and runs the infirmary. And Brother Leviticus, the gardener."

"The gardener?" Lyall questioned.

"Herbs," was all Pater Bancho said.

She was crying now, weakly and pitifully, and each sob almost broke his heart. He swiftly moved back by her side and put more cool cloths on her face.

Pater Magoon, the barber, was a tall man and he came in prepared, carrying a wooden box, which he opened and began to examine her, pulling back the blankets to her waist. "There are no lesions, no rashes, which is good." He pressed his wide thumbs on her belly and below her ribs, in the small of her throat and arm pits. He lay his hand on her brow for a long time. "Her fevers are strong and high. Her humours must be balanced."

He removed his bleeding cup and a small lancet. He lay her arm straight at her side and then looked at Lyall. "Come hold her hand into a fist, hold it tightly."

Lyall did what the monk asked, his grip tight on her fisted hand, so small his covered it. He watched closely as the barber monk made a small slice in the thin blue vein of Glenna's arm and used a flint to light small torch so he could heat the cup, which he placed on her bleeding cut and then he turned her arm, so her blood slowly filled the cup.

"Now the left side," he told Lyall. "Do the same with her other fist." He then repeated the cupping on her other arm. Pater Magoon filled the cups twice on each side, then demanded that they bring a metal tub. A bath would break the fevers, he had said, But it seemed to Lyall as if the bath made her even worse.

In came a plump little man with a face as red as an apple with a wooden tray of steaming bowls. Brother Leviticus said they must make her drink the brews, sip by sip.

"I shall do it," Lyall insisted to the men.

Brother Leviticus nodded and Pater Magoon left with the promise to come back between each prayer hour to check her humours.

She seemed to calm after the teas and when Lyall put cold towels on her, but soon her teeth began to chatter again and she twisted and fought him when he tried to calm her. At one point, he pinned her down with his body to keep her arms down and her fists from fighting him.

"I am not a brood mare!" she shouted in her delirium.

"Glenna. 'Tis me, Lyall."

"Kiss me, Montrose." She linked her arms around his neck and jerked his head down to hers before she stilled suddenly.

He pulled himself back from her. "Calm yourself. Please, sweeting," he urged softly.

Then she was crying again, her head twisting back and forth, repeating things she had said to him, and Fergus sat up on his haunches, watching her closely.

"I am stealing your horse! I have no brothers! I hate the king... Oh El! My dog comes or I do not go. Stop dawdling! Why are you begging forgiveness? I will not marry a Viking! I will not!"

Her fever raged on and Brother Leviticus tried every remedy he had from cold licorice water to a mint rub on her brow. The prior visited twice to pray over her and the gardener brought willow bark tea, meat broth, and finally vinegar with which to bathe her burning skin.

She finally became silent, her delirium seemingly controlled, but she was almost too quiet and Lyall checked twice to see if she were breathing. He sat by her side for so long his legs grew stiff. But his mind was filled with thoughts of guilt. Time passed with him watching her and asking himself he was a completely lost soul.

Later in the day, she had grown so quiet that he leaned over her, listening for her breath. She was dying or almost dead because of him, and he thought he had fallen so low that he deserved to be beaten. The warmth of her breath on his face made him take a long breath and close his eyes in relief, thanking a God he had long ago stopped believing in.

Then she punched him hard in the mouth.

He grunted, cursed, then tasted the salt of blood. Though she might appear to be weak and in delirium, there was plenty of strength in her cursed fist. She tossed and turned again and he held her until she finally quieted, and he sat there for a long, long time, holding her in his arms and watching her, wondering if each breath would be her last.

"Glenna…I'm a fool," he finally admitted to her and adjusted the blanket back over her again. He rose and crossed the room, wrung out another towel, and came back to place on her brow.

She moved as fast as a snake, and grabbed fistfuls of his clothes, then pulled hard. He fell on top of her with a grunt, and quickly tried to push up, afraid he was crushing her. Then she fought him, again, screaming and kicking, him atop her.

The prior came rushing in again, followed by three monks, while Lyall was holding Glenna down. They stood in the doorway, lined up watching, their faces serious, the prior giving him a strong, judgmental look.

He looked down, at his position, at her still fighting him. It had to look as if he were ravishing her. Lyall scrambled back, embarrassed, then stood and drove his hands through his hair as he apologized. "She's no better."

"Women are not like knights, my lord. They cannot ride for hours through the pouring rain," the prior said, giving him a direct look. He crossed the room and stared down at Glenna, who was quiet again.

"We shall pray again, my lord, for your poor sick wife," one of the monks said kindly, his prayer beads in his hand as he began reciting prayers.

"I am not his wife!" Glenna shouted so loud they could have heard her in Inverness.

The prior who had joined the praying, stopped and immediately stepped back. "What is this?"

"'Tis the fever talking, Father," Lyall said, quickly kneeling down and fighting with her suddenly flailing hands.

"I am naught but a whore," she said clearly and sadly, her eyes suddenly open, but Lyall could tell she could not see him. She was still not lucid. "I am a whore."

The prior was clearly rethinking his prayer. "Is what she says true?"

"I am a whore!" she screamed again.

"She knows not what she says," Lyall said tightly.

"This is a place of God," the prior warned. "Is she your wife?"

"As I told you.…'tis the fever talking."

"You did not answer me, my lord. Did you not claim to Pater Bancho that this woman is your wife?"

"Aye," Lyall said, trying to avoid the truth, or worse yet, the lie that could cause more trouble than the truth would. He could tell no one who she was. "She is my Lady Montrose," he lied slyly.

The prior stepped closer, frowning. "Yet your wife wears no ring as proof of the bond between you."

"She lost her ring," Lyall lied again, grabbing her fists as she tried to hit him.

"Why was she wearing the clothing of a boy when you both arrived here? Would not your true wife travel freely with you…without any need to hide who she is? And why stay you both, here, in the priory, and not at one of the manors where you, my lord, and your lady wife would be welcomed?"

Lyall felt himself sinking deeper into the hole he had dug. "You question my word when I am trying to keep her alive?" Lyall bellowed, going for noise and intimidation.

"You travel without guard or servants, my lord," the prior said to him calmly, clearly determined to find the truth. "It is my duty as prior here at Beauly and as God's servant to question you."

Lyall gave in. "She is my wife!" As long as I declare by title, that I am Baron Montrose, Lyall thought, there can be no legal bond. There can be no binding handfast. "I, Baron Montrose, declare to all here that she is my wife."

The prior wisely turned to another monk. "Go fetch your pens and parchments, Pater. You will scribe the documents immediately and my lord can mark them as proof. I see he wears his signet ring."

Lyall wanted to groan aloud. 'Twas his own ring he wore, not Montrose's.

By the time the scribe had returned, Glenna's feverish movements and shouts had stopped and she slept calmly on the pallet. The prior had been busy himself, gathering all thirty five monks in the room.

Lyall had to make his declaration. "I, Baron Montrose of Rossie—"

"Lyall Robertson," Pater Bancho volunteered cheerily. "Your family names will be best, my lord. You stated who you were at the gates. Do you have more names, my lord?"

Never in his life had he wanted to kill a man of God...until that moment.

Lined up like draughts on a game board, they were all looking at him expectantly, a room full of monks, with their neatly shaven tonsures and wearing their plain dark habits, wide cowls, and rope belts with prayer beads, some of them with large metal crosses on chains hanging from around their necks and their hands clasped before them, except the scribe who was bent over an trestle oaken table, writing swiftly, his ink quill making scratching noises on the parchment. He looked up, quill in the air.

"We are waiting, my lord," the prior said.

"I, Lyall Ewane Donnald Robertson, Baron Montrose," he told them his names but lied about the title, so he still had the hope that that one more lie might keep the document from binding him to Glenna. "Declare my wife Glenna, my lady Montrose."

"What is her surname?" the scribe asked him without looking up from his work.

"Robertson," the good Pater Bancho said.

"Gordon," Lyall said at the same time.

"Glenna Gordon Robertson," the scribe repeated, scribbling away.

"Lyall?" Glenna said weakly, opening her eyes clearly and

sitting up, holding the blankets tightly to cover her and staring at all the monks surround them.

He spun around. "You are awake!" His joy at that moment was unexplainable. He was inexplicably overcome by the urge to cross the room and hold her tightly against him. Instead he moved cautiously, then touched her brow and swept his hand gently down her cheek.

Head cocked slightly, her look was puzzled and disoriented.

"Your fever is gone," he said gruffly.

"What happened to your mouth?"

"My mouth?" Lyall raised his hand to his lip. It was swollen and sore to the touch.

"My lady," the prior said, stepping close. "Is this man your husband?"

She glanced at Lyall, but he dared not shake his head. He tried to communication with his eye.

"Aye," she said, mistaking him and agreeing quickly, then added, "I am lady Montrose." Glenna frowned at him and she rubbed her face and looked around. "What is he doing?"

"We are merely documenting that you are in truth a husband and wife," the prior said. "There was some concern when you were too ill to question. A small mistake, but all is well now that you are awake. Please tell us your family names." The prior gave a wave of his hand added. "For the scribe."

"My family name?" She frowned thoughtfully and Lyall knew the drift of her thoughts. "I used to be Glenna Gordon," she said casually, then looked up. "But I believe my correct surname is now—"

Lyall tried to wink at her but she wasn't looking at him.

"Robertson," Bancho interrupted again. "You are wed to my lord."

"Gord—" Lyall started.

"Canmore," Glenna corrected at the same time, and the monks

in the room began to quietly murmur amongst themselves. The look on her face showed she realized what she had just said was a grave mistake.

It was a mistake he would shoulder, one he must fix. "Wait." He stood quickly, laughing as if it were a jest, his hand in the air. "Aye it is the same name, and they are not related by blood. My lady wife is merely a cousin by marriage, I can assure you."

"Oh, you were thinking of the king?" Glenna laughed softly, quickly picking up on the story. "It is true. We are cousins. Distant cousins," she said firmly—her lies rang uncomfortably true, then she added a jest, "But in both family bond and...." she smiled at the prior with a look that proved her lying was equal to her thieving, "by vast distance...." She paused, then said with a smile, "Is not our king in exile?"

A moment later all the monks laughed at her jest.

"Glenna Gordon Canmore Robertson," the scribe repeated slowly as he wrote slowly, hunched over his ink pot and writing table.

She watched the scribe as if she were afraid to look away. She was still pale and Lyall wished they were alone.

The prior bent down to take her hand in his. "You have been very ill indeed. You should rest, my dear lady." He released her hand and straightened, turning to Lyall. "Come, my lord. The scribe is ready for you. You can place your mark on the papers." He faced the monks. "You may all stand as witness."

Lyall looked down at his ring, not the baron's, and he dared not look at Glenna. An imaginary noose just tightened around his neck. On the inside, he was choking.

The prior stood over him as he pressed his seal onto each parchment. "We will keep the records here with all our birth, death and marriage documents," the prior assured him and Lyall understood there was as much threat in his tone as there was promise.

Unlike Pater Bancho, there was no sweetness in the prior. The man was too sharp-eyed. All the monks surrounded him like harbinger ravens perched upon a hangman's tree.

Lyall hid his concern and blithely carried on the masquerade to the end. "'Tis very reassuring to know," he said simply. He kept his gaze hooded, unable to look at Glenna, looking down upon the documents that lay before him, knowing he wanted to burn them into ashes.

TWELVE

Donnald Ramsey, Baron Montrose, lord of Rossie, Mar, Brechin, and Kirriemur, rode over the last hill, his knights and men-at-arms flanking him and the pennant of the house of Ramsey whipping in the fresh, rain-cooled island winds. Below him stood a grass-roofed cottage of stone built into the side of a knoll and looking solitary and strangely peaceful considering the plots and skirmishes shadowing the mainland.

His first thought was that Sutherland had been right, for the girl to be stowed away in these barren outlands assured her safety. Yesterday's downpour had stopped and the sun had baked away the rain on the ground. The ship landed onto the island in the light of a clear morning, and their ride across the slopes and rises of the island had been swift because the leagues of heath and moorlands soaked up the rains and only occasionally did they hit any mud to slow them. He preferred the mud to dust which strayed into the nose and made the chest tight and breathing difficult after a few days of riding in a cloud of it.

Off in the far distance the seas were a misty purple—beyond, the unknown edges of the world—but closer, nearer to the cottage horses pranced about a paddock, the extension of a stone and plank stable also topped with a roof of bright green grass and appearing as if the hillside rolled right over it.

The figure of a young man carrying a hayfork came running over the rise from the paddock and another, taller one came around the side of the house as Ramsey and his men closed in, and when the man saw them approaching, he picked up a wood axe and planted his feet apart.

Ramsey was unsure what the two of them thought they could do with a hayfork and woodaxe when pitted against a score of trained knights and twice as many men-at-arms. Amused, he raised a hand as he reined in barely a rod away from the cottage door.

The young man from the paddock stopped next to the other, panting to catch his breath. Clearly they were brothers; their faces were the same, both with sharp, hawk-like noses and dimpled square chins. Only their hair and height distinguished them apart.

"Put down the hayfork," Ramsey told him. "No one intends to harm you."

"If you mean no harm, then there is no need for me to put down the hayfork," he said rebelliously.

The knight and men-at-arms took exception and there was clattering of drawn weapons and mounts shifting into protective positions.

"Quiet, El," the tall, ginger-haired one said and he stepped in front his brother, eyeing them uneasily.

"I've come to speak with Sir Hume Gordon."

"I am Alastair Gordon and my younger brother Elgin. Our father is dead, my lord." He lowered his weapon.

"Stand down," Ramsey quietly ordered, then turned back to the Gordons. "When?"

"Why does it matter?" Elgin Gordon asked.

"Where is Glenna?" Ramsey shot back. Her name all but snapped in the air. In the telling silence the brothers exchanged uneasy looks. Ramsey could smell trouble like one could smell bad fish.

"She is gone, "Alastair Gordon told him.

"Gone?" Ramsey paused meaningfully. "What do you mean she is gone?" Without waiting for an answer, he turned to this men. "Search inside and search the paddock and stable."

"He told you the truth. She is not here," Elgin said angrily.

"Stop, El." His brother shoved him behind him and said harshly, "Put down the fork."

"By the order of the king I am here to take custody of Glenna Canmore and provide safe escort to Rossie, where she will be under constant guard and protection. There is concern her father's enemies have learned of her. I am Baron Montrose."

"You lie!," Elgin shouted, foolishly raising the hayfork.

His men responded and suddenly closed in a circle around him, while others pounced on Elgin Gordon, disarming him and holding both brothers captive.

"Baron Montrose took her!" Elgin said.

"I doubt that," Ramsey said wryly, "Since I am the Baron Montrose and clearly I do not have her. My men wear my badges. My pennant flies thus. Note my shield."

"He had the same shield!"

The men came back before Ramsey could question him.

"She is not here, my lord."

"He was alone," Elgin said.

Despite the look they had exchanged, he saw the Gordons were not lying to keep and protect her as he had thought. A sinking feeling hit his belly. "Alone? He had no men or guard? Did you not find that questionable?" It was fast becoming clear that these men who lived in a place so far out would know little of the way of things.

"He had orders in writing from the king and claimed to be Baron Montrose," Alastair said defensively. "I can show you the papers he handed me."

Ramsey had left without the papers when they could not find

them. He had more than five shields, all stored in the armory at Rossie. Foolishly he had not been concerned about the papers.

"He was tall," Alastair Gordon continued. "With light hair—"

"—And a black horse," Ramsey finished through gritted teeth.

"Aye."

At that moment he wished he was a handbreadth away from his stepson. His anger was a live thing and his vision turned red from it. His horse baulked because his hands had tightened on the reins. He almost laughed aloud at the bitter irony. Lyall. No one knew where Glenna was but a handful of men. His stepson was not one of them.

"When did they leave?"

"Four days ago."

To think he thought this a simple errand, despite the number of men with him and word of the king's protectiveness. He had said as much to Beitris the morn they left Rossie. "I go on a simple errand. You should not worry," he had told her. Now he had things to say to her, questions to ask, and worry would be the least of what she was feeling. What in the name of God was he up to now?

"Who is he?" Alastair was looking at him, clearly concerned for Glenna. "Why would he take her?"

"He is my stepson. Lyall Robertson." He did not answer the other question.

"Will he harm her?" Elgin asked.

"No. Do not worry. I will find them and make certain she is safe." Ramsey turned to his men. We must leave now and ride hard to make the evening tide." And without another word they rode off.

Alastair and Elgin Gordon stood there, unable to move. "What have we done to her?" Elgin asked.

"Nothing we cannot fix. Get the horses, quickly, and I will gather supplies. We will ride to the Norse side. Oskar will ride back and care for the horses and one of his father ships can take us across the firth without worry about tides. We will not wait for Baron Montrose to save her. We will be far ahead of them. She is our sister and she needs us."

Dried lavender and leaves of sage floated in her bath water which was tepid now after sitting in the wooden tub for so long. There was no chill in the air. A coal burner nearby made the small room as warm as if she were bathing out in the sunshine, something she always did during summers at home.

She leaned her head back and closed her eyes tightly. At the fleeting image of the island, those horrible weak tears of hers were once again burning her eyes. She willed them away. But in her mind's eye were her brothers, nothing but small brown figures waving at her as they stood so far away, down the rolling island hills by their stone house, the paddock toward the north with colts romping and horses easily grazing, overhead the sky giant, cloudless, and blue. She could smell the heather. She could smell the hay and earthy scents of barn and animals, grains and feed, and the scents of home: El's pheasants roasting on the spit in the fire and Al unlocking the spice boxes with brass keys and carefully measuring cardamom and cinnamon into an iron mead pot.

Hands covering her face she sobbed anyway. She missed El and Al. She missed everything she had known. She even missed the lies she had lived. Right then, she thought as she took a deep, chest-shuddering breath, she did not care about lies. Those lies had been her life. Now nothing was familiar. Now nothing was safe.

Using the back of her hand, she wiped her eyes and nose, then splashed water on her hot face. She sat there still and quiet as she waited for it all to pass. The past days felt as if she had lived a year.

Though she had slept long after first awakening, she still felt out of sorts and fussy. She had not seen Montrose except once, when he thought she was asleep and came to stand over her, watching her in silence. She dared not open her eyes then, for he was such an enigma to her.

She kept splashing water on her hot cheeks and her burning eyes afraid of what this all meant, until her face was so wet water ran down and dripped onto her collarbone and plopped in the bathwater. At least now she could not tell warm water from tears.

She sat up and steeled her spine. If she was going to save herself, she needed courage and to not be a weakling, weeping over something she could never have again. Searching her mind, she tried to find some sense of anger at Al and tried to conjure up all she had felt over the last days—the hard feelings of embarrassment that she was made a fool of, of the king, her father, and all he would do to her.

A few long deep breaths and she sank lower into the water. Wafting up and around her was the sweet scent flowers and summer herbs. She began to scrub her hair and head vigorously with the ball of soap in her hand and then paused and lifted it to her nose; it smelled of wild honey and almonds, and was a gift from the shy French monk who took her morning food tray and told her he had made a bath for her, led her to the wash room, chattering in an odd mixture of Gaelic, Saxon-Anglaise and French. He said they made soap here at the abbey, much soap, and not merely sturdy lye soap for cleaning, but scented soaps sold at markets. This soap, he told her, was a favorite of the Flemish royal house, and had once been purchased by Lady Margaret Pembrooke, for Queen Eleanor.

Nobility... Did her father buy soap from this abbey? She could be using the same soap her father used. That stopped her.

She set the soap aside and slid underwater, rubbing the residue from her soapy scalp then resurfacing with a gasp, only to sink back against the rim of the tub, where she closed her eyes. Soon the chapel bells rang for Matins, sweet and sounding like angel's music and ringing through the stone hallways of the abbey and out around the abbey's wattle walls. In the distance, the monks were chanting almost song-like and she began to mentally chant her own words: *I hold my own destiny... I hold my own destiny...*

The water was cold by the time the monks' voices had stopped. Outside the tub, she grabbed a fresh linen towel from a stack near the burner and began to dry herself. Next to the towels were her clothes—all of her clothes—clean trouse, hose, tunics, hood and linen, even her gown was folded neatly, with bits of dried lavender sprinkled between the tender folds.

Not a spot of food or drink or dirt, not a bit of ash or grime or a small rip or tear was on the deep green gown when she held it up to her body, and she looked down and saw the ragged bottom was neatly hemmed with seemingly invisible stitches. She picked up the hem and studied it thoughtfully.

She chewed her lip, then and looked around her feeling somewhat enchanted. The odd thought came over her that this was a magical place, where the bells at Compline, Matins and Prime rang like music from Heaven and good things like flower-filled baths and clean, scented clothes just perfectly appeared.

Before the thought had left her, the wooden door swung open and Montrose came in, whistling some bright ditty and casually tossing a ball of saffron-yellow soap. He looked up, saw her, and froze mid-tune, sound dying on lips, which was still split and slightly swollen on one side. She could read a sudden heat of some emotion in his eyes.

In that moment of utterly silent surprise, the door clicked closed behind him and she forgot to breathe. The silken velvet gown slid like soapy water from her arms.

His face changed in a mere heartbeat. His tanned skin grew slightly flushed at the bones of his cheeks as his intent gaze roamed slowly over her, down her body to her very toes, which she curled as she stood there, feeling uneasy and confused at such a look. The expression on his face became full of meaning and emotion, odd, and as if he appeared compelled by some madness to look at her that way, as if she were the answer to all the questions in the world…as if through her he was somehow saved.

How startling, this kind of thing passing between a man and woman. She stared back at him, head cocked slightly, puzzled at what that look could truly mean. What she saw was plain: he did not want to look at her that way. Clearly he was silently fighting this some dark place inside of him.

Like sparks from the blazing blue edges of a fire, his eyes grew dark, intense, and hungry. His shoulders sank as if he had given up, or given in. "God in Heaven above Glenna… You are the most beautiful woman I have ever seen."

Though she heard his words, more so she felt his words in her heart and then at the very core of her. Her reaction was to melt again, like she had against the tree in the woods. What was this thing between them? He had not touched her, not kissed her, and she was burning up. From only those words? What was this massively frightening and compelling thing she could not control and came upon her uninvited and without warning? She understood the violence of hatred. She did not understand the violence of love.

Frightened, she scrambled to pick up the gown and cover herself. As she wrapped it around her, she thought she heard him whisper, "No…"

By the time she could find the courage to look up at him, he was staring down at the stone floor.

Had she shamed herself again? "Lyall?" she dared to speak and to her ears her voice was barely there.

He did not answer or look at her, but turned away and shoved a hand through his hair. He grabbed an armful of towels and left her with nothing to look at but the closed door.

The dark shadows of the stable hid Lyall from view and he wondered why he was doing this, why he sought her out? He stood back from the doorway in a place where he was aware she could not see him. She sat on a large stone bench in the middle of the abbey garden, combing her long wet hair dry in the warm afternoon air. Her hair glistened like onyx in the sunlight. With one hand on the bench, she leaned over slightly to run a thick ivory narwhal comb all the way through to the very ends, which flowed past the bench.

He leaned against the stable wall, crossing his arms and vowing to not move. The vision was his to watch. Back when he was part of the tourney circuit, he had for a short time taken a woman, his woman, instead of one from the army of whores that was as much a part of the tourneys as the games themselves. Knights honed their skills in the games, changed their life fortunes, and celebrated wins and healed their pride over losses with whores and wine.

She was widowed and independent enough to make Lyall as much her choice as she was his. He walked into his tent one night to find her struggling with a comb knotted in her tangled wet hair. He worked a long time to pull her knotted curls from the teeth of the comb before he continued to run it through her long hair, watching it wave and begin to shine as it dried, and finally burying his face in the clean, clover scent of it.

Combing her hair became a ritual—a prelude to bedding, as strong and powerfully captivating as his sleek touches on her skin and the moans of pleasure against their mouths. Her hair had been as pale as sunlight and moonlight spun together, gold and silver, a thousand different strands of color, and nothing like Glenna's—that midnight darkness, black, black and more black than even than darkest coat of his great horse, than a rare night with no moon, hair that now was glistening so brightly as she sat combing it in the brilliant sunshine and talking with one of the monks who worked on his knees in a garden plot.

He continued to watch her until her burst of honest laughter made him have to look away. When his woman left him, she told him she needed to return home. He heard later she had left him for another knight willing to wed her. She had lied to him as easily as Glenna had lied to the prior. He did not love his widow and never understood why she felt the need to lie to him. He could never decide if he was irritated because she left him, or because she felt he was so besotted she had to lie to do so.

Most of the knights he knew believed all women lied, that it was in their nature to confound men, believing women could not help themselves, since all were descended from Eve. But the women he had known, his mother and Mairi, told him the brutal truth, oft times hammered him with it like the best of combat knights—they hit him with it between the eyes. From what he observed, his mother and sister were like rare pearls from the twisted black mollusks along the River Tay.

He focused on Glenna talking to the monk, felt all those urges he did not want to feel and thought he was destined to have his sane mind stolen by the one woman he needed to use and forget. Why was that?

His damnation must have been wanting her to begin with, or in his own lies and deceit. He dared not cast the first stone, having too many lies and sins of his own. After the past few days...perhaps, he thought, the truth was over-valued. He watched her laughing with the monk. There was some strange kind of satisfaction in telling a good lie.

His peace was chased suddenly away when the stable lad came in tugging and half-dragging Glenna's huge stubborn hound by a leather lead. "I found him, my lord. Come, Fergus. Come," the lad said brightly. "He was hiding in the vineyard but I teased him out with some salted pork."

The dog looked at him with sorrowful eyes, white and dark and almost pleading, bending his neck to gnaw on the leather lead.

Did the cursed hound somehow know what Lyall intended? Surely an animal did not comprehend words like bath and water and soap.

"Good lad." He took the leather lead from the boy and wrapped it around his hand. The dog sat on his haunches next to Lyall's feet.

The boy pulled a small clay pot from his pocket. "This is for you, milord."

Lyall took the pot.

"Salve for the bruised lip," the boy said.

Lyall stared at the pot.

"It always works for me, my lord."

"They beat you here?"

"Nay. Not here. I should have said it has worked for me...before. I am safe here," he said with a smile that proved his words true. "I no longer need salve for bruises and beatings, for blackened eyes and swollen lips."

Oh lad, that you had some salve for my blackened heart. He pulled out a coin and tossed it to the boy. "Fetch me some more water from the barrel and then you can leave us."

The boy ran off in the burst of a young colt, and Lyall asked himself when he had last had so much vigor. He watched his tousled red head disappear from sight and thought that perhaps he had left what lightness he had at Dunkeldon so long ago, before now, when he had become as much as liar as Glenna and did not hold the right to judge her.

Before he took the dog into the stable troughs, he pocketed the salve pot and started to walk away, but could not help himself and looked out at her again. She was pointing at a bushy plant and talking blithely to the monk. There was joy in her bright face. None could look at her and believe she was a thief or a liar. Sitting there, she looked like the royal daughter she was.

Perhaps she was his recompense. His own actions and lies would lead to his punishment—her.

A sense of inevitable probability came over him—what he was going to have to do with her. Whatever distant and long-lost piece of a good heart that resurfaced ever so briefly could not change that. He felt a small ache in his chest where he supposed some slim ability to hope had just slipped away completely. The feeling was there only to haunt him bitterly. His destiny was done. There was nothing left of him to be saved.

Glenna set down her comb and leaned over the plot of herb gardens outside the infirmary, pointing to a thick green plant with white buds overtaking a nearby sage plant Brother Leviticus told her was good for melancholy. "And what is this one called?"

"That is ramsons. For intestinal worms," he said.

She made a face.

He smiled slightly. "But so is white willow bark, which I used in the tea we fed you."

"I have no worms, brother," she said indignantly.

"Nay, but it helps with high fevers and mixed with rue and mint will aid with sore ears and throat, mixed with yarrow and elderberry it will increase sweats." The brother was a cheery sort, with a face like an apple and the brown eyes of a doe. He was a small man, with breadth, and was the abbey herbalist, an expert in teas and medicinals, and apprenticed to Pater Magoon, the infirmarian. He moved across the herb bed, pulling small weeds with a weed fork and pick. He paused toward another thick green plant with small flowers, plucked off a leaf, removed his leather work glove and handed the herb leaf to her. "Chew it."

She put it in her mouth and chewed thoughtly. The flavor was strong, almost pungent, and familiar. "It taste like meat...like Easter," she said surprised.

"That's because the seeds are used to season spring lamb. This is star anise and if you chew its leaves it will help digestion...and tea from it increases mother's milk" He paused. "Do you and your lord have children?"

"Good Lord...never!" she said laughing and without thinking.

He frowned at her strangely and touched the heavy cross hanging from his neck.

She tried not to wince, her mind spinning quickly. "I'm sorry. I should not have spoken so." She looked down, then back at him, feigning a meekness foreign to her. "We have been on the road for a long time. I would not do well away from him. My lord husband enjoys the tourneys," she said vaguely, having no idea if a baron would be at a tourney. She made up her stories as she went. "I could not travel with him so readily were I with child. Surely someday...." She stood to distract him and moved toward the nearest bed, sitting on the boards and wattle that framed it. "What is this woody one with the strong fragrance?"

He dusted his robes off, then joined her. "That is thyme and it is used in salves and poultices. Wild thyme has recently been used by the local midwife to help expel the placenta, and along with yarrow can stop childbed bleeding."

"I like the smell," she said smiling."

"Many have strong fragrance. They are part of the cures. Camphor for ringworm and delirium. Rosemary is used in cooking but is made into salves which work well for wounds and sores, rashes and gouty limbs. If you breathe in the smoke it will cool hot lungs. Quince is for belly pain. Skullcap and valerian for tumors and rabies."

"You have thistle growing in the corner. What does it cure?"

He looked uncomfortable and leaned very close. Looking all around him, he whispered, "Hexes." He then he moved back and quickly made the sign of the cross.

"Ah…" She nodded, biting back a smile. "Magic herbs."

"There is no magic in God's house, my lady," he said seriously. "God gives us these plants to help us. But there is the Devil's work all about. Many must be used carefully or they will poison, such as wolfbane, and if you brew a tea too strong of bloodbane," he knelt down next to her, "and too much of this bright red plant, which induces sleep, and the patient might never awaken."

"Oh is that so? Tell me…how much should one use?" she asked casually.

He held up two fingers. "One can never use more than two leaves."

Finally, she thought, studying the red plant. Her means of escape.

THIRTEEN

The bells chimed for the next prayer hour, and Brother Leviticus pulled off his dirty gloves, tucked his weeding tools under his arm, and bid Glenna farewell as he bustled towards one of the doors. Alone, she waited, looking around the garden, past the beds and furrows of cabbages and turnips, beans and leeks, off to the distant orchard where before bells, two oblates atop a slim ladder had been picking peaches while supervised by a tall thin monk.

There was no one left. She stood then, brushed the blades of grass off her clothes. The grass grew between cracks in the stacked flat stones that formed a garden bench. Casually she looked around and moved slowly toward the bloodbane, then bent quickly and snatched a few leaves, slipping them into the woolen purse at her belt. She turned around and almost jumped out of her skin.

A ginger-haired boy stood right there, hardly an arm's length away, a wide, toothsome grin upon his face. "You are well, my lady." He sounded pleased, assured in speaking to her, and vaguely familiar, and that intrigued her.

That he wasn't looking at her hands or purse told her he had not seen what she had done. "Aye," she said cautiously.

"You do not remember me." His shoulders fell slightly.

"You took my horse when we arrived. I doused you with rainwater. Forgive me."

He shook his head.

"She frowned. You will not accept my apology?"

"We have met before," he said looking disheartened.

Glenna studied him, then something struck. "Ruari?" She paused, then saw plainly the answer to her own question. "Not remember you? Ruari!"

He grinned and she threw her arms around him and pulled him against her, laughing.

She stepped back, hands on his shoulders, now broader. "Look at you."

"I expect looking at me is more easily done when I no longer look like a bruised pig."

Another image of him flashed through her mind and she felt a pang of pity and a mixture of emotions deep in the pit of her belly, even now, more than three years past. The beating she had witnessed was unforgettably horrible. He had been so young.

With a wan smile, she studied his face and pale skin, bright with a milkmaid's color on his cheeks, not features that were dark blue with bruises or overly-swollen past recognition. His nose had healed and without crusted blood, cuts, and swelling, was quite narrow and was larger as he had grown, with a crook like a falcon; it still bore the breaks from the punches and cudgel swings.

Yet the boy's sweetness had not changed and it was a joy not to see sheer fear in his eyes when he looked at her.

"And you are now wed to a great lord," he said brightly.

She wanted to groan 'No!' but remained silent. Lying to the boy was cruel, but she could not tell him the truth and put him in the path of trouble. Lies were always trouble, even if you were fairly skilled at the telling of them. This boy who stood in front of her had already lived through too much. She reached out to touch his brow, smiling. "You have straw in your hair." She picked it off his tousled hair.

"I tend the stable and animals there," he said with excited pride, standing straight and taller, no longer cowering in fear and awaiting the next blow. He was a far cry from beaten, half-dead seven year old lad she had happened upon in the woods. "And Pater Bancho teaches me to read."

"So you are now here." She remembered his young mother, the pale woman only a few years older than Glenna, thin and sobbing, with deep dark shadows under her eyes and who cried for her child while the sheriff, Munro the Horrible, beat him so cruelly. Glenna asked quietly, "What happened to your mother?"

"She is dead. Three years now. Her lungs were weak. She did not live long past that summer, though we were safe in the high forest at that time, and she was grateful to you for that. By Michelmas she could not sleep. She coughed all night. Soon, she brought me here. Pater Magoon could not save her."

"I am sorry, Ruari."

"She is better where she is now," he said with far more maturity and acceptance than one would expect from a lad his age. "Horrible Munro would have not stopped until he found us." He shrugged. "He believes we are dead. I am safe here."

The abbey bells rang again.

He looked over his shoulder and back at her sheepishly. "I cannot stay. I gave my word to the prior I would not again miss prayer and reflection."

"Then run along with you, Ruari of Beauly," Glenna said kindly, waving her hand as he turned and ran from the gardens, zigzagging on the paths and leaping over small bushes and a bed of pease, only to plop into a small puddle of water from the stormy days before. He disappeared around a corner and left her to believe the boy's bright spirit and curiosity would make that promise to the prior difficult to keep.

She turned to pick up her comb, when she heard Fergus barking from inside the stables and spun around. Was Fergus alone in there? "Ruari?" She called out to ask him, but he was gone. She put her comb in the purse with the precious red-leafed herb, pulled the strings closed and headed for the stable.

"God's eyes, you worthless hound! Stay in the water!" Lyall leaned over the wooden half-barrel filled with water, penning the dog under him as he swept the bottom of the trough for the ball of soap he'd dropped.

Fergus stuck his wet, sloppy head through Lyall's arm, looked around curiously, wagged his long tail which sent water flying into Lyall's eyes, and then started vigorously licking his ear. "Cease!" He laughed and pulled his head away. "You surely are good for little, dog. Stop licking my ears." He grabbed the animal by the wet scruff on his neck and faced him eye to eye, almost nose to nose. "You remind me of one of the tourney whores."

"Woof!"

"Aye." He ruffled the dog's ears and head. "That you do, hound. Stop your licking." Lyall paused, thinking back. "What was her name? Hold still. Look you. I found the soap. Ah, yes. Deloys. Sweet she was…flamed-haired and freckled all over. She was the widowed sister of a mercenary from Flanders and famed from the Caledonia hills to coasts of Normandy for her long, wet tongue."

"Woof! Woof!"

"Aye, that she was," Lyall scrubbed the animal, which squirmed and fought him when he was silent. The unruly beast stood still if he talked to it. "So you like the sound of my voice, do you?" He paused. "Then to make this task simpler, I shall tell all, in great detail, the wondrous tales of my lusty dealings with

Deloys of Lille." And he began talking and scrubbing, pulling off mud clots and soaping the dog's hide clean, and in time, his talk brought back to mind all the wild, mad, and sordid tales of his tourney youth.

"...Then she got up from her knees, tied the drawstrings on my braies and held out my sword and belt. She said, 'Be gone with you now Lyall Longsword,'" he told the dog, using her name for him with no little pride. "The melee begins soon,' she said. 'You need to use your sword to fill your purse rather than fill me and mine.'"

Lyall shook his head slightly. "She was a saucy wench. Robert of Ayr once said Deloys could suck your feet out of your boots."

There was a sudden creak and a soft thump as the stable door thudded slightly against the wall. He dropped the soap, sat back and looked toward the stable doors.

Glenna was standing there, afternoon sunlight behind her, framing her in a bright glow and casting her face in dark, unreadable shadows.

He felt his neck flush hot. "How long have you been standing there?"

She was silent for a heartbeat or two and then she stepped into the light. "I just arrived. Why?"

He shook his head.

She walked toward them and her dog barked again and looked ready to jump out. "Stay!" she warned and the hound obeyed, its tail switched the air and spat water back and forth.

Lyall soaped him again. "His coat was tangled with mud."

"Aye," she said, staring at him oddly. "And now it looks as if you are wearing the mud."

Lyall looked down and saw he was soaked with stains of brown water. Flecks of hard mud were all over his undertunic. The cloth clung to his chest and his thick mat of chest hair showed clearly beneath the thin linen and arrowed down towards the drawstrings on his braies. He picked at cloth, but it stuck to his skin.

She shoved up the sleeves of her gown and knelt down on the other side of the trough. "Hand me the soap. There is still mud on him here."

"The soap is in the bottom. I'll get it." He reached down but was too late to stop her. Already she had her hands in the water.

"Here it is." She held up the soap and began to clean the dog, humming as she rubbed the soap over his thick fur. Lyall sat back, resting his arms on his raised knees, which were soaked, too.

She began to sing.

The dog stood perfectly still, and Lyall, too, dared not move, so overwhelmed was he, as if he were caught by the pure, deathly-sweet sound of a siren. What magic came from her lips was honeyed and high, as fluid as the notes of a flute, mournful as a pipe, and lilting as a lute. She sang the most hauntingly *en passant* words:

> Bird on a briar, bird, bird on a briar
> Kind is come of love, love to crave
> Blithful bird, have pity on me,
> Or prepare me, beloved, for my grave
>
> I am so blithe, so bright bird on a briar
> When I see that beauty in the hall,
> She is white of limb, lovely, true
> She is fair, the flower of them all.
>
> Might I love her, by her will I will have her
> Steadfast of love, lovely and true
> Of my sorrow, she may save me
> Joy and bliss would be, ever new for me.

The words seduced him, so true they were to how he wanted to feel—that she was his salvation, not his damnation. All too quickly the song ended and she sang the impossible words no more, but continued to hum a bewitchingly captivating melody, flowing from her mouth like the wine from Saintonge, then she paused once, glancing at him over her hound, at ease, still humming, and she gave him the softest of smiles.

The moment was almost more than a mortal man could take.

Around campfires on nights before and after tourneys, there were stories told from knights who travelled the vast and wide dry deserts of the East, where the battles fought were as much with the hot sun and terrain as from war with the Infidels. Some had seen with their own eyes men on horseback sink helplessly to their deaths into bottomless holes of sand. At that moment Lyall knew he was lost, and he averted his gaze, afraid of sinking into a place of sand from which he could never escape.

But even staring at the wet straw on the ground, he could not cut the bond between them, the warring in his head, his grand wanting of her—the mere possibility of her, of the brightness and the light, of the promise of redemption. A sudden impulse overcame him to pull her into his arms and lose himself inside of her, but some small bit of conscience stopped him. He dared not take her, not now, not ever, certainly not after she found out his protection was a lie. He sought to be stronger than his drives and wants. He sought the strength of conscience to leave her be.

"Montrose?"

He looked up, startled.

"Wake up," she said, and threw a handful of soapy mud at him, laughing.

Again the sound made his senses jump. Water dripped from the tip of his nose and dropped down to the ground. He watched it, struck dumb. A second later the hound leapt from the trough sending water sloshing everywhere.

"Fergus!" she shouted.

Across from him Glenna sat with her arms out, staring down at her sodden gown, water dripping from her face and glistening in her long dark hair. Meanwhile, the dog eagerly shook himself dry from head to tail several times, and began shaking his legs out as he walked in circles, spreading the water to and fro and sprinkling both them. They sat there, both soaked, squinting a bit because they were still getting pattered by water. Each one looked at the other for enough time to see their situation, and they began to laugh freely and then lapsed into an awkward moment of silence, both still grinning.

She lifted her chin. "I'm not as wet as you," she said to him in that imperious way she had, which made him laugh harder.

"Is that a challenge?" he asked.

"Only if you care to make it one," she said without fear.

He stood then, lifted the half full trough and pinned her with a direct and determined look. She stood her own, until he was too close for her comfort and she laughed and scrambled backwards, holding out her hand. "Nay! Montrose, you do not dare!"

That she would not be intimidated showed her will and strength and stubbornness, qualities he respected in men and in his sister, and he would do no less with Glenna. Still smiling, he turned on his heel toward the backside of the stables where there was the waste channel he had used earlier. After emptying the contents, he put the trough back by the hayforks, rakes, and groom's tools.

"Come here, you wretched beast." Glenna was on her knees in the straw, with her comb in hand and half tugging the hound back into a sitting position. "Be still, you. Your fur is all tangled and all your wiggling about will break my comb."

He grabbed a milking stool and a wad of greasy fleece hanging nearby and joined her. "Here. Sit." He set down the stool for her. "Wait before you comb him. Let me rub him down with this. The grease in the wool will make the combing easier." He knelt down and vigorously rubbed the fleece over the hound's fur and stepped back. "That should help."

She pulled the comb through easily and looked up at him, clearly surprised.

"My father hired knights from the northern regions. When I was a lad, his sergeant-at-arms showed me how he lined his sheath with raw wool. The grease in the fleece helped to keep his sword protected and made it easier to hone. His woman rubbed a small piece of fleece in her hair to remove the tangles. My mother and sister still do the same." He leaned back against one of the stalls, crossing his feet at the ankles and resting his shoulder against a rough-hewn post, lost in his thoughts of another time and place, another dog. He chose not to tell her how he had rubbed Atholl down many times after bathing him, but her hound had brought back the images, as had watching her comb her hair brought back another memory.

"You have a sister?"

"Aye, she is younger than I. You did not ask about my mother. I am surprised you did not seem shocked I had one," he said dryly. "Instead of being spawned by the Devil or sired by wolves."

"Not wolves. Banshees in the dark Caledonian Woods." She laughed at his mock anger. "And how do your sister and mother tolerate you?"

"They do not."

"Aye," she nodded, finishing with one side of the hound. "I find that understandable."

"They worship me," he countered.

"Be careful when you walk through that door, Montrose... your fat head might not fit."

"Beware how you flap that tongue of yours...I might be tempted to cut it out."

"Such threats against a poor, wee, defenseless woman."

That made him chuckle and he saw she tried not to smile, but stood instead and studied the hound, gripping him gently by the scruff and moving her face close to his dark, wet snout.

"Look at you, Fergus. You are so handsome. You look like a royal hound."

"Do not lie to the animal. He still looks like an enormous hairy rat, but with no mud on his fur."

She fluffed the dog's big ears. "Ignore him, my sweet hound. I take most of his words with a grain of salt." She surprised him, the phrases she used, and not for the first time.

"How do you know of Pliny and Pompey?"

"Alastair told me many stories. Of Aesop and Homer, Sophocles' Antigone and Oedipus, of the great tales of the Greek gods and goddesses. Those myths and poems were the heart of my childhood. My father's," she stopped and corrected herself. "Sir Hume's father was distant kinsman to the duke of Normandy and was educated in his youth by a priest and destined for the church, until some change took place and he was sent to be fostered to a family, where the house bard carried songs and poems and tales for all who dined in the great hall. He passed those stories on to his son, and he to his sons, and Alastair himself was tutored for a short time."

'Twas as if a storm cloud had descended over them, so quickly did the lightness between them change. The mere mention of her brothers stole the joy away and some part of him was sorely disappointed.

But his sense returned swiftly, and told him he was being a fool. Better there be distance between them, even rancor, than his strange weak moods of the heart.

"We will leave at sunrise," he told her.

She stood up, head down as she straightened her clinging wet gown, then opened the purse at her waist, looked inside and dropped in the comb. "Thank you for bathing Fergus, my lord. Come now," she said to the hound and snapped her fingers. The dog was instantly at her side. "We shall leave you to your..." she paused and looked at him as if she were searching for something in him rather than something to say. "...your business."

He watched her leave and stared at the empty spot where she had disappeared, unable to shake from his mind's eye the image of her. He cursed himself for starting this, for washing her hound and bringing to mind his past, one that was long since over, and worse, his future, when he would have to walk away from her, and that was the last thing he wanted to do.

FOURTEEN

Torchlight in her hand, Glenna stood over the sleeping form of Baron Montrose sprawled out on his pallet, studying the slow, even rise and fall of his chest. She took a chance and poked him in the side with her foot.

Not a sound did he make.

"Montrose?" she whispered. Nothing. "Montrose," she said louder. The man was sleeping like a drunkard. She picked up the half-full tankard and sniffed it. There was no telltale scent, nothing to warn that essence from the bloodbane leaves had laced the beer. Montrose had no warning of what was coming.

For reasons she could not explain, she was not proud of herself, and uncomfrotable with her moment of conscience. Still she stood there longer knowing there was no time for regret.

But part of her still wished….

What good were wishes? Pah! She hurried around the room gathering her packs together. Soon after she'd left the stable earlier, she had done as Montrose asked and packed up what she had and changed clothes. Her gown was still wet when she rolled it up, but she sprinkled it with some fragrant dried lavender leaves from that morning, before tucking her green gown and the rest of her things tightly into her saddle roll.

Fergus was eagerly up on his haunches and watching her as

she pulled her things into a corner before loading herself up with gear. Over one shoulder she slung the braided leather cord on Montrose's fat waterskin, then shifted, adjusting it more comfortably next to the thick satchel strap that was already cutting into her slightly from the weight. She also stole his knife and a bag of silver marks.

A woolen cloth filled with food and tied tightly together would have to wait for the second load. She would not be as foolish as before and leave with nothing to eat or drink. One quick look at Montrose; he looked to be far, far from awakening. But she had no guarantees he would not wake up soon after she left. She was new to this drugging ploy and had been somewhat afraid to use too much and kill the man.

To Fergus she said, "Stay. Lie down. I shall be back." He obeyed but rested his ragged snout on his paws. His eyes were big and wide and innocent, still watching her as she slipped quietly out of the room.

With the pack, her satchel, other goods slung about her shoulders and wrists, she moved down the abbey's narrow maze of dark hallways, being careful as she passed the dimly lit corridor that led down towards the front doors.

She looked around the corner.

At the end of the hallway, under wane of a flickering rushlight, Pater Bancho dozed in a niche by the large oak doors while slumped in a heavily carved wooden chair. She tiptoed quietly past the opening and moved swiftly down the halls to the back doors that led to the gardens.

Outside, but for the click of insects and the slight sound of her soft and careful footfalls, it was quiet, being well past the night's last chiming of the bells. Soon she would be free and away from the threat of her birth, away from her fears, and away from Montrose.

An uneasy feeling ran over her arms like chilblains at the

image of him when he awoke and she was not there. She could almost hear the bellow. And this time, she felt no urge to laugh. Somehow, besting him now held little satisfaction for her.

She began to run, heavily with her load, but run she must. She needed to run from his image, from the mere thought of him and the questions that came into her mind, far away from what she was feeling.

Above her, the twinkling of stars scattered as if thrown across the sky, and the thin splinter of a moon stood off toward the southwest where the edges of the horizon were still the late summer color of heather. She crossed the last distance of the garden, heading into the orchards where the fruit ladder was light and easy enough for her to carry to the south outskirts of the abbey garden and pull up after her whilst straddling the lime-washed wall, and then lean down on the other side, where she climbed outside the grounds and ran into a nearby copse of thick rowan trees.

Tied to a tree in the woods, Skye whinnied softly and Glenna pulled out a handful of oats and let her eat from her hand. Her horse had been waiting there most of the night. She secured on her packs and ran back the way she had come. She entered as quietly as she had just left and slipped into the room, where Montrose was slightly snoring in his drug-induced sleep.

No…she was wrong. It was not Montrose who was snoring.

She took down the torch and moved to the dark corner, where Fergus lay on his side, snoring,….next to the over-turned beer tankard. Had it not been half full? Now there was not even a puddle of liquid. She squatted down and whispered harshly, "Fergus!"

No response.

She shoved his body, shook him. "Fergus!"

Her dog was drugged. She groaned miserably and sank her head into her hands, just sitting there, feeling a little lost and defeated.

What had she done?

Lifting her head up, she glanced at him again, the slow rise and fall of his furry chest, lying on the floor as stuporous as was Montrose himself. She sat there for long moments, each one essential to the success of her escape, knowing she had made a muck of things.

This was perhaps her only chance on the journey to run. She stared long and hard at Fergus. She prided herself on out-thinking people, on proving she was smart. The best thing for her own survival would be to grab the bag of food and leave. And break her heart. Running away without her dog was not an option she would consider, no matter what was the best move.

Without another heartless thought, she lifted him into her arms...Lord, but he was heavy, and floppy, and awkward—dead weight—and positioned him over her shoulder like a wheezing sack of oats, dipped her knees slightly to pick up the bundle of food, and she made for the door.

Pausing, she looked back and whispered, "Sweet dreams, Montrose."

Lyall's mouth was as dry as the deserts of Outremer, and tasted oddly sweet and bitter, as if he had drunk bad heather ale. He rolled over—a monumental effort—and groaned, his body like dead weight and stiff, muscles aching up and down his limbs and back with the merest of his movements, the way one ached after sleeping in one position all night.

His hand and arm were numb; he flexed his fingers, staring up at the blurred beams above him. His head throbbed and was not much better than his numb hand.

Where am I?

He shook his head and blinked several times, adjusting to the dark, and could make out the carving in the thick wooden beam overhead, a familiar psalm for pilgrims: *Thy help comes from the Lord, Maker of Heaven and Earth.*

He was at the Abbey at Beauly. Under that beam he had knelt by Glenna, held her down during her deliriums and prayed over her to a God he'd had little communication with since he was ten years old. He sat up and glanced opposite him, where her pallet was empty. Thinking she must have gone out to the privy or taken the hound out, he tried to clear his head, knowing he needed to get up. It must have been near dawn and any moment he expected to hear the bells of Matins.

Today they were facing another long ride, but in the windowless room, he had no idea if it was yet close to sunrise or past it. He stretched, pulling his muscles tight, then relaxing and wiping his face. Odd how he felt as if he could fall back asleep. Even after his most drunken of nights, his head had never pounded like it did now, thundering across his scalp like horse's hooves.

He pushed himself up and the room swam. He swore then scratched the back of his head. Out of sheer stubbornness he stumbled to the laver, filling it from the ewer and splashing water on his face.

As he toweled off his face, the bells rang...the bells rang the number for Terce, late...midmorning. The towel slipped from his hands, and he glanced over at the empty corner, where last night she had stacked her packed possessions. He was out the door in a heartbeat.

Before long all was clear. Glenna, it turned out, was nowhere to be found. The orchard ladder was left on the ground near the south wall. No horse. No hound. He looked around him and cursed himself a fool. His 'wife' had taken off sometime during the night, and he was forced to leave the abbey with great speed and a lighter purse (much lighter considering one bag of marks was missing). less a substantial sum to the abbey to pray for his heartless soul.

On horseback outside the gates, he winced up at the blurred sun, which added to his blinding headache, but all he could see clearly was the vision of her talking to the monk in the herb garden. So much for all his long well-thought stratagems. She had outwitted him, and if he weren't in a temper at his piss-poor self, he might have paid silent homage to her actions.

There was no doubt in his throbbing head and unlikely sluggishness that the little witch had drugged him. As he knelt by his horse outside the abbey wall and touched her trail marks in the soft wet ground, followed them into the woods and tracked the deep, sunken hoofmarks heading away to the south.

What was that she had said when she was fevered? *Applecross, Dingwall, Suddy, Cromarty, Plockton, Garve, Kyle, Avoch, Knockbain, and Wester.*

So he knew where she was not, and knew, too, that when he found her — and find her he would — there would be hell for her to pay.

There would be hell for his stepson to pay when he found him.

Smelling of horse and dust, driven by lack of sleep and anger, Donnald Ramsey took the castle stairs at Rossi two at a time. He crossed the solar, pushed aside the thick brocade curtain to the bower, and stalked into the open room looking for his wife, who was not there. Maids were busy scouring coal smoke from a stone wall and, on hands and knees, cleaning the flagstone floor. One turned from the wall, saw him, and dropped her bucket to the floor with a clatter. The others turned in unison, looked at his face, and quickly curtseyed.

"Where's Lady Beitris?" His voice sounded like thunder.

One woman paled while another gaped, open-mouthed. He seldom shouted.

"She has gone out to the kitchens, my lord."

He swore and left the room, ran back down the stairs and across the open bailey to the cook sheds. Inside was absolute chaos, which was appropriate considering his last couple of days. Kitchen lackeys were beating out a spreading fire near the wood larder, leaving him unnoticed, while the cookwas shrieking that whole place would be up in flames and 'my lord would hang them from the towers and rip off my thumbs.'

Two castle guards came running past with buckets of water from the castle well, so he grabbed one and doused the fire in sizzling burst of smoke and steam. All turned in unison to look at him, and the shed was suddenly silent, while they stood staring at each other, smoke swirling, the taste of burnt wood in the air.

One of the lads averted his wide eyes, but Ramsey caught his expression—so fearful and pale he was on the edge of bursting into tears, probably at the image of hanging from the east tower by his neck.

"No one will hang from my towers," he said in a suddenly calm and quiet voice. Except perhaps Lyall, he thought, glancing over at the cook, a wiry man with a thick thatch of coal black hair who had cooked at the castle for more years than Donnald cared to count and had the priceless skill to make plain mutton stew taste tender and spicy and like no other. "And were I to cut off your thumbs, man, how in God's name would you prepare my meals?"

The man set a jug down and then laughed and said, "Thank you, my lord, my thumbs are quite necessary for butchering spring lamb.

"Where is Lady Beitris?"

"In the buttery, milord," the lad volunteered quickly, his color returning.

Ramsey decided he needed to have harness made for his wife. As he walked across the bailey yard, he realized he was more tired and disappointed than angry. Between the island and Rossie he had stewed in his anger until it turned into a highly cooked rage and he thought his head would blow off by the time he approached the castle gates with a few of his men. Now, he was resigned. Lyall had chosen his path. What was done, was done.

Inside the buttery, barrels of ale and a few hogsheads of wine stamped with winery marks were stacked in straight rows along the freshly limewashed stone walls and Beitris stood inside, directing workmen in the restocking of recently delivered Angevin wines. She demanded precision in all things—the position of stored goods, the perfectly aligned rows in the castle gardens, the table settings in the great hall, the exact placement of a carpet upon the stone floors, the tapestries on Rossi's wall, even their clothing on the rods and in the coffers of their bedchamber; and he wondered if that perfection was all there only to compensate for what she felt when she touched her face or looked at her reflection in the polished surface of a metal mirror.

"Beitris," he said quietly, his voice sounding as strained as he felt.

She turned quickly and her hood slipped down. Her hand went to her face and she quickly pulled up the hood, turning away so she stood in profile, the unflawed side of her face all he could see. Over the years she had learned to judge—also with precision—the exact angle to hide the scarred side of her face.

But he had known her since she was ten and three and barely betrothed to Ewan, who she had wed three years later. From first sight of her, Donnald was smitten. She became part of him; she haunted his secret dreams and was what made his nightmares. Ewane was his friend, yet that did not stop him from coveting his friend's wife. Time and their destinies had changed all and she was now his wife, her beauty had naught to do with anything. She was his heart. He cared not about the appearance of her face and would give all he had, including his soul, to take away the shame she felt.

Had he known what their future held could he have controlled his own deep desires? All thought him to be an honorable man, yet he knew the truth.

"I did not expect you for days." She paused. "What is wrong?"

What was wrong? So much, including the fact that he was her husband and she need not hide from him. He had seen her face despite the darkness she begged for. He turned to the workers. "Leave us."

When they were alone he sat down on a ale keg, hands hanging down almost uselessly between his legs, him staring at them and searching for the words to tell her what her son had done. His mind found a fine use for his hands...he wished to strangle Lyall. "Tis about Lyall."

"Is he dead?"

"Nay," he said, and told her all. His words were crushing her, he knew, for Lyall's actions were treasonous. Whether Ewane had betrayed the king or not no longer mattered. Because her son had.

She stood there for a long time without saying a word, battling the demons of motherhood.

"Did he say anything to you?" Donnald asked. "Did he meet with anyone recently?"

"He said naught to me." Her words were terse and she looked thoughtful. "We should send for Mairi. Perhaps she will have some knowledge." She shook her head and stared off at the wall for a long time. He could hear the choked tears in her voice when she said, "Is there naught you can do, Donnald? Can you not find him and stop him before all is lost to him?"

"I sent men in all directions looking for them, and I rode straight here."

She placed a gentle hand on his shoulder and said, "You must be exhausted. Come inside where you can bathe and have some wine."

"Wait." He pulled her into his lap and she quickly maneuvered so his face was next to her unscarred side. Leaning against her soft skin, he closed his eyes, took in the weak, sweet scent from the rose petals she used to store her linen underclothing, and deep in his heart he wished she loved him enough to let him lean his brow upon her scarred skin.

FIFTEEN

"Applecross, Dingwall, Suddy, Cromarty, Plockton, Garve, Kyle, Avoch, Knockbain, and Wester," Glenna recited. Places to avoid. She led Skye not in the southern direction she believed Montrose had been taking her, but due east from Beauly, where at first she had gone through the woods in a southerly direction, then guided Skye along a stream and doubled back, twice and in two different directions, covering her tracks, and leaving false ones.

He would never know she was headed for Inverness.

For half the day she had crossed through the long, wooded grounds of the Great Glen, riding through streams of water and away from, or skirting around, villages and hamlets she and her brothers had plundered.

Her brothers' sweet faces came flooding into her mind and she wondered what they were doing this day, and did they miss her as sorely as she missed them, as if she had left part of herself with them, an arm, a leg, a piece of her heart. She lost herself in thought for a few memories, ones that stole some of the life from her.

The silence stretched onward, until she heard nothing but the crush of Skye's hooves on the leaves and pine needles beneath her, and then her heart beating loudly in her ears. The realization hit her that she was more alone than she was comfortable. On the island, the quiet had always felt peaceful, soft, and not empty like it did now. She had sought out time by herself. She was quickly becoming a stranger, she thought, and rode onward.

At the place where the stream turned to falls, tumbling down to a river below, she stopped to refill her flask and remounted. As she moved on, the song of a lark made her look up through the trees, but it stopped singing when a devilish black rook shrieked loudly and flapped its wings, diving like a spear and scaring the lilt and bird music before it flew away.

Overhead, a patch of blue sky stared back at her as if it had eyes.

The clear blue of his eyes.

A hare suddenly scampered out from beneath a fern and her heart caught in her throat.

Overhead a hawk circled, only to light in the high branches of one of the tallest trees and she could hear the sound of an animal thrashing through the brush, eerie and strange and a little frightening.

It was as if there was no other living human soul in the world. Urging Skye forward, she held her breath, and then finally exhaled as she rode out from under a dark stand of larch and pine and reined in, sagging slightly in the saddle, her heartbeat slowing and her hands relaxed.

Before her spread a vast and open river plain and the air was dry and warm as a fur-lined cloak, and tasted of summer, unlike the fecund and verdant dampness of the woods—a metal taste reminiscent of blood on the tongue. The high sun had cooked away the last of the night's dew on the grass, and to her left, a marten scurried through a crackling nest of needles and larch leaves to disappear into a hole.

Skye shied slightly and she controlled her with slight pressure from her knees, which were fairly numb from her dog's weight. Fergus lay limply in front of her, slung like a grain sack across the saddle, unmoving. But once she shifted, one of his eyes popped open and he was staring dully up at her. "You are awake. Poor dog." She stroked his neck, feeling like the worse kind of monster. "Beer is not for hounds, you foolish thing." A couple of breaths and his sad eyes drifted closed again. "And spiked beer is for big, brawny barons who...." Her words trailed off. She couldn't muster up anything horrible enough to squelch her feelings of guilt.

Had he awakened by now and discovered her deceit? He would be angry enough to spit daggers, that she knew. His expression of anger was burned into her memory, so different from how he looked at her the day before.

The image of him in the stable at Beauly came flooding into her mind, Montrose laughing, his eyes the exact color of a perfect sky, crinkled at the corners and changing his whole face and demeanor, the flash of white, even teeth, his ample height and impressive breadth, looking ludicrous in the way his clothes and face were dripping water as he stood threatening to soak her to the bone.

Her mind's eye switched to the tender, odd look in his eyes when she was singing—a look she had never seen on a man—and then the stiff tension in his muscles and the sense of panic emanating from him as he ran down the narrow abbey hallways with her shaking in his arms...the warmth of his body when she was ill, both there and on the ship's crossing...his mouth on hers.

Such thoughts. She was twisted up inside them, these games inside her head, trapped, and tangled in even sillier dreams she dared not allow herself to think about. Montrose, Al and El, her father dying...her father lying...not her father after all. Her *father*, the king.

Would the king ever let her be? If she could stay hidden for a long time would he forget about her? Would she ever be free?

Men, she thought with disgust. May St. Columba take them all! If she were violent, she would want to hit something. "Yesterday does not matter," she said aloud stubbornly, as if by doing so she could believe it as truth.

The past was merely that: past.

She used her hand to shade her eyes against the startling bright sun, as her squinted gaze followed the bare leg of road cutting through viridian grass and a lazy scattering of chalky rock; it led through the last span of land between her and the port burgh of Inverness, which was large enough to keep her safe, with cross streets and its trade market.

Cast in the blue haze of distance and perched on a distant crag was the castle; she could make out the notched teeth of its crenelled walls. Below it, a wide silver ribbon of water, the River Ness, which curled off into Moray Firth and was trimmed in lines of the town's staggered buildings a good league away. From here, they looked like nothing more than a game board of merels.

A startling shout, the snap of a whip and a curse to the "slowest beasts this side of Cromarty" pierced her lonely silence, and soon the slow, creaking sound of a wain came from a nearby bend in the road. Oxen, huge and horned and knotted, pulled a lumbering wagon which slowed as it grew closer. Stacked up the sides of the cart bed, burgeoning bundles of plump corn threatened to burst from their tethers.

"Good day to you, lad!" The driver wrapped the thick leather reins securely around his fist and pushed back his hood of brown wool worn above a saffron tunic of trade's linen. His face was kindly, eyes bright and cheeks red as island deer, but the right side of his face was misshapen and twice the size of his other.

He rested his reins on his knees and uncovered his head to reveal hair the color of iron, blackish flecked with gray. The oxen must have stopped, although considering how slow they had been moving, Glenna wasn't certain. "Good day," she said.

"What have you there?" The man sounded as if he had a mouthful of stones and she stared without thought at his swollen face. He was looking at Fergus—a large furry lump in front of her.

"My hound."

"Is it dead?"

"Nay. Dead drunk," she fabricated, figuring it was a half-truth. "He lapped up more ale than a brewer earlier."

The man gave a bark of laughter then grabbed his cheek and groaned. "This blasted tooth!" He pulled a small pot from his cloak, dipped in his fingers and rubbed them on the back of his mouth. "Wintergreen oil," he explained and tucked the pot away. "Barely a league of road left ahead of me and I can seek out the clever hands of the town barber. Won't be too soon enough, I say. With this fat load I should be wanting to head straight to the mill, but—" He put his hand on his fat cheek. "I will stay in town for I cannot take another eternal night of this. You're headed for town, laddie?"

"Aye."

"I'd welcome the company. Will take me mind off the Devil's own throbbing pain." He cast a quick nod toward the wagon and winced slightly. "The hound can rest in the back of the wain."

She looked down at Fergus, knowing he would be most comfortable in the wagon, sleeping off his stupor on a bed of corn husks rather than ribs rattling as she and Skye rode on." And his weight was causing her limbs to go uncomfortably senseless. She eyed the man's wain and its precarious load and wondered where Fergus could sleep safely and not fall off.

"Do not fash yourself. We've plenty of room for him. See? There is dip in the midsection." He stood. "Come. Hand him up to me, laddie, and rest your animals for a while."

So with Skye tied to the back of the wain and Fergus asleep in the middle of the load, Glenna took to posing as the lad Gordon of Suddy, the best she could invent in the spur of the moment, and she rode companionably into the town of Inverness on a sunny afternoon settled on a wain bench next to the loquacious Heckie of Drumashie. He told her tales of his past and his family, his wife who was the daughter of a sea merchant and, he, with hectares of fertile land given him as reward for saving the son of his overlord, a story he chewed her ears over with flourish and as much drama as an Angevin bard.

Heckie of Drumashie was a man of many words and even more gestures.

Soon black-faced sheep could be seen grazing contentedly on the low rises, and dairy cattle munched on fathoms of clover speckled with yellow flowers. Scattered along the outskirts of town were perimeters of low stone fences and crofts covered in thick thatch, built of solid wattle and daub that sparkled in the sunlight with newly lime-washed walls, surrounded by freshly mown fields, one with a lumbering spotted sow and gaggles of children laughing, chasing.

A woman with her blue skirts tucked up into her girdle stood hoeing rows of turnips and onions, and another tossed feed to red-brown hens with feathers all-a-flutter as they pecked heartily at the ground near her wooden clogs. Off in the distance, men tilled the grain fields and others were bailing up huge rolls of fresh golden-green hay, while large-bedded hay wagons lined up to be loaded. Wagons stacked high with faggots cut from the forest for cook fires moved past the town's perimeter ditches and disappeared into the bowels of Inverness. Everywhere she looked was another teeming eyeful. To see so many people caused a humming deep inside her. She was not so alone, and she smiled.

"Aye, 'tis a sight, is it not?" Heckie said with admiration. "To see a holding where the lord and the sheriff don't bleed all the wealth out of the land and its people. Even the likes of Munro the Horrible wouldn't dare plant his greedy feet onto charter land of the king, Himself."

Her smile disappeared. She didn't know which name upset her more, Munro the Horrible or her father 'Himself.' She paused before speaking. "When the king Himself has been living in exile for so many years past?" The words spilled like toads from her mouth. "What king does not rule his land?"

She could feel Heckie's look without a glance.

"I would expect a laddie from Ross-shire to know more of how the winds blow," he said quietly and pulled on the reins.

She stared at her hands in her lap, knowing she could not tell him the truth, that she knew little of kings and politics living not in Ross-shire but in the isolation of the outer islands, where rare news was more of the Norse machinations than much of their own homeland. That she was not a lad.

What would he say were she to pull off her hat, let down her hair, and declare she was the daughter of Himself?

Did that make her Herself?

If Heckie of Drumashie knew he was sitting next to the daughter of the king she suspected the news might actually render the man speechless.

She searched for a lie and settled on the truth. "I do not know much of the workings of politics and the rulings and rights of kings. I never dared ask why he is in exile, having lived with the belief that the king was so far from my place in the schemes of the world and therefore had nothing to do with me. I have only known that the king has been away for as many years as I have breathed this air."

So Heckie explained the king's exile, the great battle on the day she secretly knew she was born, and Heckie's story made her understand betrayal on a grander scale than she would have ever thought she could fathom before the last few days.

".... And later we heard that the great and lovely queen had died, with her newborn child, in a fire in the woods, while the king was taken prisoner, and none ever knew if it were the king's enemies that got to her."

From Heckie she heard of such tales of the treachery that for the first time she understood the thin thread of control and slim trust available to anyone with royal blood. He told her of the king's cousin, who challenged her father's right to rule through his mother's line and with coffers of gold and silver from his many ransoms bought easy rebellion from some lords who swore fealty to her father, but behind his back plotted to oust him.

"He came back to Scotland once, Himself did," Heckie said. "But a traitor was privy to the secret plans, and as the king and his men rowed ashore, the barons and their mercenaries attacked and he took an arrow deep in his side. On the ship was a man from Jerusalem who studied Eastern medicine, and he held the king together until they landed in Brittany. The French king's chirurgeon brought him back from death throes, but his recovery was long and difficult. 'Tis said he was betrayed by one of his closest friends…the name bandied about was Sir Ewan Robertson.

For a brief moment she wondered if she had misjudged her father. She still ached from her own experience with betrayal.

"There is fresh rumor brewing about. First heard a fortnight ago."

"What kind of rumor?"

"That Himself is coming home."

She knew the rumor was no rumor but the truth. Her father was coming back. Would his enemies again try to kill him? How could he ever trust anyone?

Heckie was watching her quizzically.

"I do not know what to say except it would seem to be folly for him to risk his life again. Why would he?"

"Because his blood is that of kings," he said simply.

He spoke with honest reverence about her father and his courage, and his tone was filled with pride. She felt suddenly small, and for the first time she wondered at her blood. What did she carry beneath her skin that drove her and made up her being? So many unanswered questions.

They drove past the deep defense ditches lined with stone and into Inverness proper, where buildings huddled close together like foot soldiers, shoulder to shoulder, as if there were only bare enough plots of land for the four corners of each one. Up from the dirt street, a blanket of dust swirled around the ox team, dusting their black coats with a fine veil of red dirt.

That the thoroughfare was not muck-ridden was extremely rare.

From what Heckie said, drain gutters and cess channels were built behind the buildings, as they were in Edinburgh and London. And though there were dogs and pigs and chickens occasionally roving in the streets, there were far more people moving to and from the market crossing; it stood ahead them, where the crowds thickened and one could hear the hawking of goods, pipe and drum music, and the buzzing voices of trade.

Heckie turned the wain down a side street and stopped in front of a narrow, stone based building with blood-red painted shutters. A barber sign swung on an iron hook above the door, a thick oak timbered with red and white-lime painted trimwork. He assured her he knew of a stable where she could safely board and care for her horse and hound while she explored the temptations of the market. In exchange she would stay and watch the loaded wagon while Heckie took care of his tooth pain.

Glenna knew she could not stay in the town indefinitely—she would have to move onward—but the size and crowds of Inverness afforded her more anonymity than a village and she needed supplies. For a short time, perhaps a few days, she could lose herself here.

Lyall lost her trail again. He reined in and rubbed his brow, took a long deep breath before he glanced up through the trees at the sun to gauge how much time he'd already wasted.

Too long. For every movement of the sun across the broad blue sky, she was getting farther and farther away.

Frustrated, angry at himself for letting his guard down—and wanting to whack the little witch for being so quick-witted—he turned around for the third time and went back to the place where she had entered the stream. He dismounted and carefully tracked her on foot, walking on the rocks and stopping to examine anything, until finally he found one deep hoof print between some rounded stones, not on the east side as he had expected, but on the west side of the stream.

West? He stared into the trees. He didn't for a heartbeat believe she would go back toward the abbey. He looked westward, then north, checked both directions for trees with broken twigs and branches, marks that proved she had ridden past, and then searched the areas for hound and horse dung, anything to give a clue of her direction. But he found nothing.

Back by the stream he kicked aside some fallen leaves, hunkered down. There, finally, he saw a trace of hoofmarks that had been brushed away. He shook his head, half admiring her.

The trail led in a wide circle back to the stream. So it was no surprise when he found she had pulled the same trick again further upstream, only this time the hoofmarks were headed north, and again she had covered her tracks back to the stream— which meandered westward before turning into a rock falls down a hillside near the eastern edge of the woods.

He followed her trail, trusting his instincts, which had yet to lead him false. Only when he let down his guard did his plans go awry, he reminded himself. Something to keep in the forefront of his mind when it came to his thoughts and plans and feelings about Glenna.

Eventually he rode out of the woods to face the road to Inverness, the sun far behind him, and he spurred his mount forward, riding hard and fast—a wolf on the scent.

As she sat on the wagon seat waiting, a familiar panting sound came from overhead, and she leaned to the side and glanced upward to see Fergus, snout resting on his large furry paws atop the piles of corn, eager eyes wide and looking down at her. She could hear his tail thumping on the husks. He whimpered and crawled forward, so she stood and wrapped her arms around him, burying her face in his fur then letting him freely lick her face.

"I swear I will never again spike a tankard of ale." She gripped his wrinkled furry jowls and faced him nose to nose. "I am sorry, sweetling."

From the barber's open shutters, a loud, drawn-out shout of pain cracked through the air, and Fergus lifted his head, ears perked. Glenna winced, then shuddered slightly, thankful for every tooth in her head, even the crooked two on the bottom.

Time slogged by. She began to tap her feet.

The finally door opened and Heckie came out, a leather flask to his lips. He wiped his mouth with the back of his hand, and climbed up into the wain, the overly pungent scent of usquebaugh tainting his breath.

He sat down and weaved a bit, then gave her a silly drunken grin, revealing a large bloody gap where his bad tooth had been. "Gone. There…see? I'm grateful, lad, for staying with the load." He inhaled deeply, whistling slightly. "I see your dog is awake. Good…good. Now we'll be off to find your stables." He paused, shook his head and moved his mouth oddly slipping his tongue into the space where his tooth has been. "This fresh hole in my mouth is making music. I breathe and whistle." He inhaled. "There. Did you hear that?"

Before she could agree, he was off talking about the barber and how much the usquebaugh burned his mouth and throat but lessen the pain greatly, except for when the hard grip of the barber's tool clamped onto his deviled tooth, and he snapped the reins and continued to blather on…only twice as fast and loose.

'Twas not long before Glenna had bid a sweet farewell to Heckie, who drove off to take his load to the mill for grinding, talking avidly to the ox team and occasionally taking another sip from the flask. Skye and Fergus were fed and boarded in backstreet stables owned by the town's well-trusted alewife, so Glenna moved without worry down the short maze of narrow alleys.

With her coins safely tucked inside her chest bindings, and a few more in her boot (no thief would be fool enough to carry a purse about a market that would no doubt be crawling with divers and pickpockets) she stood at the edges of the market cross and took it all in.

After purchasing apples and root vegetables for the road, the thought came to her that it had been a long time since she'd entered a market without being there to stake out the easiest victims. She felt easy, light of foot and mind, and she hummed a merry tune as she moved from booth to booth. The scent of warm oat and cinnamon honey cakes wafted from nearby and she bought one and ate it like a child given a treat for the first time.

Colorful flags and tent awnings were trimmed brightly to catch the eye. The unmistakable scent of fresh bread and the sweetmeat call of pieseller's booth drew her into the thick of things, past the dancing of tumblers and the lively song of bonepipe and naker drum, on to the tented booths where huge cheeses were sold by the slice and crusty bread made with light flour were all but impossible to pass up.

Munching on her third mincemeat pie and feeling fat as that spotted sow, she paused at the mercer where silk as fine as hoarfrost hung next to stacked bolts of Flemish velvet softer than feather down, and shimmering metal threads of thin gold, copper, and silver lined the back shelves. What would that silk feel like against her skin?

"You, lad." The mercer whacked her hand with a measuring rod.

"Ouch!" She pulled back quickly and the pie slipped from her other hand. Wincing and stunned, she rubbed her throbbing hand as tears burned the backs of her eyes.

"Little bugger!" He waved the measuring rod in her face. "Keep yer greasy fingers off the goods!"

She bit back the urge to curse him to the bowels of hell and instead looked down to hide her tears. Her pie lay broken in two on the ground. A large boot of oxblood cordovan leather smashed the pie, and she slowly raised her face upward.

A tall knight with bright red hair stood but a hand's breadth away, staring down at the pie oozing up from the edges of his boot. He looked at her and his dismayed frown faded. "Lady Caitrin!" He gaped at her with an expression that was almost comical...until he said, "We left you at the castle. How did you come here? Surely you are not alone?" He looked around swiftly. "Finn will have your head...wearing peasant clothes again. What were you thinking, woman? He whispered harshly. "You swore you would obey all his commands." The knight grabbed her arm tightly.

Lady Caitrin? "Let me go, sir." She pulled on her arm but he had the grip of a giant. "I am no lady. I am Gordie of Suddy."

"Aye...and I am St Columba facing the great monster of the Ness." His hand moved so fast she hadn't time to stop him. He jerked her hat off her head and her braid tumbled down her back.

There was a gasp from the crowd nearby, which was growing, a sea of curious, wide-eyed faces.

She snatched her hat and crammed it back on just as he began to drag her away. "You, my lady Cait, will come with me to find Finn, and you can then tell your husband your boldface lies."

Oh God... She dug in her feet, and bit him hard on the arm, her hand going for the knife in her boot.

He swore in a huge and loud bellow.

She kicked him first in the knee and again between the legs.

With a loud "Offffff!" he doubled over.

She snatched away her arm, cut his purse from his sword belt and ran, weaving in and out of the crowd, crawling under displays and leaping past anyone who got in her way, leaving a path of overturned carts and tables and spilt goods, screaming merchants and utter chaos. Scrambling on hands and knees, she crawled away from the center of the market, under a rack hung with tunics and braies, (she grabbed one of each and a handful of crossgarters, tucking them in her trouse) and scurried around a table stacked high with bolts of wool and linen. Over and behind the booths and carts she went, weaving like a frightened hare.

Creeping along behind a line of tailors' displays, she managed to pull a dark woolen cape from a corner hook undetected, before she ran on and snatched a green feathered hat with two more just like it from a plumer who had turned away to watch the commotion. For protection, she sliced open a large sack of his down and sent a cloud of feathers into the air, before ducking, tucking up her hair under the hat, pulling closed the cloak, and within moments she had made her escape.

The north end of the market was already chaotic with the business of cattle and horses being bartered by raucous copers, and men racing swift and agile Arab and Barb-blooded mounts for betting stakes. Losing herself amongst the crowd, she slowed to catch her breath, staying in the thick of them, and she wove her way north, away from the main market cross.

She reached the high end of the market at the tinker's corner and heard a horrific, angry shout.

"Cait! Caaaait!"

She swung around as a tall nobleman in a red tunic plowed through the crowd and leapt over one tinker's booth before knocking down a stack of copper pots. His intended path was straight towards her, hands out, and he looked as if he were preparing to go straight for her throat.

"Bugger!" She took off northward, heart pounding in her ears, crossing the road and ducking down an alleyway, running for all she was worth. She took another side path then slipped into recessed doorway and pressed back against the door, holding her breath as she heard the thunder of more than one person's bootsteps running down the alleyway, coming nearer...then past.

"You men! Get your mounts and ride to the town gates. She will not escape again!" came the man's angry shouts.

Panting in time to her beating heart, she closed her eyes. She knew the man who was coming for her. His overly handsome and striking face was memorable, although she recalled him more clearly with his bare chest...and bare arse. He was the drunken lord whose horse she had stolen, the first man she had left naked in the road.

Who was Lady Caitrin? Whoever she was Glenna pitied her, surrounded by men who bellowed at her, handsome, naked, or no.

She counted slowly and waited, listening in case it was a trick, then counted again before she stepped away from the door and edged back toward the alleyway, back pressed against the stone wall of a carpenter's shop—she could hear the sudden pounding of a hammer, and when she felt safe, she doubled back and made her way to the alewife's stables, sought out the woman and used some of the knight's coin to pay for the feed and shelter.

Inside, Fergus spotted her and sat up, tail wagging, a look of adoration on his silly face. "Hullo, Fergus." She fell onto a pile of hay, drew up her knees, slipped her arms around him and laid her head against his warm fur when she realized she felt lost and a little alone. She grabbed Fergus's floppy jowls and shook his head a little. "But I am not truly alone. I have you, do I not?" she said to him, putting her face up to his. He still smelled like the abbey soap. Suddenly she could hear the memory of her own laughter echoing in her head, as if she were back there again.

For that one single moment, while bathing Fergus, there had

been nothing on her mind but the joy of her laughter and a natural warm bond with Montrose, the kind she'd had with Al and El—a rare occasion in her life now, when she wasn't worried about what she had to do next and how they were going to go on.

Why did that make her belly churn and her chest ache, as if she had lost everything all over again? One breath more and tears burned in her eyes and she sniffled, wiping her nose with the back of her hand. She lifted her tunic and pulled the spare clothes she'd stolen from her belt then added the knight's coin purse on the pile next to her.

Staring at her plunder, she felt nothing good. They were not hers, she thought, in a rare bout of conscience. Stealing was no lark, held no happiness for her, anymore than being alone was any kind of lark or pleasure. Being alone was just that…alone. Empty. For the first time she could ever remember, she was truly afraid to go out into the world. She was afraid to leave the hay she was sitting upon. Al and El were no longer part of her life. They did not ride at her back or laugh at her jests or hug her just because she was their little sister.

A long and quiet time passed before she looked at her situation without self-pity. She had spare clothing and more than plenty of coin. She dumped out her boot and removed the money she'd carried inside her chest bindings. But she had no supplies. Her plump bag of apples and turnips were back at the mercer's booth, and she dared not return to the market, now being unmasked and a woman.

To stay in town was no longer safe for her. All was ruined. She closed her eyes and took a deep breath, searching for some of that infamous courage in the blood of kings. Perhaps Montrose and Alastair had lied about her father, she thought, having no great surge of some magical, instinctive feeling that made her want to rush out and face warriors, naked noblemen, or her unknown future.

She got to her feet, picked up her saddle and readied Skye, cinching the belly strap, tying on her possessions, moving by rote. She left the stables, Fergus following and looking none the worse for wear after his encounter with Montrose's spiked beer, but she did not head for the western walls where those men were looking for someone named Lady Caitrin. To the east stood the castle on its great crag, and to the south was the wide stretch of the River Ness—another ferry crossing—which she dared not chance, and that was the only way to the southern side.

Instead she moved past the alehouse and into an alleyway that circled to the northeastern edges of town, heading swiftly towards the old northern gate. Seldom used since the treaty with the Norse rendered the town no longer a target, the back gate was forgotten—a place where she and Al had crept into town once before—and where she now left Inverness and rode into the slough marshes, through the reeds and peaty black water that dirtied Fergus' clean paws and belly hair, out over the Great Beyond, heading westward across the northern lowlands and towards all the places she was supposed to avoid, because she had no other choice.

SIXTEEN

Lyall quickly stepped back into the shadows when he heard the clamor of men and horses, then eased deeper into the depths of the alley where he knew he was out of sight and moved over to the opposite wall for a better view. Across the way, a tall, copper-haired nobleman came out of a tavern to join a troop of men-at-arms waiting in the narrow dirt street. Lyall recognized the badges and the Douglas device.

"The alewife says she paid for boarding her horse and hound," the man told Finngal Douglas, tall and mounted at the head of his guards on a fine piece of Barb-blooded horseflesh that shifted spiritedly, hooves dancing in the dirt.

"What hound?" Douglas asked, frowning. "Cait has no hound."

"Based upon her history for trouble, Finn, she could have most easily found herself a hound…no doubt one that once guarded the River Styx."

"Aye. Do not remind me of her propensity for trouble. She is my curse for every wrong I've ever committed."

"Was like trying to cull coin from that alewife's purse to get her to tell me what little she did spill. Seems she took a fancy to the poor laddie."

"The poor laddie, my bride," Douglas said, shaking his head.

"The puir wee laddie who stole my purse."

"She will pay you back, I will see that she will regret this day."

"She is a wonder, the way she can twist people around her finger. The old alewife gave me the evil eye for daring to ask about her or imply the lad was in truth a woman."

"Cait does not have me fooled. The moment my back is turned she is gone, out traipsing the countryside on a lark, dressed as a lad or servant, unprotected….again. How many times is this?"

"Five," the knight said, "If you count the time she dressed as a nun.

Douglas drew a gloved hand through his dark hair and scowled. "God's Legs….if anything happens to her, Sutherland and my father will have my head on a pike."

"Aye, Finn," his friend said sarcastically. "Keep telling yourself 'tis all about the earls' tempers," he paused. "And that you care naught a fig for her."

"I care," Douglas said briskly. "I care to make the little shrew regret disobeying my orders."

The knight shook his head. "I would wager a year's income—should your wife not steal it from me—that she is no longer in Inverness. She was most likely out the gates before we had gathered the men in their saddles. We have searched the town twice over."

A look of pure determination washed over the face of Finn Douglas. "Then mount up and we will ride hard to Killencraig. I feel the sudden itch to beat my wife."

"And come out the worse for it, I'll wager. You are dealing with the Lady Caitrin. What do you suppose she will throw at you this time? You had good a lump from that apple. I would have never believed fruit could be an effective weapon. Mayhap we should store a barrel of them along the curtain walls."

"I didn't see it coming," Finn groused. "And stop grinning like a fool. I know all too well this old trick of hers—heaving of missiles. I'm familiar with her diversions."

"Perhaps to protect your head, my friend, you might send a man ahead to clear out the sharp objects—and fruit—from the castle solar." The man was laughing as he mounted and moved his horse to Douglas' side.

"I intend to get my hands on her first...but I'll remember to wear my helm."

"And to duck." Laughter followed the men's comments as they rode off toward the town's western gates.

Lyall stared at the dust swirling in the empty road, lost in thought. Finngal Douglas was heir to the earl of Dunkirk, a strong ally and sword-arm to Glenna's father the king, and a man who was close friend to the most powerful noble outside the crown—the earl of Sutherland—whose tight ties to the English crown, to Ireland and the Norse made him untouchable by anyone, even the king's strongest enemies. Sutherland also happened to be the king's most loyal friend, his eyes, and his ears, and a man Lyall's father had known well.

Before his father had been condemned as a traitor, both Sutherland and Dunkirk had come to Dunkeldon on the king's business. Though he was merely a young lad at the time, Lyall still remembered their colorful arrival through the gates of Dunkeldon.

He had been more than curious about the king's great earls, and so he had hidden in the galleries above the hall, hanging on every word as he watched the king's earls dining and drinking with his father, talking politics. When talk grew more intensely heated, they moved their conversations to someplace more private than the Great Hall.

Too young then, he had not yet honed his skill of listening at doors, back when the name he carried was not one of shame. A few years later, his ear pressed to doors was the way he could keep his single-minded goal before him. In time he learned all about manipulation and whether honor mattered in the Great

Schemes of man, and he learned about desperation, the dark shadow of which was now always with him.

Sutherland and Dunkirk were assuredly at the helm of whatever plan there was for the king's return. But he knew little of Douglas, the son, except by reputation, acknowledged wealth, and word he was a man whose name garnered respect and reaction. He then remembered Mairi and his mother gossiping the last time he was at Rossie, some maelstrom regarding the recent wedding of Lord Finngal Douglas, the king's champion, to Sutherland's ward.

Interesting...that Douglas was searching for his errant bride—a thought that gave Lyall a moment's pensive pause where every muscle in his body stiffened as he suddenly pieced all of it together for the first time. Glenna and her hound, not Lady Caitrin.

Lyall stepped out of the alley and moved swiftly toward the tavern door. Inside, the crowded alehouse was darker than the evening sky and smelled of beer and burning mutton tallow from the candle pricks on the smoke-burnished walls. Barrels of mead and bigger hogsheads of ale were stacked up in back behind a thick, solid slab of oak that served as the board, where stood the alewife, as stout as her beer, with face flushed from a nearby coal brasier and the kitchen fire in the rear, looking as weathered as a dried apple. She moved with speed that belied her aproned girth, down the line of tankards filling each from a frothy ewer as she gave orders to her lackey.

Lyall crossed over toward an empty seat in dark corner, used his boot to pull out a chair from a squat table, the opposite side of which was set with a trencher of stewed meat and a half empty beer mug. Straddling the chair, he sat and stabbed his jeweled dagger into the tabletop.

The lackey came running over and set an ale tankard in front of him.

With a swift nod of his head toward the meat trencher, Lyall said, "I'll have the same." As the lackey moved away, Lyall drank from the pint, not realizing how thirsty and hungry he was until food and drink were both less than a cubit away and the scents were unavoidable.

Studying the room as he drank, Lyall searched for parties to question, besides the alewife. Since Douglas' man had just questioned her, and apparently had trouble, Lyall understood he would need to choose most carefully. He did not want to raise too many questions. But still he needed to know how much time had passed since Glenna had been seen.

A freeman dressed in hood and gorget came scurrying in from the back, probably from the latrine, since he was busy adjusting his braies. He did not notice Lyall until he was already by his abandoned seat and he looked up and stared across the table as if hit. His eyes grew wide and his manner servile. Bowing slightly, he started to pick up his food with both hands. "I'll leave, m'lord."

"Stay where you are, man. Sit." Lyall sheathed his dagger and pulled out his eating knife. "I welcome the company and will gladly share your table."

The man sat and was saved from having to speak by the lackey who placed a steaming trencher of lamb stew in front of Lyall and refilled his ale before taking the ale pitcher around the other empty pints in the tavern. They both ate in silence as thick as their trenchers, but every so often Lyall caught the man staring at him over his food with wide, white eyes.

Lyall tore off some more bread and sopped up the stew, chewing, then he set down the knife. "I have only just come to town," he said, easing into the conversation.

"Aye, m'lord. I, too, drove in with a wagon load from Drumashie just this morn. Left home the day before."

"And I come down from the North coast," Lyall said vaguely, since the isle was to the north and had plenty of coastline.

"I am Heckie, the corn farmer," the man said, and with a sudden burst of words he began to talk about his farm and wife and the wain's load, the mill and a bad tooth. Lyall stared at the chattering little man whose face was slightly swollen on one side and listened with half an ear until Heckie the corn farmer said, "The laddie and his dog."

Lyall did not move for a long moment, but then his hand was inside his purse. "A laddie and his dog?"

"Aye. Gordon of Suddy the lad was."

Gordon? Lyall almost laughed out loud at the irony: she sends him on a false trail three times in the woods and then uses her foster family's name. He laughed to himself instead. Luck was his, this day, perched upon his shoulder like a falcon.

"And that hound...What was its name?" the corn farmer said absently. "Drunk as a wounded mercenary, the hairy beast was." The man frowned slightly. "Fergus! That was it. A sweet laddie, that Gordon and his droopy-eyed hound named Fergus."

Sweet laddie, my arse.

When the man took an odd, whistling breath, Lyall leaned forward slowly, forearms on the table, setting some coins between them where they caught the candlelight and gleamed bright silver.

"This could be a day of fine luck for both of us, Heckie of Drumashie," he said easily pushing the coin closer to the man. "I am on the trail of some important information...."

Ramsey paced in his private chamber, hands locked behind him and dictating a message to his scribe, when three small children came running across the stone floor shrieking, "Greatpapa! Greatpapa!" and they were suddenly shimmying up him like the odd, agile monkeys he once saw in London. As those small hands and feet frantically covered him, his mood lightened and his precise and careful choice of words written to the earl of Sutherland were quickly forgotten.

"We will finish later," he told his scribe, who quickly gathered his precious writing tools close to his chest. All knew Mairi's young and curious children had free reign at Rossi to destroy whatever they could, at their whim, and the scribe rushed the room as if his hair were on fire.

Ramsey pulled Duncan and Gregor into his broad arms and Robbie, the eldest, was already hanging from his back.

"Be the bear, Greatpapa!"

So he growled and carried on, juggling his grandchildren, step grandchildren if one wanted to be accurate, as he prowled the inner chamber like a dancing bear and nothing near to an infamous warrior or a baron. He was at that moment merely 'Greatpapa,' a name Robbie had come up with mixing up great and grand, and despite all Mairi's scolding, nothing could change Robbie's name for him. Secretly Ramsey cared not what the lads called him and thought his grandson's stubbornness was a good trait, and at one point, he taught Duncan to call him *the* Greatpapa, which, when Mairi caught him in the act, earned him a weak scolding from his laughing stepdaughter.

For Ramsey, the sound of children's voices echoing off the stone walls of his castle gave him great joy, and was something he had longed for. All his wealth and power could not give him sons and daughters. No babes had grown from the wombs of either of his wives. He had his two stepchildren—though he could not wait to get his hands on one of them—and he had Mairi's sons.

By the time he and the lads were all tumbling upon the thick carpet he had brought back from his youthful journey to the Holy Land, Beitris and Mairi came inside arm in arm and stood watching and shaking their heads, ready as usual to put a halt to their antics.

"Come along you," Mairi said as she began pulling children off of him. "Leave Greatpapa be."

Robbie puffed himself up, "I am the great knight Sir Robert of Glamis!" He held up a mock sword. "I shall save all from the mad bear!" He kissed the imaginary sword and acted out jabbing it into Ramsey, who rolled and groaned and moaned, flopped and twitched like he was dying, then flung his arms outwards and lay perfectly still on the carpet, while Robbie rested his small foot on his chest and bowed victorious to all.

"Enough foolishness," Mairi said, but her voice held no censure. "Come. Cook has warm honeycakes waiting for you."

The children froze and looked down at him as if to judge which was more desirable, Greatpapa or sweets. "Go on with you," he said, winking. "But save me the heftiest honeycake."

The women gathered up the bouncing children, who were now arguing over which would choose first, and sent them off with two capable nursemaids, so Ramsey leapt up easily and ran a hand through his tousled dark hair which was just beginning to show the steely edges of some gray, and he grinned sheepishly at his wife, then turned to his stepdaughter. "Come and give an old man a proper greeting."

"What old man? I do not see an old man," Mairi said and nestled into the crook of his arm, hugging him.

"Two score and five this coming year," he declared. Spoken aloud, the number sounded old to his ears. He slipped his arm tighter around her and he thought perhaps she had finally began to put some meat back on her willow-thin bones.

"You are so good for them," she said quietly, her cheek to his chest and her voice thick with emotion.

Widowed just over a year ago, Mairi still looked wan and lost without Robert Gray. Her husband died in a shipwreck off the coast of Ireland while there as an emissary for his maternal uncle, the earl of Pembroke. Ramsey knew she would need another husband to protect Grey lands for his grandsons, and while many believed he should marry her off to another quickly, Ramsey wanted Mairi to be content. She, like Beitris, had had enough pain. For now, he held guardianship over her and the lads and provided their protection, because he knew his strong-willed stepdaughter could not yet face another marriage.

Beitris handed him a large goblet of wine and turned slightly away...taking another small piece of his heart as she did so. "Sit," he released Mairi and took a drink of dark wine that suddenly held little flavor. He sat down heavily in a chair, his long legs out in front of him.

"Tell me what was so urgent to send guards to escort us here immediately," Mairi said.

Mairi and Lyall were close as a brother and sister could be.

Beitris stood next to him, her good side to him, her unscarred hand resting gently on his shoulder. She understood how difficult this was for him. If only she understood what she meant to him.

He took another drink and set down his goblet, talked to Mairi about the importance and secrecy of what he was about to tell her...and he told her what Lyall had done.

Mairi swore like a man and her mother flinched and made the sign of the cross.

"My exact reaction," Ramsey said grimly.

"Lyall stayed with you for most of the spring and half the summer," Beitris said. "Did you see or hear anything?"

"Aye," she said, still clearly angry. "Months back, in the late spring, he received a message and rode out with a de Hay knight."

All was becoming clearer and more treacherous, Ramsey thought.

"God, no... Are you certain it was de Hay?" Beitris asked, her voice high and her hand tightened on his shoulder.

"Aye. I saw the man's badge. When Lyall returned his mood

was changed. He was not himself. I asked what had happened and he claimed it was something to do with Isobel."

" 'Tis unlikely since Isobel's been dead for three years," Ramsey said wryly.

"And once she died, Lyall wanted naught to do with the family. In particular her father," Beitris said, not bothering to hide her anger.

"Only because Dunkeldon was lost to him," Mairi said aloud what Ramsey was thinking.

"Dunkeldon will be the end of him," Beitris said clearly unable to comprehend her son's intense and bleak ties to his father's lands.

Ramsey did understand Lyall's torment. A man's lands gave him worth in a world that judged him on his possession and sword-arm. But Lyall's drive and his pursuit at any means and in the face of the unattainable was like watching a caged boar beat its head against the iron bars.

"He is a fool," Mairi said, but the words carried a great and heavy sadness that spread through the chamber.

"He will be hanged for this," Beitris' voice cracked and she buried her face in her hands and began to cry.

"Mother…" Mairi ran over to her.

Ramsey stood and started to reach for his wife but someone called to him from behind the chamber curtain. He crossed the room and swept aside the curtain to come face to face with one of his house knights.

"We found their trail, my lord, near Inverness. I rode like the very devil to get here."

"Good." Ramsey clapped him on the shoulder and looked out the tower arch. "We have enough time before the sun sets. We will leave immediately. Go find a fresh mount."

"The grooms are saddling one now, along with your horse, my lord."

"Go then and have some bread and ale, man—see the cook—while I speak to my wife. I will meet you in the stable." Ramsey went back inside their chamber. Beitris was sitting in the chair, Mairi kneeling at her feet and holding her hands. She had stopped crying and looked up at him, forgetting in her sorrow to hide half her face.

"My men found their trail."

"Donnald..." she stood and Mairi stood with her. "Please find him. Save my foolish son from himself."

"I swear to you I will find them." He reached out and gently touched her scarred face and she suddenly remembered and her hand quickly covered his and he could read the shame in her large eyes. He shook his head, pulled her into his arms and kissed her hard before he turned and left.

Glenna dug her knife into the dirt and pried loose a skinny bunch of carrots, stuffing them into a sack with a few turnips and an onion, and she placed a silver coin worth a hundred bunches of carrots next to the hole, before she crawled down the dirt row to another, where she inhaled the strong scent of leeks. A moment later a handful of leeks hit the bottom of the sack and she left another coin before she glanced up to keep an eye on the moon still hiding behind thick, approaching storm clouds.

Candlelight flickered dimly from a nearby manor house, and the wind carried the soft, distant voices of the guards whose shadows paced watch near the walls. She was somewhere north of the Ness and east of Beauly, smack in the middle of some of the Gordons' prized pickings.

She sat up, resting back on her heels, eyeing the outlined shadows if the garden bed. Taking only a few vegetables was all she would allow herself—despite the coins she left—because she was still not completely comfortable stealing from crofters, even those on a wealthy estate. Circumstances were such she could not be selectively generous about who she stole from.

The lands surrounding the manor were rich garden furrows of root vegetables and lush, fruit orchards. In the distance, sheep huddled together in a large cluster of white and the soft, satisfied lowing of cattle came from the byres attached to the crofts. A mill with its distinctive waterwheel stood near the river. All was only a short walk down the grassy hillside. There was not much distance between her and the guards.

Still, leaving the money made her feel less guilty.

What she could see of the manor house up the slight hill was impressive, with a Norman glass lancet on the top floor set inside thick window buttresses and stone walls. A thin thread of pale smoke came from the thumb-like shadow of the closest chimney above the pattern of roof tiles.

Some wealthy noble's hunting lodge? Its position sat near the Great Forest which was filled with wild boar, pheasant, hare, and hart.

A few guards walked out the gates and stood on the hillside for interminably long moments. Had they seen her? She dared not move. Perhaps she should have waited longer.

Certainly she'd had plenty of close calls, the last one when she'd barely managed to cross the peaty slough to the north of Inverness and escape into the shadows of the trees before himself, Sir Naked-in-the-Road and his troop thundered past, heading like fire for the northeast. A few heartbeats less or had she merely made one stop to rest and she would have been crossing the meadow and out in the open as they came around a hill, stirring up red dust like a wind spout.

She tucked the money pouch into her tunic and then froze. One of the manor's guards shouted to a dog.

Oh lud! Would they send a dog or pack of hunting dogs to

search outside? A nobleman's trained hound could easily catch her scent, bark and give her away, or worse yet, follow her.

The racing shadow of a large hound scurried around the guards in playful circles and then disappeared inside the gates chasing the stick, while the guards laughed and followed it inside, stopping to stand just inside the wall.

Rain began to splatter down in huge, hard drops and glimpses of silvery moonlight snaked downward through holes in the thick, roiling night clouds. A gust of wind swirled and curled by. Still talking, the guards moved back inside, so she crouched up and scurried to the closest fruit tree, grabbed some low-hanging plums and quickly slipped back down the damp hillside, disappearing into the great wide forests that ran between the lowland glens and high granite crags.

She followed the deep path she had taken earlier into the fecund depths of trees, where fallen leaves and mulched ground swallowed the sound of her footsteps, and the air carried the thick taste of dark, dank moss and fallen needles. Overhead, light shot down as the moon came out from the clouds as big and bright as a silver coin, but she could still hear the patter of the rain hitting the ground behind her and, as she moved deeper, a slim scattering of raindrops hitting the sky-high crowns of the forest trees.

The small clearing was dark, but Skye stood contentedly tied to a tree and turned her big eyes on Glenna as she came through the bushes and flung the bag on her saddle. She turned, frowning. "Fergus?"

He was not by the tree where she'd left him.

Squinting slightly, she scoured the area, hoping with a suddenly wan heart that he was only a few feet away. "Fergus!" she whispered harshly.

Oh, no! Glenna untied Skye and pulled her along as she half ran back towards the edges of the forest. Before she ever reached the rim, her worst fears were realized when chaos sounded from the manor. Chickens loudly squawking and sounding worse than a cockfight. Men shouting.

The moon was bright now and the clouds and rain had moved passed, carried away on the high whipping wind. Grasses swayed slightly and took on a new color as their dew and dampness glowed slivery in the moonlight. There were few shadows for hiding, just the light illuminating the land and gardens and trees, even the faces of the guards at the manor.

Just then, Fergus came racing out of the manor, squawking chicken in his mouth as he sped down the slope low and as if his tail were on fire. Her heart sank when a man came out on the heels of her dog, carrying a torch in one hand and a raised sword in the other, followed by another guard, and a bowman, too, as dark arrows began to shoot down from just outside the manor's wall.

She heard the men shouting orders into the wind in what had been a silent, quiet night. Her eyes stayed with her dog. She dared not step into the open to be seen so easily and he was headed too far west. Quickly she mounted, then turned Skye westward, leaned low over the saddle, ready to run, and she gave a single, sharp, piercing whistle.

Fergus changed directions in a heartbeat, scampering towards her. She waited until he was close and she kicked Skye forward and out of the thick trees, where she was free to run hard, Fergus at their heels, and she rode like the wind along the dark line of the forest.

An arrow shot past her shoulder to hit the trunk of a nearby tree with a singing sound. Another whizzed by her ear. And another.

She spotted a clearing between some of the forest trees and headed straight for it, disappearing into the dark trees, slowing to a canter as she heard another arrow hit nearby and another to the east of her. She all but lay on the horse's neck, snapping her fingers to keep Fergus at her side and still riding hard as the trees grew thicker and more protected and the skies overhead were black from the hidden moon.

Fergus yelped.

She turned in the saddle, looking back.

He was still with her, but his lope was slowing, chicken dead and hanging limply from his mouth and a trail of moulting feathers drifting to the ground behind him, and a deadly looking arrow was sticking out of his bloody side.

SEVENTEEN

Above the pinewoods, high up along a wild and rocky ridge with a wide, dark corrie set into its ribs, horses' hooves clopped along the narrow ridgeline above the Great Forest. Sharp pairs of eyes searched the moonlit treetops for signs of who they sought deep amidst the thick pine trees and in the hazel and birch woods that edged the lower elevations of the forest. They spoke only when they must and communicated with merely a look. Their mission was personal.

There was a broad meadow below and beyond, and in the distance, a manor house with small croft cluster and sheep scattered across dark and rolling hillsides. A snaking river skirted a sprawl of oak trees in the distant glen toward a mill, where silver arcs of wheelwater caught the moonlight. Below, flicks of torchlight circled the wide glade as men scoured the grasses and riders disappeared into the forest.

At the same time, opposite the high rock ridge, across the forest and meadow and glen, a single rider came over the top of a northeastern hillside and reined in, wrapping his cloak more tightly around him. When he saw the torches and action below he moved deeper into a copse of birch trees, hidden and watching intently, knowing instinctively that what he saw was trouble.

And from the southeast, some distance away from all the fray, where a wide glen rolled for leagues and leagues and the River Beauly made its way from the inlet at Inverness, a troop of heavily armed men wearing Ramsey badges left Inverness and followed another trail, one that led to where the cloaked rider was now hiding.

The shepherd's hut deep in the wooded hills smelled of old, wet wool and mud, but it gave Glenna cover from the hard wind as she added more sticks to a small fire and talked softly to Fergus, lying on his side next to her with his terrible wound. Around the arrow, the blood was thick. It had stopped seeping out bright red. Every so often he would whimper and his legs would quiver in pain. But if she dared to touch the arrow, he would yelp and snap at her.

She placed some more tree moss around the wound and had used a small pot to make some willow bark tea, like Brother Leviticus had done for her. She didn't know if it would help, but willows and hazels were scattered through the woods, a godsend. "If only I had some of that red bloodbane, sweeting, or even some ale for you," she said to Fergus as she stroked his neck and one floppy ear. She leaned closer and plucked a few more red chicken feathers from the corner of his mouth, tossing them into the fire where the culprit chicken itself slowly cooked on a spit she had made of slim branches.

Whenever she turned the bird, the juices spilt and spat in the fire and Fergus had lifted he head and wiggled his nose. A good sign, she believed, that in spite of his horrible wound he was still hungry. Perhaps the meat would help him. She felt helpless, as if her hands were bound by her doubts and a lack of a way to fix this. She did not know what to do for him.

At some point, she must remove the arrow. But she was afraid she was not strong enough to hold him down securely and use her knife to pry loose the arrow.

"You foolish, foolish dog, you. Chickens have always been trouble for you." Her voice cracked and she covered her mouth with her hand, unable to look away and scared he was going to take his last breath there before her eyes. His body moved slowly as he took shallow breaths and his big wide eyes looked at her beseechingly. Just watching him broke her heart.

She had few choices. Beauly was only an option if she could reach Ruari without being seen. How would Fergus make the ride there? With an arrow deeply imbedded in him and riding with the pounding of Sky's hooves would jar his body and perhaps kill him.

Above the shabby roof, the wind howled like hungry wolves and the air growing cold. She shivered, glanced around her, warmed her hands over the fire, and when a branch broke in the wind and fell to the roof above her, she wrapped her arms around herself. There was also another problem: she had no idea what had transpired once she left the priory…or how Montrose had left things.

His image came into her mind and she felt something deep and sorrowful. She closed her eyes and willed his image away, while in her heart she wanted him there at her side, knowing with a surety that he would save Fergus…that he would save her. For the first time in her life, she understood the value of a man's protection.

Had she grown so used to looking out for herself that she was blind to what other choices she might be given? To have the refuge and safe shelter of someone whose duty was only watch and guard her was a gift she had never known she desired, and something she had run from.

Now, as she sat alone in the shed, she regretted some part of running away from him. From her earliest memory she had been her own keeper, since her brothers doted on her, and she usually managed to get them to do what she wanted...even steal. Her brothers were just that, not a father really, but her brothers, and their adventures together were larks and exciting and somehow more like children's play than the reality of the laws they had been breaking, the risks they took, and the consequences they could face.

Hidey ho! They were a pack of thieves...even Fergus she thought miserably.

She glanced down at him. Poachers were hung for stealing less than a chicken, for snaring a scrawny wild hare in the distant woods. Would the guards let it be, or even in the wind and darkness would they search them out? She had no answers and watched the rise and fall of her hound's chest.

For him could she sneak back into the priory and trust the monks? How could she help him here, inside this shed? For how long would they be safe here?

She would ask herself these questions again and again, chew on her guilt and more while she fed Fergus small bits of roasted chicken, which he ate slowly with large sad eyes. He lapped up some of the willow bark tea and soon he was breathing quietly and looked to be asleep.

After eating some of the chicken, she sat alone by the small fire, knees hugged to her chest as the huge trees outside creaked ominously in the wild winds, while she felt even more alone and frightened and miserable. Glenna cried so hard her eyes burned like fire and finally, when her chest stopped hiccupping, when her eyes could hardly produce anymore tears, she pulled her cloak more tightly around her and tied her hat down so it covered her cold ears, and she lay down, her hand on Fergus' neck to feel his reassuring heartbeat.

Soon she closed her burning eyes and tried to forget for a moment how terrified she was, and exhausted, she fell fast asleep.

The dream was back—the rook flying in the blue skies. Feathers black as night shone and caught the sunlight, glistening, beautiful and free above moors that were the bruised and purple color of a sunrise at dawn, and she flew higher and higher, aloft in the warm summer air, wheeling to the sweet sound of a minstrel's song, singing the tale of a great and magical love, of a brave and valiant king and his beautiful Norse queen.

With a suddenness of the blink of an eye, the sky turned gray and the winds blew in winter, clouds rimed in ice and with almost black edges, wind that cut like ice made flying through the air more strained and difficult. Snow fell like downy feathers and the black rook could feel the flakes begin to coat and weigh down her wings.

She flew lower and lower, gliding down into the thick forest trees, past the tall larches and firs to where flames in a clearing suddenly shot high and sent her soaring up and up, far and away from the smoke and the flames, back into the icy storm, back to where her wings again caught the snowflakes even though the sun still shone.

Summer was blue and golden and just ahead of her...if only she could fly faster. If only the ice would melt. If only she could keep flying away.

She soared above the high nests of other birds, above where grass as green as spring covered the ground and could silence the footsteps of anything smaller than a great war horse.

From above her came the call, "Kee-oo, kee-oo!" A hawk bore down upon her, determined, brown and black and white, feathers wide and striped like enemy banners, flying faster than her smaller wings would allow, and she dove and wove and spun in and around the sky, yet the hawk flew back, kept coming, almost at her tail, and he lunged at her.

She spun downwards, flying straight down...down...towards the silvery lake below, surrounded by thick, green bushes lined with deep red roses and where a beautiful white swan wearing a golden collar cut languorously across the peaceful waters.

The rook called out and the hawk shrieked his deadly call, diving closer, and the swan looked into the deep blue skies above her, and seeing the poor and frantic rook, she drew her long neck up and opened her wings wide and grandly, almost standing on the water, and the rook swooped down under the swan's wing, taking shelter as the swan lowered her grand wings, one cradling the black rook next to her downy body and safe from the claws of the deadly hawk.

Heart beating hard and frighteningly, Glenna's eyes shot open, unseeing, her breath still caught in her chest, her blood racing, sweat beading on her brow. The dream had come back, the same dream....

She moaned slightly and blinked.

Before her eyes, in the dim light of the coals, a large pair of dark boots stood planted firmly apart and were cast in red from the glow of the fire. A shining, deadly sword tip lowered into her line of vision, stopping barely a palm's breadth away from her nose.

EIGHTEEN

Fergus gave a low growl, tried to rise on his weak legs, but yelped pitiably and sagged back on the ground, still emitting a long, feral growl. She was too frightened to move and waited for her eyes to adjust to the dark. Overhead the wind began to howl and the trees creaked and rocked. Red coals from the dying fire cast the sword tip before her eyes as deep a red as the fires of hell, and Glenna looked up slowly along the length of the sword's blood gutter.

Above her, his teeth shone white in the dark and the sudden flare of a torch limned him from behind. He moved the sword tip to her neck and pressed hard enough that she dared not move and barely breathed.

"I could kill you here and now," he said, and she felt the tip cut slightly.

She stifled a cry.

Someone waved another torch and a pair of bats shrieked and flew down from the roof, drifted menacingly over the heads of the men then out the wide open door. Torchlight hit his face. Above her stood the devil himself, the one man she never wanted to see again. Looking down at her was the deadly, cruel face of Munro the Horrible.

"You are a fool, poaching from the manor of the sheriff?" he said.

She was frozen in terror, but desperately tried not to show it.

He was a squat, thick man with long and powerful arms, large hands, an expression of evil…and the coldest eyes she had ever encountered. He pressed the sword even deeper.

Unable to stop herself, she sucked in a breath at the pressure of the sword tip.

"Nothing to say? Someone must have cut out your tongue. Hmmm…" He rubbed his bearded chin.

"I can speak."

"Ah, so you can, lad," he said pensively, staring at the chicken bones next to the fire and what was left of the few vegetables she had roasted. "Perhaps I will cut out your tongue before I cut off your hand or I could choose to hang you. I have options. However, I have found there is nothing better to dissuade others and save our game from greedy hands than a body hanging off the gates."

Fergus growled ominously.

Munro pulled back his sword and quickly turned to his men. "Take this thieving fool who sleeps so easily after feasting on my birds. The lad is under arrest." He sheathed his weapon and turned away to walk from the shed.

Two men jerked her up by her arms, Fergus acted up again, and while one tied her hands behind her back and the other called out to Munro. "What should we do with the hound?"

Glenna didn't breathe. *Do not kill him…please do not.*

The sheriff turned and gave Fergus a cursory glance.

Her poor dog lay on his side, the arrow sticking out of him, his black lips curled and his long canine teeth bared at Munro.

"Leave him. He will be fortunate to last another day."

Glenna exhaled the breath she'd been holding at the same time the truth of his words struck deeply into her heart. She looked at Fergus as the sheriff's henchmen each grabbed an arm and dragged her from the shed. Fergus tried to rise again, viciously growling.

"No, Fergus!" she shouted. "Stay! Stay..."

Outside, the fire from the torches lit the small clearing, where their horses were gathered. They had not found her horse. Skye was tied deeper into the south side of the woods, where there was grass and she would not be seen. They stopped next to a large bay and one of the men tossed her up in front of the saddle and mounted behind her, warning, "Do not think ye to escape, lad. 'Tis a far way down to the ground and Thor's hooves will crush your bones."

Glancing towards the shed, she could barely make out the silhouette of her hound lying by the dying fire, then the men all closed in around and with Munro leading, they rode down into the darkness of the trees.

No one spoke as they rode and time passed tree by tree, the only sound that of their horses hooves on the leaves and twigs covering the floor of the forest. The sudden wind had calmed down to a occasional gust high in the treetops. Whenever there was a break in the forest, she could see a few stars hanging high in the sky. The moon was gone, and the path ahead and behind them dark. She was numb with fear, contemplating her fate.

For a fleeting moment she wondered where Montrose was. She closed her eyes and tried to imagine his face, and absorbed deeply all of her regrets.

She didn't know how long it took to reach their destination— back to the manor on the hillside. She was panicked and lost in thought, but it was still dark outside when she caught a glimpse through the open shutters of the setting moon. There was no wind, no rain, just quiet. She stood before the sheriff in a chamber inside the stone and timber manor hung with tapestries. Logs crackled from a blazing fire burning in the huge stone hearth and the flames reflected on the stone floors. Iron lanterns with thick, sweet-smelling candles spread warm amber light down from iron hooks in the walls, and a bowl filled with fruit next to a plank with dark bread and cheese sat waiting on a table next to Munro's huge carved chair.

He studied her silently over the rim of a large silver wine goblet trimmed with jewels she would have loved to show off to her brothers. She stood quietly still, taking long deep breaths to quell her fears and mask her weaknesses, like her sudden urge to cry at the sweet images of her brothers. Would they hear what happened to her? Would she hang? Or would they wonder about her and think of her living in the king's castle as his lost daughter, not a thief hung or maimed. She thought of what he had done to poor Ruari.

Munro rose from his chair and slowly walked toward her, sword in his hand and he lifted her tunic with the blade, touched the ties on her trouse with the sword tip. "I wonder how repentant you can be?"

She dared not breathe.

"How much do you wish to live lad?" He touched her face and she wanted to wretch. "No sign yet of a beard," he laughed.

His pleasure was for young lads. Her mind raced toward a single idea—a great risk but her only chance. She stepped away and shook her head violently, until her hat fell forward and her long braid cascaded down.

She could see his reaction in those icy eyes.

He grabbed the neck of her tunic and ripped it to reveal her breast bindings.

"I am no lad," she said defiantly.

"I can see that," he paused. "I know you. You're the horsethief."

"I am not."

He waited a heartbeat or two and spun around. "Jock!" he called out to one of his men, who came rushing inside. It was the stocky, red-haired guardsman who had lifted her into the saddle and had been dragging her all about.

"Look what we have here. What do you think?" Munro asked him. "Would you care for this wench?"

The man eyed her as if she were covered in honey.

Oh lud! She fumbled to lace her tunic closed.

Munro was watching her reaction and he began to laugh. "Give us your name, lass."

"Rot in hell!" she spat.

He only laughed more but his eyes...his eyes bespoke murder before he turned and walked away. "I believe you will serve as a grand incentive for my men."

"I am Glenna Canmore," she said. "I am the king's daughter."

He was still as a rock, then he laughed loud and hard. "Aye. The king's daughter...a horsethief. A lying horsethief." He picked up his goblet of wine and drank, leaving his words to do their work.

"I *am* Glenna Canmore."

"You aren't even a good liar. The king has no daughter, or son." He set down his the goblet and said, "Lock her in the pit cell."

The man set his hands on her shoulders.

"And do not stop for your own pleasure, Jock. I will check on her."

His man angrily pulled her from the chamber, shoving her down narrow hallway with his hands on her buttocks, stopping to squeeze and fondle her, and she stumbled away and hit the wall. He pinned her with his body, pressing his hips against her. "I can give you this. Munro will never know." He forced his fetid mouth on her and bit at her lips. "I can ride hard and long, wench."

She wanted to fight. She want to knee him. She wanted to wretch. He would no more believe who she was than Munro had so she pressed her chest to his and said breathily, "Wait. He will catch us." Like a hungry tavern maid, she licked her lips provocatively.

He bought it and seemed to think she had a point and dragged her by the arms once again into another room, an interior room most likely toward the rear of the manor, with four rounded stone walls dotted with lit candle pricks.

She thought he would ravish her and looked for some kind of weapon as she backed away from him and the hungry look in his dark eyes. Her leg hit something and she looked behind her.

Then she saw an open trap door in the ground. She looked down into a small and narrow black hole and panic hit her. *The pit cell*. She turned back to him. "Please. Wait. Do not put me in there…please."

He paused thoughtfully, as if he might actually give in. His hand went between his legs, massaging suggestively the weight of his genitals. "I will give you this when I come back…later." He grabbed her by the hair. "You can suckle me…hard."

Suckle him? Oh God… He meant…. And before she could quite comprehend, he shoved her down inside the pit and slammed the trap door.

Damp dirt crumbled down from above her into her hair and face.

"Come back!" she shouted, panicked. "Come back!"

Overhead she heard the bolt slide closed and the distant, muted sound of his footsteps.

Glenna blinked, trying to make her eyes adjust. The pit was dark as a rook's feathers. She touched the walls, which were jagged stone and hard clay-like soil. Raising her arms, or even her elbows, was not possible. She had perhaps only a hand's breadth on each side from her shoulders to the walls. It was as if she were being buried alive.

A sob escaped her and she sucked in a quivering breath. The

air was small and tasted and smelled of dank dirt. She could kneel but her shoulder caught on the wall the space was so narrow, but it was slightly wider on the lower half. Like a blind woman her hands slowly swept over the ground, where there were deep-angled divots as if left from the shovel used to dig the pit.

Standing took some work in the small space and she tried to quell the fear that overwhelmed her. Above her was the trap door. She jumped upward trying to hit it, but her fist barely tapped the surface of the wood.

With every breath she took the air changed. A great and powerful fear raced through her, soaked deep into her very bones, and she felt a panic so intense she could only scream and scream and scream, until the shaking stopped and her voice was raspy and almost gone, then she collapsed into a knot on the dirt, knees wedged to her chest, toes against the opposite wall.

She lay her head on her knees and she tried to breathe calmly, breathe slow breaths. The air was getting hotter yet she was shivering as if she were exposed in the dead of winter.

Footsteps sounded, soft thuds coming closer. If the guard was coming back could she get away? Mere minutes had passed...or was it hours? She pushed up the walls, the only way she could actually stand and the trap's bolt shot.

The door opened, blinding her from the change of light. Munro stood above her. She could feel his aura of evil before his face appeared.

"Well, my dear, how do you find your new home? Looks to be a perfect fit," he said, laughing. "I have brought you company." He stepped back.

One of his henchmen came close to the edge. Over her head, dangling from a hook in his hands, was a twitching snake. She could catch glimpses of the distinct pattern on its back and she stopped breathing.

"Drop the adder!" Munro ordered, his face intense.

The snake fell on her, still twisting in the air, its cool skin across her neck and shoulders and she panicked, flailed in the pit and scratched her arms on the rough stones sticking out of the walls. She began crawling up the wall, desperate to get away. She heard the snake hit the dirt just as the light disappeared and the trap door had closed on Munro's vile and wicked laughter.

"I am Glenna Canmore! I am Glenna Canmore! My father is the king!"

The footsteps didn't stop....

"I am Glenna Canmore!"

....They merely disappeared.

She hung her head for a hearbeat, then kept crawling upward, her back pressed to one side of the pit and her feet against the other. Her heartbeat thrummed loudly in her ears and in her chest.

Below was the adder. She could hear it moving in the dirt.

Above was the bolted trap door. Trap...trapped. It was so dark her eyes could not adjust to see anything. Her back ached from the pressure of the jagged rocks, but she dared not relax, wedged as she was she was safe from the adder.

She took long deep breaths and focused on her position. In time, her mind wandered. If she fell, how many snakebites would it take to kill her?

If only...if only...

Her concentration broke and she slipped a bit, but pressed so hard against the wall the rocks felt like knives in her back. She gripped her knees, willed away the pain in her back, and prayed for the strength to stay as she was, prayed for the power of lust to overcome the guard who had promised to come back.

Lyall adjusted his rough woolen hood and shifted, tugging at the tight peasant's tunic that pulled at his arms and chest whenever he moved. He snapped the reins and drove the heavy, creaking wain stacked with firewood up to the posts of the manor.

"Where is Cam?" The sheriff's man asked casually.

"Broke his arm, he did. I am Frang, his brother," Lyall said, his hands tightening slightly on the reins of the ox team pulling the wagon. Cam was, in truth, tied to a tree up on the rise above the glen.

"Pull your wain to the side and stack the wood there," the guard said without question and he pointed beyond the gates and around to the back side of the manor house.

Lyall steered the team as told, his gaze darting, taking in the number for guardsmen, the rear gates, lackeys and workers moving about. A groom lugging buckets of water to the stables. The hot iron smell of a smithy. Baying, barking hounds in the kennels and screaming peafowl in pens next to the chickens. He jumped down from the wain as a tall, willow-thin older woman came outside from the open kitchens, eyeing the load of firewood and then eyeing him.

"Where is that Cam?" she said and held up a hand not waiting for an answer. "Foolhardy he is. The mon cannot hold his beer." She placed her hands on her hips. "Ye look brawny enough to carry wood, mon. Stack it there. When yer done ye can bring some logs inside and stock the wood boxes." With that, she disappeared inside.

He needed to find Glenna. But the yard was bustling with guards and workmen. Lyall grabbed the woodman's gloves from the plank seat but they did not fit his hands, so he tossed them aside and unloaded the wain barehanded, stacking wood, watching and studying the place until the bed was almost empty and his hands and clothes were filled with splinters, wood dust, and dried flecks of old moss.

As he brushed off his tunic, he looked up. A milkmaid with her milk pails hanging from a wooden yoke was coming towards him. As she passed by him, she struggled and milk sloshed onto the ground. She gave a soft cry, her creamy skin flushed and her eyes panicked. He steadied the yoke, lifting it easily off her shoulders before she spilt the whole lot of it.

The maid thanked him sweetly and looked up at him as if he were God Himself, and Lyall thought he had found his means of information. He had watched them bring Glenna in, but where they were keeping her?

"Where is Cam?" The maid asked shyly, eyeing him up and down.

"Broken arm," Lyall said and changed the subject. "Where do you want this milk? I shall carry it for you."

"Here," she said, opening a large oaken door. "Follow me." She went down some stairs that led to a cold room beneath the ground floors. He carried the milk and set the buckets down.

Inside the dark room, Lyall easily got the information he wanted from her. A poached chicken, a hound, and some lad the sheriff tracked down in the high forest. One relief—Glenna's guise was safe—until the maid went on about how she pitied the young boy who would be used so cruelly by the sheriff.

"I heard the boy is locked in the pit," she told him.

"The pit?" he asked. "What is this pit?"

" 'Tis a dirt hole with trap door."

"Have you seen it?" Lyall asked.

"I saw it once, not much bigger inside than an ale barrel, and 'tis in a round room deep inside the manor, close to the master's chambers. Some say for his convenience." She paused. "I am not allowed inside, except in here and the kitchens." She looked down, clearly ashamed of her limits.

"Were I sheriff, a pretty lass like you could roam the whole of my manor," he said kindly.

Her expression was open—the sweet, carnal invitation in her eyes. There was a time when he would have taken this maid because that was how men proved their manhood. A youthful ideal—one that changed drastically when he stared down at the broken body of his young wife.

He reached out and touched her jawline. "You are a lovely lass."

She cocked her head and looked at him with an odd expression, curious. Then she smiled tenderly. "Another holds your heart."

Her words made him immediately uncomfortable. He shook his head, denying what she thought.

" 'Tis the truth. Whether or not you choose to believe it."

"Hullo! Worthless woodman! Where are ye?"

" 'Tis the cook," she said. "Go. Hurry. No one should see us."

Lyall went up of the stairs. The cook stood near the woodpile with her arms crossed. "There ye be, mon. Come. Fill yer arms with wood." She clapped her hands impatiently. "Come. Come!"

He carried in armloads of wood to stock the kitchen fire boxes, before he volunteered to take wood to the rest of the manor and into the master's chamber, receiving for his good offer, exactly what he wanted: directions to the sheriff chamber inside the manor. Arms piled with wood, he moved toward the chamber.

Munro was slumped in a chair, his chin resting on his chest, either asleep or drunk or both.

Lyall quietly lay the wood near the hearth and he left the room, moving down the opposite hallway until he opened the door and found the round room.

A red-haired man lay face down on the floor, dead or unconscious. Lyall caught the rise and fall of his shallow breath. Unconscious.

He crossed the small room to where the trap door was open and grabbed a candle from the wall prick. He knelt down, holding the candlelight and he looked down into the pit, where a snake stared back at him with yellow eyes.

NINETEEN

Glenna hung down from the manor wall, her arms scraping against sharp stones as she dangled there. Looking down, she adjusted her hands, her weight pulling and making the stones cut into them, too.

Take a deep breath and let go. The ground looked far, far away. The guards walked slowly around the manor but still she had little time.

Let go...

She could feel her hands began to slip and closed her eyes, praying for courage. The sound of Munro's wicked voice echoed in her head and she saw the vivid image of a coiled adder in a dank pit.

A moment later she hit the ground hard, her bones ringing on impact, and then she was running across the grassy field and sliding down over the next slope, tumbling out of sight and rolling over rocks and into bushes, numbed by fear. She got up running her heart beating in time with her swiftly moving feet and her breathing grew harsh.

Behind her, no shouts came from the manor for the guards to run after her, but she kept her ears sharp, expecting with her next breath to hear them shout and begin the chase.

Still, there was no sound but the pounding of her feet and

heart. At the arc of another hill and where the terrain went flat, she turned and glanced back, then stumbled on a willow root and fell hard, biting her tongue. Pain shot up her ankle and she tasted blood, but she scrambled up and hobbled toward a skeletal copse of trees ahead of her.

With the cool, dark shadows of the rowans around her, she bent down, hands on her knees as she tried to catch her breath. Soon her lungs had filled and stopped burning, and she slowly straightened, resting her hand on a tree trunk with rugged bark. Nerves raw, she looked back.

No guards streamed out from the gates. In the distance, sheep calmly grazed, the mill's waterwheel slowly turned at the river beyond, and the valley looked quiet and peaceful and nothing like the place of evil she knew it to be.

She took a long deep breath. It was over, yet her heart still beat like the drums of Morris dancers and in her mind she could still taste the dank scent of the pit; she could still feel the presence of that snake almost as if it were there with her now; she could still feel Munro's voice. The shaking overtook her, uncontrollable; it started with her hands. She stared down at them as if they belonged to someone else.

You escaped... The words echoed in her head like a monk's chant. *You are free...you are free....*

Laughter boiled up and out of her. Relief. She stumbled deeper into the woods. Away. Farther away, and her frantic, odd laughter was the only sound around her. She sagged back against another tree as if her bones had turned to eel jelly.

Eyes closed, she leaned her head back, and her laughter suddenly changed and she was crying, hard, shuddering, wracking sobs. She wrapped her arms around herself, sliding down the tree into a puddle, and just sat like that, crying in the woods as she rubbed her ankle and rocked and hiccupped and silly tears spilled shamefully down her face like water from the mill wheel.

It lasted a long time—her misery, her fear, her relief. Rampant emotions she couldn't control.

Soon her crying slowed and she sat there, aware she was completely alone. She closed her eyes. *Fergus....* And she started crying again, giant sobs that wracked her body.

Looking up, the huge crown of the tall trees made her feel small and lost. She took long, deep breaths to calm herself.

He was a strong hound. Perhaps....

Haunting her was the image of him wounded yet trying to get up to protect her. She could see his sad eyes as she told him to stay. Was he alive still? She had to know.

"Foolish hound...stealing chickens," she muttered miserably, rubbing her ankle. And Skye was most likely still tied to a tree, she thought. Sitting there crying was doing no good. They both needed her and she needed them.

With a sense of determination she stood and dusted the leaves off her trouse, and she began to walk, hobble really, since she accepted that she could not run, at least run well. She had been walking a while before she realized that her ankle no longer sent shooting pains up her leg and the dull ache was waning.

The shed was far up into the forest on the opposite side of the valley and below a tall ridgeline of granite that stood to the south. Keeping to the woods kept her hidden, but how long before they discovered she was gone? Could she still run if she were forced to? She had no pain and she could walk.

Be thankful, Glenna, for that, she thought. She trudged on, looking up at the sky through the trees to judge the daylight, aware there was still more than half the day left. She could make it before nightfall. One step in front of another over leaves and mulch as the sun slowly moved across the broad blue sky.

Eventually she crossed into a clearing with hard-packed ground that made her ankle ring with dull pain. The trees grew thicker and needles covered the ground and less and less light shone through to the forest floor. She licked her lips, which were as dry as her throat and tongue. She needed water, but she moved on. There was water in the shed. She'd pulled it from the stream near where she had tied Skye.

Fergus…please be safe. Please be alive. She concentrated on walking…walking…. walking…walking…. Mouth dry. She just needed to get there. She had to get there.

A sharp, distant sound broke her focus. She glanced up to see nothing, then quickly darted behind a nearby tree and paused only a rapid heartbeat before she moved to another with a low branch, swung up, scrambling higher and up into the thicker branches, into heavier leaves, hugging the trunk before carefully settling quietly into a crook. Her heart was thudding in her ears as she tried to listen.

For a long time there was nothing. She slowly counted. Waiting. Listening.

The noise sounded again. The softest of sounds…just a barest crushing of a step. A horse? Boots?

Suddenly as quickly as it had come, the sound disappeared and there was a strange almost heavy silence, as if all the birds had flown away and there was no life in the forest but hers and whomever was out there.

Again she held her breath, ears sharpened, listening. There was nothing. She dared not move and she took short shallow, quiet breaths, afraid to give herself away.

There it was again…so close this time: the softest of footfalls.

Someone was below the tree.

She heard him breathe.

Oh Lord… She shifted ever-so-slightly to try to look through a small opening in the thick leaves.

"Hallo?" came the voice of Montrose.

Lud! Glenna's heart jumped into her throat.

Was it really him? She sagged forward as if her bones disappeared and clung to the tree branch.

"How long are you planning to stay up there?"

"Montrose! It is you!"

His voice had come from the back side of the tree. "Montrose!" she called his name as she scrambled from the branches, sliding down the tree trunk before she hobbled to him. Nothing could have stopped her as she threw her arms around him. "You are here... Montrose, Montrose, you are here..."

He pulled her up against him. "Ouch!" He stepped back quickly, rubbing his chest. "What *is* that?"

Glenna pulled the silver, jewel-encrusted chalice from beneath her tunic and held it up. "A gift from Munro."

Lyall took the cup, frowning at it as he twirled it in his hands, then held it up. "Look there. Is that hair?"

Strands of coarse brown hair were caught in the large rubies on one side. "Most likely. Before I escaped, Munro's head came in hard contact with it."

He smiled slightly and handed her back the chalice, one arm still protectively around her. Looking down at her, his expression became almost unreadable. He seemed to be searching her face for something important and he raised his hand tenderly to her cheek, his thumb stroking her cheekbone. "I want to beat you senseless for running away." His expression and tone belied his words, spoken tenderly and without anger.

"Nay...you do not," she said spritely, overcome by a sense of joy she did not want to over think. The look they exchanged then was powerful and made the racing in her heart earlier seem like nothing. Why, why him? Why did her mind go weak whenever he looked at her...whenever she thought of him....whenever he stood so close that goosebumps broke out on her skin that had nothing to do with the weather? Her hand went to her belly because it did some kind of somersault. She understood then, what she was feeling, and curiously, she did not try to pretend or tell herself she did not love him. How could she deny what her heart held so deep within it?

He moved first; his hand slid to the back of her neck and she was back into his arms, where she wanted to be. For just a sweet moment she was overcome by a powerful sense that she was truly safe. She closed her eyes and just let him hold her. He was warm and his body muscled and solid as the protection of a stone curtain wall. She took a deep breath and smelled leather and horse and pine. Montrose was here. She relaxed for the first time. His hand rubbed her back and he did not move; he did not step away. He just held her. The only thing better would have been if he kissed her.

She lifted her face upward.

Kiss me... Kiss me...

Mentally she tried to will the idea into his head.

But he merely held her. Then his hand left her back, stopped rubbing it.

He pulled some leaves from her hair and softly brushed at the hair at her brow. "You've lost your hat," he said gruffly.

"Because of Munro. I had to let down my hair to save myself from his lust."

His eyes narrowed and his expression grew harsh and black. "What did he do to you?"

"Surely not what you are thinking. He was much more interested in doing something other than hanging me when he thought I was a lad. Women hold no interest for him, other than to torture. He is so evil—the man who beat Ruari till he was almost dead. Did you know that?"

He shook his head.

"Munro would strangle cats, probably pull the wings off of butterflies, and beat children. He locked me in a dirt pit with an adder!"

"Aye," he said, tightening his arm around her. "I saw the snake."

She pulled back. "You were inside the manor?"

"It matters not." His arms fell away from her and he was all business. He glanced around the woods cautiously. "We need to leave here." And he started to turn away.

She grabbed his arm. "First we must go to Fergus. They shot him with an arrow, and they took me away from him and left him to die. We were hiding in a shepherd's hut high in the forest. There." Her voice grew higher pitched and faster as she spoke and she pointed toward the ridge and said in another rush of words, "Skye is there, too. She was tied to a tree in the woods behind the hut. We must go. I must go."

"Calm yourself. We will go to the shed."

Why had she thought he would argue with her? He did care...

"But come now," he said. "We need to move swiftly." He took her hand and strode toward the denser woods and she had trouble keeping up with him. He stopped turned back and caught her hobble. He looked at her foot. "What is wrong?"

"I fell. 'Tis nothing."

The next thing she knew she was up into his arms as if she were merely a bag of goose down. She didn't protest, but slipped her arms around his neck and leaned her head on his shoulder until they reached the black and she asked for water and drank from the skin he had until she thought her belly would burst.

He took the empty skin. "There is water all through these woods. You did not know? You could not stop?"

"I dared not. And Fergus and Skye must need water as much as I do. If they go without, I can go without."

"You would do them and yourself little good if you wither and drop to the ground from thirst," he said, shaking his head in that way men had when they were exasperated with a woman and he set her on his horse and mounted, settling into the saddle.

She slipped her arms around his waist and said cheerily, "I am stronger than you would believe."

"But more stubborn than I can even imagine."

She smiled. "Aye, we are much alike, I think."

He laughed.

"You have a new water skin."

"Aye. Someone took mine."

And she leaned her head against his back as he spurred his horse towards the high forest.

With her directions, they reached the stream in the woods behind the shed, where Skye was munching on grass as if she hadn't been abandoned there overnight and half the day.

Montrose dismounted and handed Glenna the reins of his horse. "You stay here," he said quietly. "I will go get your hound."

"But—"

"Someone could be waiting."

She nodded.

He moved swiftly toward the trees, then stopped and turned back to her. "Do not move. You can take the horses to drink and fill the water skins."

She nodded, watched him disappear into the trees with his sword raised, aware he gave her something to do to keep her from following him, which she was not planning to do anyway. She went to the stream, filled and rehung the water skins on his saddle and waited long moments as the horses drank noisily. Ears sharp, she listened for the sounds of swords and heard nothing but the watery noise of thirsty horses.

Her mind wandered and played its own game of magic thinking...if this, then that. *If Montrose comes back carrying Fergus, he is alive. Please... Please...*

She paced in a small circle, placing her foot in the same place where she had just walked—it kept her mind occupied, then she felt Skye nudge her and turned to stroke her muzzle. "I am sorry you were alone, sweet. I am sorry, so very sorry. Skye…Fergus has to be alive."

A crunch of leaves made her spin around, her breath held tightly in her throat.

Montrose appeared out of the trees, sword sheathed, and his arms empty.

Her hand covered her mouth to stifle her cry.

He looked at her with an odd expression. "He is not there."

TWENTY

"I will not leave," Glenna said, standing inside the cool dark shadows of the shed, toe to toe with Montrose. "Fergus! Fergus!" she kept calling out, desperate and panicking. Did he crawl away? "He is here somewhere. He has to be here."

"There is no sign of him, Glenna. No trail. I looked for him. You can see…here. Look about you."

"You do not believe me. You think I am lying. That he was not here."

He ran an impatient hand through his hair. "I believe you, but that does not change the fact that your dog is gone."

She searched the dark corners of the small shed. "He must have crawled away."

"There are no prints in the dirt."

"But there was blood on the ground. By the fire last night. He was bleeding. It was there." She moved to where a small stone ring held blackened fragments of burnt wood and ashes, and she went down on her knees. "It must be here."

But there was no sign Fergus had ever been there. There was no sign of the blood she had seen. She stood, looking at the spot where he had lain, frowning. "There are no footmarks of mine…or of Munro and his men."

"Which is why we are leaving." He grabbed her hand. "Come. We cannot stay here."

She pulled her hand from his. "I will not abandon him again."

"You are not abandoning him. He is not here."

"I will not leave without Fergus!"

He took her by the shoulders, clearly angry. "Do you wish to come face to face with that snake again?"

Silent, she crossed her arms and stuck out her chin. "I believe I am looking at him now."

He swore, quickly picked her up, and threw her over his shoulder, in spite of her threats and shrieks, then strode outside and towards the stream.

She punched him hard in the back with her fist. "Put me down! Oaf!"

"Be quiet, Glenna."

"I'm glad you did not kiss me," she mumbled, trying to decide where to hit him where her fist could cause the most pain.

"What did you say?"

"Rot in hell, Montrose." She hit him hard in the ribs for good measure before he set her down (dropped her really) by the horses. She shoved her hair out of her face and gave him a look that could melt a steel blade. "You have a hard, black stone where your heart should be."

Silent, he turned his back to her and checked his saddle bags.

She looked from him to the black. "You do not take the time for the mere thought to give your horse a name." She laughed without humor. "Why would I expect you to care about my dog?"

His hands stopped moving. He stood still as stone.

"You are a heartless man." Words, bitter and ugly like toads, just spilled from her mouth.

He took a long, deep breath. "Perhaps I am," he said evenly and adjusted his saddle strap. He did not face her. "But we are leaving." His voice was gritty. "Mount your horse or I will do it for you."

"If you ever have children what will you call them? Boy? Girl? What did you call you poor wife? Woman?" Still he was annoyingly silent. "What do you call her now…dead?"

"Enough!" He moved so swiftly she swallowed her words. His sword tip was at her throat. "One more word and I will call you dead."

"I am not afraid of you."

He groaned and let the sword tip fall to the ground. "You have no sense."

"You have no soul." She began to cry she was so angry and frustrated and hurting…and she was ashamed of the angry words she could not seem to control.

He looked at her, then turned back to his horse and mounted, his back to her as if he could not stand to see her cry. She, a weak and sniveling woman. She wiped her tears , sniffled, and found her pride.

Once in the saddle, she kneed Skye forward, her head high despite what she was feeling, and she stopped beside him. "'Tis so cruel to leave without him," she said quietly, her voice bitter and accusing. "You do not know what you ask of me."

He turned in the saddle, his eyes glistening and his jaw so tight it looked carved from granite, and he said, "Ride."

Tears streamed down her face. She hated feeling helpless and trapped and angrily swiped at her damp face. He would not know she was crying.

Let him ride like the devil himself.

And he did. They rode swiftly once they were over the ridge and down into the open lands to the south, and in silence, headed toward a place only Montrose knew. No matter how many times she had tried to pry their destination from him, he had denied her, saying only 'to the south,' or 'the east' or her favorite response, 'You will know when we arrive.'

Alone with her own thoughts, she tried not to think of Fergus, to be brave and say goodbye, because she knew despite how much she wanted the truth to be otherwise, her beloved hound was gone.

But no matter how much she tried to send her mind elsewhere, Fergus' silly, big-eyed, shaggy face came unbidden before her eyes: him loping beside her as a gangly pup; jumping up onto her cot in the small niche that was her room back at the island; chasing birds through the heather moors, and tragically, running across a grassy field with another bird—a chicken; and lying on his side by the flickering fire, blood dripping on the ground and an arrow sticking out of him.

To her horror a loud sob escaped her lips; it just seemed to spill from her throat.

Montrose cursed loudly and slowed, placing his hand on the cantle as he turned back in the saddle.

By then she had covered her mouth with a hand.

For a long moment he eyed her strangely. She had a hard time holding his gaze when everything inside of her wanted to turn away and sob.

Finally he said in a voice that was not unkind, "I must think of your safety, Glenna. I could not stay there and search."

She dropped her hand and gripped the reins, rising in the stirrups. "I know that! I am not the village idiot."

"But you often behave like one."

She raised her chin and scowled at him.

He scowled back. "Your dog is gone," he said sharply, almost shouting before he turned around and rode harder than before.

"Fergus!" she called out, urging Skye forward. "He is not *Dog!*" She would keep up with him if it killed her. He could not ever accuse her of holding them back. And she raised her voice as loud as she could and shouted, "His name is *Fergus!*"

Her words echoed back, sounding hollow and distant and dying.

Night was chasing them, turning the skies a deep purple as the stars began to shine in the clear sky, and the moon rose huge and bright from the east. They dodged hart and hare that came out in the dusk and soon they neared a wide rushing river. When he finally reined in, they had ridden inside yet another forest flanking the river and to a small spot where darkness was beginning to fall through the leaves. There had not been another civil word between them, and she was fine with the heavy silence. She would be fine if the oaf never spoke to her again. At least that was what she told herself.

The night was calm and the air still; it tasted clean, of pine and moss and rushing water. The trees were tall and she spotted flat rock ledges between the openings in the trees. He reined in when they came to a glade, where moonlight lit the grasses on the ground and the sound of the river was loud. She could see its lush and rocky banks were barely a fathom away.

He dismounted and began to remove his satchel and bags so she swung down from the saddle as if her legs were not jelly and her body not numb. She was determined he would not see any weakness from her. No more tears.

Montrose turned and casually tossed the water skins at her feet.

She stared at them. Surely he did not just throw them at her? She opened her mouth intending to voice a series of cutting words for him, but she snapped it close. She would bite his head off and what good would that do? And she was weary of arguing, weary of crying, weary of the loud, shrewish voice that sounded as if it belonged to someone else—someone she didn't know and someone unlikable—and she was weary of hiding her tiredness and feelings…she was just plain weary.

"You can fill those skins at the river," he said matter-of-factly and without a single glance in her direction.

Over the river, the moon shone as bright as a lantern, the water gleaming silver and rippling with a swift current flowing away and down a slight rise to rush over rocks and grow wider before it disappeared into the dark, sawtooth outline of tall trees. It was the kind of river filled with fish and ran clear and down in falls from the high granite cliffs. That he had happened to stop here was sheer blind luck, she told herself.

"The water is easier to reach down the lower bank, over there by the big tree."

What was it about men that made them think they knew the lay of every thin plot of land, even a strange river bank in unfamiliar woods?

Once, when Alastair had sold three prime horses to the son of a Norse earl with holdings in the northern borders, she had spent a miserable half a day in the pouring rain and hail following Elgin in circles because he said he knew where he was going. Had she not found a road and stopped a passing carter to ask the way of things, they might still, two years later, be riding in useless, cold and muddy circles.

Ignoring Montrose, she silently tossed her saddle bag and blanket on the grassy ground, then removed her woolen cloak and made absolutely no attempt to bend down and pick up the skins.

Throw water skins at me and blurt out commands as if I am his lackey.

When she turned, she found him looking pointedly at the skins and back to her. She gave him what she felt was a scathing look of disdain.

She did not like the smile that teased his mouth; it showed a dimple in his right cheek. She did not believe ogres had dimples when they smiled.

He was shaking his head. "You might not feel or think of yourself as being born of royal blood, Glenna, but that look down you just gave me, down your noble little nose, is more proof than any decree or document or witness. Trust me, you are your father's daughter."

She did not know whether she should feel happy or angry, so she kicked one of the skins with the toe of her boot.

"Do not take your foolish anger out—"

But before he could finish reprimanding her, she kicked the skin up in the air like the finest of jugglers—she'd learned the trick from one—caught it, then turned her back and with her heel kicked the other skin backwards into the air and spun around and caught it, too. Tucking the skins under her arms with a smug smile, she walked past him, her head held regally high.

Lyall walked toward the fire pit he'd dug and dropped an armful of wood into its center, and dusted off his vest and tunic. Odd how he had realized for the first time that his walk was different here, on this ground of his childhood, his step lighter, natural and less careful than when he walked upon land elsewhere, where a man had to watch his step because he knew not what he would face next, and because his heart held no bond to those soils, no familiar scent or comfort, no knowledge of those places, just instinct to protect him from the unknown.

Outside of Dunkeldon, he felt forever like a stranger in a foreign land.

But here, for a time, his youth had been idyllic, growing up in the warm, lactescent breast of Dunkeldon, where the castle had sat upon its motte like a giant game piece, facing the road that led to its gates, surrounded by a velvet green robe of a forest with trees so tall and full of majesty they became the giant warriors he fought in his child's mind—the enemy he vanquished in his youthful dreams toward greatness. He was shaped by this plot of land, the forest and the ever-changing river, where trout sought him out and salmon leapt into his hands, where a tree cradled him as he dreamt the dreams of young lads who believed in the existence of honor in men.

High in the treetops, the wind sang it's languid, plaintive song and overhead the stars were beginning to shine as the sky grew into the deepest purple. If he were a lad, he might still believe in the magic of this place.

The night was unusually bright. A misty ring hung around the full moon; it would be cold tonight. Odd, he thought, the things that stick with one long after they should be forgotten.

His mind went back in time to when his father told him about moon rings and the weather—and how much more he had learned that single night. They had been standing together on the roof watch of Dunkelden, his father's hands secure on his shoulders, making him feel safe even when the drop was dizzying and the ground looking far, far below. Lyall never liked heights. When Malcolm would dance over the walks along the guard walls, Lyall seldom followed. He preferred his feet to be flat on the hard ground.

That singular night, his father had shown Lyall each of the distant borders of their land. The misty ring legend originated from Ewan's father, who first told it to his son on a cool, autumn night long ago and Ewan passed it on to Malcolm, and then to Lyall, those stories handed down through the male line.

His grandfather Robert had been a mariner who traversed the seas and rode with other men into Outremer, and who came home to lands that were dowered to him when he married the youngest daughter of one of the old Celtic earls. Lyall never knew his grandfather, who died before he was born. He had only his father's stories and Malcolm's thin memories of a large man with golden hair and a laugh that echoed in the rafters of the greatest halls.

But on that same night when he stood with his father, something else happened. Perhaps it had been the tone of his father's voice when he spoke that night. Perhaps it was the way his father hunkered down and pointed in the distance, his arm on Lyall's shoulders as if he were not just a lad but a man grown. Perhaps it was because Lyall had been born there, and his destiny was blood and bone of the place—the parts of a man that made him hollow and dead if you took them away.

On that night long ago, Lyall began to understand the rite of passage between fathers and sons, rings around the moon, the traditions in a man's life, and the reverence of a man for the lands that gave him worth and defined him. As his father showed him all the places that marked their borders: the granite rock shaped like an angel's wing; the distant hills, two in row, camel-like in their twin humps; the hook in the river where the wild aspens grew—what became clear to him, even as young as he had been, was that Dunkeldon and the ground upon which it was built, was the passion that fueled Ewan Robertson's lifeblood. When Lyall turned away from the passionate light and pride in his father's eyes to look out past the light of the moon, in the path of the stars over the trees and the river and grasses he had seen a thousand times and never thought twice about, he saw and felt something else. What it was, he did not truly understand, but felt deep in his bones the very seeds of something important to his measure.

He understood it all too clearly when it was too late, when he buried his brother in the chapel next to father, when he walked over that drawbridge and saw the traitor's flag, when the stars misaligned and he had to turn his back on his father's legacy, Malcolm's and his own. The gift they could have given to their sons was suddenly gone with the first snap in the wind of a vile yellow flag.

So under the night's moon with a ring around it, Lyall sat back on his heels in the clearing in the forest and studied the sky, watched the colored edges as they deepened into almost black, the bright spots of starlight some claimed were small holes in Heaven that shone down to mortal men the merest glimpses of its bright light.

Lyall found that fable of Heaven unlikely, but then he did not believe in much anymore. Life and years had changed him. He had lost his belief in the alignment of the stars and the warm, fate-changing glow of magic trees, and even his belief in the goodness of man.

Away from the vastness of the night sky, he glanced at the river. Glenna was gone. Where was she? Her horse was still there by his. He moved swiftly, calling her name. At the river's edge, he found one of the water skins in the thick grass alongside one of her shoes.

Had she fallen in? He cupped his hands about his mouth. "Glenna!"

There was no sound but the rush of water over some rocks downstream. A hot wave of panic swept over him. He shouted, "*Glenna!*"

No response.

His vest hit the ground and he stripped off his tunic and boots. A heartbeat later he was in the river. "Glenna!" he called out, standing in the water with his feet wide apart to counter the current, and he looked around him and off towards the blackest edges of the water, where the moonlight was blocked by the shoreline trees stretching out along the opposite bank.

He saw nothing and his heart pounded, his panic grew.

"*Glenna!*"

"I am here," she said calmly and came striding through the water easily around a small bend, pulling herself along by exposed tree roots along the river's edge, seemingly unaware he wanted nothing more at that moment than to strangle her. She stopped when she was a few paces away.

Fortunately for her...out of his reach. He stood chest deep in cold water and glared at her, overcome for a moment with relief made his chest ache strangely as if bound by tight ropes. He took a long breath and wiped his wet face in frustration. "You could not find your voice long enough to answer my call *before* I jumped into the water?"

Her back was to him as she tossed the water skin she carried onto the grass near the bank and spun in slow circles, looking down to search the water around her and completely unaffected by anything he said. "I've lost my shoe."

"You have what?"

"I was filling the skin, and it slipped, and I reached out to grab it and fell in the water, and so I caught the skin, but now I cannot find my shoe." She faced him frowning, clearly annoyed—she, who could not find her voice a moment earlier.

He spotted her shoe caught in the roots to her left, and next to what looked like a fat cluster of river mussels. He waded closer, took out his knife, cut the mussels away, and tossed them on the bank. Then he found another cluster under the waterline. Now they had food. He put away his knife and faced her. "This shoe?"

"Oh! That is quite wonderful. You found it. I was certain I was going to be riding around in a clog and boot." She grinned, her eyes bright. "See? There was a reason you jumped in."

"Aye. I wanted to freeze to death tonight."

"Cease your grousing, Montrose. 'Tis not all that cold and you were beginning to smell like your nameless horse." She paused. "Do not glower at me like that. I speak the truth. I would know since I had to ride downwind of you. And I...I smelled of that pit," she said viciously as she shivered slightly and grabbed a handful of roots to pull herself up the bank.

"Wait! Glenna...do not move."

Of course she turned around, and her movements sent a strong ripple over the surface of the water. "Why?"

It wasn't enough she had disturbed the water. She also had to speak. Standing still as a stone, he swore under his breath and said evenly, "Do. Not. Move."

"Why can I not move? You said yourself the water is cold. You do not have to—" She shut up as he tossed a large, spotted trout high over her head and well onto the bank, where it flopped and twisted in the grass, its scales sparkling like jewels in the bright moonlight. "Good Lord in Heaven...." She turned and looked at him, stunned.

He stepped closer and used his knuckle to close her open mouth. "You might catch waterflies, love." In a blink he picked her up and plopped her on the bank, then jumped up and joined her, both of them soaked and dripping water, and he looked down into her amused face and said, "I assume you are as hungry as I."

She laughed. "How did you do that?"

He shrugged. "It swam into my hands. There would be two fish had you merely obeyed me and ceased your talking." He stood then and water dripped down his chest and onto her head and he bent to gather up the mussels. "All your chattering frightened the other one away."

She picked up the fat fish and followed him, a slight smile on her lips. "We have mussels to eat and this fish. Looks to me to be plenty for both of us," she chattered.

TWENTY-ONE

The pearl was the size of Lyall's fingernail, yet perfect and round, with the same milky sheen of the moon. River pearls came from the mussels that lined the shores of the river. They were small and imperfect, in colors of pink and brown and gray, with knots and marks and sometimes they had large dark holes in them.

He had found river pearls when he was a lad, years back, another lifetime ago, when he was careless and young and free to comb the shores of the river, innocent enough to make wishes on magic trees, to fish and play at war and pretend life was less idyllic than it had been, back when he roamed the wild woods not comprehending the hard truths of life.

But he had never found a pearl like the one he was staring down at. Nestled in soft, tender and pale flesh, surrounded by the pearlescent wall of the shell, the pearl was huge, it was flawless, and it was in the last mussel...the one they argued over....the one he offered her...the one she had insisted he eat.

Glenna stared at it in such shock, almost as if the pearl had spoken. He knew that because of her life as a thief, she understood its value and its rarity. When she finally spoke it was with the reference of a truly larcenous soul. "It is beautiful."

He glanced down at it, then held out the shell. "Here."

"I cannot take it." She looked up at him, clearly stunned, and said quietly, "'Tis yours."

He shook his head. "What am I to do with a pearl like this? I have jewels," he lied. His stepfather had jewels. "Take it, Glenna."

"Nay."

"If I keep it, you will merely steal it from my bags at some point," he teased, knowing it was most likely true.

"You do not trust me," she said, but even she could not pull off that false humility; it just was not the Glenna he knew.

"Nay, I am not a fool." He laughed. "How much silver have you taken from me?"

"I have not counted," she said proudly, chin up a bit. However, she had not taken her eyes off the jewel he dangled right in front of her nose. Had wealth a scent, her nose would have twitched.

"If you do not take it," he said casually. "I suppose I shall be forced to throw it back in the river."

She looked from him to the pearl and paused—oh, she wanted it—but she stubbornly shook her head. "'Tis yours, Montrose."

He sighed heavily. "Then as mine, I can do whatever I wish with it." He started to rise. "Even toss it back where it came from."

"Nay! Nay!" She scrambled over so swiftly to grab his arm she almost made him light-headed. "Montrose! Do not!"

Moments later she sat across from him, crossed legged, with the pearl cupped tentatively in her hands as if it were more delicate than a robin's egg, her expression filled with awe and a little touch of avarice that was Glenna.

He wanted to laugh out loud and his first instinct was to swing her up into his arms and kiss her senseless. But he stopped himself and stayed there, savoring what was an odd feeling—a great and overwhelming sense of gratification at merely watching her.

Not much later, he had second thoughts, after he had banked the small fire and before they had made pallet on the ground or gone to sleep, that she came over, pearl clutched tightly in her fist, and placed her other hand on his chest as she stood up on tiptoe and gave him a tender kiss. "Thank you, Montrose. This is the loveliest gift I have ever been given."

He called himself a fool as he watched her walk away from him, Glenna Canmore, the king's daughter, with the chance at a future full of more than pearls, more than jewels, and he turned away from her and all the fine sense of joy left in her wake.

His hands clenching into fists at his sides and his face skyward, he stood there powerless. Everything he saw, even with his eyes closed, was tinged in bitter yellow—something else passed from father to son, he thought as the taste of betrayal swelled in his mouth.

And for a mere moment, he had to fight the sudden urge to hang his head in shame....because of what he was going to do to her.

"What in the name of Heaven and Hell are you doing to me, witch?"

Glenna froze. She was lying on the ground and tucked snugly under her woolen blanket. Yet Montrose was talking? She lay still and stopped breathing, and didn't dare open her eyes.

Did she actually hear him speak? Or had she imagined it, a dream or wish or mind-trick? Did he believe she was still asleep? Was he even really there? What would she do if she opened her eyes only to stare back into his?

Oh God's toes! She could not see a thing with her eyes closed!

He began pacing the grass for so long the monotonous sound of his footsteps might have lulled her into a soft sleep if not for the possibility that he had said those words. His voice had just come to her as real as if he were standing over her and talking.

She kept her breathing soft and slow and even. Before long some part of her could feel the heated warmth of his eyes on her. Oh, he was surely standing there. She knew as instinctively as she knew how to lift a purse.

Odd how she always knew the exact moment when he was looking at her, a kind of sixth sense came over her, a feeling of unearthliness, like when bees hovered right in front of one's eyes or when the birds vanished just before lightening would strike the earth and set it on fire. But the feeling, the sense, happened with him alone, as if they were invisibly chained by their thoughts and minds as well as the wild emotion she was keeping secret deep inside her heart.

He wasn't pacing any longer. The absolute silence came in the amount of time it took for her heart to beat once, like a moment of emotional clarity, or a snatch of color in the night—something warm and pink, like alpenglow, rare and only there in the last breath before night fell or the first glimpse of dawn.

But then the real sounds of night invaded her sense: the chirping song of the insects, the distant rush of river water over rocks and small falls, and the pounding of her own foolish heart.

"I am bewitched," he said. "And destined to hell. Why do I care about you when I dare not?" His voice was real and it was heavy with emotion when it drifted off. "I cannot...I will not." He cursed in a low voice and walked away, his footsteps swift and growing distant.

She opened one eye, then turned over just as he disappeared through the trees. Kicking aside the blanket, she knew there was no way she would let him walk away from her after what he'd said, whether or not he'd spoken only because he believed she was asleep.

Up on her feet, she slipped on her shoes and moved stealthily through the woods, staying back far enough for the moon to light his shadow. The woods grew thick, then opened up. When the roots of a giant, old yew tree almost tripped her, she placed her hand on the bark to steady herself and almost cried out, looking down at her hand as if it were suddenly burned. She stared at the tree, almost expecting to see a handprint where she had touched it.

Carefully, tentatively, she reached out and then touched it with one finger. No burn. The tree was cool, the bark rough, like every other tree in the woods.

Still, her hand throbbed, and she stared down at it expecting to see something like a slave brand, but her palm appeared perfectly normal. Yet something…there was something. She stared at the tree, then shook off the strange thoughts that made gooseflesh of the skin on her arms. Silliness. With no time to dawdle, she rushed on to stay in sight of Montrose, who was moving again and even farther away.

Eventually, he stopped at the top of a rock ledge and stood looking into the distance, his strong profile, sleek nose and square jaw limned in the moonlight like the effigy of an ancient god. She hung back, unable to see past him or the woods and tall fir trees flanking his sides. The vision he made reminded her of him poised on the prow of the ship the morning after the storm, and made her breath catch. She could not have looked away had lightning come down and flashed right there before her eyes.

Suddenly swinging his arms out into the air, he leapt down to the forest floor with a soft thud and a whoosh of breath, and he began to run. She moved swiftly to the ledge, which she found was perched at the forest's edge, where a short, gentle slope rolled down into a small clearing.

There, she spotted his dark figure running across the field towards a sight she never expected. In the distance, the dark, burned out ruins of a castle stood atop its motte, looking like the island's Celtic stone rings: staggered, jagged and great, black against the iridescence of moonlight that shone down turning the field a silvery white, almost as if it were not a night on the cusp of the end of summer and beginning of autumn, but a night in the height of the coldest winter. She moved down from the ledge and onto the slope.

Around the castle was a wall of thick bushes and brambles and brush, and he ran to a spot that sloped downward into the wall of weeds, and he disappeared. She moved fast, running breathlessly across the silver field, keeping her eyes on where he had gone and once there, she moved down where a small cave-like tunnel, a black hole really, shone where its weeds were freshly torn aside and its bushes trampled.

Without hesitation she stepped inside and all light disappeared. She froze. Chills ran up her arms. Inside, it was as black as the pit and to her horror it smelled the same. Her skin crawled and she shivered, looking for courage which had disappeared the moment she stepped into the tunnel.

In a weak moment she turned back, catching and swallowing a sob that threatened to escape her lips, and she took a step toward the entrance, where there was moonlight and fresh night air. At that moment she heard the hollow echo of his running footsteps deep down the tunnel and she moved away from the safety of the entrance, cautiously touching the damp walls only to keep her balance on the stone and uneven rocks underfoot, telling herself she was not afraid. But it was a lie. Her fear was tangible.

She rounded a bend in the walls and stepped back quickly. At the far end, light shone down from an open trap, revealing the carved rungs of a wooden ladder. She took five slow breaths, then ten, and edged around the corner just was the trap door snapped closed and the tunnel was bathed once again in darkness.

Before long she stood at the top of the ladder, feeling for the door. She counted to twenty before she opened it—not wanting to come face to face with Montrose—barely enough to see and she panned the grounds, then flipped open the trap and climbed out, kneeling down to quietly closed the trapdoor.

For a sweet moment she just breathed in the cool night air and composed herself and her fears. She was outside in the open air. No more dark, dank-tasting tunnel. No imaginary adders under her next blind step.

Around her, the castle was eerily abandoned, with debris covering overturned wagons and the remnants of animal troughs, the gate from an old pen and pieces of burned walls still sitting atop stone bases, all covered in old, broken pieces of burnt wood and years of weeds and dead leaves.

As she moved, she could mark buildings that had been, the stable, stalls broken and charred, a large center building that had crumbled, caved in from the sides, with pieces of stairs piled upon each other, and another building nearby with a tall stone fire hearth like that used by a village smithy.

A cross hung at an odd angle over the lone door in the midst of a small burned out chapel; that was where she spotted him, standing at what must have once been an altar, the raised stone dais covered in debris starting at the very toes of his boots. He looked as if he was unable to go any further.

She watched him for a long time, soaking in any clue she could from studying him. Before long, she could almost feel his sorrow, palpable and like the waves of the sea coming at you. Whatever this place was, it was painful to him.

He seemed so far away, a tragedy standing raw and open, his hands open and out in front of him as if in supplication, and she understood she could see him this way only because he believed he was completely alone.

She had not known that such emotion and pain could be found merely in a man's posture, but there she saw a crushing sense of isolation so clear, as if he were in another world... alone, deserted, adrift and looking lost, the emptiness of which she understood all too well. He was a man at Gethsemane.

The overwhelming need to reach out to him came to her, but she felt if she did so, somehow she would violate him when he was already wounded. Watching his pain made her belly turn and she placed a hand over it and closed her eyes. If only she could know what was wrong, perhaps she could find a way to help him.

Before long watching him in such a state and saying nothing was too difficult. She felt if she stood there longer, she would have to pull him from the depths of that black place he inhabited, so she decided to leave him alone with whatever demons he possessed. She took a deep breath that turned into a sigh, and he spun around, his face hard and his eyes moist, glaring at her as if she were a rude awakening.

"What are you doing here?"

Caught, she had no out so she looked him in the eyes and admitted, "I followed you."

"I can see that."

Now, without the need for excuses, she walked toward the altar and looked down, where he had been cutting away the weeds and brambles when she first spotted him. There before him lay two old graves—one covered with a square stone plaque carved with a man's effigy, and the other a cairn—a crude piling of old rocks. "Who are they?"

He was stonily silent, unwilling to let her in. There were moments, she noticed, like now, where his solitude was like a shield he forced between them and his response was strong enough to make her believe he would gladly turn that shield into a weapon and wield it like some battering ram on anyone who tried to save him. "They are my ghosts."

"Not any longer," she said lightly, bending and gently pulling more of the weeds from the cairn. "I am here." On her knees, she dusted off her hands and glanced up at him. His expression she could not read.

"Uninvited and unwelcome," he said.

"Nevertheless, you must deal with me." She continued to pull the weeds from between the rocks. "Why is it secret?"

He was weakening. His hands gave him away; they were in fists at his side.

"I will not leave until you tell me," she said.

Still, only his glare and silence met her unwavering and calm gaze. *Let me help you.*

He looked away from her, away from the graves and up to where some rooks were perched ominously on the highest part of the burnt wall, where a half of an old carved cross still hung. She looked from him to the graves set into the altar like those of ancient kings.

"And you call me stubborn." She brushed the leaves and grass from the stone carving of a man's face. Sitting back on her heels she looked up at him and said, "He looks like you."

It was a long time before he spoke. "'Tis my father."

"And the other?"

"Malcolm, my brother."

She frowned and stood, then looked around her and at the ruins. "These are your lands?"

"No!" he said sharply.

She stepped back as if his voice slapped her. In that single word, she heard the sound of a dark soul.

"I draw strength here. As I stand before these graves I do not forget." With a deep concentration she could almost feel, he stared off at some distant memory and time. Both elements hardened his features and it seemed as if he was somewhere desolate and vast; he looked as if he what he carried was insurmountable. "You cannot understand."

The rooks suddenly cawed and flapped away, one flying after a darting sparrow. When he did look at her, she caught a swift glimpse of emotion she could not name—something fragile and breakable behind the hard mask he wore and his often harsh manner.

Then it was gone, lost in a slim moment of a time, and he said coolly, "We should leave this place."

The part of her that loved him could not ask him to explain the deaths; she could not ask for more from him. He had needed to be there and she accepted that. But not even to satisfy her natural curiosity could she make him stay where he was a wounded soul, open, bleeding. "Aye. We should leave," she agreed.

His expression held a hint of an apology and something else, another kind of sorrow, perhaps the same emotion she couldn't read before. She held out her hand to him.

At first he stared it at as if touching her would be a mortal sin. Waiting for him felt natural to her, as did walking by his side when he joined her, and as did the feel of his warm palm against hers, and the silence cloaking them not in awkwardness, but one of those moments where words spoken aloud were unnecessary.

Each was a little puzzled by the other and lost in the curious darkness of their own thoughts and, hands still clasped, they walked out of the castle ruins together.

TWENTY-TWO

The bright morning sun bespoke of a hot day to come and brought with it some clarity for Lyall. He stood on top of the stack of rocks where years ago he had watched Dunkeldon burn, and he concentrated on the single thought that he had a mission to complete: to trade Glenna for Dunkeldon. Only one more day was left, because tonight would finally end this. Tonight, he would walk away from her.

To most, Dunkeldon was nothing but a burnt shell of a keep, a place with its glory lost except to his own memory. What value did it have? Perhaps only to de Hay and his allies who sought to gain their desires by dangling his family ruins before him.

He leapt down onto the ground and moved through the woods, his head clear, his mind focused on his goal. But before he was halfway back he stopped at the edge of the small clearing where he had played war games back when he was not living his own war.

The last place he expected to see Glenna was beneath the ancient yew. But she stood there, talking to it.

"Did I imagine what I felt, Tree?" She touched the bark and stared curiously at her hand. "Do you hide fairies under your roots? Does magic pulse beneath your bark? Must I believe you are simply an old tree and my mind is bewitched?" She placed both hands flat on the trunk and leaned into it with all her weight, looking up into its wide crown. "Do you make wishes come true?" she asked and Lyall was struck by the coincidence, her image so like his own had been as a lad.

Something else hit him—a strong sense that the two of them were bound by some emotion that was kindred and otherworldly. He felt her coursing through his blood and in the marrow of his bones, and some place he could not name. His heart? His soul? His evermore?

"Hallo, little bird," she said then she began to sing, siren music that pulled at him like before. "Bird on a briar, bird, bird on a briar..."

His resolved shattered as her song spun up into the air and around him, lifted him with its joyous notes, as if she were his hope, and the next thing he knew he was standing next to her, his arms out to her. She turned as her song waned. Under the shade of the ancient tree, she stepped into his embrace, and he made the fatal mistake of looking at her mouth.

He kissed her, because he had no other thought at that moment except to taste her, to hold her soft body to his, and yet he knew he was a madman to do this. His whole path was mad, and now his sanity constantly fought with a great and driving desire. His head cleared for a single thin moment of time and he pulled back as if he had touched hot coals.

The sense of awe in her eyes made him unable to stop himself. His mouth was on hers again, denied the strength of will to leave her untouched because of the innocent hunger he saw in her expression, her own desire clearly there for him to read and try to not act upon. He was not that noble or valiant. He had no power of self-control...only the knowledge of what was right, and he had long ago given up on doing what was right.

His mouth moved on hers, and as he pulled her against him, he knew he should turn and walk away. Some voice in his head said *Go! Leave! Release her!*

Her hands were flat against his chest, warm, and she pressed, resisting. His hand gently cupped the back of her head and he softened his mouth, gave her sweet small kisses, his lips on her hers, sipping, before pulling back, kissing her again, and pulling back, so she knew he would not force her.

Yet his intent was clear; he knew he was seducing her. Only his wants drove him. No minute slip of lost conscience miraculously appeared. Getting closer was his goal, inside of her. There was one truth in all of the desire and want. Some truth in his head told him if he could get inside of her heart, she could save him from himself.

Then she surrendered to him and kissed him back, linked her arms around his neck; she was warm and fluid, melting into him. The longer he held her and kissed her, the closer he grew to her, the more he understood he was a doomed man. The taste of her mouth was all he needed for the rest of his life. Thoughts ran rampant in his head, fighting with the powerful emotion of what he was feeling.

The precious daughter of the king? She was the farthest thing from safe, so why did his instincts tell him she was his salvation? He was mad…mad…mad….

His mind reeled backwards to another time, another woman who had jumped from a tower to escape his desire. Although everything that was right in the world shouted for him to cease this insane act now, his passion flared like oil on fire, blinding him with its intense light and burning through his doubts and whatever handful's worth of conscience and honor he might have had left.

There was nothing but her soft mouth open and yielding, nothing but his need to get inside of her innocence. There was her tongue against his, her scent swirling around him as if the air held nothing but her.

The time for his salvation was past. He was too far gone to

save. But for the sweetest of moments, he found a taste of the life he could never have.

Just one more moment, he told himself.

The passion, brilliant and golden, began to wane and a heart-crushing sound, pitiful and innocent, made him freeze.

She was crying.

As recognition cracked through his senselessness, he broke the kiss. His kisses, gentle though they were, had made Isobel cry. He stepped away, needing some distance between her soft body and his.

She cried out softly on a breath, and her moist eyes flew open. Her expression told him she was unable to understand what had just happened. Bewilderment, the same confusion he felt, pain and something close to horror ran across her expressive and lovely face. And it was like watching someone crush a perfect rose in their fist. Tears fell from her eyes. Her hand went to her mouth and she looked up at him with honest desire and something else he wished he did not see there.

Her heart was on her sleeve, and his heart was in the way.

Lyall wished he were capable of love, of believing he could put himself in someone else's hands, but he might as well believe that if he held very, very still, a bee would never sting him.

"Do not look at me like that," he said gruffly. He was a man who could never love. His love would be pure destruction and he would take down with him any poor female soul who believed he was worth loving...worth saving.

As she searched his face he forced himself to look passive, unwilling to give anything, afraid if he did he would take her to hell with him. He could never let her see he had almost given into everything he was feeling. So he grew tense, and she looked down—shamed by him. He had taught her that with their first kisses—to be ashamed. Proof of the bastard he was.

She turned her back to him, a sorrowful cry escaping into the air.

He stepped forward, his hands on her shoulders and he pulled her back against him, resting his chin on the top of head, closing his eyes against all that was going through him.

She was quivering like a frightened hare when she said, "I am supposed to feel ashamed. I am ashamed this time."

"No, Glenna. You are innocent."

"But you do not understand. I want you to kiss me. I want you to touch me. Oh, how I regret what I feel!"

He turned her around and she would not look up at him. He lifted her chin with his knuckle. "You have nothing to regret or be ashamed of. Your heart and what you feel is pure. 'Tis not you, but me."

She gave a quick and humorless cry and shook her head. "I do regret what I am feeling because of how you look at me when we stop. As if this is horrible, what I feel. It consumes me and I cannot stop myself."

He laughed bitterly then because her words were the same as his thoughts.

She stepped out of his arms and faced him. "You can stand there, as I bare every thought in my head and feeling in my heart and still laugh at me?" She stared at him in disbelief. "I unfold the deepest of my secrets and you mock me?" She was truly angry and her face crumpled as surely as if he had crushed it in his fist. "I think at this moment," she said. "I truly, truly hate you."

Perhaps hate was the best thing between them, at least he could let her believe that she hated him. It was not true. And if nothing else, she deserved some truth in this whole tangle of lies.

Lyall took a long breath but his chest was so tight he could barely fill his lungs. When he spoke, the words were the most honest he had ever spoken in his whole miserable life. "What we feel is not hate."

He turned then and walked away. He had said all he could.

'Twas not hate he felt, but the opposite, yet there was no possible way he could ever say the other words to her.

The hot midday sun beat down on the links of Donnald Ramsey's cowl, cooking his head like a roasted boar…all he needed was an apple in his mouth. He signaled for his men to stop. The thunder of horses' hooves ceased pounding the ground and a cloud of dust swirled up around the troop, now speckled with pieces of sun-dried grass.

He tightened his grip on the reins as his horse danced along the wide, dry crest of high ground overlooking the valley to the west that cradled the Beauly River, its abbey, and in the distance, a sparse pattern of crofts. Off to the west stood the blue shadows of the western coast. They, however, were headed south, and east of Ben Nevis, which lay far in the distance like giant sleeping cattle.

Ramsey pushed his cowl back and took a drink from a skin of water before pouring some of it over his sweaty head. He swiped at his brow to keep his eyes clear and took another drink, then exchanged a look of misery with his men at arms. "I do not know if we should pray for rain and suffer battling the rust, or continue on only to swallow more dust than air."

"'Twill only become worse if we keep following this trail another twenty leagues," said his captain.

"There is a small stream and falls over that distant rise, my lord," offered another. "We can rest and water the horses."

The rise was in the wrong direction but Ramsey knew he could not ride his men and their mounts into the ground, no matter how desperate he was to catch Lyall before he destroyed his future and made himself into the traitor Ewan had been. The horses and men needed respite from the sun. His itching, sweaty skin and dust-burned eyes could use some shade and water.

"Aye. We'll ride to the falls." He pulled his cowl back over his damp head and waved his men forward.

The falls were wider than he had expected, with clear water rushing downward over granite rocks edged in lichen, trees cloaked with moss, lush patches of long grass and circles of cool treeshadow. Mist rose up from the spill of the falls and rinsed the dry, dirty taste from the midday air and cooled their hot, flushed skin. The horses drank for a long time, their tails flicking lazily at flies, and his men rested in the shade, many of them sitting in the grass, some in their linen and soaked from a quick swim in the cool waters, now chewing on dried meat and crusts of bread.

Ramsey wrapped closed his food cloth and tucked it inside his satchel. He winced when he felt the leagues he had travelled in his stiff muscles and rattled, creaking bones.

By God's eyes he was getting old. Too old to rescue a young man from himself. They had been riding for a long stretch without stopping, compelled to stay on Lyall's trail from Inverness. Although he had joined his men late, after riding straight from Rossie, and they were still a merry distance from where he expected to find Lyall. He did not believe the lad could pass remotely close to Dunkeldon and not go there, so they were headed that way.

And there had been more news. Seemed that there was word the Gordon brothers were tracking and asking questions, too.

Ramsey's instincts were high and strong. He would find Lyall. But he could not say if he could find him in time. His instincts seldom let him down, except perhaps in the glimmer of honor he'd thought he had seen in his stepson all those years back. Where did that lad go?

He glanced at his men and thought to give them more time, so they could ride even harder. He had men in eight different directions, like the one who discovered the Inverness trail, lone riders who could ask questions and find answers.

Another smaller contingent of men were with his captain, heading in a different direction, toward de Hay lands, but more as a precaution after what Mairi had revealed to him about Lyall's father by marriage. Isobel's father, Huchon De Hay, was a weasel of the worst kind, conniving in his practices and treasons. De Hay's unfortunate ties by his own marriage to a powerful Norse earl as well as a blood bond as a distant cousin to the king of France had provided him protection for all too many years.

Would De Hay dare to conduct his treasons in his own nest? Did not seem likely. He was too sly to tempt getting caught. For all too long the man had managed to straddle both sides of the power struggle for the crown, waffling over and placating each side, while subversively aiding the other, hoping to make his own gains amidst the chaos.

In planning the king's upcoming return, Sutherland had found enough evidence to suspect de Hay's true loyalties lay among the Norse earls, or at least with their gold and promises. The wealth and power of those earls had been threatened by the true king's marriage and the short peace that marriage brought before the young queen had died. That peace had put a stop to the earls' constant, lucrative raids down into the southern isles and their drive to continually encroach upon northern borders. Rebellion and a king in exile kept their coffers filled and their lands expanding southward.

'Twas in the Norse earls best interests to feed a war over the Scots throne, allying and abetting Argyll, the most powerful lord in the west, and continuing to light the man's hungry desire for the power of the crown itself and using the well-known greed of England's Henry to aid in his schemes.

But William, the true king, was soon to be free. All the plans were set, the ransom grudgingly set and agreed.

Except that Lyall's stupidity and single-mindedness was about to ruin his own obligation and part in those plans, and jeopardize the safety of Glenna Canmore. All those years of hiding the king's daughter were about to be made worthless because years back Ewan Robertson had been a traitor.

Lyall, where go you? Foolish, foolish lad to involve yourself in this. The noose is tightening about your neck, son.

Ramsey stared out at the misty dark outline of Ben Nevis in the distance, and felt as if the road he faced ahead was like climbing that great mountain on foot. His stepson had grown up determined, but lost, unable through his years of trying to in any way redeem his name, to extirpate his father's treason. It seemed to him that Lyall had eventually given up and tied himself to de Hay with that disaster of a betrothal in a desperate attempt to regain his family's lost lands. The meek Isobel De Hay had been raised in a nunnery and was unable to face wedding anyone other than her own God.

Since that disastrous day when Lyall had stood over her broken body, he had built a wall of solitude and isolation around himself, which led him on a dark path to destruction, all because of the pain and guilt the lad carried. That determined boy with the bow and quiver, and eye of an eagle, was slowly decaying and destroying the man he could be. Lyall was compelled by some demon of legacy to make the same mistakes Ewan had. And if Lyall was condemned to hang for treason, Beatris would shatter as easily as a clay pot dropped from the hall rafters.

Beatris.

The image of her as Ramsey had first seen her so long ago was always close to his mind. Back then, on that singular day so many years past, she had worn no hood or veil to hide her face. There was no need. She had been young and bright, with skin like the shine of the moon, her eyes the color of the firth in summer, and her hair—the darkest, deepest color of a ripe apple—long and waving down her back. She had been laughing, the sound like bells in the wind, and running into the arms of his closest friend.

The memory faded then, growing dry as the dust on the road they had travelled, leaving the same taste of failure in his mouth as those times when his wife hid her face from him. His Beatris could not survive much more suffering. Ewan's betrayal wounded all of them in a deeply profound way.

There was only trouble ahead, for despite his compassion for his stepson and his great love for Beatris, his loyalty was first to his king. Above all, Ramsey knew he must keep his pledge to protect the king's eldest daughter and if that meant Lyall would be sacrificed, then he little choice.

One of his men stood up abruptly. "My lord!"

Ramsey rose more swiftly than his muscles wanted.

"A rider!" More men shot to their feet, weapons ready as one of his outriders rode toward them with great speed.

Ramsey sheathed his weapon as the rider reined in. "Argyll is trapped and sent for aid from de Hay at Kinnesswood, my lord."

De Hay at Kinnesswood? That was Frasyr's keep and Frasyr was Argyll's cousin. But the castle was solid and impossible to attack without tenfold his current number of men. If Glenna Canmore was there she would be in the hands of the king's opponents.

"There is more," the rider said seriously and he pointed down into the glen. "Look there."

Two riders were crossing Beauly glen, heading south and west. Ramsey watched them long enough to recognized them by the mounts they rode. The stride of the horses was swift and nimble, bred from the finest of Arab bloods, distinctive in their size, color, and motion.

"The Gordons," Ramsey said.

"They have been asking their own questions, my lord, and had left just before I heard about Argyll's messenger."

There was no doubt what they were about. The Gordon brothers were looking for Glenna. "Mount up!" Ramsey said, wincing slightly as he followed his own orders and his legs and hindside ached sharply when they hit the saddle. He gathered the reins and held up a hand. "Wait... Let them go over that next hill and then we will follow. I suspect we are headed toward the same destination."

His sharp eyes followed the black outlines of the Gordon brothers riding in the distance, heading south and west toward Loch Lisson, where Kinnesswood stood towering over the water from a solid rock island in its center, a castle in a key position and impregnable to attack.

"Ride!" Ramsey ordered and they took off, heading toward a quest that appeared to be impossible.

Clouds rolled in on gust of strong wind and the dark sky overhead seemed unpredictable. There was no bright shining moon in the night sky, no trout cooking on an open fire, or starlight over the ruins of a burnt castle, just the high clouds over the black darkness of a loch and distant silhouette of a rock island in the middle of the loch, and above it, the staggered shadows of a castle tower and wall.

Glenna pulled her woolen cloak more tightly about her as she sat in the boat while Montrose rowed them across a lake toward their swiftly approaching destination. What was inside that castle ahead of them? Along its crown were the jagged crenels, looking like a demon's bite. She closed her eyes and sought some sense of courage she doubted she had left; but she needed some strength of heart for the unknown she was about to face.

Montrose was silent. For the whole day he had withdrawn again, erected a stone wall around himself, and nothing she could say would break through to him. That hardness, that silence, carried into the night.

The night air went suddenly still, as if someone swallowed the wind and left only silence that was pierced only by the rhythmic slap of oars as Montrose drew them through into the water.

'Twas odd. She looked around her.

The brush lining the shore was thick and dark and still. Her mind was mad, her instincts affected by her fears. The trees and bushes had no eyes.

She faced forward, calling herself silly. Her heart was affecting her head.

Behind Montrose, the image of the castle was growing larger and more imposing, and with each oarstroke her hands began to shake more. The wind picked up again, a small gust, then another, bigger and higher. She could hear a tree bend, the rustling of leaves. Hair pulled from her braid to cut across her mouth and whip into her eyes, for a moment obliterating what was ahead.

When she tucked her hair back, before her was their destination and the knowledge she was one step closer to the moment she would face her father, her fate, her failure and whatever horrible humiliation her future would bring. At that moment she would have given anything to be a crofter, a milkmaid, a goat girl…anything but the daughter of a king.

She tried to quell the rising tide of her fears. Montrose's lack of speech became too much for her. "Will my father be there?"

"I was told to bring you here. Whether it is to await his arrival, or to meet him, I do not know." His deep voice sounded cold and tight, his words sharp. He'd had a hard time looking her in the eye since he'd left her standing alone by the strange old tree, confused and feeling adrift.

"I merely wondered if perhaps he had come back undercover for his safety, rather than arriving from a ship like before to face his enemies and their arrows."

If Montrose had heard her, she would never know. He chose to remain stonily silent, but she could not. "I do not know what he expects of me."

There. She had spoken her fears aloud. She admitted what she was afraid of.

I wonder if he knows that I trust him enough to tell him this. Then she asked herself why that mattered.

The oar locks creaked as he increased his rowing speed, and she could hear the cutting of the water, the draw of the oar and the ripple of the water on the surface, and then his breathing. Not a word from him. There was only an occasional gust of wind over the land and trees.

"Talk to me, Montrose. Please..." Her voice caught a little and sounded as pitiful as she felt and she hated that.

"You are his daughter," he said heavily after a moment. "No doubt when you do finally meet he will expect to see a young woman."

"When we do finally meet?" she repeated, almost leaping upon his words. "You know something! You know he is not there."

"I know nothing," he said sharply, continuing to row.

"Then why did you say when we finally meet?" She could feel his tension and hear a slight strangle when he said her name aloud. "What is wrong," she asked.

He shook his head and looked out at the water. His voice was emotionless when he said, "From what I remember of him, you have his looks."

"I do? Hmmm. If that is supposed to reassure me, it does not. I do not know if having his look is a good thing. They say the queen, my mother, was a rare beauty." She grew thoughtful about her mother, speaking of her aloud, and she wondered about all those things a girl who never knew her mother wondered and longed for—someone to guide her and explain her feelings and wants and needs, so many things she never could understand.

Her mind flitted from one fear back to another. "But if I looked like her, I might remind him of his loss and he would ban me from his sight. And of course if I am not beautiful enough, then he might ban me anyway." She faced him. "Do kings not have pride? Many say they have all too much pride—the cause of wars." After a moment she threw her hands up. "Oh, none of this matters because once he knows me, he will probably banish me to some tower or if facing a war, he'll marry me off to an enemy to forge an alliance. I know little of politics and the power struggles of men. How am I to survive? How?"

I only know how to steal a purse.

Panicking, she blurted out, "What if my husband is old? Or worse?" She paused, then whispered, "What if he beats me?" She wanted to bury her face in her hands and sob. Instead, another horrific image came to mind, one worst than the closing of a trap door. "Montrose?" She almost choked on his name. All her fears and feelings were stuck in her throat.

He was silent.

She lowered her voice and said, "Did you know Germans bury their wives alive as punishment?"

The oars stopped and the oarlocks grated loudly. Montrose cursed viciously. "I cannot do this," he said, and a moment later he had used one oar to turn the boat.

As the boat spun around, racking raggedly, she gripped the sides. "What are you doing?"

"Be quiet, Glenna."

The wind picked up and boat moved swiftly.

"Why? We are not hiding. No one is around. I can speak."

"I am beginning to feel a great kinship with the Germans." He pulled the oars through the water a good three times faster than before.

"This is no time for jests."

"What makes you think I am jesting?"

"But what about my father? Why are we turning back?" She looked around her. "Montrose? What are you doing?"

"I'm going mad. Now do not say another word or I swear I will steal a shovel and make you dig your own grave."

"Ha! You would not dare."

"Good. You have stopped your crying," he said.

"I was not crying!"

The boat hit the bank. Before she could move he pulled her out, gripping her by the shoulders. "I believed I was stronger than I am. I believed I could let you go, could turn and walk away. I cannot. I do not know what you have done to me. You drive me mad."

"I do?" she asked, suddenly warm. His hands gripped her shoulders and made her feel warm, warmer still from the look in his eyes. He wanted to kiss her. His words to her at the tree came echoing back.

He released her as if she were made of Greek fire. "Despite what I need to do, you are forever in my head, deep inside. Here." He pointed to his temple, then to his chest. "And here."

On his face he wore the truth: that he was not pleased about what he had just told her. But she was. "You love me," she said, trying not to smile.

"Glenna...."

"You love me. 'Tis true. I shall not argue with you about it, Montrose."

There were deep furrows in his brow and his hands were in fists. He was battling something strong, and having a great deal of trouble.

She watched him pace the grassy bank like a cat caught in a pen. "Scowl all you want, my lord."

"I am *not* your lord. I am not anyone's lord!"

"Fine but I'm still confused. How does what you feel, Montrose—please note I did not call you 'my lord'—have anything to do with your taking me to my father?"

He drove a hand through his hair. "Lord above, woman! I am not taking you to your father!"

"I do not understand. Where are you taking me?"

Torchlight and swift moving shadows came out from the trees, and suddenly a troop of armed men surrounded them. A deep voice came from the midst of them. "He is taking you to me."

TWENTY-THREE

Luck was with Lyall because de Hay had no clue he had changed his mind. The man had only heard the end of his conversation with Glenna. She stood before them in the dank hall at Kinnesswood Castle—the holding of one of de Hay's men, Coll Frasyr, who was cousin to the king of Argyll and who Lyall had known through the tourneys and had, after Frasyr was awarded his own lands, once sought betrothal to Lyall's sister Mairi.

The thick candles guttered and smoked from mutton fat, and the wax spilled in long yellowish trails down the blackened walls to pool and congeal in the corners. Light from the torches and candle pricks flickered over high walls covered in sooty tapestries, and glinted off Glenna's dark hair, shiny at the crown and falling into one long thick braid down her back. Her bedraggled peasant clothing was speckled with leaves and grass and her shoes were stained and crusted with dried mud. A mangy grey cat with half a tail threaded itself in and out of her legs, rubbing against her calves before it sat abruptly, scratching vigorously at its fleas and nits. Behind her, a couple of hunting hounds were busy gnawing on venison bones near a hearth that was stained with smoke and the rushes on the floor were old, infested, and smelled of grease and neglect. From the condition of his household, one truth was clear: clear Frasyr still had not found himself a wife.

Lyall looked back to Glenna. He was acutely aware they were standing a short distance apart from each other and yet acting as if they were in different worlds: she was her father's daughter to the bone and stood before a room filled with armed strangers looking misplaced in their midst; while he stood shoulder to shoulder with her father's enemies, caught in the teeth of his own misdeeds.

De Hay studied Glenna for a long time before he said, "Interesting." He moved closer and tilted her chin up so she had to look up at him.

To stand passively by and watch was not easy; he wanted to pull de Hay away from her.

"She has his look…without the fire. But one could expect little substance from a woman, even one with royal blood." De Hay turned and stepped away, half-laughing. "Not that she looks like one."

Glenna did not show any emotion, nor did her eyes appear to make contact with anyone in the room. After de Hay stepped away, she stared down at her clasped hands. Lyall could only admire her ability to not give an inch and to hide her feelings, something she never did with him.

What was she thinking now?

Did she long to stick a knife in his ribs?

Whatever was going on inside her head would only be inflamed as his father by marriage explained, rather cheerfully, her use as a mere pawn in the plot to overthrow her father.

"Woman!" de Hay barked. "I am speaking to you!"

She raised her face and looked past them all.

"Your father's men sought to protect you, hiding you away for all these years. You are the eldest, I'm told," de Hay said, casually.

Lyall caught Glenna's blink, the only sign that she'd just received the news she was not the only child of the king. His own decision to not tell her the truth had more to do with ease of his mission than protecting her. And there was little that was true in what he had done. Why, he thought bitterly, muck up all the lies with one truth?

For days the feeling haunted him that his life had changed forever. Once again he tried to summon up some kind of protection from what he felt for her, a wall to erect between them—like he had done before—but something warm like pride washed over him as he watched her unflinching strength.

To deny what was between the two of them was no longer possible, a bond the seeds of which had been there from the moment he held a knife at her throat in that stable, a bond he would have never thought possible with anyone who was not his blood. Only his mother and Mairi touched him in the same intimate way. But unlike Glenna, they were safe from his treacheries.

The deed was done. His fate was set. Her fate was truly no longer his concern.

Then he watched her knuckles slowly turn white and felt a deep and abiding regret and worse…shame.

"Sutherland, Douglas, and Ramsey foolishly bet on the secrecy of your existence to remain a secret. Fortunately for us," de Hay put his hand on Lyall's shoulder. "Roberston here wants Dunkeldon enough to give you over to us." De Hay laughed with an ugliness that proved him to be an arrogant, manipulative bastard. "Some persuasion on my part, the bribe of the lands, and here you are."

Glenna did not look at him, but stayed stoic.

"At one time there were rumors the queen was with child, but they were put to rest after her death," de Hay continued. "Until a few months ago, no one knew of your existence, Glenna Canmore…or that of your sisters."

For a mere heartbeat Lyall dropped his head back and silently cursed, but Glenna appeared calm as a rock when she looked at de

Hay blankly. He could only imagine what it took for her to remain passive, given the Glenna he knew and what she'd just been told.

"I am no fool and have heard you speak, girl." de Hay goaded. "You are not an idiot. Do not pretend to be one. Have you nothing to say?"

"Aye. I have something to say."

Lyall almost winced, expecting her to fling de Hay's words back in his face.

"I do not know my father anymore than I know you, sir." She lowered her eyes. "I am but a woman raised simply to be nothing close to what I was born into."

Lyall choked on his spittle and began to cough so long and hard that Frasyr thumped him on the back a few times.

Meanwhile Glenna bent down and picked up the flea-bitten cat, and Lyall was reminded how much she had lost in a matter of days: her beloved fool-faced hound, her home and brothers, her life as she had always known it.

Her face was placid as milk when she shrugged. "I care naught for the machinations and workings of men." She scratched the cat's flea-bitten ears and rocked slightly, cooing at it. "I have never known a throne, jewels, or fine gowns. Until this moment, I have never been inside a castle.

"And you expect me to be loyal to blood and bond and a name I have never known?" She laughed softly and looked evenly at all the men who stood before her. "I care not a flea on this cat for kings and crowns and the power plays of men…or what any of you do. I care only that I have a safe shelter, food, and a bed in which to sleep," she paused, then said, "…covered with furs."

One of the men snorted a laugh.

Glenna blinked twice, a performance the finest Lyall had ever witnessed, and she looked at them all wide-eyed. "Have I said something humorous?"

"Nay," de Hay cut in, bored with her. "If what you say is true, your stay with us should be simple and uneventful." He dismissed her for the meek, simple woman she was playing, and turned to one of his men at arms. "Lock her in the tower room." He paused, then added, "And make certain she has her furs."

Before the man led her away she looked directly at Lyall, and for the merest of moments her eyes narrowed when they met his, then she turned, cat still in her arms, and calmly followed the men up the stone stairs.

The mangy grey cat was perfectly happy in her arms as Glenna followed the guard passively, watching for the right moment. The stairs led up a thick side wall from the great hall and at the top, the guard turned and they passed by a small grouping of chambers, some with their doors open, and a wide open room with a huge hearth and pallets on the floors, clothing, armor and weapons strewn about, and the strong stench of male and animal sweat.

They continued down a hallway with little light, and up a narrow staircase that went round and round, seemingly forever, and at the landing at the top of the stairs, she took what she knew was her last chance. "Sir, please…I beg you. Stop. The stairs are so high… Why…why my head is swimming!" she cried out weakly and stumbled into him.

The cat screeched and leapt from her arms onto the guard, so he struggled to catch her and dislodge the flying cat, and suddenly the three of them were a knot of flying arms and claws, and her swooning knees.

Just the chaos she needed. She and the cat both fumbled over him as his arms clamped around her, and he dug in his footing and steadied her.

"There. I have you," he said not unkindly.

"Thank you," she said, wide-eyed, one hand behind her back. "'Tis terribly high up here...like standing on a cliff, and so terribly dark." She shivered for effect.

When he turned and moved toward a single door with a heavy iron bolt, she hid his dagger up her sleeve, and his slim purse up the other.

Weak candlelight dimly lit the tower room. The furnishings within were few, a long and narrow wooden table and a single small chair. Nearby a braiser provided a circle of warmth by a large wooden bed topped with an uneven straw mattress and rough woolen blanket. On the opposite wall an arch was shuttered closed with an iron bold and lock, but drafts of the wind outside still blew through the gaps in the wood and through the staggered arrow slits at opposite sides of the room.

"There is water in the ewer. And food," the guard said, standing in front of the door.

On the table, a bowl of plums and figs sat by a loaf of bread and platter of cheese, a ewer of water, a small cup and laver flanked the rough hewn edges of the table. Fergus loved plums. She saw his silly, shaggy face. He used to toss them like a ball, then eat, jowls cavorting, and spit out the pit the way El taught him.

She felt a sinking feeling in her belly and placed her hand on it. But he was gone. El was gone. And look where she was.

The wind outside picked up and a gust blew in, swirling 'round the room. One of the candles flickered out. Suddenly the room was all shadows.

"Good night, my lady."

Her burning eyes adjusted and she wiped them and turned quickly. "Wait!"

The guard started to close the huge door.

She rushed forward. "My furs....and a flint and oil reed? To light the candles?"

He glanced at the candle pricks and nodded. The door closed and the bolt swung into place with a loud scrape, leaving her alone as the sound of his bootsteps disappeared down the tower stairs.

An empty feeling inside her, she stared at the closed door, confusion and despair fighting for control of her thoughts. Montrose? But he was not Montrose. She placed her hand on her belly as it turned over and she felt a sharp pang in her chest. She bit her lip and closed her eyes, and the image of him came into her mind, a man desperate and alone, standing before two graves in a burned out castle.

An image she understood. She knew desperation. The first time she had stolen from anyone it was for food. They were starving. Their stock was gone, except for their own mounts. They had nothing. Their father had been dead for four years and her poor brothers had struggled. So she stole first, and they got by.

Aye, she understood Lyall's actions. Desperate people did desperate things. She did not believe for a moment he had been pretending to care for her anymore than she had been pretending. She loved him, and in spite of himself, she believed he loved her.

I cannot do this was what he had said. Now she understood.

Oh, Lyall, what shall we do?

She closed her eyes. Her mind was full.

I have sisters. She was not the only daughter.

How could she have sisters? Did the king hide all his children? She laughed then at the madness of it all before she grew thoughtful. If she were the eldest, then they could not have shared a mother. If she was hidden away, they must have been, too. Could they be as rough and wild as she was?

Or was she the only pawn, the eldest, the man called de Hay had said, and supposedly worth something to the father who had never met her and worth all that much more to his enemies.

If there was one thing she would never allow herself to be, it was a pawn.

Lyall's eyes remained locked on the empty spot at the top of the stairs where Glenna had disappeared, and told himself that regret was for those who had a conscience, and he never claimed to have one. Why then did he have the urge to draw his sword, grab her, and die if he had to, fighting to get her away from this place to which he had brought her?

Long ago, he knelt and avouched to a life of honor, only to have his honor questioned again and again because of the name he carried—his father's black legacy. He was the son of a man who had no honor, and in time, he learned there were not enough vows in the world to change the dishonor of his name.

Around him, men's voices pierced his consciousness.

"The armorer overcharged me. I threatened to take his fingers one by one if he were to act the fool again."

"…came walking out of the hayloft after the milkmaid only to have her young brother conk him out with a barrel stave."

"Aye…the best piece of horseflesh I've ever cast these old eyes upon. 'Tis a smaller, swifter breed of palfrey, bred in the west, on the isles, from Barb bloods and another desert breed. I would give a year's wages for one."

Lyall cast a quick glance over his shoulder. Frasyr's man at arms was the one lusting after one of the rare bloods, those the Gordons raised, smaller, swifter breeds of riding mounts like Glenna's Skye.

A vision of the island swam before his eyes—fields covered in heather, Glenna riding with her romping hound, her laughter or a challenge…all that was left in her wake. So bright was the image, so strong the sound her voice, that his breath caught. His clothes felt suddenly small, and he tugged at his tunic as if he could cover up what he was feeling—the most intense sense of loss. Part of him wanted to sink into the ground.

In a shadowed corner, de Hay was talking with Frasyr. Meanwhile some of the guards were beginning to sprawl out on wooden benches and pallets, some went abovestairs as pages brought lavers for washing and thickly frothed ale for them to drink themselves to sleep. Before him a maid with a ewer of thick brown ale ran into a bustling squire who precariously balanced a flagon of wine on a tray and had not been paying attention. Brown ale went everywhere, and the two began bickering until they were quieted by a sharp command.

"I will have a word with you, Robertson."

Light from a candle suddenly appeared at his shoulder. De Hay was standing next to him, and he took a goblet of wine from the squire and demanded Lyall follow him from the hall.

Inside a private chamber with plenty of candlelight, Huchon de Hay sat down in a chair at a wide hewn table and set a coffer before him and unlocked it. Without looking up he said, "Is she as simple-minded as she appears?"

"More so," Lyall lied.

"Then your task cost you little trouble to earn this." De Hay held out a parchment. A thick gold ring with a mark Lyall had never seen was on his long fingers.

Lyall steeled himself to look into his eyes and appear passive. When unrolled, the papers revealed a sealed and witnessed document bequothing all of Dunkeldon and its lands, borders, crofts and income and tax fees from the village of Dunwood and the nearby Tay crossing to Sir Lyall Robertson and his heirs.

Lyall's hands shook slightly as he read it.

De Hay stood. "Dunkeldon is yours."

"Aye," Lyall said, lingering in his own hopelessness, unable to know how to act or what to do next. He half-expected the parchment to burn its image into his palm. He finally held in his hand all that he had craved for more years than he had lived on Dunkeldon lands.

"You may go," de Hay dismissed him, and Lyall walked out to the great hall. As he walked away without purpose, he realized the place stank of burning mutton and sweat, ale and wet, fetid rushes. The stink grew stronger. He needed fresh air. Smell was his only sense, and it was acute and overpowering.

Had someone touched him, he doubted he would feel it. Had the Devil himself arisen there before his eyes, he would not have seen him. Had the ground opened up and the screams of Hell surrounded him, he would not hear them.

The coward in him wanted to run, an urge he had felt often in his lifetime but never admitted or acted upon. He didn't have the courage to be a true coward. He walked on, feeling nothing, yet wondering if betrayal carried a stench.

Outside, he headed straight for the stable, saddled and mounted his horse, paid the guard a pretty sum to open the gate, and rode out, only to have to bribe the castle ferryman to barge cross the lake. The wind was picking up overhead, and it blew water from the white-capped lake into his eyes and face, and rocked the wooden raft so hard he had his hands full calming down his high-spirited horse.

On the opposite side he eased his skittish mount off the rocking raft to soft ground, and he kept along the edge of the lake as the wind calmed down, and in time, so did his horse. At a break in the trees, he dismounted and his horse was happy to eat grass. But Lyall's state of mind was in turmoil as he paced across the damp grass in the dark.

Dunkeldon was his. After all the time and the pain and disappointment. After keeping his eye on the prize with a single-mindedness that had gone on for so long, eventually he drove himself from the hearts of his family.

What price so dear one pays....

He was alone in the grand quiet of the moment he had waited for, yet there was great noise inside his head he could not shake off.

At the edge of the lake, he stopped. The waters spanned out before him, past the castle rock, and into the great beyond, proving itself broad and distancing and making him feel small. Now the prize was his, and instinct told him that he needed to remember his father and Malcolm; all he had done had been for them.

He closed his eyes to take his memory back in time. But he saw nothing familiar. No features he could remember, nothing but the shadows of two men.

What punishment was this? He could no longer conjure up their faces. When had that happened? How long had it been since he could see their features in his mind's eye, since he could hear their voices in his head? He could not remember if or when he had tried. He massaged his brow and frowned, then swiped his hand over his mouth and chin, rough with beard.

The images were lost to him, and he understood like a fool does after acting the idiot that he had traded his memories of his father and Malcolm for the land. Their images were gone, wiped clean from his mind and memory. He had lost everything, and justified doing so by telling himself the greatest lie: all he had done, he had done for them.

His gaze went to the castle tower, where dim light shone vaguely from an arrow slit. As clear as a summer sky he saw Glenna Canmore walking regally up the stone steps and taking with her his lost soul.

Lyall could not breathe. He fell to his knees, his control gone. Suddenly all the air in his lungs had been stolen, then next...the blood in his veins disappeared, his bones felt brittle and dry as an old corpse. He was empty.

Dunkeldon was his but at what cost?

He knelt there taking long breaths and staring at the flickering, distant light in the tower, until he flung his head back and cried out, a sound that was like that of a lone wolf who lost its mate, a sound that echoed out over the water, into the ground under him and through his body, a cry that filled his throat and left it rough and scratched, and when he found his voice again, the words from his mouth were, "What have I done? *What have I done!*"

A moment later a knife pricked his throat as someone gripped his hair tightly in a fist. "It matters not what you have done because you are a dead man."

TWENTY-FOUR

The tower room door opened to the squeak of rusty hinges and the guard's gruff voice. "I have your furs, my lady." He stepped inside, and the grey cat rushed in between his legs. "You devil of a cat!" He tossed an armful of marten furs on the bed and grumbled, "That's how she lost her tail, skulking through open doorways."

The cat sat looking back and forth between them.

Glenna picked it up, scratching it under the chin. "Look at you…"

The guard was halfway out the door.

"Wait." She stepped forward, holding out the cat for him.

He looked at her kindly and said, "You keep her, my lady…for companionship." He closed the door on her protest.

"But—" Her voice trailed off as the bolt slid into place. She groaned, then held up the cat and looked into its bright and curious eyes. "You are a problem."

The cat blinked.

"You see, I have no plans to stay here."

It's expression changed to a sloe-eyed look of superiority.

"Such as it is. Whatever you are about, silly puss, you are stuck here in this tower. I, however, will not be." She set it down, and the cat prowled over toward the table, leapt atop it, and sniffed at the cheese.

"Hungry are you?" Glenna unwrapped the cloth and pinched off a soft cheese piece for the cat, then wrapped up all the food, including the plums and tucked them inside the deep pockets of her trouse.

With her ear pressed to the door, she waited until she was certain no one was outside. She slid the knife in the thin gap between the door and lifted up... The bolt moved free from its slot.

Could her escape be so simple? She pushed the door open, peeking outside through a slim line of vision. One waning candle cast a pale amber light on the landing, which appeared empty. She opened the door far enough to step out and the cat rushed out and stood in the middle of the round room.

"Bugger!" she whispered sharply.

Facing her, the cat sat down, swished its tail, and stared at her, looking half bored and vaguely intrigued.

Glenna leaned out and hissed. "Come puss. Come here..."

The cat did not move.

She needed a bribe. Digging around in her clothes, she pinched off cheese from her stash and squatted down in the door, a cheese morsel in her open palm. "Come sweet cat," she whispered sweetly. "Come to me..."

The cat eyed the cheese, blinked, and a heartbeat later took off down the dark stairs, leaving Glenna to stare at the empty spot where half of a grey tail had just disappeared. Muttering under her breath, she closed the door behind her.

If the guard saw the cat, she would be a cooked goose.

She edged down the stairs quickly, moving blindly away from the light into the dark depths of the tower stairwell. Her hands ran along the wall, feeling her way down as her feet edged uneasily onto each unfamiliar stair tread.

As she neared the bottom of the tower, there shone a dim spill of light from one of the nearby chambers, but she heard there no voices. Before she passed the open chamber, she moved to the opposite wall, listening sharply for sounds, and when there were none, she hurried past, keeping against the wall.

Four more chambers had their doors closed and then she was looking down into the hall, where pallets were scattered and men were sleeping lumps...except for two men talking quietly near the stairs. If there was a way past them, she could not see it.

The cat was back, and it made a plaintive meow. Quickly she stepped back, pressed again the wall, her heart beating in her throat.

Be quiet, cat.

There was a long, empty and quiet pause, then suddenly the beast was making enough noise to awaken the hall. She bent down to grab it and it shot away from her, plopped down and started all over again.

"Meow, meow, meow, meow, meoooooow..." The cat sounded as if it were a Gregorian monk on the feast day of Saint Columba.

Belowstairs someone cursed.

Please let there be a dozen cats in the castle.

"Meow, meow, meow, meow, meoooooow..."

Quickly Glenna searched for some way to escape and prayed the guard who knew the cat was locked in the tower was sleeping soundly.

"Someone drown that cat." A gruff voice carried up from the hall.

"Here take my sword and cut its throat," groaned another.

A loud and vicious curse came from inside the nearest chamber, and Glenna quickly ran into a dark corner as the door cracked opened and a boot flew at the cat, who screeched and disappeared down the steps.

Glenna held her breath as the door stayed open, and then

slowly began to close. She dared not move until the door closed enough for her to sneak down.

From below came a familiar voice, "The cat's out!" cried the guard.

Her heart sank.

There was a roaring shout to find her. "Quick! Up to the tower."

She closed her eyes and stayed into the corner as the clatter of weapons and running feet carried up the walls. Men came up the stairs and passed by in running shadows.

She had nowhere to go.

From the open room nearest the tower stairs came two men, armed, and followed by three others carrying swords and reed torches. Light flooded out into the darkened halls and the door next to her flew open and her captor came out, barefooted but strapping on his sword belt.

Her heart was beating so loudly in her ears.

"Meow!" The cat was back and moved straight for her. "Meow!"

Huchon de Hay paused, then turned. He was looking right at her. She was staring at his sword blade.

She covered her head with her arms and cowered, whimpering softly. "Do not kill me. I beg you, my lord. The guard did not bolt the door," she lied and looked up at him from wide eyes filled with tears. "Can you blame me? Would you not have tried to escape, my lord?"

"She is here!" he called out to his men and continued to stare at her from eyes that told her nothing about what he was thinking. He lowered the sword and said to her, "Stand up, woman."

The horrid guard cat stood near her feet, as men at arms began flanking de Hay.

"Take her back."

Already her mind was working. How long should she wait before she tried to escape again?

"And this time..." His pause was poignant. "Place a guard at the door."

Bugger!

Lyall looked up into the angry eyes of Alastair Gordon.

"*Bastard!* Alastair hissed viciously. "Where is Glenna?"

"Let me cut him, Al." Elgin Gordon said, holding the knife at his neck. "I want to cut him for what he's done."

One quick slice of his arm to Elgin Gordon's knees and Lyall knew the knife would be gone. But he did nothing. Alastair twisted his hair harder and the pain grew in Lyall's eyes. There was not enough physical pain in the world to match the pain he felt inside.

"The real Baron Montrose came to the island. We know all, you lying bastard! Where is she?"

Lyall swallowed hard and felt the prick of the knife tip. "In the tower."

There was dim light coming from one of the arrow slits and Lyall wondered why. It was well into the early hours. Did she need a candle lit to sleep there? Was she frightened? When she snapped at him, when she threw his words back or made him feel like a witless goat, when she acted her most prideful, she did so because she was afraid. That he understood so well her whims and moods reminded him of what he'd given up, of his failure and his betrayal.

Alastair cursed and released Lyall's hair, but a sword tip was now poised at his ribs.

"Step away El."

"I was not going to give her up," Lyall admitted. "We were surrounded. I had little choice but to play along."

"And we are supposed to believe you suddenly speak truths

from your lying mouth?" Elgin laughed bitterly. "Please Al...just one good slice so I can watch his life's blood bleed out of him like the stuck pig he is." He flipped the dagger over in his hand and pointed it at him.

Elgin was impulsive, but Alastair Gordon was not. Lyall glanced at the sword he held, an elegant weapon, honed and oiled and perfectly capable of sending him to his place in Hell....for a man who knew how to wield it. But he believed Gordon was no trained warrior. Still his grip was correct. "Do you know how to use that weapon?"

"He can wield a sword," Elgin said with pride. "He can slide it into you easily. He was trained by our father. But I want to kill you myself."

"Killing me will not help you get Glenna out of that tower."

"Perhaps to you, nay, it would not," Alastair said unfazed, and the weapon he held so threateningly moved dangerously close to Lyall's throat. "But seeing you die would give me such great pleasure."

"I have a way inside," Lyall told them.

There was a shout, and all three men looked toward it. The loud clank and rattle of heavy chains drawing the castle gate carried out over the water. A dark silhouette of a single rider disappeared inside the castle.

"The messenger," Elgin said to his brother.

"What messenger?" Lyall asked, and a twig cracked loudly and all three men turned.

"The rider from Argyll," came another voice.

His belly turned. Lyall knew that voice all too well. *Ramsey.*

"The rider who led us here to you, son."

Before him stood his stepfather, armed and tall and none too pleased with him, flanked by a large troop of men, men who knew him and who he knew, their swords drawn, looking as ready to fight as the Gordons.

He looked at the expression on his stepfather's face, the disappointment and anger coming from him filled the air and was palpable. Lyall could not move. He could not look any of them in the eye, because he was acutely aware at that moment he was living, breathing proof of what everyone believed: that bad blood bred bad blood. He was nothing but his father's son.

She hit him with the laver.

The poor guard crumpled to the floor, and the food tray she'd begged for, cried and sobbed for, despite the hour, and because she was 'so famished,' crashed next to him. Glenna leapt down from the chair and ran out of the tower, almost flying down the stairs. She moved through the hallway in the dark and started down the main stairs to the great hall, keeping to the wall.

A door flew open below and someone was running into the hall. "*De Hay!* A messenger!"

Glenna ran back up the stairs and into the hallway, looking for a place to hide. Across the narrow gallery, she hid in a small niche covered with a tapestry. But it only ended at her knees. She stood with her back pressed against the niche and prayed it was dark enough for no one to notice.

"My lord! My lord!" came the call, and she heard two men run up the stairs. Someone pounded on the chamber door of her captor.

De Hay's gruff voice called out for them to enter.

She stood hidden, her heart beating away time, knowing how little she had left. She had to escape. She would not be the power for her father's enemies or the tool to bring him down, no matter who or what kind of man he might wed her to.

There was a sudden and loud call to arms.

She mentally groaned. Caught again!

But from here abovestairs, men were running past and down into the great hall. The clank of weapons and boots, excited voices, and calls to get their mounts ready told her this was something other than her escape. The noise below was waning, so she shifted and tried to look out. There was no one about, but the door to de Hay's chamber was open and she could hear the men talking.

Moving quickly, she headed for the chamber next to his, slipped inside, and sidestepped a large cache of weapons thrown on the floor. She hid behind a clothing rod hung with men's robes and tunics. Breathing softly, heart beating hard, she slid a robe aside and took a look.

The room was completely empty, except for a long desk and chair and a massive carved wood bed that dominated the center of the room. But no one else was there now, though the bed linens were tossed aside and appeared slept in. She stepped out from behind the clothing, wondering how she could possibly escape.

The clang of weaponry came up from below and male voices filled the hallway.

A sudden sound of running steps from the tower made her freeze.

"She's escaped!" The guard's voice came through the hall. "She's escaped!"

Panicking, she dropped to the floor and crawled under the large bed, and was immediately assailed with the strong odor of urine. Wincing, she pushed the pisspot away from her head. A man came inside the room and she watched his feet. He stopped at the clothes rod and he began to dress quickly.

Glenna held her breath, afraid he would hear. She dared not move.

A loud curse came from the next chamber and de Hay bellowed, "Can you idiots not keep one woman locked inside that tower?"

"She hit me in the head with a laver!"

"Find her! Now!" There was a pause, then he shouted, "Frasyr!"

"Aye? In here!" the man in room called out, and de Hay came inside.

"Your cousin has sent for aid. They have been attacked. I must ride, and ride hard, yet I cannot leave until I know she is secured," de Hay said angrily and he began to pace. "How can one feeble woman cause so much trouble?"

I am not feeble, she thought. You witless oaf.

"I would guess she is not the meek, slow-witted lamb she appeared to be," Frasyr said.

She smiled.

"Of course she is not." De Hay stopped pacing. "You will have to stay to keep her safe. I cannot risk taking her outside this stronghold. Your defenses here are strong. I trust you can keep her secure without my troops."

"No siege could take Kinnesswood.," Frasyr boasted.

"Aye, she is safest here...as long as we can manage to keep her locked up," de Hay said dryly. "You might want to shackle her to the bed."

"Spread-eagle," Frasyr said, laughing.

"You forget yourself," de Hay said without humor. "She is still the daughter of a king, whether or not we support his right to rule. No harm must come to her."

"I was jesting. I am well aware of her price."

"I expect her to remain unharmed...and untouched. You do understand?"

"Aye," Frasyr said with quiet seriousness. "She will be safe here. I give you my word."

They spoke of Frasyr's cousin, the king of Argyll, but she stopped listening when four grey furry feet padded into the room. The feet stopped beside the bed. The guard cat was back. The beast went down on its haunches and stared at her. "Meow..."

Bugger! Glenna wiggled away, back toward the head of the bed.

"Meow, meow, meow, meow...."

There was long, telling break of silence, and she had nowhere else to run, then both men were on either side of the bed looking at her from narrowed, angry eyes.

Never had she been intimidated by male anger. She didn't give in, but scooted all the back against the wall. They grasped for her but she moved out of reach, so they split up to each side of the bed, moving closer and grabbing for an arm or leg.

She scampered back and forth, until they were half under the bed with her and she shimmied down for the foot of the bed, but one of them got a leg, and another, an arm. They tried to drag her out, but she fought madly, kicking and biting, clinging madly to the support ropes on the bed, as more men came and they each pulled and yanked until her poor body felt stretched to the breaking point and her strength waned. Her arm slipped from the ropes, burning her skin as she was dragged out, still kicking and flailing.

At the last moment she grabbed the pisspot and threw it on the man who pulled out by her ankles.

Sir Coll Frasyr dropped her and cursed so loudly his voice echoed overhead. She swung her feet up and kicked the other man hard in the jaw, scurried up, pulled her knife and faced eight men, while more men came running in the room. Frasyr was dripping in yellow piss and his face was almost blue he was so angry. She looked from one man to another. Where was de Hay?

She shifted, her weight on the balls of her feet, searching the crowd of male faces, the knife poised to strike. "Any one of you tries to touch me and you'll find yourself gelded."

She felt a sword tip at her back. "Drop the knife," de Hay said.

"You will not harm me. I am worth too much to you."

"What you do not understand is I can, and will, wound you

enough to make you drop the knife. You are caught. There is no escape. Look around you. A wise woman would do as I ask. And I do not believe you are without wits." He pressed the sword into her back, deeper. She did not budge. He pushed it deeper, and deeper. She stood unflinchingly strong.

And he pushed harder. The sword cut into her. She cried out at the pain, but reacted instinctively and gripped the knife even tighter, pulled back, felt the sword tip pop free, and she spun and threw the knife at him.

De Hay sidestepped and the knife flew past him to stick with a loud thud in the wall. "Take her!" he ordered through a tight jaw and slammed his sword into the floor.

The first man who grabbed her she bit, hanging onto his skin with her jaw clamped tight and she heard him hiss in pain, and then yell when she bit even deeper. The second she kicked in the groin, the ribs, and the jaw, then there were more men pulling at her, strong hands and arms everywhere. She twisted and scratched and pounded with her fists, and kicked hard with her feet, but too soon her strength was gone and futile against so many.

She had the will and the determination. But she did not have enough hands and feet to fight them all.

The sun was rising when the gates opened again and a large troop of men rode out of the castle and began crossing the lake in large numbers, on three ferry barges, one after another.

"Huchon de Hay," Ramsey said under his breath as if the name was profanity, but he made no motion to arm or give chase as the men rode onto shore and gathered, ready to ride.

"You will not go after them?"

Ramsey shook his head. "My duty is to claim and safeguard the king's eldest daughter." To Lyall he turned and said, "You say you have a way inside. The position of the keep is near impossible to lay siege. Since you are the reason she is not safely tucked away at Rossie, I will hear your plan."

His stepfather sarcasm was not lost to him, but Lyall's mistakes were done, so he refused to cower and or labor over what he could not change. He told them of his conversation with Frasyr's man, then explained that along with Glenna's brothers and their horses, they could infiltrate Kinnesswood under the pretext of offering the horses for sale to Frasyr's man. His stepfather listened without comment, then joined the discussion and questioned him about the lay of things inside the gates, and the plans began to grow, take form, and become the single path that made the most sense, except for the matter of trusting him.

"How do we know you will not give us up to Frasyr?" Elgin Gordon asked, eyeing Lyall with contempt.

"You cannot know," Lyall said. "But without me, neither have you a chance in hell to get inside, so you have little choice."

TWENTY-FIVE

A group of men-at-arms stood guard outside the tower door. Earlier, when Glenna put her ear to the door, she could hear them talking and dicing. After her third foiled escape attempt, Frasyr stayed true to his promise and sent for the smith. She was leg-shackled to a pin in the wall beneath the shuttered arch with just enough chain for her to reach the edges in the room.

The traitorous grey cat lay curled nearby, contented and purring so loudly it sounded like the recoil of a bowstring. The beast was not part of her plan. She had tried to get rid of it, had pounded on the door when she discovered it was locked in with her again. "Guard! Guard!" she had called out.

"My lady?" came the voice through the door.

"You need to take the cat," she said. "It wants out."

"Nay. She will stay with you."

"But—"

"Good night, my lady."

"Guard!" He did not respond. "Guard! I had not wanted to hit you with the laver," she said truthfully.

Still nothing.

"If your sister were held captive, would you not want her to do the same?"

But she found she was talking to dead ears, and was stuck with the cat.

For a while now, she kept busy by cutting the support ropes from bed with one of her three stolen knives. She crawled out from under the bed, dropping some of the ropes next her, before she cut the last two and watched the straw mattress fall to the floor.

Done!

She sat back on her heels, wincing as she rubbed her ankle, which was red from the thick iron shackle. Then, for the third time, she hunched over it with the smallest knife and worked at the lock, but she could not seem to pick it no matter how she turned it.

"What is wrong with this lock?" She looked across the room, where she had picked the shutter lock without a problem. When the manacle lock would still not open, she dropped the knife in frustration and groaned under her breath.

The cat opened one eye, annoyed.

"This is all your fault".

Unfazed, the cat went back to sleep.

The sun was up and though it was still cool in the tower, 'twas lighter now in the daylight and with the shutters open. She rose and moved toward the arch, leaning a shoulder against the shutter and looking out while she waited for some renewed patience to test the manacle lock again.

Outside, there was a huge, bright blue sky with a few, fleece-like clouds floating by. The breeze coming in carried the moist scent of morning dew, and spread out before her, the wide forest beyond the lake stood in the great shadow of Ben Nevis.

A movement caught her eye near the edges of the lake, and she leaned forward, searching the shoreline and the trees.

Montrose?

He was not Montrose, really, but Sir Lyall Robertson. To her he would always be Montrose. Again and again she perused the area, but there was no one. Her eyes were playing tricks on her.

After they had pulled her out from under the bed, when they had dragged her away, she'd called out for him, out of instinct, perhaps. For her instinct told her Montrose would never let her be harmed, or hurt, that he would save her if she were in trouble and called out for him. He loved her.

De Hay had laughed at her when she had called his name and said, "Montrose? He is not Montrose, you foolish woman. You think that Robertson will rescue you? That coward? He took the deed to his lands—his thirty pieces of gold for bringing you to me—and he was out the gates moments later without a word or a look back."

She had bitten de Hay for those words. Montrose loved her. If it were not true, what kind of fool would she be? He loved her. Yet when they closed the door and she was alone again, battered and bruised and feeling trapped, she weakened and asked herself if he would really walk away so easily.

She thought not, but then she remembered her own escape from the abbey, running away because she was trying to ignore what she felt for him, and still stubbornly sticking to her vow to not be a pawn for a father she did not know.

Self preservation.

But Montrose loved her. She believed that more than any single thing, and perhaps, the only thing left for her to have faith in.

But until the oaf realized what he had done and how he felt, she would be forced to save herself.

Below, the lake shimmered silver in the sunlight, and from the tower, it was a straight drop down to the water. She turned, hands on her hips as she studied the room. There had to be something else she could use to pick the lock.

She began rummaging through all of her plunder and lay

them out on the table. Five purses lined up in a row on the table, some plumper than others, along with two jeweled rings and the three knives, one with an emerald-encrusted handle that at some point Sir Coll would see was missing from his person, along with his purse—the plumpest—and a lovely brooch with a huge ruby in its center. Though its pin was narrow, she pulled it from the brooch, held it up and eyed the tip.

Perhaps....

She sat down with her foot on the edge of the chair and tried every way to pick the manacle lock. There was a loud snort, and the cat, asleep on its side, began to run, its paws moving furiously as it slept. She should hate the cat, but she couldn't, even though the little beast kept her from escaping. The cat was only was acting on instinct, something she understood.

A vision of Montrose came to mind, and she felt a deep pang. De Hay had been wrong about Lyall. He was not a coward, driven by greed. Emotion drove him, and perhaps some misplaced pride.

A loud shout pulled her from the chair to the open arch, then came the creaking of the gate chains and the sound of horses hooves. She could see nothing, even when she tried to lean out. She sagged back against the shutter and closed her eyes.

Come to me, Montrose. Please come.

She opened her eyes and searched the horizon again, but saw no sign of him. Sighing in frustration, she slumped to the floor and stuck the pin back in the cursed lock.

One slight twist and it magically clicked open. She was free! Well...she was free of her chains. Laughing, she rubbed her ankle, so relieved, and then, she pulled the ropes toward her and set to work.

The mattress took a while to tear apart, the straw took some time to spread out in piles about the room and in front of the door. At one point, the cat woke and moved to one of the straw piles, curled up for a nap, refusing to leave even when Glenna scolded it, hissed at it, and tried to shoo it away. Finally, she picked up the cat and fashioned a sling to hold it.

The flint sparked readily, and before long, the oil reed flamed. Fire ready, she looked around her, took one deep breath, and she was ready, aware of the great risk she took if her plan did not go well.

His plan was not going well.

The first guard went down easily, but the second guard had Lyall pinned on the battlement with his head and shoulders hanging off. Below was a huge outcropping of jagged rocks that would break a man's back should he be unfortunate enough to fall upon them...and he was close.

From his first few steps across the battlement, he had been in trouble. After fighting with the guard he'd met on the stairs, Lyall opened the wood door and ran out on the wall, then made the mistake of looking down. The height threw him off, and when he turned about, he faced an archer the size of a yew tree.

Disarmed too quickly, they struggled man-to-man, his only weapon his strength with his sword out of reach. The man pushed harder, a hand on Lyall's throat, and from the corner of his eye, he caught a glimpse of the rocks so far below.

Fear broke out in beads of sweat on his brow, but he kept the heel of his hand pushing the man's head back so he could not shout any warning. One alert and the castle would arm, then Ramsey and his men would never get inside the gates. And he hoped to God that Elgin Gordon was where they had left him, still manning those gates.

He felt the prick of the man's dagger at his throat and found another burst of strength, and tried to reach for the man's arrows, but his arms were not long enough. The knife tip was dangerously close, and his opponent did not budge but his face was red as apple.

With his boot to the man's gut, Lyall tried to shove him off, but the man gained momentum, then lifted him and started to push. He began slipping over the side and fought to not slide any farther, which took everything he had and his arms began to shake.

The guard gasped suddenly, and made a sick groan of death. There was no more struggle and Lyall was freed, as Alastair Gordon shoved the man off him.

Panting, Lyall pulled himself up and sat there, his breathing labored, cold sweat pouring like water over his face, his worthless life still passing before his eyes. He took a moment, then grasped his sword and looked up. "God's ears, Gordon. What took you so long?"

Alastair gave him a hand up and boasted proudly, "I had three guards to overtake on the eastern wall."

"Only three?"

"Aye, but all at once," Gordon lied.

"I'll wager they weren't the size of two men." Lyall cast an uneasy glance at the man laying next to him, and knowing he owed Alastair Gordon his life.

"I would not have thought you were so worthless in a fight, Robertson."

"Aye. Merely ask any one of Ramsey's men. They'll be all too glad to tell you what a coward I am." Spoken too many times before, the words came from his lips easily. "'Tis is in my blood," he said simply. "Now grab that pennant from its mount, and stop your cockcrowing. Someone has to signal Ramsey."

Just as Gordon began waving the pennant, Lyall looked into the bailey, where a man had crossed and was just entering the gate house where they had left Elgin.

Lyall cursed silently.

There was a shout, loud enough to cause an alert. A moment later the gatehouse door opened with a loud scuffle and Elgin Gordon and the man tumbled out, Gordon clearly outmatched.

Alastair spun around. "El!" He took off through the battlement door, but Lyall looked on as his brother was already sprawled on the ground with a sword poised to kill. Frasyr's man raised the weapon, ready to skewer Elgin.

In a the time it took a heart to beat, there was a whistling thud, and guard fell forward, an arrow in his back and piercing straight through his heart, his sword falling harmlessly from his hands.

Alastair Gordon came running out from the bottom of the stairs and straight to his brother, who lay there alive and stunned, pale and staring at the dead guard. Alastair turned and looked up as Lyall lowered the bow.

Two groups of Ramsey's men had crossed the lake and were riding off the barges onto the island, another was already nearing the castle entrance.

"The gates!" Lyall shouted, then ran for the stairs.

The castle was arming.

At the bottom, he ran out, sword raised as Frasyr's men swarmed out into the bailey. But the Gordons had managed to open the gate, and half his stepfather's men were already inside and had the advantage of fighting on horseback. The fight struck hard and furiously, with sword clanging against sword and men began falling.

Lyall ran through the melee toward the keep, and inside, running past Frasyr's men, who were flooding out like ants, strapping on weapons, and did not question his presence.

They must have thought he had never left.

Ahead of everyone else, he took the stairs from the hall two at a time, finding speed he did not know he had. He ran down the corridor and up into the tower, where he threw two guards down the steps and kept going until he faced and fought the other guards posted outside the tower door. His strength felt like a gift from Heaven and he fought as powerfully and unrelenting as did the huge archer on the wall.

The ring of metal against metal was still in his ears when he used the guard's key to unlock the door, only to be stopped in his tracks by an orange wall of burning flames, and over the top of them, the horrific, haunting sight of Glenna leaping out the tower arch.

TWENTY-SIX

The lengths of rope Glenna had tied to the manacle chain ended only halfway down the tower, where she was dangling. She looked down. It was a sheer drop to the lake below. Too late now, her great idea to escape down the outside of the tower didn't look so brilliant from her current vantage point. She felt as if she were hanging off of Ben Nevis. The cat, an added nuisance, was looking at her contentedly from the sling around her shoulder. The little beast had no idea what was coming.

Clinging to the rope, Glenna used her feet to push off from the tower wall, swinging outward, trying to find the courage to let go and fall into the lake. She kept touching the wall with her feet, and shoving off, touching the wall with her feet, and shoving off....

"Glenna! *Glennnnn-na!*"

"Montrose!" Startled, she looked up and there he was, her beautiful golden knight, half hanging out of the arch, black smoke billowing up above him. Coughing, he tested his weight on the rope, then pulled off his smoldering gambeson and tunic in one swift motion, and crawled out, barechested, then shimmied down toward her.

A breath she hadn't known she held escaped in relief. Her knuckles grew white she held onto the rope so tightly; it swayed and shook from his motions. Tears burned her eyes.

He had come for her. He had come for her!

Then he was there, so close the warmth of his breath touched her face and ruffled her hair. She felt his strong arm wrap firmly around her. His mouth closed over hers, and she was swept up and carried away as if lost in the waters of Lethe. There in his arms, it mattered not that they were hanging off a burning tower. She felt safe, as if she could fly like the gulls that wheeled over the sea, like the eagles that circled the treetops, or the plovers skimming across fields of heather. She clung to him as if he was her breath and blood, her heart and life.

Longing and relief ran through her veins and felt so joyous and natural and pure she questioned if those emotions came from her or him…perhaps, from them both. Together, they were different than who they were alone; they were solid and strong and one. Loving him was everything, a power to which she could surrender because instead of weakening her, loving him made her stronger.

Montrose. If she fell to her death at that moment, she would have died in complete elation, because he was holding her and kissing her, because he loved her.

The cat mewed…loudly.

He pulled back. "What have you there?"

The cat stuck its mangy head out from under her arm and looked up at them from eyes the color of the island summer sea.

"I couldn't very well leave it to burn," Glenna told him.

"Aye. The room is well gone. I almost didn't make it to the arch. The floor collapsed behind and under me." He looked down, paused, then said seriously, "You know we must jump. There is no other way."

"Aye," she said with mixed emotions. That water looked far, far away.

"And yet, here you are with a cat hanging off of you."

"I planned to hold onto this cat tightly when we hit the

water," she said brightly, as if fear were the farthest thing from her mind. "And here you are with me hanging off of you."

"I plan to hold onto you tightly when we hit the water."

"We would not be in this situation if I'd had—"

"—your bow and arrows," he finished.

"At least you can admit it." She gave a shaky half-laugh, nerves still raw. "Montrose?"

"You need to stop calling me Montrose."

She looked at him and said, "And you need to start calling me, your highness."

He smiled. "So you have decided you like being the daughter of the king."

"Only if being one gets me what I want."

"You are prolonging this, Glenna. Look up there. Smoke and flames are coming out the arch. We have to leap."

She nodded, suddenly as serious as he was.

"We have to let go."

"Are you afraid?" she asked in a rush.

"Frightened witless," he said calmly, taking a firm hold of her hand. "We'll push off from the wall three times, then on my command, we'll let go of the ropes together."

She nodded and kept her eyes on his, as they planted their feet on the wall side by side, and shoved off, once, twice…thrice…

"Let go, my love," he said as simply and evenly as if they had been walking in the woods.

Hands threaded together, they fell through the air frighteningly fast, like heavy stones, and echoing out over the water, his scream was as loud as hers.

The water was cold; it slapped and stung and was endless, swimming through it was truly endless. When Lyall feet's finally hit the silty bottom, he pulled Glenna into shallow water, while the mewing cat, slung over his shoulder, squirmed and scratched at him. They stumbled together onto grassy land, breathless, spent and soaked.

Lyall dropped the sling between them and lay there, then rolled onto his back, breathing so hard it hurt and staring up at the blue sky, the grass feeling strangely warm beneath him.

"Solid land has never been so welcome," Glenna muttered, laying face down on the grass next to him, her head buried in her arms. "Do I still have arms and legs? I cannot feel my limbs."

The cat coughed and sneezed and spat, and sneezed again, shook itself and sent water in all directions. It looked like a drowned rat as it butted up to Glenna, and sat there with a thoroughly puzzled look that said, how could you do that to me? When she ignored it, the cat squealed plaintively and batted her with its paw.

Glenna opened one eye, stared at the cat for a moment, then said, "Vengeance is mine, puss." The cat only meowed and ran off into the bushes. "Traitor," she muttered. "I save you and you go running off for a life of your own."

Her words were never more true. She had a life of her own, the future she was born into. Lyall watched her. She did not know he was trapped by his actions, nor that his stepfather would make him face what he had done. Bits of moss clung to her long hair and her face was smudged with dirt or ash. Water dripped from her tunic, trouse and head. She was soaked from head to foot, and she had just leapt from a tower. Lyall closed his eyes. *What have I done to you?*

As if she had read his thoughts, she turned to glance at him, and frowned. "Don't look so fretful, Montrose. A little water never hurt me."

He shook his head and said, "We just leapt from a rope that was hung from a chain in burning tower that belongs to one of your father's enemies—a tower I was responsible for putting you in—and landed in a lake...with a cat. I am not certain what your father would have to say about all this but I expect he will say plenty."

"Since my father—a man I have never met, mind you—is not, nor has been, on home soil for most of my lifetime, I do not believe he has any say in what has gone on with me...and you. I am alive. He should be thanking you."

"I do not think royal gratitude is in my future," he said dryly. "You are his daughter."

She scrambled to her knees and leaned over him, her hair dripping on his chest. "Aye. I am his daughter and you have my gratitude." She leaned down and kissed him, softly, tenderly. "My eternal gratitude," she murmured against his mouth, and his hand cupped the back of her head. "Kiss me, Montrose."

"There is where we have a problem." He picked a strand of lake moss from her hair. "I am not Montrose."

"Kiss me, Sir Lyall Robertson," she said laughing. "Kiss me now! I love to kiss. Consider it a royal command."

He looked up into her eyes, filled with humor, with challenge and that fine line, the spark in her eye that bespoke her deepest desire, along with a touch of avarice. "You look at me the same way you eyed that plump pearl."

"Aye," she said nonplussed. "I have a keen eye. I can gauge your worth."

His worth? What was his worth? He no longer had his good word and felt as if he were searching for the good in himself somewhere in the depth of her eyes. He wiped the wet hair from her cheek, moving his thumb to her mouth as he drank in her face, drawn to her because of that odd thing she seemed to see in him— something worth saving.

He came close to believing it was true....close.

"You love me," she said, in almost a whisper, but without

hesitation, and as if she were telling him a secret no one else knew.

He was not a strong man. He could not fight this. With all the lies he'd told her, now he owed her the truth. "Aye, witch, I do love you. But I believe you are the only one happy about it. You forget. I am a traitor and you are the daughter of the king."

She gave a sharp and bitter laugh. "You are no traitor."

"You say that after what I did." He shook his head. "You forgive me far too easily."

"Aye, if there were anything to forgive. I know why you did what you did. How else were you to get Dunkeldon? I have spent most of my life taking what I want." She shrugged. "You bartered me for what you wanted. Why would I not understand?"

He looked at her for a long time. "What do you see, that I cannot believe?"

She lifted her hand to cheek. "I see the man I love," she said simply.

"Your father could hang me, Glenna."

She grew serious and stared at him, clearly thinking. "I will not let them hang you. I am the daughter of the king."

"You are a woman, whose power is, in truth, only that which your father allows you, your father and the man you will wed."

"I want no other man," she said stubbornly. "I am yours. I give myself to you, Lyall Robertson...only you."

But her words, the gift of herself, the truth she spoke, her devotion, her troth, all of it broke his heart because he could not have her. Still...he was a weak, weak man, who had no strength to fight the bond between them—he wanted her with a fever as hot and scorching as the fires of Hell—and he could do nothing but pull her into his arms and try to find the strength to let her go.

She lay her head down and he stroked her wet hair, tangled and spilling down over his ribs. He closed his eyes.

"I hear that sound," she said. "Your heart beats here." She placed her hand on his chest. 'Tis mine, this heart of yours that beats so," she said softly. "Say the words to me. Say them and then take me. We will be wed and there will be nothing anyone can do."

To say the words would be fatal, for her more than him. He wanted her. He would wed her without a hesitation were she anyone but the king's daughter, his first born daughter at that.

He could promise me to anyone. Did you know the Germans bury their wives alive?

He closed his eyes, searching for the will to do what was right. Her mouth moved close to his but he stopped her, a finger to her soft lips, and he started to say nay, we cannot do this, but he whispered the words that would bond him to her, "I give myself to you, Glenna Canmore."

She smiled slightly, and her turned-up mouth, so full and moist, found his, and he rolled over in the grass with her, covered her body with his own and gave in to the sweet, impossible fantasy that she could truly be his.

Ramsey rode into the small clearing, some of his men in his wake, and he took one look at the couple rolling in the grass, a tangle of legs, a tanned hand on a pale white breast, the long waves of shiny black Canmore hair next to a head of golden hair exactly like that of his old friend, and he bellowed Lyall's name like the most foul, most blasphemous of curses.

The two broke apart as if touched by fire, showing flashes of skin and wet, twisted garments that were difficult to pull into place. But his stepson helped to right her clothing—had he only shown such gallantry before he ravished her on the grass—and then took to straightening what little he wore, unable to hide his erection in his wet, sodden hose. Her mouth was swollen and pink, her cheeks rubbed red from Lyall's beard, and her face was that a woman flushed with passion, damp and loose and ready to swive.

He recovered himself quickly and ordered his men to stand away and waited until they left the clearing. He spurred his horse forward until he was close enough to see the sweat beading on his stepson's brow. "In the name of Heaven are you daft? Rolling around on the ground like some lackwit itching to plough the milkmaid?" He lowered his voice and his hand went to his sword hilt instinctively. "She is the king's daughter you witless fool! I swear by all that is holy and right, at this very moment I could easily beat you boneless."

Ramsey stared hard at Lyall, then at Glenna. Neither of them appeared to be the least repentant, humiliated, even mildly contrite, and as he continued to look at them, he thought the top of his head was going to blow off. "You have nothing to say?"

Lyall placed his hands on her shoulders. "Glenna, this is Donnald Ramsey, Baron Montrose, and my stepfather."

Her dark eyes bright and quick, Glenna Canmore assessed him with one solid, slightly familiar royal look. "My lord."

Lyall leaned down and whispered something in her ear. When he straightened again, Ramsey saw that his hands still rested there.

She looked up at Lyall over her shoulder, her expression saying clearly that whatever he had said was asinine. "I do not care. I will not deny you your place in my life." She looked Ramsey in the eye, her expression the image of her father, and said without fear or any emotion other than absolute conviction, "It is done. Lyall is my husband. We have promised to each other."

Ramsey pinned his stepson with a look he hoped struck hard. "Is this true?"

"Aye."

"Speaking in the present tense?" Ramsey shot back pointedly, aware a handfast had two binding conditions, vows spoken in the present tense and consummation.

Lyall gave a sharp nod.

"Such a marriage is not binding unless consummated."

Glenna immediately looked up at Lyall, and he frowned and shook his head slightly to warn her, but when she faced Ramsey, she did so without any fear and with conviction. "We became man and wife in the forest of Dunkeldon, by the River Tay."

Lyall stared at some distant spot over Ramsey's shoulder, his brow furrowed slightly, but said nothing.

She pulled a small purse from her trouse and spilled a large, impressive pearl into her palm. "He gave me this. A bride gift for my innocence, which I gave to him gladly, my lord."

Racing like Greek fire through Ramsey's head were the eventual reactions to this news from Sutherland and Douglas and worse, the king, Himself. Completely disarmed, Ramsey understood he had failed his duty in an insurmountable way. Not only had he allowed Glenna to be captured, handed over to the enemy, locked in a tower, but wed by custom, rather than ceremony to his own stepson, certainly not the king's choice of husband for his eldest daughter.

Perhaps with enough silver the validity of the marriage could be put to test, particularly with no witnesses. "We will see what can be done with this union after the king's councils hear of it. Witnesses," he said pointedly, "are of great importance at a royal ceremony."

"'Tis binding law of the land, how we are wed" Glenna argued stubbornly.

"And I am still bound by my word to keep you safe." He held out his hand. "Come Glenna, you will ride with me."

She looked to Lyall, which annoyed Ramsey, having his orders questioned.

"Go," his stepson said to her.

"You, also, Lyall," Ramsey said coldly. "Pick one of the men with which to ride. Once I have secured Frasyr and disbursed his men, we will make for Rossi, where your mother is most likely pacing the solar floors bare." Ramsey paused, noting the uncomfortable look on Lyall's face, then he added pointedly, "Aye, lad. And Mairi is there. Your sister longs to speak with you."

TWENTY-SEVEN

Inside the hall at Kinnesswood, Alastair Gordon grabbed a couple of ale tankards from a passing server and sat down next to Glenna at a table away from the others. She was petting a scrawny-looking gray cat that had followed her inside. He shoved one tankard at Elgin and took a long swig of the other. "For someone who has just been rescued from a locked tower you look fairly glum."

"What?" Glenna asked distractedly, then smiled up at him. She touched his hand and El's. "I'm glad you are here."

"I, too," Alastair said. "Now what is wrong?"

"Is that blood on your tunic?" she asked.

He looked down at his leather tunic. It was ripped and slashed, covered with soot and dirt, splattered and stained with blood and mud. He smiled.

"Aye," Elgin said before he could answer. "Alastair, Lyall, and I used a ruse to pass through the gates. Here to sell mounts to Frasyr's sergeant. But once inside, we overpowered the gate guards and the sergeant. Al fought like the greatest of knights. He managed the guards on the east and south walls by himself." He paused. "Father would have been proud."

Those words were invaluable to Alastair, as he remembered the scrawny lad he'd been when he father spent mornings teaching him to wield a sword or mace until his shoulders ached, his arms were numb, and his ears rang with the sound of metal clanging against metal. At El's words, Alastair tried to not wear his pride too obviously and give himself away, but Glenna was never one to miss much.

He'd once had a dream, too, to be as his father had been, a knight, a man of substance and pledged to a king, with duties of a grand scale, to earn his spurs on the battlefield as had his father before him. But his promise to his father on his deathbed to care for Glenna and El made those dreams impossible. His fate had been decided and his duty was to his sister and brother. He shifted the tankard in his hand and looked at Glenna. "You have changed the subject, sister. Twice."

She sighed heavily, so he slipped a comforting arm around her. Time had not passed well, and the days without her had not gone by easily or without guilt. To have her lean on his shoulder like she had for years made him feel whole again. For so long he'd had a purpose—seeing Glenna raised and safe—and when it was done and she had gone with Robertson, his life felt hollow, and each day echoed her absence. "Tell me, goose, what is bothering you."

"Oh, Al...." She shook her head, staring into a full goblet of watered wine. "Everything...nothing...I don't know." Her voice trailed off. She glanced across the hall looking distant.

He exchanged a worried look with El, who was watching her and frowning.

"Yes, I do know!" Suddenly Glenna slammed her fist on the table top and the cat shrieked and leapt down, then moved to curl in and out of a server's legs, causing him to drop a platter before it scurried safely into the kitchens beyond.

Alastair turned back just as Glenna faced them both. "Lyall needs me. I trust him, and I believe in him. No one else does. Look!" She gestured angrily over in a corner of the hall where

Baron Montrose looked to be verbally hammering Robertson with words.

Alastair watched them for a moment. Robertson stood stoically, his profile immobile as stone and letting the baron's angry words sluice off of him, while he acted as if he cared not a whit for what he had done. He showed no emotion, no reaction. But Alastair suspected he cared deeply, and all was an act for his stepfather, a way to shield the rage coming at him and what turmoil he felt inside. 'Twas a man's way to hide his shame and anger, a technique he'd used when faced with his own father's wrath.

"He's a good man," she said.

"Aye. He saved my life," Elgin said, then told her how close he'd come to death and how Lyall's quick skill with the bow meant El was there with her again and not buried in the ground somewhere.

"He's brave," Glenna said knowingly. "And he doesn't realize it."

"He surely realizes what he'd done and how he feels about you. But I'm not certain that is a good thing," he pointed out to her.

"How can loving someone be a bad thing?"

"I somehow doubt this love is good, Glenna, and none of that matters much because you have others to answer to."

"My father?" she said. "Bah! A pox on him."

"Glenna!" Elgin hissed. "He is the king. To speak such is treason!"

"What is he going to do, hang me? Believe me when I say he will wish to hang me the moment we meet face to face, so what I say and how often I curse him does not matter one whit to me."

"You cannot change your circumstances, or your birthright," Alastair told her.

She dropped her chin into her hand and stared sourly at the tabletop, then said quietly. "I know." She glanced up and looked off at Lyall again. "Baron Montrose believes our marriage is questionable. Another reason to not be the daughter of a king," she muttered. "It seems a handfast could be declared unbinding. Royal marriages need to be witnessed."

"So you did wed him?" Elgin asked. "At Beauly, Ruari and one of the monks both claimed you were wed. I did not believe it. We thought he had forced you or was lying, but—"

She stood up suddenly. "The abbey!" She grabbed Alastair's tunic and half pulled him up off the bench. "The prior has a document. I had forgotten! They witnessed our claim as man and wife, though it was not true then, but that does not matter," she said with a wave of her hand. "What matters is there is witnessed proof." She laughed. "Writ, signed, and sealed. Oh, who now shall win this battle!" She looked up at him, a plea in her desperate expression. "You have to go. You have to get the proof, Al. I need proof so they cannot dissolve the marriage. I beg you."

The determined and anxious look in his sister's eyes was one he knew well. She would have Robertson no matter what obstacles were in her way. She was not one to give up. "You are certain this is want you want?"

"I want no other than Lyall," she said firmly, and her attention went across the hall to him again, still standing with Montrose. "I love him," she said with quiet sincerity.

"We can fetch the proof," Elgin said firmly and rose to quickly come around the table. "We must go there to check with the healer to see if—

Alastair kicked his brother in the shin before he spilled the truth.

El flinched but stopped talking. Al had already warned him not to tell Glenna they had found Fergus and taken him to the abbey, even though Glenna had told them when they reunited about losing him, about the arrow, and her heartache, and her anger at Lyall's refusal to search for him.

Would she have felt better knowing they had found him, only to be told he had later died?

Alastair had spent his life protecting his sister, and his instinct to protect her had not waned. He would not take the chance of telling her, only to make her mourn the loss of Fergus all over again. Until he knew if the dog lived or died, he did not want to tell her they had found him, particularly when the monk doubted Fergus would make it.

"Swear you will help me," she said.

He nodded. "We will ride to the abbey."

"And you will bring back the proof to the baron's keep?" Glenna said, more of an order than a question.

"Aye. We will bring you your proof."

She threw her arms about him as she used to, covering his bearded cheeks with silly kisses. "Bless you, Alastair, my dear brother. I know you will not fail me. You never have."

He kissed the top of her head and stepped back, feeling as if he were suddenly taller, and still her brother. "Come El, we must help prove our sister is wed to that horse's ass."

"Alastair!" she said, but she was laughing.

"The horse's ass with whom you fought side by side?" Elgin said.

"Aye."

"The horse's ass who saved my life and that of our sister's?" Elgin grinned.

"Aye. The horse's ass who started this whole thing." Alastair clapped his arm around El's shoulders as they left together.

And Glenna's quiet voice carried back to them. "Remember, that horse's ass is your brother. He should fit in well."

The inn where they had put up for the night was too small for the contingent of Ramsey troops now escorting them back to Rossi. Lyall lay on a straw pallet on the floor of the taproom, surrounded by sleeping men. His stepfather was taking no chance of losing Glenna.

Whilst still at Kinnesswood, Ramsey had called in more of his men from other nearby positions. Soon after, they left Frasyr and his keep under guard by two of Ramsey's most trusted knights and their retainer troops, amounting to enough men to hold off a siege on a land-locked castle, much less Kinnesswood with its lake-midst position. Even Argyll would not dare try to free his cousin.

The night felt long and Lyall folded his hands behind his head and stared up at the dark roof beams, listening to snoring men. He caught a movement from the corner of his eye and raised up slightly to look. The guards stood quietly posted at the door. One leaned against the jamb and the other shifted his weight from one foot to the other, but their eyes remained sharp.

He lay back down. There would be more men outside. His stepfather was thorough. Others stood at watch by the kitchens, and the stairs leading up to the rooms where Glenna was safely sequestered, and where his stepfather holed up for the night, likely dreaming of vile punishments for him. The rage between them and their words haunted his thoughts.

"Sweet Mother Mary and Joseph!" Ramsey had raged. "She is ruined! Even if we can find a way to annul this union, you have ruined her. What have you done? Where was your head, man? She is the daughter of a king!"

"And I am the son of a traitor."

"I did not say that."

"You didn't have to." Lyall knew what he was.

His stepfather's piercing look was almost more than he could bear, knowing Ramsey, his mentor and more, was a man of honor and his word was his life, something Lyall had almost believed in, back in halcyon days of naïve youth when he thought it was possible to live down his name. "I rode ahead of you by days,"

Lyall answered without emotion. "And I convinced Glenna and her brothers I was you and there on your mission. 'Twas simple to take your weapons from the armory, one of your shields, the message and proof of the king's demand sent you by Sutherland."

"I know what you did. But I would know why," he'd paused and his spoke with less rancor. "I cannot believe it was only for Dunkeldon. Tell me, son."

But Lyall knew he was not Ramsey's son. The name of Ramsey carried no shame. He could barely remain standing from the monstrous wave of bitterness that came over him, battling with the shame he carried in the black cold impregnable place where hope had once, long, long ago, lived and breathed within him. Long moments passed as his stepfather waited. "What does it matter?" Lyall said coldly. "Neither of us can change what I have done."

"I do not like your tone."

I cannot speak and still hide what I feel. So he stood before his stepfather, stonily quiet, refusing to speak again because there was nothing he could say, and speaking from his heart was not an option. He had no defense to make.

Even now, in the middle of the night as he lay in thought amidst the Ramsey men, words and reason escaped him, even sleep alluded him. He stared overhead. The coals in the waning fire beyond turned everything red as if limned by hell. Nearby, a man sighed and shifted, and another snorted and mumbled a curse before he quieted. The fire snapped and popped...a log fell. Again something flashed in his periphery, and he looked the side window, where Glenna's head suddenly popped into view for barely a heartbeat before it disappeared.

What was she about? How did she get outside?

He was on his feet and feigned stumbling drunkenly over to door. Bracing a hand on the wall, his head down, he growled, "I have to piss."

The guard let him pass, and a few steps away he found her waving him over as she huddled behind some barrels beneath the window. He squatted down. "What are you doing?" he hissed. "How did you get out of that room."

"Quiet! Not here." She grabbed his hand and pulled him down at the sound of voices from beyond and behind the inn.

She was mad as he was.

They huddled together behind the large barrels, bodies close and still, her breast resting softly against his wrist, their breathing so shallow it was like holding a breath. Some of Ramsey's trusted guards crossed the path near the inn's back kitchen, their boots crunching on the rock, their voices muted, until one of them laughed quietly.

Glenna was still as a rock. His heart pounded in his ears. The men circled past the barrels to the front of the inn, and stopped at the corner to talk. He knew there were men sleeping outside, and others in the stables. *How foolish was this!*

In time, a hundred heartbeats, a thousand? The men disappeared.

"Quickly," she whispered and stood, forcing him to follow her to the east side of the kitchen shed, where she shoved him through a door and down into a cold room dug into the ground. The scent of brined meat, dairy and onions filled his nose, and the temperature dropped to that of a mid-winter day. She closed the door behind him and threw her arms around his neck. "Kiss me," she said.

He grabbed her wrists firmly and pulled her arms from around his neck, setting her back from him. "We are surrounded by guards."

She grinned and bit her lower lip, then admitted with a wicked gleam in her eye, "I know. Makes the idea of what we are about to do all the more keen, does it not?"

His head filled with the image of them swivving against the

wall whilst guards walked by, stood at doors unknowingly, and slept soundly overhead.

Lyall groaned her name.

"Do not make the grand risk I have taken all for naught. Kiss me, Lyall. I want you to kiss me."

He came back to reality, took a long breath and said evenly, "First I will have an answer from you. How did you get out?"

"Maggie," she paused. When his mouth had barely formed the word who, she added, "The maid. I told her the horrid, long and trying tale of how we were being kept apart by our cruel, cruel fathers. She was terribly sympathetic."

He shook his head and could only imagine her vivid words of their great and troubled romantic history. "I imagine with your glib tongue she was sympathetic." Most likely whipped up into a state of tears, he thought.

"She showed me a hidden staircase from my room down to just above here." She pointed to the dirt ceiling. "Now I would kiss you with this glib tongue."

"Glenna...."

She slid her hands flat against his chest and rubbed him, murmuring his name.

Looking down at her was his perdition, for she looked up at him dreamily, still innocent yet seductress. Her heart was clearly his and she understood her power—he had taught her well. She was all dark eyes that sparkled and beckoned as did the stars over the River Tay, lashes long, with black tips like marten fur, lips moist and dark and sweet as the flesh of a ripe plum at summer's end. There was nothing in the world he wanted more...and he wondered at the God whose hand ruled the fates of men.

A strong and honorable man would have had a hard time turning away from her when she begged for exactly what he wanted...and more, when she offered herself to him so readily, so easily. Could something he desired in his treacherous and stormy life truly be his so simply?

Her body was against him, all softness and woman, so different from his, the fullness of her breasts in his hands, the tightness of the small tips when he ran his thumbs over her, her palms flat on his chest, and so hot was her touch he had the insane thought he could feel Eve's temptation in the outline of her fingers.

He slid his hands down to press flatly against the softness of her bottom, to bring her against him. His mouth and tongue ravaged hers and he walked her back, pinned her to the wall and held her up with his thigh between her legs. Their hands moved over each other. Sweat began beading on his brow and down his back despite the temperature in the cold room. He was on fire for her, burning hotly from the inside out.

"Take me, Lyall, take me and we will truly be wed. My oath before, sworn to the baron that we had been lovers at Dunkeldon will no longer be a lie."

From somewhere far away he caught her words, and their meaning. His stepfather's accusation came charging back to him clearly and as if he were there shouting into Lyall's ear. *You have ruined her!* The thought was like being doused with a bucket of melted snow. He pulled away, trying to gain some sense of control. The air he needed had disappeared and he panted, searching for the breath he needed to cool him down, another dousing. His body throbbed from his cock to his head.

"Lyall?"

He held up a hand to warn her, the other clutched into a tight fist and the urge to pound the wall hit him hard. The ability to speak escaped him. He did not move. He couldn't look at her. Somehow he would do this. "Leave."

"Nay. I will not."

"I said leave!" he hissed in barely controlled anger, facing her.

She did not back away, but she was shaken.

"Go," he said in a low rasp and pushed her toward the door. "Go! Get out! I swear on all that is holy in this world, Glenna, I will call out to the guards if you do not leave now."

She shook her head.

He picked her up and she fought him, silently, but kicking and pounding him with her fists. She connected with his eye as he shoved her out and closed the door, leaning against it as he felt her hit it with her fist. Through the door she spat his name as if it were a vile curse, then wished him an eternity in hell.

He was already there. His back blocking the door, he stayed that way, breathing hard, head thrown back, eyes tightly closed, his teeth clenched and his hands shaking. He fought her; he fought himself; he struggled, while the last flicker of hope—that his life was not lost—died inside of him.

TWENTY-EIGHT

The shadows were lengthening as they rode over the crest topping another hill, and past the lush forests to a point where Baron Ramsey reined in. Glenna had not seen Lyall since that morning at the inn, when he chose his position at the rear of troop. Their eyes met once, enough for her to see what she knew—that he was far from through with her, and she was even farther from through with him. The baron had been kind to her, and she knew he had not missed nor was unhappy about the distance Lyall had put between them.

As they stopped, one of the knight's palfreys nipped Skye and reared, almost throwing the man from its back, and loud curses flew through the air. The men closed ranks about her as Skye sidestepped uneasily, forcing Glenna to quickly control her or be thrown. But she knew horses well, having been in the saddle since she was three, and she knew Skye more so. When the elegantly bred mare calmed down with little trouble, some of the men murmured appreciatively. Glenna settled into the saddle with the sound of creaking leather, and the baron leaned over and nodded to the valley below. "There is our destination."

She followed his gaze and experienced her first sight of Castle Rossi. Her breath caught at the immense impression it made, and the reality of it frightened her to death.

Built in an opulent and fertile valley and spreading out in the wingspan of a great walled city, the seat of power for the barony of Montrose was a massive stone structure with towers at each corner, and thick outer walls which were turning pink from the setting sun. The nearby river was wide and turbulent in places; it snaked along the castle's southernmost edge, gleaming eel-like and silver, winding its way through rich farms dotting the eastern plains and out into the deep, blue waters of the great firth beyond.

As the contingent rode down into the glen, the walls of Rossi loomed closer, and Glenna's fears grew. She sat rigidly stiff, her eyes straight ahead while mad thoughts and images flew through her head. Lyall's mother and sister were inside the keep. They would be the first women of the new life she would be forced to face.

You have sisters.

There was the true curse: more women she would have to face. She closed her eyes and white-knuckled the reins. She could not bear to think of her unknown sisters, women of the same blood who never existed in her world before, and to imagine who they were and how they would view her was enough to make her run away with her hair on fire. She had been raised with men. Sisters were as foreign to her as was a father who was king.

But now, ahead of her, she must confront the two most important women in Lyall's life. And they would judge her. That's what strangers did. They would have expectations, and would take one look at her and form their opinions.

The sunlight was waning fast and night descending, but not quickly enough or dark enough to hide who she was.

The women inside that keep would stand there in their beautiful gowns, their hair coiffed and hands soft and uncallused, pale, with their practiced ways and natural status, and look down their noble noses at the sight of her and her tangled hair, worker's hands, and peasant clothing.

The cold meat and bread she had eaten earlier now roiled in her belly, making her want to retch into the bushes, but she pressed a hand beneath her ribs and sought some kind of courage. Her pride was her only asset, and her shield against the expectations she was certain she would face...and would surely fail to meet.

Surrounded by more than two hundred men and the Baron Montrose, she rode up to the perimeter of the castle feeling completely alone. A call came from the guard above the gatehouse and the heavy portcullis rose like an iron smile to the sounds of chains and cranks, and the hollow clatter of horses' hooves on the drawbridge. They rode into the outer bailey, past Rossi's villeins who watched or stood poised at the edge of a garden with hoe in hand and eyes on her, while others rushed out from their huts to wave at the baron on his great horse, riding with pennants flying at his side, and the strange woman with him. She sat even more stiffly, trying not to show her fears and weakness to all and sundry.

Inside the walls was like a village, complete with smithies working the bellows and hammering out red-hot iron, and outbuildings sheltering workers, animal pens with sheep and pigs, a dovecote, and huge stone wells where water was drawn or cooked and stirred in giant vats of laundry, the linens hanging from ropes that crisscrossed from heavy posts in the ground.

Glenna could still feel the curious gazes of the baron's people watch her as they rode past and through another thick wall to the inner ward, where many of the knights were greeted happily by their women and children. Behind the families, there were household quarters along the walls and an enviable stable large enough to house all the men's horses and more, filled with working farriers and grooms, and the troop reined in before the massive keep. There was a flurry of squires who came rushing out from the yard and milled around the chaos of dismounting men, taking reins and orders from the Montrose knights.

Her breathing froze in her chest and her hands gripped the reins in the busyness and blur of their arrival. As if he had appeared out of thin air, Lyall was at her side, and that surprised her, since it had been the one place he had avoided all day. He seemed to fill the space, so tall and golden, the last glow of the setting sun behind him and casting his face in shadows and angles. She blinked and looked at him, his face unreadable as he stood next to Skye, his arms reaching up to help her down from the saddle.

The words 'why now?' were on the tip of the tongue, but a sound pulled her attention away to the enormous doors of the keep, which opened slowly. *Oh, lud!* She closed her eyes. The women….

A strange roar sounded in her ears, like nothing she had ever heard, and her blood seemed to grow warm, too warm. Her vision changed suddenly and grew foggy. As if her bones had melted, she slipped from the saddle and felt Lyall's strong arms catch her, then heard the worried tone of his voice when he said her name, but it sounded as if it came echoing out from a cave, then the whole world went black.

To the sound of his stepfather's shouts, Lyall ran through the open doors of the great hall with Glenna unconscious in his arms, and almost trampled over his sister. "Mairi!"

"This is the king's daughter?" Mairi whispered in a rush of worried words. "My Lord in Heaven, Lyall, what have you done to her?"

A hundred answers came to his lips, none of them good. "Everything," he said quietly.

But his sister must not have heard him because she pulled on his arm and said, "Come quickly."

He followed her up the stairs and into her chamber as she called for her maid.

"Lay her down...gently. Aida! There you are. Send someone to fetch some watered wine and my herb bag is over there in the chest. The lemons, aye, bring some of the lemons my lord just received from Amalfi." She stood in the center of the room, frowning. "Let me think...."

Lyall straightened, staring blankly at Glenna's pale skin, feeling uncomfortable and unable to think clearly. He heard his sisters words but he cared not what she was saying. He sank to his knees by the bed and touched Glenna's face with his hand. Her skin was clammy and cool.

A water-filler laver cradled in her arm, Mairi edged him aside, but he took the damp towel from her hand and stepped in front of her. "I will do it."

"You should leave."

"Perhaps I should, but I will not. Glenna? Sweetheart?" He used the towel to wipe her brow and face.

"What happened? Lord, Lyall, what else have you done to her?"

He froze, aware his sister was angry and she blamed him. Her beliefs were well-founded. "She swooned. I merely had the foresight to be standing there to catch her." He eyed Mairi's sweaty hair, pulled from its braid and hanging around her flushed face, and the old woolen peasant gown with the patched sleeves and covered with a stained leather apron. "Perhaps the prospect of meeting you frightened her,"

Mairi swiped at her brow self-consciously. "I was making candles, Lyall Robertson! More like the prospect of being handed over so freely to the likes of Huchon de Hay. And do not be so thick-headed!" She lowered her voice and hissed, "How could you kidnap the king's daughter?"

"She didn't know she was kidnapped," he said flippantly.

"She thought I was taking her to her father. Ouch! The Devil's blood! You have boney knuckles."

"Knuckles? I should clobber you on the noggin with a flail, crack it open and hope some good sense might fly in. You gave her to *de Hay*?"

"And your old swain Colin Frasyr."

"Do not, Lyall. I cared not a whit for Frasyr and you well know it. And he has a blood bond with his cousin so that he was involved is not a surprise. I doubt he would harm any woman, but de Hay? He is cruel. Why did you do it? Tell me why?"

"You are a woman. You cannot understand what was at stake."

"What I cannot understand is stupidity. You imagine yourself part of some brotherhood misunderstood by mere women whose minds are frittered away on such things as velvet and pearls."

Lyall did not respond.

"I cannot understand? That is what you men say when you do something we women know is harebrained. Do not tell me I cannot understand. My husband was the king's own diplomat. You think we did not speak of things? You think he did not value my thoughts? My opinions? You are a fool, brother. And I understand all too clearly that you have no excuse for what you have done."

"Dunkeldon—"

"Curse Dunkeldon! Curse it to hell and back! Curse it to the hell it has taken you to, Lyall Robertson. We walked away all those years ago and still you cannot leave it behind you. You are my brother and I love you, but you have made a grave mistake, out of guilt you should not feel, for events out of your control, and the foolhardy idea that Dunkeldon is more than just a burnt old ruin—one that has ruined you! It has." She looked away from his and shook her head in disgust and frustration.

When she looked up again, she placed a hand on his arm. "Do

you not see? This is not a mere sport, some lark. 'Tis not a mistaken marriage, the lure of bonding yourself to the man who held our father's lands or a marriage to some poor lass far from willing. Dunkeldon has driven you too far this time. It has driven you toward treason. You gave the king's daughter to his enemies. You could lose your knighthood. Your name could be listed, Lyall. You could be imprisoned, or hanged." There were tears in her voice when she said, "Did you learn nothing from what happened to our father?"

"How could I forget? I bear his name...you do not. You married Robert. Mother wed Ramsey. I—" he tapped his chest angrily, "I alone carry his name, and his shame."

"Mama! Mama!" The boys came running in.

"You lads be quiet. What are you doing here? Oh, where is their nurse?" Mairi ran toward the chamber door and called to their maid.

The nephews spotted him and shouted his name louder than Norman tourney caller, and suddenly he had boys all over him.

"Mama? Is that the great lady?" The child's voice came from far away.

Where am I? Glenna's head was foggy.

"Aye, Duncan." The woman who answered did so kindly, her tone soft and lilting.

"What is her name?"

"Lady Glenna."

"Why is she on the bed?" Another child asked, his voice higher and with a slight lisp of a child still learning to sound out his words.

"She's dead, Gregor!" Yet another piped in with a wicked, teasing tone, before he lowered his voice ominously and said,

"She was poisoned by the vile, dark witch who lives in the forest and eats foolish lads with red hair and spots after she boils them in oil."

"No witches are in the forest. You lie!" But poor Gregor's voice sounded doubtful and as if he were going to cry.

"Why won't she wake up?" Duncan asked.

"She will."

Lyall?

A small finger slid open her eyelid, and startled, she was suddenly staring a small lad with bright red hair and no front teeth. "Hallo." His freckled face squinted at her and he removed his finger from her eyelid. "Are you dead, my lady?"

Glenna opened both her eyes.

"Mama! She's awake," he shouted. "The Lady Glenna, is awake!"

"Glenna!" Lyall was suddenly kneeling by the bed, her hand in his. His face was covered in road dust, caked along his lips and jaw, and his hair was stuck to his head from his helm. But there he was, so close, looking contrite and overly concerned, his brow furrowed and his eyes red with road dust and moisture.

Was this the same man who shoved her away last night, who ignored her all day?

He reached out to lovingly take the cloth from her brow and her hand shot up and gripped his wrist hard. He looked at her hand and frowned.

She took the wet towel and whacked him with it.

"Oh! Did you see, Mama? She hit Uncle Lyall!" The oldest lad was pointing at her and jumping up and down.

"She will not have sweets for a whole day," Duncan said seriously.

The children's nurse came into the room, looking harried and out of sorts. "I'm sorry, milady. They escaped. Come along, lads. You were not supposed to leave the kitchens." The woman shooed them toward the door. "Now be off with you. Hurry."

The children's voices waned as they ran down the hallway, and room was suddenly silent. Lyall looked at Glenna and said, "What was that for?"

" I shall tell you. Gladly. I wake to you kneeling by my side? This is far cry from the tail end of the contingent, is it not? All day you avoided me." She lowered her voice and said, "I hope you ate enough dust to choke on. Now suddenly you choose to be near my side and all concerned?" She gave a sharp laugh. "You are an ass, Lyall."

"You make no sense woman. You do not get angry…you do not hold me accountable when I turned you over to your father's enemies, when you are locked in a tower—"

"She was locked in a tower?" The young woman standing behind him interrupted, only a voice behind Lyall's big, broad-shouldered body.

Glenna tried to lean enough to see her but could not.

"Aye," Lyall said quickly, "which did not affect you, apparently. Yet here you glare at me and beat me with a towel for not riding by your side?"

"Nay…" Glenna sat up on an elbow and spat, "For last night!" She flogged him with the towel twice more, but the third time he grabbed it mid-air and jerked it from her hand.

"Perhaps that is why I chose to ride in the rear position…my lady," he said sardonically and stood up, calmly dropping the towel in the laver by the bed.

"Coward," she said with barely controlled contempt.

"Exactly." Lyall gave her a forced and icy smile that held no humor. "I have never claimed to be anything but." And with that, he bowed stiffly and strode from the room.

TWENTY-NINE

Run away. Walk out! I do not care! Glenna glared at the wide open door, then realized her hands were in fists and she relaxed. She looked down, surrounded by lush furs and thin fine sheeting on a huge soft bed, candlelight everywhere from over a hundred candles in the room. Then she remembered she wasn't alone. Also left in the midst of the opulent and massive chamber was another woman. Lyall's sister?

They exchanged an odd look of surprise, suddenly alone together, strangers, then the young woman burst out laughing. "Oh, what a dear you are!"

She had the most lovely colored red-gold hair, not Lyall's gold, but redder, like the rare, pinkish-gold hammered wristbands from Byzantine Glenna had seen in a seller's stall once and could not bear to steal. But those strands of that hair fell all about her face and shoulders, not unlike her own wind-tumbled mop.

Where was the velvet gown? Where were the jewels? Where was the smug look Glenna had expected? Except for her clear skin and soft, noble features, Lyall's sister looked like a chorewife at the end of a long, hard day. Glenna was shocked silent.

Still laughing, Mairi said, "I have wanted to hit my brother with more than a wet towel!"

"Aye, you poor thing. Truly." Glenna looked at the door, then shook her head. "I have been stuck with him for mere days, yet I cannot imagine the trial you had growing up with him."

"Oh!" Mairi gasped, then in a laugh she snorted like a pig and put her hands to her face, which was bright red. Her giggles and embarrassment were infectious, and Glenna laughed, too, completely taken aback and loving Mairi's open and blunt manner. No coy noblewoman here.

The young woman closed the distance between them and gave a slight curtsey—an odd and uncomfortable gesture for Glenna to receive—holding her stained , dark leather apron and rough, worn, woolen gray gown with the torn sleeve and spotted with bits of hardened wax and splatters of oil. "Lady Glenna, I am Mairi Grey, Lyall's sister and widow of my dear lord Robert Grey, and mother to those rascal lads who were bothering you."

"They did not bother me, Lady Mairi."

Mairi shook her head. "Listen to us. We are not at court." Mairi grabbed her hands and to her surprise and relief, Glenna felt as many calluses as she had on her own palms. "We are to be friends, I think, Glenna."

"Moreso. Sisters," Glenna admitted quietly.

"Sisters?" Mairi frowned, then her eyes grew large. "Lyall and you?"

Glenna nodded.

"Oh, Mother Mary and Joseph!"

Glenna winced a little, suddenly having second thoughts about spilling the truth—the lie?—so soon.

"You cannot be wed."

"Aye." The more people who knew, Glenna decided, the more she told, the more tight the knot would be around them and harder for Lyall to back away from her, and perhaps, the more difficult 'twould be for her father or his councilors to dissolve the marriage. She had no choice but to fight for Lyall, though she was not pleased with him at that moment and he still was not convinced how badly he needed her. Hardheaded, beautiful, stubborn man.

"But you are royalty."

"So they tell me." Glenna frowned and looked down at her pitiful clothing, then shrugged. "I look nothing like one."

"Oh, you need not worry," Mairi waved a hand casually in the air and if the news were nothing. "I have gowns for you, bolts of fabric, and more."

Gowns? Glenna's heart caught slightly. *Gowns?*

"My mother and I, along with some of the other women, have been stitching our days and nights away, but later with all that."

"What kind of gowns?" Glenna whispered, almost afraid to believe the words she'd heard, afraid to ask, and thinking of her precious green velvet, far too big and that hung from her shoulders down to its ragged, knife-chopped hem, rolled up tightly in her satchel with her too-large red leather boots. Could she have two gowns, maybe three? What if one of them were silk? She could barely breathe at the thought.

Mairi must not have heard her because she continued pacing on the thick carpet in the center of the room, then she stopped and said, "How can you be wed? Any marriage you make must be made with the king's approval and witnessed."

"We spoke vows to each other."

"You handfasted? Lyall should be flogged with more than a towel. It matters not. You needn't worry. A handfast cannot be binding. You are not a crofter or freeman. You are a Canmore. Any declaration of man and wife surely must be witnessed for legitimacy."

Glenna started to tell her there was a witnessed document, but bit her tongue. She had best keep the proof to herself for now.

Mairi faced her, frowning. "I cannot believe Lyall is caught up in another complicated union."

At first Glenna was deeply hurt, then she said, "Another?"

"Aye. He did not tell you about Isobel?"

Glenna shook her head. "He did say to me once that his wife was dead."

Mairi came and sat on the bed next to her and her expression grew serious, "It was a terrible, terrible time, and a poor match, but Lyall was on his grand quest for Dunkeldon. Do you know about Dunkeldon?"

"I was there, but I did not know its significance. I found your brother standing at the graves of your father and brother. I had to prod to find out that much. He would not speak of it, and I did not push because of the deep pain he carried in his eyes when he was there."

Mairi nodded. "That is another story for another night. 'Tis enough to know our father was declared a traitor days after his death and Dunkeldon burned to the ground. Our older brother died that day and our mother was left scarred from the burns she suffered. The lands were taken. We were very young. It was many years later that Lyall approached Huchon de Hay, whose only daughter Isobel's dower lands included Dunkeldon, the very land our family had lost. Our stepfather tried to talk some sense into Lyall but he would have none of it. His decision was made so the family stood by him.

"Isobel de Hay was raised in a convent, sheltered, and not the right match for my brother. She was as fragile as spun sugar, and about as sensible," Mairi added in a wry afterthought. "I believe she always thought she would become one of the sisters and wed her God, but her father never would have allowed it. She was too valuable to barter. The blood bond through Lyall to the Ramseys and the barony of Montrose, our stepfather and close friend and council to the king, was all too tempting for de Hay."

A daughter's barter value. There was something Glenna understood and she experienced a moment of deep sympathy for Isobel de Hay.

"Isobel was naïve, and after they were betrothed, she was exposed to gossip and lies and manipulations of others with hard hearts and jealousies. My brother had been very successful on the tourney circuit. He had grown rich as Croesus from his prizes and purses, was acquiring the respect for the Robertson name—he wanted so badly to vanquish all that had tarnished our name—and most expected that at some point, our stepfather would make him his heir to the barony.

But Lyall often kept to himself. There were not many he trusted, my husband, and at one time, another seasoned knight I only met a few times, Sir Ellar of Herth. So often he was without close friends to stand by his side, and that time of the wedding was no different. Isobel was a twit who listened to gossip. The night before their wedding ceremony, when the de Hay castle was filled with wedding guests, she wailed and pleaded with her father that he had betrayed her, that he had shamed her because he gave her to the son of a traitor. Lyall heard her. We all heard her."

Glenna closed her eyes. She could only imagine what that had done to him.

"The wailing was horrid. I wanted to gag her. The next morning they wed but soon afterward, while the celebrations were going on, she snuck away. Lyall was the one who found her body at the base of the tower, dead, broken." A haunted look came over Mairi's expressive face and she was pale. "I have only seen that look on my brother's face one other time, and I was so young. That was how my brother had looked when he buried Malcolm and we left Dunkeldon."

Glenna wanted to know what happened to them, but she could see the telling of his story was painful enough for Lyall's sister.

"By law, the dower lands stayed with de Hay because they had not yet consummated the marriage."

"The betrothal was not binding enough?" Glenna asked.

"Not for the dower lands. The betrothal was the promise of the contract, but the wedding itself and the act of the marriage bed secures the deed. Lyall was left more broken than that poor, sad, young woman. Not because he had lost the lands, but what her words did to his pride. He blamed himself for her death and said had he treated her more kindly, she might not have chosen falling to her death over being wed to him. What she did to him." Mairi shook her head. "She broke his desire to even try to reclaim honor for his name, then finding her body seemed to break something else.

"In what way? He changed?"

Mairi nodded. "He put up a wall that none of us could break through. He had been close with Donnald, the baron, who has been a good father to us both. But Lyall blocked him out. He ran wild and drank and disappeared for days at a time. Finally, he came back one day, looking like he'd been to hell and back, and he let his squires and other men-at-arms go, found them positions with other houses, and other knights, and he struck out alone and none of us could stop him. As far as I know, he never again joined another tourney."

"Where did he go?"

Mairi frowned and shrugged. "I saw him only a few times before last year. He came back when we lost my dear Robert—he and Lyall were close and had served together as pages, then squires for my stepfather. After Robert died, Lyall stayed at Greystone Manor with us. I believe he and my stepfather thought it best the boys and I were not without family close. My sons adore him, and I think after some time, they were good for him. There were days when I thought perhaps he might be coming back into himself again, but then de Hay contacted him."

Glenna was as quiet as Mairi as she applied the knowledge to Lyall and his manner and actions. My Lord, what had he thought when he came rushing into the tower at Kinnesswood as she jumped?

The door opened and a young, fresh-faced maid came in. "Milady?"

"Aida. Oh, I had forgotten."

"The bath you ordered is ready, milady."

"And becoming cold whilst I stand in here yammering?" Mairi gave her maid a wry smile. "We will be right there. Forgive me, Glenna. I forgot myself. You must long for some comforts."

Glenna thought the soft bed and furs she was sitting on was the finest comfort she'd ever experienced.

"There is a meal waiting for you and a bath. In your chamber." Mairi extended an arm. "Come. We will see to your needs."

Glenna followed her, pensive, but no longer tentative, and wondering if she could be so very wrong about the people in her future.

Nights were cooling off and the sun setting earlier, signs of autumn and the changing of all things about them was edging out summer. Owls flew across the sky, landing on trees near the river, calling to the moon. But within the walls, noisy frogs had left the water ponds in the last weeks, making the air in the baileys quiet and peaceful but for the hum of insects. The air was brisk enough to make the ground cold and wet early in the morn, to turn the grass in the meadows silver with dawn dew. The time of year to think about what had passed and what was coming. A time for changing with the season.

There was slight wind when Ramsey opened the thick oaken door to the eastern wall and found his stepson leaning against the stonework with his elbows resting on a parapet, hands relaxed, face reflected in the moonlight as he stared out at the countryside.

Only if he could get inside his stepson's head and his thoughts. Perhaps he could understand the demons driving him to commit the worse of mistakes and pretend he did not care. Lyall was not that shallow. The lad had not been, and the man could not be, though at that moment he was still angry and disgusted enough and ready to beat some sense into Lyall.

Ramsey closed the door and walked along the wall. "I have been looking for you."

"And I have been avoiding you." Lyall turned away from the parapet and faced him, that cocksure attitude in every nuance of his body.

It angered him, how Lyall would go out of his way to not let anyone help him, to not change but continue on some bitter, self-destructive path to a hell of his own making. Ramsey believed life served up its disappointments. How one dealt with them proved the measure of the man. "You are a thick-skulled son of a bitch," Ramsey said, aware of the sunken, angry depths to which their conversations had come.

"You think so little of my mother?" Lyall quipped.

"Nay, I think so little of her son."

His cruel words hit their mark. Lyall chewed his lip and his jaw tightened. Ramsey regretted saying them the moment they came from his mouth. Yet nothing moved his stepson. So their conversations were insults and anger, barbs and truths hidden behind sardonic comments meant to stop the talk between them.

"I am sorry for that. It is not true. My anger speaks before my head can." Ramsey sighed and ran a hand over his face. "I am weary of this hostility between us, Lyall. I want to understand you. You stop me at every turn. Where is the lad who pestered me senseless, the one who was determined to prove his worth and his honor?"

"Buried under a yellow cloak of dishonor. Ironic is it not? I am held fast amidst the black muck of disloyalty by the family name: traitor. Bad blood breeds bad blood."

"You will let the words of a young woman with no knowledge or life outside a nunnery define who you are?"

"Life has its lessons. There is the truth of what people think, but don't say. That is what follows me and my name. The name of Robertson is like carrying manure on your boot, except it does not wash off."

"I have never believed that," Ramsey said and tapped his fist against his heart. "You are still here, son. Despite all that you do otherwise, I believe in your good soul. Would that you were not so determined to prove me wrong." Ramsey paused, then added, "But that is not why I have come."

"Why then? To tell me why I cannot be wed to the fair Canmore first born?"

"I suppose there is that, too. But I desire information. I want to know how you knew I was ordered to escort and protect Glenna."

Lyall straightened, frowning, clearly surprised by the question. His expression changed from sardonic to serious, signaling he was willing to talk straight. "De Hay told me. He knew of the orders and papers and letters. He knew about her, where she was. I knew nothing of it or her existence until he summoned me."

Ramsey was afraid of that. He began to pace and took a long breath. "Then there is a traitor among us. A spy for those tied with de Hay to Somerled, someone with close access to information, even the most secret communications between Sutherland and myself. The existence of the king's daughters was kept between only three of us and those trusted with protecting them for years. But now the truth suddenly comes out after so many years. Something reeks."

"What of the other two?" Lyall asked. "Her sisters. You think they are in danger? De Hay was the one who told me Glenna was not the only daughter. He seemed to have plenty of information."

"One is Sutherland's own ward, and I am certain she is safe. The other is in a convent. Both have protectors. But we thought we were working without suspect, and to have the knowledge of their existence in the hands of the king's enemies..." Ramsey shook his head. "Who knows what is happening as we speak. I have sent word to Sutherland, but I fear we might be too late, that other plans are in motion." Ramsey paused again and looked at Lyall. "In a perfect world, I would have wished that you would have come to me after de Hay summoned you."

Lyall was silent, staring at his hand.

"We could have worked together to fool them into thinking you were working with them and still have kept Glenna safe. But then 'twas all for Dunkeldon."

"At first. Now the land does not seem so important. That has surprised me." Lyall gave a short laugh. "I have writ to the lands and I no longer care."

Ah! There was the sad truth of it. "That is often the way of things, son." What he saw in Lyall could only make for more pain, pain Ramsey had known for all too many years to count. "She is the daughter of the king. Far from your reach, Lyall."

His stepson said nothing.

"Do you love her?"

"Aye."

"Then make the sacrifice and stay away from her. No good can come from this, no matter what has already passed between you."

"She is not defiled. She lied," Lyall admitted.

Ramsey was relieved and surprised, but he masked it, still acutely aware of what that cost Lyall to admit, and it gave him hope that the man was not lost. "You need to keep her that way. She is not yours for the taking, no matter where you believe your heart is. Whom she weds is her father's choice. And he is my liege and I will protect his right and his daughter, even if from my own stepson."

They exchanged a long look, not unlike two hounds, each sizing up the other. Lyall gave him a quick nod.

"Were she anyone else, I would be happy for you," Ramsey told him.

"Were she anyone else, there would be no reason to be happy." Lyall did not look at him, but continued to stare out at something or nothing.

"Come, lad. Your mother has ordered a meal for us."

"I need more air. 'Tis quiet here." He gave a sharp laugh. "I had thought this spot was one where I would not have to answer for my actions."

"We always have to answer for our actions, son. Our choices in life can help us or haunt us."

"Or haunt those left behind," Lyall said pointedly. "Go. I will be down shortly."

Ramsey nodded and crossed the wall walk, but he paused at the door and looked back at Lyall, and he saw not his stepson, but the tall, golden ghost of his closest friend.

"This is your chamber while you stay here," Mairi said as Glenna followed her inside, then stood with her back pressed against the door.

"Glenna?"

"Like it? Lud!" She laughed and faced Mairi. "'Tis a far cry from two room cottage with a grass roof, built into the side of a hill on the outermost edges of a remote island."

Giant timber beams crossed the high ceilings, and in the room's center, a circular iron candelabrum as wide as a trestle table well hung down from heavy chains bolted into the beams.

Near a stone hearth that climbed clear upward to the roof, stood a large wooden tub filled with water, and a stool nearby held a bowl of small round soaps with flower petals in them, rare lemon citron with a long iron file, and a stack of towels folded while others warmed from a wooden rack set in front of the fire.

"The servants will bring more hot water for your bath, but there is food here."

The table in a corner near the windows was laden with a feast large enough for five of her. She bit into a hard, sweet apple and her belly rumbled loud enough to make Mairi giggle and say, "Look at the sweets, honeyed figs, candied plums, and these spiral wheels are Catherine cakes, made with currants, almonds, cinnamon and caraway. Cook has unlocked the spice coffers in your honor." She plucked up one and popped it in her mouth, humming as she chewed, and exchanging a gleeful look with Glenna, who tore off a piece of crusty bread swiped it over the butter, and dipped it in dark red jam. She was in heaven!

Mairi grabbed two more honeyed figs and crossed the room, moving past a large bed, where Glenna's gaze stopped and the bread fell from her fingers.

On the bed was a gown made of the most glorious deep crimson velvet like that of her infant coverlet, but the gown had an embroidered silk panel of vines and roses made of silver thread, and the neck was trimmed in white snowy fur, as were the long sleeves. She walked over to it and touched the silken fabric, then stroked the fur, unable to believe what she saw before her eyes.

"We finished it yesterday," Mairi said with pride in her voice. "It is the gown for a king's daughter, the ermine fur, the fine silk velvet, and it is yours."

Glenna lifted the gown and held it up to her body, moving and watching the skirt dance with her. The hem was perfect. The gown was hers!

"Behind this curtain is your clothing rod, and there hang the gowns we have made so far, and the cloak, but you will need more. I particularly like the deep blue. My mother chose the fabric and her handmaiden who is the finest seamstress in a hundred leagues did the embroidery on the sleeve edges. But the green is lovely, too. Your shoes are in that chest along the wall, my favorite are the green embroidered slippers with the satin ribbands but you can certainly decide your favorites. There are a dozen or more to choose from, and the cobbler is still at work. Your sleep gowns and chemises are here. The silks are so wonderful to sleep in. I stitched the red birds along—" She turned around and stopped abruptly. "Glenna? What is wrong?"

Glenna was no longer standing. She sat cross-legged on the carpet, clutching the red velvet gown to her, the ermine against her neck felt as soft as the breath of angels, and she broke down sobbing, loud throat-catching sobbing. She pointed to things in the room but sobbed nothing coherent.

She could not speak the words. After her grand fears and doubts, to stand in a room so big one could fit inside the whole cottage in which she grew up, to see the fine, large hanging tapestries, the heavy carved furniture polished to shine like metal, a stone floor not needing rushes to cover the hard dirt, but huge deep carpets with rich designs woven into them, so clean, and a bed like that on which she had awakened with fine linen sheeting as white as snow and pillows of silk and goosefeathers, fur throws and deeply embroidered heavy draperies to keep out the cold.

Even the food on the table was beautiful, apples and plums so polished she could see her reflection on their skin, the bread's crust shining with some kind of glaze, meat of a rich dark color in a sauce that smelled of wine and thyme, small whole carrots cooked with their green tops, long beans and turnips in bright colors, a slab of the palest butter she had ever seen, and apple and pear compotes, a small cup of bright marmalade made from bitter orange, pork and cabbage, and hard boiled eggs topped with salmon roe, marzipan birds and hares and swans with candied wings atop small golden meringue boats.

Food for a royal table.

She was unable to stop her silly crying, pointing around the room, and she shook her head at Mairi, who looked horrified. Nay! Nay! All is wonderful, she thought, and raised a hand for Mairi to wait until she could get control and find her voice. "Please. These gowns," she croaked, her breath shuddering in her throat. She took another long and deep breath and hiccupped.

"I am so sorry. What is wrong with them? I swear to you. We will fix whatever is wrong. Please do not cry."

"Wrong?" she gasped out. "Nothing is wrong! They are perfect. More than perfect. I am such a goose." She wiped her eyes and sniffled.

Mairi cocked her head, still frowning but clearly ready to listen.

"My story is...difficult to admit," she stared at her lap and began. "I grew up with two older brothers, Alastair and Elgin Gordon. I adore them. I know nothing of kings and courts and nobility. When you curtseyed to me I was secretly horrified. Truly. My brothers raised me after our father died when I was barely four. The cottage I spoke of was smaller than this room, and it is the only home I have ever known. My days there were spent in the paddock or the stables, or roaming the moors and coves. For most of my life I have only worn trouse like these." She pulled on the homespun fabric covering her legs.

"To everyone here I am the king's daughter. But I am not. The truth is I am a thief," she admitted. "We were thieves. Al and El and myself. Until I stole a gown, I never had one to wear. The only things I own I did not steal are my dog, my horse and my infant coverlet made for me by my mother, and I only just saw it for the first time when your brother came to the island.

Mairi's look softened with kindness and understanding and she gave her a wan smile. "Glenna, what happened to you was certainly out of your hands."

"But it does not change who I am and how I have lived." Glenna looked at the crimson velvet gown in her arms. "Look at this. 'Tis the loveliest gown I have ever seen. For me...the lass who can muck out a stable, groom, feed, saddle, and break a horse. The thief who can cut a purse from a man's belt in a heartbeat and steal even lint from his pocket without him knowing." She ran her hand along the seams and looked up. "But my skills matter little, because I cannot sew a stitch. To see all of this. To have it made for me, I am..." she paused searching for words. "I am...more than grateful, particularly when I feel unworthy and so wanting."

Mairi came and joined her on the floor, settling easily next to her so their shoulders and knees almost touched. She straightened her work apron as if it were a gown as fine that the one Glenna held. "You do not have to be grateful, dear Glenna. We made them for you, our gifts, gifts we wanted to give you, and now that I have heard your story I want to give a hundred more!" She leaned her head a little closer and said quietly, "I am certain thievery is a most helpful talent. Would that you could teach me to lift the cook's keys to the sweets coffers!"

And when Glenna laughed, Mairi patted her hand and laughed with her, then said, "But the best secret is this: you are a king's daughter. You do not ever have to sew a single stitch."

THIRTY

Glenna sat by the fire with Mairi, belly full, bathed, a maid combing her long clean hair dry, and listening to Lyall's mother talk about her son.

Beitris Ramsey was a thin and delicate woman, who had greeted her kindly, but seemed cautious and curious like a bird on a window sill, which made the meeting more than awkward at first. As the women ate together and attended Glenna, Lady Beitris soon relaxed.

Her first impression was striking and unique, made so perhaps by what she chose to mask. Dressed beautifully, in a gown of deep blue and gold brocade with velvet braided trim, she moved around the room with grace and elegance, a quiet step and straight, high back. Her belled sleeves long and elegant, yet she wore a tight silken glove on one hand. To cover the burnt, puckered skin? That she was scarred was made apparent by her manner of dress. But Mairi had warned her, and Glenna understood it was to protect Lady Beitris as much as to prepare Glenna.

Half her face was covered with a dark veil connected to a circular cap that tied tightly under her chin and again at her neckline with a wide collar. The visible half of her face was lovely with her soft white skin, wide eyes the exact blue color of Lyall's, and a full mouth that showed little age and was as pink as late summer's campion bloom. Her red curly hair hung down her back in a bright, thick braid encased in a slip of icy blue silk and wrapped with gold and copper braided ribbands. As she sat near Glenna, the braid draped over her shoulder, hanging past the chair on which she sat, and there were small gold pendants in the shapes of crosses, stars, suns and birds decorating the twists of ribbands.

"What he shows the world is a mask to protect who he is inside," Lady Beitris said, a woman who certainly understood the art of masking things. "The idea he is a coward?" She shook her head. "That is not my son."

"Not the brother who saved me," Mairi said, and when Glenna asked a question, the women told her the whole story of the day Dunkeldon burned.

"He was ten years old," Mairi finished, "when he carried me on his back and took mother's hand and we traveled alone to Rossi. He was ten years when he faced the wolves who attacked me. He saved me," Mairi said quietly.

"And lost Atholl," her mother added.

"Atholl was his beloved hound," Mairi explained. "They were always together, my brother and that big hound. It slept at Lyall's feet, followed his shadow, obeyed his every command."

"We had been walking for two days by then, and we were resting against some tree at the edge of the great woods," Lady Beitris told her. "My burns were so painful, I could not go on, and Lyall was trying to cool my skin with a cool rag. I was crying. My skin felt as if it was still on fire." Lady Beitris looked down, the memory obviously still painful in a different way. "Mairi wandered off into the woods."

"I was chasing butterflies, or something equally foolish."

"Atholl followed her," Lyall's mother continued. "We had not noticed she was gone, until we heard the wolves. My heart was in my throat. All that we had lost and then Mairi, too? 'Twas too much for me."

"I had no idea what danger I was in until I looked up. Before me was a line of them, snarling, and so close I could smell their fur." Mairi shuddered. "They pounced, but Lyall beat them off and carried me back to mother. But Atholl…" She paused. "He could not save us both."

"Lyall never said a word but he never spoke his name again. He merely grew more quiet and inward. At some point Donnald tried to give him another hound from one of the litters here at Rossi, but Lyall refused. He never wanted another pet."

And, Glenna thought, he never again named another animal.

"'Tis a sign of a great heart, and his greatest curse, that my son does not forget those he loved."

Lyall could not forget her. He tried. His stepfather's words haunted him, echoed about his mind in an eternal headache, and defied who he thought he was, while keeping alive some part of him that still had the essence of a conscience. He ate little, under the assessing eyes of Ramsey and the worried glances of his mother, but went back to pace the parapets again, walked the halls of Rossi, and finally sat down and played chess with an old knight he found sitting in front of the huge hearth near the keep's back entrance, long after the castle was quiet and abed.

"You have lost thrice now. If an old man did not know better, I would think you were throwing the game, lad." Sir Magnus had been with Ramsey for more decades than Lyall knew and had trained Lyall in service when he was first at Rossi. "Get yourself to bed."

Lyall rubbed a hand over his face in frustration, then rested his hands on his knees and stared at the fire. "I cannot sleep."

"What is this sleeping excuse from one as young and strong as you? I am old, which is a fine excuse to be awake at this hour—too many aches to sleep through the night, too many broken bones."

And I have a broken heart. Until he had just thought the words, he had avoided the core of his troubles and what was truly bothering him. Now it was there for him to chew on.

"Based on the confounded look you wear, I will venture a guess that a fine ankle and a pair of breasts are involved," he laughed wearily. "'Tis only women that inspire in a man such utter despair and complete confusion."

Lyall gave a wry laugh. "A fortunate guess."

"In my six hard fought decades, I have seen too many men felled to their knees by a fair maid. Few men are immune. Kings and princes, earls and freeman, even the baron himself.

"Ramsey?" Lyall laughed.

"Aye, he suffers still."

Lyall doubted that piece of frippery. He shook his head. "He is a large part of my problem. The lady is willing. My stepfather threatens me to not act on it…on her."

"I am not surprised," was all Magnus said.

"My orders are to keep her safe."

"Safe? Matters of the heart are seldom safe, and power, title, name and wealth provide no armor. My own dear Aileen ran me a merry and frustratingly long race from a nunnery to the Cairngorms, to Normandy, Outremer and back. Aye, 'tis a lass who gives a man that lost look."

"I look lost?" Lyall said, not really a question. Was he that weak. A lost lamb? He'd rather think of himself as a coward.

"Oft times you have been lost. You have not made good choices over the years. But this manner you have is different. You do not look driven by fire and vengeance."

Magnus and his brutal honesty. Lyall gave him a square look.

"I, too, have lived with the fires of youth. Vengeance and greed have ruled my life. I do not condemn you, lad. You have followed what you wanted unflinchingly. And that is not a weak trait, Lyall Robertson." He paused meaningfully. "Now you need to decide what you truly want—make certain it is what you want—and chose your path without regrets. If your path is truly your own heart's desire, you will have little to regret when you are my age. The trick is to find the truth in your desire. To not chase after something for the wrong reasons." He stood and stretched, wincing with his joints snapped aloud.

Lyall stood out of respect for him.

"I told you years ago, when you first came to Rossi, that a man must choose his battles. Do you remember?"

"Aye, but in truth I have not thought of it," Lyall admitted with a wry laugh. "Or I would not be in this fix."

"I somehow doubt that, lad." He clapped Lyall on the shoulder. "You must learn which battles are worth fighting. Now I am off to bed and you should do the same."

Lyall watched him leave, then took a candle from a stanchion to light his way through the halls and arches, and went up to the next floor, Magnus's words alive in his head as he passed by Glenna's chamber. He stopped and walked back to the door.

Inside, the room was still dimly lit from too many candles that been forgotten and the glow of the banked fire in the hearth. At first glance, the room appeared ransacked, but with a closer look, he realized that was not the case. The clothing rod was empty and the drape that covered it wide open. The chairs, stools, benches and tables were strewn with gowns of every color. Shoes were lined up by each gown, some with long toes, some square-toed with no backs and small heels that might bring her closer to his chin, shoes made in leathers and fabrics of every color with silver buckles and ribbands. Shifts and chemises, other underwear and thin, delicate sleep gowns ladies favored, some in a bleached stark-white spilled from a large open clothes chest lined with hand stitched sachets of flower petals Mairi always used and that made her smell like a spring garden.

He looked at the number of the thin sleep gowns. Ironic, since Glenna lay asleep on the bed wearing a thick, finely-woven wool robe and hugging a red velvet gown with fur trim to her chest like a coverlet, and on one foot was a green slipper with gold ribbands and a purple kid ankle shoe with red laces on the other.

Watching her, a smile curved his mouth and felt sweet, and something like happiness swelled within him, the first he'd felt since he'd been home. His heart was in his smile, but it was safe now, to reveal his deepest and secret feelings inside this room, because no one could see.

There was the chance he could spend every night of his lifetime watching her sleep, seeing her at peace, and by doing so, feel at peace himself—a miracle of sorts? In her he felt the wonder of miracles, the truth of life and God and man, the reason to be alive and to walk the earth. There was no other woman he had ever looked at and imagined fat with his child, imagined faces and bright eyes and small hands, with no other woman had he seen his sons and daughters until now.

What had Magnus said? Reasons…reason.

There was no wrong reason for Lyall to go after Glenna. He had never set out to make her his and prove or avenge something. But what would their being together do to her? There was the true issue. Who would be most hurt? Ramsey was certain something dire would happen. Would she look at him someday with regret?

As he left her chamber and moved down the hall toward his, he knew one certain thing: with her, he would never have a single regret.

———⇒⋅⇐———

The next morning was filled with busyness that started barely after the cock crowed. Prayers in the chapel, where Glenna knelt quietly between Lyall's mother and sister until her knees were sore and her quiet words ran together in her head, then off to break fast with the women in the solar over bowls of stone fruit, a platter of crispy fried trout and hot pepper bread with warm honey and crunchy, oat cakes fried and dusted with cinnamon. Mairi's boys joined them, romping like spring colts, while they asked Glenna enough questions to fill a coffer, and eventually their nurse took them off to run wild outside rather than in. The room felt the sudden quiet.

"They are a handful," Lady Beitris said as she rose from her tapestry stand and placed a hand on her low back. "Enough stitchery."

"Not for me," Mairi said looking up. She bit off a thread and rummaged through a basket of spools. "I want to finish this today."

Lady Beitris took Glenna's arm and slid it through her own, patting her hand. "Come along with me, Lady Glenna. 'Tis a lovely day. I will show you about Rossi."

And that was when the day took a different turn. As the women walked the castle gardens, moving from the rows of roses and bellflowers, past the great cabbages and root vegetables, to a large, flat herb patch with clumps of marjoram, thyme, thick, sharp rosemary tuffets, and the wide frosted colored leaves of the sage plants, chatting, a wide brown leather ball flew behind Glenna and crushed a corner of the herb garden.

Lyall came running around a wall, laughing and teasing, with one of his nephews in his wake, until they came face to face with the women. He stopped, his eyes on Glenna.

"Ladies," he bowed and said, "Make your bow to the ladies, Duncan. That's a good lad."

"Look at my herbs!" Lady Beitris scolded, but there was no anger in her tone.

Lyall picked up the ball and tucked it under his arm. "Fluff your grandmother's prized weeds, Duncan."

"Weeds!" Lyall's mother gasped. "You are incorrigible, Lyall. These weeds are what make your winter mutton palatable."

But Lyall was still staring at Glenna, until she finally looked away from all the feeling she saw in his eyes, and she flushed when she realized Lyall's mother caught their exchange. The pensive expression on the face of Lady Beitris was telling.

"Come along, lad. Your brothers are waiting." Lyall nudged his nephew into a race and they disappeared behind the wall.

By afternoon Glenna had a few moments to herself, and for the first time since morn she was alone. She went down to the stables to see Skye.

"Hallo, you worthless nag," she said, stroking Skye's muzzle as she fed her a summer apple. When Skye was done nibbling, Glenna started to wipe her hand on her clothing by rote, but stopped. She was in a gown, the plainest of the lot and made of finely-woven, thin violet wool, with simple sleeves and shoes of calf that fit her feet like gloves. She squatted down and wiped her hand on the clean straw then straightened, looking around her, liking the familiar scents of the stables. She had missed this.

Leaning her head against Skye's neck, she thought back to days on the island, when her life was simpler and all about horses and feed and manure. She closed her eyes as her mind drifted back over time.

"Thinking of me, love?"

Her eyes flew open and she stepped back. "Lyall!" *Was he everywhere?*

Handsome as the Devil himself, hair golden, eyes the color of cornflowers, grinning wide enough to show a rare dimple in his cheek, he stood there, arms resting on the stall gate, intent on watching her.

"Thinking of you?" she repeated sweetly. "The baron might have to enlarge the castle arches so you might manage to get your head through. And if you must know," she lied, "I was thinking of how to scrape the manure off my shoe." She pulled up the hem of her gown and showed him her shoe.

"And a fine shoe it is, as is your lovely ankle. But I was recently warned that a fine ankle is trouble."

"What do you want, Lyall?" she asked in a flat tone, feeling mixed up and annoyed, happy to see him, yet confused, and wanting to throw her arms around his neck and cover his face in kisses.

His look changed, the joy in his expression vanished. "Want? Something I cannot have," he said seriously and the moment died. "Good day, Lady Glenna," he added curtly and walked away.

Her heart sank, and she cursed herself for dousing their fire.

But they were not done and the afternoon and evening continued to play cruel tricks on her. They crossed paths repeatedly, almost as if they were dice in hand of God. When Glenna took Mairi's lads to the kitchen for a sweet, rewards for napping quietly, Lyall was standing with his arm resting atop Cook's head as the short woman who ran the castle kitchens looked way up, waving a wooden spoon under his nose as she pretended to scold him for sticking his fingers in the plum sauce, both of them laughing, until Glenna and the boys interrupted.

Later, as she raced from her chamber to go to meet Lady Beitris in the solar, she and Lyall came out of their doors at the same time, both froze in place looking down the long hallway at the other. Later still, when she was speaking with Mairi in her chamber, Lyall came in without knocking, asking his sister a question before he looked up just as Glenna dropped her wine goblet on the carpet. And when night had fallen and the moon began to rise, when the stars overhead blinked in the darkening sky, when the castle was just beginning to quiet, they met on the dark narrow staircase, each heading in a different direction, and they stared, startled, frustrated, then turned to edge by each other.

But quarters were too close and her breasts brushed his ribs, making her breath catch. He looked down, their mouths were almost level, with her on a higher step and him on a lower. His breath was warm on her cheek, and she could smell the scent of cinnamon and allspice from the stew served earlier, and feel the intense heat coming from his body.

His hands touched hers, and something glinted in his eyes, before he pulled away as if burned and continued down the stairs without looking back, his voice quietly saying, "I cannot do this. I am done."

And as she watched him walk away, shocked by his words, she vowed, "You might think we are done, but I am not done."

THIRTY-ONE

The moon was higher in the night sky when Lyall turned at the sound of the door and there she was. "Glenna," he spoke aloud, her name coming naturally from his mind to his lips. She was not a ghost of the woman who had haunted him, that he had seen around every corner as he tried to hide from her and what he felt.

Flesh and blood Glenna stood inside his bedchamber, a royal daughter in a deep green gown, fitted to her body and with gold embroidery along the neck and in panels at the sleeves, looking like an angel, a siren, and a witch, the beautiful sorceress placed in this earth to test his mettle.

He had known she would keep pushing, that he would see her again, but not now, not when he was tired of living with himself, and the disappointments of those who should matter in his life.

Not now when he'd been tested all day by face to face encounters and still tried to feel nothing. He could not find release from how he felt. And here she was. He was all too aware of the determination in her manner, the gleam in her eye. She came to him in the way a knight charged after the quintain. He took a deep and long-suffering breath. Her scent filled the air, that of a summer field full of flowers, reminding him of moments when he had held her. He crossed the room putting some distance between them, and he blew out a candle, then pushed aside the chair and braced himself against the edge of the table, crossing his feet at the ankles and acting as if she did not affect him as she did. "I know why you are here."

"And you are not pleased," she said moving near a chair, where she stood on tiptoe and took a candle from the wall prick, using it to light another.

"You wish to save me."

"Someone has to. They will not dare to hang you as my husband, and were anyone to try, I would go to my grave fighting for you." She moved by the bed and lit more candles, one, two, five, six... "'Tis the simple plan, Lyall."

When she faced him, he saw she truly thought 'twas all so clear and sensible. But nothing in his life was simple. She stood before him, a Trojan horse in the guise of a small black-haired woman who would be his champion.

"Aside from that," she admitted. "There is another reason. I have a selfish motive to save you."

He gave a short laugh. "Because you gain a husband who will not bury you alive."

"Aye. There is that," she agreed.

"So you imagine I am safe. I think your father, his councilors, and my stepfather all would argue that point, sweetheart."

"I do not care," she said stubbornly.

"But I care." He straightened and turned his back to her, unable to look her in the eye with what he was about to do. "With all of your grand ideas you have not considered one thing."

"What would that be?"

"Why should I exchange one shackle for another?"

She paused about one heartbeat, then laughed at him and did not budge.

Stubborn, mule-headed and foolish woman!

"Oh, Lyall, really. What a poor liar you are."

"You should leave, Glenna."

"Perhaps I should, but I cannot. I dare not leave you again. I love you too much to let you keep running away from this…from me." She came close and stopped next to him, so close he could hear her breath, and she lit the candle he'd blown out. "From who we are together." She looked at him from beneath the darkest thick lashes, a sultry look that was far beyond her experience. She pulled the gold combs from her hair and shook her head, and her hair tumbled down as black and shiny as a rook's wing.

The king's daughter was bent on seduction. Her eyes met his and the gauntlet was down.

"You are only afraid of who you are and what you'll have to face, of your father and his decisions," he said truthfully. "I am merely the simplest answer to your problem."

"Aye," she nodded without hesitation. "That too is true. Convenient is it not? I can save you and you can save me." She smiled at him, a smile that was easy and free and unconcerned, a smile that drew him unwillingly into the charms of it. "Seems the simplest of all solutions. I expect that you would leap upon this opportunity if you cared nothing for me."

Her words struck. That she knew him so well was different, and not so very comfortable.

"You claim you are a selfish coward," she continued. "But a true coward would never walk away from the simple answer to a problem. I think you are no coward. Why do you do this but for my sake?"

He had no answer because she spoke the truth. And that was how he was caught in his own game. He could not do with her what he did with others in his life: act as if he didn't care. She saw him for exactly who he was, not on the surface, but deep, deep inside, the place scorched by all the hurts in his life.

"The more you balk, Lyall, the more you prove that you love me more than yourself," she said.

He chewed it over—this whole thing between them. It was a

long time before he admitted, "You are a thorn in my side. A stone in my boot. A pain in my—"

"Aye," she agreed easily.

He looked into her eyes, so clear and trusting, so unafraid yet he was scared for her. All she felt for him was revealed in her look, open, loving, and there was nothing more he could hide from her. "You do not give up." He shook his head and sank into the chair with almost no fight left in him. "What a warrior you are."

She smiled and moved into his lap, linking her arms about his neck and her head lay softly and easily on his shoulder. Her breath whispered against his neck and for a long time neither of them moved. They sat as they were, her nestled against him as a great sense of peace came over him, and with it waned the one thing that had held him back, his will and need to save her from himself. "We should not be here."

Her lips brushed his neck, then his jaw.

"Leave, sweetheart. Leave while you can. Run away and save yourself."

When she did not move, he pulled back and she grabbed his tunic in her fists, her face a handsbreadth away, suddenly full of emotion. "Oh lud! Do not dare put me through this again. Do not dare choose a higher road, Lyall Robertson! What I do need is not for you to decide to be honorable and walk away from me, or for you to send me away again all because you have some kind of hairy idea—foolhardy at best—that I am too good for you."

He merely looked at her, searching for some strength and losing. To which, she crossed her arms, tossed her chin, wiggled her bottom, and glared at him.

What was not being said made the silence louder. Then his burst of laughter was like a clap of thunder; it echoed and rang and was honest and contagious. He pulled her to him. "My Glenna. My warrior," he murmured softly against her lips, perhaps to himself more than to her, and he kissed her without hesitation or any feelings of regret.

When he was done with her mouth, he pulled back and capitulated with a sigh. "Do not fret, I am still the coward. I am still selfish. I surrender. If I do not, you will harangue me, chase me, seduce me, tease me, flog me with wet towels for all eternity. In the face of that and with all my weaknesses, I have not the courage nor inclination to commit the most noble of acts—that of protecting you from your poor choice of a husband."

"Lud, I would hope not." She eased back against his arms. "After all we've been through, I would hate to think I misjudged you and found myself bound to a man of morals."

"I have no morals, love.

"Someday we will discuss the root cellar at that inn," she said with a half-smile and glint in her eye that promised more than retribution.

Laughing, he spun her around and began working at the ties on her gown. "Let's rid ourselves of all this clothing."

She turned back and did not stop kissing him, small light touches of her lips along his neck and jawline, distracting him from his task at the ties of her gown until he tore them apart and the sound of rending fabric made him groan and her laugh, giggling with her lips against his mouth. She cupped his face in her hands. "For a man so quick to leave me, you seem to have little patience with my clothes.

"A cursed thing, these clothes," he said, scooping her up in arms and he carried to the bed, pulling back to draw open the heavy bed curtains so he could see her completely in the amber candlelight.

"You have on more clothes than I. Take them off," she said, laying back with her ebony hair spread out behind and beneath her, blending with the furs on the bed, a dark halo framing her pale skin and dark eyes, her wine-colored lips, moist from his kisses, her arms raised as she lay there calling to him in ways he could not name, but only feel.

He pulled off his tunic and linen chainse.

Her eyes did not leave him. "More," she said, and he stripped off his hose and loincloth and stood before her, bare of body and bare-souled.

Overwhelmed by the sight of her and needing her body against his, he crawled onto the bed and rolled over with her wrapped in his arms, pulling apart her clothing. First her gown, tugging it down over her buttocks and she kicked it off, then he grabbed the thin chemise with birds stitched carefully along the neck, and she stopped him.

"Do not tear it! Please. See the birds? Mairi stitched it for me. It is the most beautiful thing I have ever worn against my skin," she said reverently.

He slipped it off her shoulders, one at a time, and down to her waist. Turning over, his hands spread open on her ribs, amazed that they were so small, then slowly his hands moved upward to take her breasts, thumbs stroking. She sucked in a breath, and he lowered his head, her hands splayed in his hair and held him to her, her breathing in small gasps.

They kissed each other in every way, mouths seeking and tasting, lips touching, tongues and hands, discovering new ways to give and take pleasure. Desire was a force beyond them and they rolled all over the bed and each other, absorbed beyond thought in the wild vortex of it, soft breast to hard-muscled chest, the tease of tight curly hair brushing against soft skin, a strong knee between her legs and they touched and found each other's secret places, learning the textures and scents, the soft and hard places where sensation lived inside their bodies.

On his back, Lyall kissed her deeply and wrapped her long hair over them, and it cloaked them like the shadows of the night. And when he looked at her, her face was flushed with love and her eyes misty with passion. There were men who traveled leagues and whole lifetimes, across mountains and seas and hot desert sands, in search of miracles, and yet here he had found his. Glenna...his Glenna.

"You are the most beautiful thing I have ever had against my skin," he told her.

"Lyall," she said his name.

He gripped her soft buttocks and rolled over, settling inside her legs and he kissed his way down her body and back, tasting and pleasuring, her skin so soft he could lose himself in her. Drawing up her knees, he slowly sank into her and they became one heart.

"My love," he murmured. "Look at me, sweetheart."

She opened those black eyes of hers. He braced himself on his elbows and held her head in his hands. "You are almost mine. Almost."

"Take me. Fill me."

He thrust forward catching her sharp cry with his mouth, and he did not move, but waited. At that moment, so sweet, so pure, so deeply inside of her, he was someplace he had never been, almost like heaven. *I could stay here forever.* And he had no idea he'd spoken aloud until she laughed and smiled softly before she said, "I doubt we would get much done in our lives."

He laughed then, dropping his brow to her chest. "Do you think we would care?"

"Nay," she said. "Kiss me. I love your mouth over mine."

"You and your kisses."

"Aye, me and your kisses."

At her wit, he smiled, this joy inside him a foreign thing, then as the moment passed into passion, into desire, and their looks melted into one another. "'Tis the moment." He grew serious. "I am going to make you mine completely." Gently at first, he began to move. "I am going to swive you slowly, stroke inside you and thrust until you cry with joy, my love, and spill my seed deep into your womb."

He moved with exquisite slowness, feeling each sensation, sliding into her as she grew hotter and he stroked faster, their breathing rapid and their bodies moving together, a timeless rhythm. She began to whimper and clutch, growing closer to completion, and he kissed her open-mouthed, his tongue mimicking his staff, again and again, and she cried out his name and clutched him with deep spasms. He came hard, spilling inside her, and he shouted his love for her, his voice like an echo in his own ears.

I love you, I love you, I love you…

Some part of him was dying and he arched his back, taking all of her deeply until it was done. As he lowered his head to the crook in her neck, he felt all that he doubted leave him, all that he hated disappear, and all of the past fly up and away and out of the present. His life, for what it was, had at that moment, begun again.

Glenna awoke to the odd silence of dawn and new twinges and small aches she had never felt, in places virgin before, proof what she'd experienced was not a dream. Sighing she slid a hand across the bed linen, but there was no hard muscled body beside her, so she sat up, the warm furs falling to her side. The heavy bed curtains were open to reveal his silhouette at the window.

He wore nothing but the pink light of dawn, and she could study him without scrutiny, his tall form and wide shoulders, his narrow waist and muscled buttocks, the sinew of strong leg that belonged to an experienced warrior, a man who could control a great and wild war horse with his thighs and knees, or use the same to pin her to the mattress and love her all night long.

There was a white scar along his hip. She knew that now. The secrets of his body were hers, the touch of his hand and lips, his skin, his scent and the sound of his voice when he said 'I love you.'

He is thinking about us.

Tossing the covers aside, she left the bed and joined him, slipping an arm around his waist and he shifted so she was tucked safely against his side, her cheek touching the short curly hair on his chest and her hand resting on his strong, broad ribs.

"See that tree down by the bend in the river?" he said.

"Aye."

"When I was young, that first summer here, I used it for target practice with a bow and arrows until the bark was all gone and the trunk was chipped." He laughed softly. "I cannot believe it still stands. One good wind should have toppled it years ago."

"A bow and arrows?"

"Aye."

"A bow and arrows," she repeated indignantly.

Laughing he said, "If you only had your—

"—bow and arrows," she finished and smiled, her mind's eye imagining the determined and strong-spirited brother Mairi had told her about.

Below, a dairy maid in a work gown and blue apron, wearing wooden clogs moved across the bailey toward the dairy byre swinging empty milk buckets on a wooden yoke. A laundress came out and another followed, talking as one lit a fire under a huge, black clothes kettle with an oil torch that made the air smell like the grease from roasting meat Moments later they carried out overloaded baskets of dirty linens and laundry they stacked between the clothes poles and the cooking kettles, still chatting amiably. Their work day was beginning, as was her life.

That new beginning sun was whole now, balancing precariously on the edge of the horizon, fiery and colorful. A sharp whistle made her gaze follow the sound. In one of the crofts beyond the wall, dog trailed after a shepherd boy with a long pole who was skipping and side-stepping as the hound barked and happily frolicked after him.

She took a long and quivering sigh and closed her eyes for a moment.

"I'm sorry about your hound," Lyall said quietly.

"Fergus?" she said and he looked down at her.

"Aye. Would that it had been safe to stay behind. But 'twas not."

Can you not even call him by his name after he is dead? But she could say nothing aloud after Mairi's story about her brave brother and a hound named Atholl. She leaned her head against his chest, because that was where she felt comforted. "I miss him."

"I know, sweetheart." And she understood he knew better than anyone else. His hand slid up and down her back, soothing her with a tender touch. They stood like that, arms about each other, holding together, the day dawning before them in light the color of the flesh of a salmon, each lost inside their own thoughts. He turned to her, lifted her face with gentle hands and kissed her.

The chamber door flew open with a bang and the baron filled the doorway.

Lyall turned her away to shield her from view with his body. "Get out."

"What did you say?" The baron's red face turned redder. "I am the lord of Rossi."

"You should know to knock at a closed door," Lyall said unfazed. "Else I will have to find another place to sleep."

Ramsey angrily pulled the sheet from the bed and tossed it to Lyall. "Cover her."

The Lady Beitris came rushing in, tying a belt at the waist of the thick, damask robe she wore over her sleeping gown. About her head was a tight silk cap that still hid half her face behind a deep blue sarcenet veil. She looked at them, naked and in each other's arms, and her hands went to her bright face as she said. "Oh, Lyall no... You did not!"

Those few words held such disappointment that Glenna flinched slightly and looked down, staring at the pale, golden hairs at the bend in his spine. She felt Lyall's hands tighten on her.

"See how your son defies me under my own roof?" Ramsey gritted and stormed from the room.

Lady Beitris looked from Lyall and Glenna to the bed. She walked over and picked up her chemise and held it out to her, her voice unemotional, "Get dressed, Lady Glenna."

"We are husband and wife, my lady," Glenna argued from behind him.

"Do as she asks, love. Trust me. This is not yet done." Lyall turned and his hands were soft on her bare shoulders. He gave her a slight shove towards his mother.

Glenna obeyed and slipped the chemise over her head. When she slid her arms into the green gown it gaped open in the back, and Lady Beitris pulled the pieces of torn ties together, knotting them in each eyelet again and again, tightening them before finally clucking her tongue. "Really, Lyall. This gown is just made."

"I would advise you to make future gowns with fewer ties, Mother."

Glenna glanced at him over her shoulder, and they exchanged a private look. She thought he might smile, something like one teased the corners of his mouth, but his stepfather came back in the room followed by three armed men.

"Shackle him," the baron ordered.

"Donnald!" Lady Beitris rushed to her husband, her hand on his arm. "Nay. I beg of you. Do not do this."

But the baron spoke directly to Lyall and 'twas clear his rage had not waned. "I have somewhere else for you to sleep," he said, throwing Lyall's defiant words back at him. "You are under the mistaken impression that you have the freedom to leave. You do not." The baron turned to the men who were standing by Lyall, holding his arms as the other clamped thick iron manacles on his ankles and wrists.

Lyall stood there with his head up and his eyes unseeing, not showing that he was vulnerable, wearing nothing but the iron clamps and chains. But Glenna could see something else. For a man so strong and tall and acting emotionless, something about him he tried to hide from the world was fragile as spun sugar, ready to crack and shatter into a thousand small pieces.

"Take him to the cellars and lock him up."

"Nay!" Glenna cried "You cannot! He is my husband. I am his wife," her voice caught and she felt her throat tighten.

The baron looked at her, startled, and his eyes cooled and his expression softened. "That decision will be for the earl of Sutherland when he arrives, my lady. Until then, my stepson will remain locked in the cellars."

"Donnald," Lady Beitris said quietly, her voice filled with emotion. "His clothes."

Glenna ran to Lyall and locked her arms about his waist, her cheek to his skin. "You cannot take him." She clung to him.

"Do not, sweetheart," Lyall said softly.

"You must take me, too!" Glenna said firmly and she looked up at Lyall. "I will not leave you."

Mairi came in the room, frowning. "What is this?" She faced her mother, then looked at the baron and Lyall. "What is happening here?"

"They were together after your stepfather forbade Lyall to touch her," Beitris stated unemotionally.

"But 'twas I!" Glenna cried out, looking back and forth between Lyall's parents. "I came to him! Do not blame him. We are wed." her voice cracked. "'Tis the law! You cannot deny 'tis the law. We have a right to share a bed."

"Beitris, Mairi," the baron said firmly. "Take the Lady Glenna to her chamber and see to her needs."

Tears burned her eyes and she looked up at Lyall. To her horror she felt them spill down her hot cheeks.

"Do not cry, love. Go."

"Nay, Lyall. I beg you. I love you." She was sobbing now and could not stop, her breath hiccupping in her chest.

"Go," he said softly and full of emotion, as if watching her was torture.

They gently pulled her away from him, but still she reached out, "Nay... Nay..." Her crying bordered on hysteria, her breath hardly there, the noises coming from her mouth and throat pitiful, and yet she had no pride when it came to him. She would do anything. "Please do not take him. Do not blame him..."

The baron looked away from Glenna and threw a coverlet over Lyall's shoulders, and gave Lady Beitris a look of concession, before he said, "Take him away." And he left the room.

Behind him, the guards led Lyall out, her love, her husband, in chains, and Glenna slipped out of the women's arms and sank to the floor crying, left with nothing that mattered.

THIRTY-TWO

'Twas not long before something mattered to Glenna. Getting to Lyall. She made seven unsuccessful attempts to sneak, lie, and scheme her way past the guards into the cellar, but had only managed to make the baron so red-faced and angry that the entire the castle was talking and its routine was turned upside down.

Failure did not stop Glenna, since she was mere staircases away from him. How difficult could it be? There had to be some way. Another way....

So she merely gave up that course, and instead, went on a new plan: a starvation fast.

Glenna set the third supper tray, untouched, outside the chamber door and with one more starved look at the food on it, she shut her eyes and the door, leaning against it. Her belly rumbled and tried not to think of roasted duckling and root vegetables in a marmalade wine sauce, the stewed cabbage with bacon and onions, and the hot crusty bread and butter that she had left on the tray.

The plum tart.

Was not long before she heard the baron bellow, "This is her untouched supper again? By God thumbs, I swear she will eat something soon or—"

"Donnald," Lady Beitris' voice interrupted him. "Calm down. You cannot make her eat."

"I could debate that wife," he grumbled.

"She is the king's daughter. You cannot force her to do anything."

"But what if she never eats? I cannot present her to Sutherland , 'Here my lord, is the king's daughter…his eldest daughter, the half-starved one.'"

"Come with me, dear," Lady Beitris said. "Let us retire to our chamber, where I will pour you some wine, and call the lute and flute players. The music will calm you down. You can put your feet up and forget about all."

Glenna exhaled when she heard their footsteps wane, and she listlessly crossed the room, leaned against the small table, filled a goblet with watered wine and sipped it slowly to quiet her belly.

The baron's mood grew increasingly foul the longer she refused to eat. She had told him the first night she started her fast that she would eat when he released Lyall from the cell, but not until then. He refused. The poor man had not butted heads with her yet. Her brothers could have warned him. Oh, where we they? If only Al and El would return with the proof of witnesses.

Her belly turned again. She stared down at it. How could something so empty make so much noise? She placed her hand on it and willed the idea of food away.

You can do this….

There was a slight and quiet tapping at the door and Glenna called to open. Mairi stuck her head inside, looked at Glenna, then quietly closed the door behind her. "Are you well?"

Glenna nodded.

Mairi pulled a bundle from her skirts and unwrapped it. "Come. Look here. I have bread and cheese and a little meat, not much but I saved you a duck leg and a stewed apple from my own supper."

The food called to her, as if meat and bread and cheese had soft and haunting voices were singing, *Come to me....Come to me....*

Glenna spun around, eyes tightly closed, her hand up warding off the idea of eating, of even looking at the food. "I cannot!"

"Of course you can. No one need know."

"I shall know," Glenna said firmly. She could do anything for Lyall.

Mairi rolled her eyes. "Really, Glenna. From where comes this sudden need for valor?"

"You think I cannot starve Lyall free? I can," Glenna insisted.

"Of course you can." Mairi waved a hand as if to add 'you silly goose.' "But actually starving is not the point. The point is to make everyone think you are starving, in particular my stepfather Now come here and eat."

"I cannot," Glenna said, having eyes only for the food. "I must grow weak enough to swoon."

"Lud!, Glenna, swooning is simple. You have done it once already."

"Aye, but I did not know I was swooning."

"Swooning is an art, not unlike your swift and thieving hand — which you still have promised to teach me, do not forget — now you will need some swooning practice. Here, watch me." Mairi crossed over near the bed and flexed her knees. "The most important thing to remember is to position yourself so you will not be hurt when you sink or to make certain you have something to fall back on depending upon which method you choose. Something soft like this mattress is always good."

"There are methods?" Glenna repeated.

"Aye. I believe the most realistic is to let your knees kind of turn to water and just sink to the floor like this—"

One moment Mairi was standing and the next she was on the floor, half on her back, arms back by her head and her lower body turned slightly, her knees bent.

Glenna burst out laughing and ran over to her. "That was quite wonderful!"

Mairi popped upright, eyes wide and grinning. "You liked it? Good." She scrambled up. "Stand here, and you try. Remember to keep your breathing very shallow."

"Can I eat first?"

Mairi grabbed the duck leg and handed it to her. "Eat this while I show you 'the fall upon something' method. This is for furniture or someone's lap or a chair. You will need a more exact position, since you want to land on a bed or chair or a nobleman." As Glenna chewed on the duck leg, she watched Mairi who taught fall gracefully backwards on a chair, and then upon the bed. Glenna stood beside her, half-eaten duck leg between her teeth.

Mairi said, "Go!" They both fell back on the bed at the same time. Mairi began giggling and Glenna sat up and chewed on another bite of duck, brandishing the bone, both of them laughing.

And that was when they turned together and saw Lady Beitris standing in the room watching them.

The cellars at Rossi were built deep in the ground and held barrels of ale and mead made at the castle brewery, and an entire room of wines, many imported at great cost from Bordeaux, Bruges, Briones, and Crete. The iron gates at the cellar's entrance were locked, and the anteroom, before the barrel storage rooms, served as Lyall's cell. He lay sprawled on a straw pallet on a corner as he tilted to lips a clay jar of wine, Ramsey's costliest from Malvasia, rattling the chains clamped onto his wrists and wincing as the manacle clamp caught and twisted the hairs on his arm.

He squinted inside the jar's short neck. "Good stuff," he muttered, since talking to himself was his only option. Then he drunkenly toasted his missing stepfather and took another swig.

Footsteps echoed in the dark recesses of the stairs. The guard had been gone for some time, since he took away Lyall's supper.

Within moments of being locked behind the gates, he was bored almost senseless, and his remedy was to raid the wine coffers and drink himself to sleep.

Lyall called out the guard's name, and his voice echoed in the stone rooms. Where was he? He had known the man for years.

More footsteps.

"'Tis about time you came back here, you worthless bastard! I uncorked some Malvasian. I'm willing to share!"

Glenna stood at the base of the stone stairs, a beautiful dream in blue, her hair down and shining, her look all for him, the way he saw her every night, the way she haunted his mind so vividly there were moments when he actually believed she was there and his weak mind was not playing tricks on him.

This time she held a candle in her hand when she said, "Lyall!"

The dream speaks! For the maddest of moments he thought he heard her voice. He held up the wine jar. "Little wonder Ramsey pays dearly for this. 'Tis powerful stuff."

"Then pour me some," she said clearly and used a large key to unlock the gates, stepped inside, closed and locked them behind her.

"Glenna? 'Tis really you?"

She faced him, hands on the hips of her gown. "Nay, fool, 'tis Mary Magdalene come to pray at the foot of your cross."

"Glenna?" He stood up and had to steady himself with a hand to the wall. "Glenna...."

She threw her arms about him then he had her in his arms, really holding her. He staggered back against the wall, "My love...my love..." She was all he ever wanted.

Covering him with kisses she was real, her body soft and warm, her kisses—Glenna and her kisses, he almost laughed out loud, the feeling inside him bubbling up. She stopped and pulled back, looking up at him. "You've been drinking?"

"For three days," he said brightly, then frowned. "Or at least three suppers." He waved a hand behind him. "See there. I have access to all of my stepfather's cellars."

"What were you planning to do? Drink him dry?"

"The thought crossed my mind. How am I doing?"

She wrinkled her nose and waved a hand in front of her face. "Smells as if you are almost there."

She had two noses. Beautiful noses, and her face was moving. Lyall staggered back against the wall, his head swimming, hugging the wine jar, and he ran a hand over his face. "What are you doing in here?"

"I wanted to see you."

"And you managed to steal the key? I expect someone will come drag you away soon. The guard is missing but he will be back soon. The world is against us."

"That's not true. And the guard is gone for a reason. We have all night together, and your mother gave me the key." She waved it under his nose.

"I am piss-drunk." He shook his head and it almost felt as if it rattled. "I thought you said my mother gave you the key."

"She did."

"Why would she do that?"

"Perhaps she understands."

He grew quiet, taking it all in, and he slid down the wall and landed hard onto the pallet, legs out in front of him. Back against the wall. He thought it might be holding him up. "I'm drunk. So very, very drunk."

She came over and sat down beside him, slid her arms around his chest and held him, her head on his shoulder "Then sleep it off. I'm here. I will stay with you. I will be with you." She moved down, nesting into the curve of his arm and she placed her hand over his heart, as she had done before. "There is nowhere else I would want to be," she said. "When I close my eyes, here is where I am safe. I know you are no coward, because it is here," she patted his chest, "where I can always hear how strong your heart is."

He closed his eyes, the warm feeling of peace around him and sweet oblivion just an arm's length away. "Do you regret us?" he asked her.

"Never," she said so fiercely he almost believed her.

"How can you be so certain? How do you know?"

She was quiet, then asked seriously, "Do you think someday you will regret us?"

"Nay. Never." His lips brushed her brow.

"How do you know?"

He had his answer, and he smiled.

A shaft of light woke Ramsey from the dregs of a deep and dreamless sleep, and he turned away from the open bed curtains and reached out for Beitris. Her side of the bed was empty, and the linens were cool to the touch. As he lay there, he could hear her moving around their chamber, poking the wood in the fire, the slight clunk of setting something down on a table, the shuffle of her slippers on the stone floor, then suddenly muted by the carpet.

He tried drifting back to sleep, but his head throbbed, and when he took a deep breath, his mouth tasted as dry and trampled as a tourney field. Sour. Then he remembered the wine, goblets and goblets of undiluted wine. He sat up and winced, hunching his shoulders, and emitting a quiet groan. He felt as if someone dropped an anvil on his head. But he rose and used the garderobe before he burst.

He heard a gasp and looked over his shoulder to find a maid

with her hands over her face. "Where is milady?" he asked the horrified maid.

"I am here," Beitris said, standing in the door, capped and veiled and gloved…all imperfections covered, a ewer in her hand. "You may leave," she kindly told the maid and shut the door after her. She crossed the room to a table near the bed and filled a goblet from the ewer. "I'm afraid seeing you, my lord husband, in all your morning power and glory was too much for her."

He snorted and scowled at her, aware that his nose was numb. "I have a bone to pick with you, wife."

"I can see you do."

"Do not try to deflect the subject with sweet talk." Ramsey shook his head and winced. "Inside my head there is a full battle going on." He touched the tip of his nose and frowned again. "I cannot feel my nose. You got me drunk last night."

She turned around to fidget with something but he caught her guilty look, at least half if it before she showed him her back.

Staring at her, waiting, he wondered how early she had risen. *Time enough to hide half of herself from me, still, after all these years. The same ritual of hiding herself every morning and every night.* "Beitris. I would know what you are up to."

"Up to? Here drink this." She held a goblet out to him. "You will feel better."

He drank the potion down, handed her the empty goblet and swallowed a belch. "You have not answered my question."

She stood with her back to him for a long time under the pretense of placing the goblet on the table, then turned finally around, her expression serious. "Glenna is with Lyall."

His reaction to her news wasn't immediate. But then everything about him had slowed down. "If I shout like I want to, my head will crack in half," he said and sank down into a nearby chair, one hand holding his throbbing brow and the other resting on his bare knee. "I am too angry to speak."

Naked, stripped to nothing but crapulence, he sat there exposed. Yet his wife was swathed in cloth and veils and caps, covered like a sister of God, well-hidden with the scars she would never love or trust him enough to let him see. They were like two chess pieces at opposite ends of the board, one white, one black.

And the king's daughter, his responsibility, in his protection, defied him, was no longer chaste and loosely wed to a scoundrel, his fool stepson, and both were down in his own cellars doing God only knew what together.

With the morn barely begun, what else would happen?

Beitris, who had remained silent, walked around the bed and stopped. "Donnald," she said in a soft, frightened gasp, and he looked up in time to see her swoon.

"Beitris!" By the time he was at her side she had fallen on the bed, her arms flung back and limp beside her head, her breathing so shallow he had lay his head on her breast to hear it. He patted her face and kept repeating her name, then bellowed for her handmaiden, but his wife opened her eyes and said his name.

He held her hand and said, "Do not move. I want to send for the chirurgeon."

"I am fine." She started to sit up but he slipped an arm behind her back and helped her, noting her color was fine.

He poured her some of the potion she gave him and handed her the goblet. "Drink it."

She wrinkled her nose and took a sip.

"You cannot be fine. You did swoon. I have never known you to faint. Have you done so before?"

"Apparently not often enough," she murmured into the goblet, confusing him.

A guard outside the door called out for him and pounded. Donnald shrugged into his robe and opened the door.

"A rider has come with news, my lord. The earl of Sutherland is near. He and his party should be here before midday.

He dismissed the guard and began to dress.

"Are you going to the cellars?" Beitris asked anxiously. "If so, I want to go with you."

"You just swooned. You should lie down and rest.

"I have not eaten," she protested quickly, standing up. "My faint was from hunger." She took an apple from a nearby fruit bowl and took a bite. "See? I shall be fine. I will not be left behind, Donnald," she said fiercely, and he knew that tone in her.

He should just give in now. Or continue to merely feel as if he were beating his head against a stone wall. In the end, he would give in. So he did not deny her.

Was not long before they were together near the base of the cellar stairs, and she stopped him with a hand on his arm. "Let me go first."

"Why?"

"Because I ask it of you," she said.

Wordlessly he stepped aside and watched her as she reached the bottom of the stairs and paused, then after a moment waved him down, her finger to lips.

Lyall and Glenna were asleep on a straw pallet in the corner, Lyall's back against the wall, Glenna tucked under his arm, her head on his shoulder. Then he noticed her hand was on Lyall's chest, resting above his heart.

Ramsey's mind went back to another time and place, and he felt Beitris' arm link through his. *Did she remember?*

Once, long ago, they lay in each other's arms on a pile of warm hay, her head on his shoulder and asleep like Glenna. That day was everything, the kind of day where a man could believe that life did have its pure and tender moments, that love could heal a man's soul, a day of revelation. In a moment of whimsy that day she had listened to his heartbeat, and made him listen to hers.

"They beat together as one," she had said to him.

To this day he could remember the sound of every heartbeat.

When she had looked up at him. He found himself staring into the color of the sky, on that happiest day of his life. But she did not have to tell him what he already knew. He understood how much he loved her, and yet barely a fortnight later, he chose what was best for her and walked away.

He could feel her gaze on him now, and he looked away from her son and into her veiled face, her eye still the exact color of a cloudless sky. She placed her gloved hand over his heart and took his and placed it between her breasts. "They still beat as one."

Her words stirred the dreams still in him, the memories of a love that was the single thing in his life he longed to relive, to relive the choice he'd made to let her go and then spent the rest of his life regretting that choice. Brushing aside part of her veil, he lowered his mouth to hers and she didn't stop him. The kiss was theirs for a long time, and in that touch of their lips was a love that covered more than half a lifetime. When he pulled back, she straightened the veil back into place, looking down. She was still hiding.

But her hand over his heart, and her words…they were enough for now.

He glanced back into the cellars to find Lyall staring at him, his look unreadable. Ramsey's gaze went to the key in the gates' lock and turned a questioning eye to Beitris.

She knew his question before he could speak and said bluntly, "I chose to give them last night."

"What is happening?" Glenna said in a voice raspy with sleep. She was awake and frowning.

Ramsey saw her arms tighten around his stepson, who pulled her even closer to him as if he had to protect her from them. The chains that still bound him rattled, a telling moment, and Ramsey had the thought the two were as close as links on a chain, and trying to look as strong and unbreakable. Something in Ramsey changed as he watched them, and some doubt ran through his mind, adding to his confusion.

His wife opened the gates and held out her hand to Glenna. "The earl of Sutherland is but a short distance away. I shall help you change before he arrives."

Glenna didn't argue, but paused to look at Lyall.

What Ramsey saw pass between them was too familiar to not cause him pain, and produced a moment that was uncomfortable enough to make him wonder what was best, rather than what was right.

She got up, giving Lyall, a wan smile before she left with Beitris, and he and Lyall were alone.

Ramsey knelt down and unlocked the manacles, then tossed them aside. Lyall winced and rubbed his ankles, while Ramsey fought with himself over what to say and chose silence. He rose and moved away, holding the cell gates open. "You need to prepare for meeting with Sutherland." He gave a quick nod. "You can go."

Lyall walked out of the gates, but stopped when he was next to him. They were of the same height and could look each other in the eye, which was a curse more than a blessing when it came to reading each other. "I want you to understand something, Donnald. I know what I have done, and I know what I did after you strictly forbade me." He paused after this honest admission, then placed a hand on Ramsey's shoulder. "I could say no to you, but I could not say no to her."

THIRTY-THREE

The earl of Sutherland and his contingent approached Castle Rossi to the sound of heralds trumpeting their arrival and with all the pageant possible, pennants flying from lines of mounted squires in the earl's colors, and so many troops that in the distance they looked like ants flooding down from an anthill.

"How many men do they believe it will take to keep your brother and I apart?" Glenna asked sarcastically.

But there was awe in Mairi's voice when she said, "He is the most powerful earl in the land, chancellor and council to your father the king. A travelling contingent such at that one commands instant reverence."

"Or fear," Glenna said, fully prepared to dislike this man who represented her father, her father who she had already decided she did not care for despite their shared blood. She knew nothing about this great earl except that everyone seemed to quiet when his name was mentioned. "Can men not understand that respect is earned?"

"I suspect the earl does not worry over such things. And respect is due and required by men of rank and birth. You have lived outside the life you live now. You did not see such on your small island. But our land is wild, and there are men who would change the way of things, men who would be cruel and murder and take what they want. In your father's stead, the earl alone is Scotland's great protector."

"Alone?" Glenna laughed. "He and his five hundred armed men?"

"Impressive, though it is to behold from here, that is but a travelling contingent. Were he coming for a battle there would be five times the number of riders, along with warriors on foot and a legion of archers." She paused and turned. "I have never heard that he is a cruel or unfair man, Glenna."

Glenna closed the shutters and said, "It matters not to me because I am prepared for battle."

"Aye. You have fire in your eyes." Mairi said and began to help her dress and braid her hair.

The earl and his men had long ridden through the gates when both women finished. Glenna stood fully dressed and coiffed, brushed and braided, decorated and standing in the center of the large chamber, her nerves growing raw, her heart beating too hard, a bead of sweat on her upper lip, and her mind thinking of a thousand possible answers.

A knock came at the door and Mairi answered it, saw Lyall and slipped out.

He stood there, tall and gloriously handsome, dressed in a rich, dark blue long tunic with gold design that was his own over dark hose and soft boots. His face was clean-shaven, his golden hair touched his shoulders, and heavy jeweled rings adorned his fingers on the hand he held out to her. His smile for her was clear. His love for her in his eyes.

Lud, how I adore this man.

"Come, love," he said easily. "We will face them together."

Without hesitation, Glenna reached for him. His warm hand closed over hers, and she was struck by a wonderful serge of power and sudden strength, and they walked toward the hall, and down the stairs side by side.

Before they reached the stairs, Lyall touched Glenna's hand and she glanced up quickly and gave him a smile—one he could see did not quite reach her eyes—then she looked straight ahead, her mouth in a thin line of determination though he knew , she was frightened. Her back was straight. Her chin was high.

"You are so beautiful," he said casually, not looking at her. "I am the most fortunate of men."

He felt her glance up at him, and he gave in looked down at her sweet face, something he could do for the rest of his days. From beneath feather-thick dark lashes, her eyes were so ebony that they looked as vast and fathomable as the deepest forest under a midnight sky. She chewed on her lip, her guard down.

He gave her wink and she recovered quickly, a clear smile on her lips. She gave an exaggerated sigh. "I would argue I am the most fortunate of woman. Who is the more fortunate?"

"Let me think," he said thoughtfully. "Perhaps we are both wrong and the most fortunate man in the world would be he who holds the heart of Old Gladdys."

Laughter burst from her, hearty and honest, and for a moment he thought her fear might have subsided. Lyall patted her hand reassuringly before they reached the bottom of the stairs. She was a grand sight, dressed to impress. She was breathtakingly lovely, the unforgettable kind of woman whose image was burned for an eternity in a man's mind. Like the Canmore she was born to be, she was the image of the regal daughter of a king in the gown she had clutched to her chest as she slept. The color could only be worn by those of the highest birth, crimson, and fitted of the finest velvet warped with silk, rare and woven with a discriminating Flemish skill and eye, expertly decorated with silver embroidery that hinted of his sister's fine stitches, trimmed in royal ermine and girdled over her rounded hips with a heavily hammered silver belt set with rubies.

Her black hair hung in stormy waves down her back and past

her buttocks, but the hair near her temples was drawn back in twists of thin braids decorated with red ribbands from which hung silver pendants in the shape of stars and drops of perfect white pearls the color of her pale skin. The pearls in her hair matched the wide necklace she wore around her throat: three tight stands of large, round pearls with a ruby set in the center, the necklace and the long jeweled belt gifts from his mother and the baron. He, too, had a gift for her, one he now wished he had given her, but 'twas too late.

At the bottom of the staircase, the cacophony of voices in the room slowly waned as many curious eyes lit upon them. The sudden silence grabbed the room's attention as quickly as the ringing of the supper bell. In the center of the great hall stood a tall, powerfully-built man with a stark white streak in his dark hair. Next to him were Lyall's mother and stepfather, and all were surrounded by clusters of retainers—Sutherland's contingent of knights along with the Montrose household knights and their ladies.

The great earl of Sutherland, Lord Chancellor ,Valan de Carleone looked up, then faced them. His wide earl's belt glinted in the light and his eyes immediately lit upon Glenna. His expression froze and the color drained from his face. "Cait?"

There was a frantic and sudden murmuring from many of the earl's men. Glenna stopped and looked behind her, then back again, frowning, but Lyall merely ignored the strange reactions and murmurs, stayed calm, and moved them closer.

Ramsey stepped up and pulled Glenna into the group. "Lady Glenna Canmore, my I present to you Lord Valan de Caleone, earl of Sutherland, Lord Chancellor of Scotland, and old friend and council to your father. Earl Valan, you remember my stepson Sir Lyall Roberson."

The earl had been studying Glenna as if he were seeing a ghost, but made a quick bow to her and acknowledged Lyall with

'Sir Ewane's son.' Lyall wasn't certain if he meant to insult or not, or perhaps considering why they were there, he meant to remind him exactly who he was.

But Lyall quickly gauged there was no intent, in fact the earl barely paid attention to him because he was so busy studying Glenna.

When the earl took her hand he said quietly, as if talking to himself," 'Tis uncanny."

"What is uncanny, my lord?" Glenna asked.

And his look was assessing, then he gave a slight smile and shook his head. "Just fancy, my lady. An old man's eyes play dark tricks. Come with me. I believe we need to speak privately." He threaded her arm over his and gave Ramsey a nod, asked for two of his knights to accompany him. "And you Robertson."

An urge came over him to tear her from Earl Valan's arm, to place his body between them and shout that this was all his fault, but his stepfather was talking to him, asking a casual question and demanding his attention and walking close to his side. His guard? Lyall made a vague comment, but never took his eyes off of Glenna, watching her straight shoulders and stiff spine, her chin unduly high in the presence of her father's most powerful ally and friend, attuned to her nerves, her every motion and look. Lyall did not want her hurt. She was trying to be his champion. They all walked casually through the hall—a designed parade to keep tongues from wagging—and went into a room off the main hall, where there were many candles lit, a table with benches and two tall heavily carved chairs at either end. A ewer sat at each end and a tray of goblets. Two squires in the earl's colors were already positioned unobtrusively in the back corners, and the knights stood back as the earl led Glenna to a seat at his right, gestured for Ramsey to take the other end and for Lyall to sit on his left.

"Ramsey tells me quite a story about the two of you." The earl raised a hand by the ewer and each of the squires moved swiftly to the table, pouring and serving the undiluted wine while the Earl Valan settled in and leaned back in his chair, fingers on one hand drumming on the table.

Not a good sign, though his voice was even and without animosity or anger, and Lyall wondered if that might be all the worse for them. The look Glenna wore was stubbornly intent and he loved her for it, but he rose and spoke before anyone else. "I have acted foolishly and have been driven by my past and my desires. Glenna was a victim." Lyall gave her smile. "She has championed me, to save me from the consequences of my actions, and has forgiven my lapse in good sense."

Earl Valan gave him an arched look that questioned his choice of words and demanded plain speak.

Lyall raised his hand. "She calls it a lapse. I know what I have done is most serious. I failed and betrayed my stepfather, you, and my king." He paused. "And her, the one who holds my heart, my today and my tomorrow." The look they exchanged sent a pang of meaning through him and the realization she was his reason for living. He did not take his eyes off of her as he continued. "She is my wife, in body and heart and mind, and I swear on my own black soul it is I who will defend her best because I will do so with my life. I would give everything I have, down to my blood and bone, to live out my time on this earth with her by my side, so I will not step away, as I was asked."

Her smile softened. Without her, there was nothing. He faced Sutherland. "Know this...there is no other man who will protect her as I will." He tapped his heart with a fist. "So dear she is to me."

The earl was an experienced diplomat and his face revealed nothing. "Glenna believes that she can save me, because I am now her husband and she is the daughter of the king." He looked down, laughing in self-deprecation. "But the truth is: what is between us is my greatest gift and I would willingly hang tomorrow knowing that she has been mine for these few days."

Her expression told him that his words troubled her, and she slightly shook her head, warning him to stop.

"You can take me away, my lord," Lyall vowed. "You can lock me up, shackle me to castle gates, stick my sorry head on a pike or draw and quarter me, but I will not deny her. Glenna Canmore is my wife for my life." He paused. "However long that may be."

The thought of losing her, thus losing the man he could be, made his eyes burn and he looked away...unfortunately, right into the intense and thoughtful face of his stepfather.

Was that compassion he saw? If so, he deserved none.

Glenna stood abruptly and faced the earl. "You tell me I am the daughter of the king. Then hear me when I say we are wed. You harm my husband and you harm me." She flattened her hands on the table and leaned forward. "He *is* my husband."

Earl Valan laughed softly and shook his head. "Why do I think you want to add 'you oaf' to your last comment?"

Her brow creased but she said, "You think you know me that well?" She laughed without humor and moved to the window, leaned against the wall not looking at any of them.

"I know I saw a sudden gleam in your eyes, and you moved away to hide it from me. Know you this. I have been called such names many times, my lady. I understand you more than you can fathom."

Glenna refused to look at the earl, but stood with her arms crossed, her shoulder against the open shutter.

Lyall spoke from his heart, but he was at a loss now of what else he could say, and he sat down and took a sip of wine, hoping to calm things somewhat while his mind searched for another way to persuade them.

"I would not condone what my son has done, my lord," Ramsey interjected. "I would say that he has acted without thought and selfishly. But he has taken something valuable from all he has done. I believe I know Lyall, perhaps better than he knows himself.

Consider this: there are those who would say he does not have the wealth or position due a man wed to the daughter of a king. I would petition now, at this moment, to make him my heir."

Hearing that was like being hit in the head with a flail. Lyall expected to argue with Ramsey for him to not dissolve their marriage...not to hear defense and support for him, support he did not deserve and was difficult to hear. He stared into this wine goblet.

Anger he could defy. Kindness? He wanted to hang his head with shame at his actions, at how he had let bitterness consume him, and with that shame came a great regret. To be standing there now, so clear eyed and aware of what he knew he wanted, and aware of how he wasted it and risked his future, was strangely comforting. He had no doubts. He wasn't fighting his conscience, perhaps because this time what he wanted was not about his pride. With Glenna, his pride was not all twisted up inside of his desires.

The earl gave his stepfather a direct look. "Well and good, Ramsey. However, we are not here to debate whether he is suitable."

"Nay, you are here to dictate the validity of our marriage," Glenna said quickly. "To twist and turn my life so that I cannot follow my heart but understand my worth is only to be bartered to assist the Crown. My marriage is sacred to me. A handfast is the law of the land."

"That is true, were you not who you are. There *is* no royal marriage without witnesses. That, my dear, is the law as it pertains to you."

"What would have happened, had I, Glenna Gordon, wed a sheep farmer before my father the king decided I could come out of hiding?"

Lyall had to look away. The idea of her wed to a sheep farmer almost made him laugh out loud.

"You believe that such was possible?" The earl looked amused. "You believe you were free to marry a pig farmer?"

"Sheep farmer," she said tightly.

" 'Twould never have happened, my lady, and I prefer not to waste words arguing over the impossible."

"I did not think any of us was wasting words. But I would now question the truthfulness of the stories we have heard about the grand romance of my parents. Was it a grand romance? Is only my father allowed to marry for great love? And if I am my father's daughter, is not fighting for my right to the man I love in my very blood?"

Now there, Lyall thought, was the best question.

The earl watched her for a long time. Glenna was trying desperately to make him angry. He did not bluster and order them about, a sign of how Sutherland had risen to his high position. The man was thoughtful, and Lyall had to admire him.

"Watching you, my lady, I wonder…" Earl Valan said quietly. "You are quite fearless."

"Thank you."

"That was not a compliment," the earl said bluntly. "You are also quite willing to speak your mind." When she started to speak he held up his hand. "Also not a compliment. It has been my experience that speaking out is not the best way for a woman to get what she desires."

"Neither is becoming a mute, and I did not know you had experience as a woman speaking out, my lord earl."

Lyall bit back a laugh but his stepfather did not and Ramsey shook his head, still laughing. "She has you there, Valan."

The earl exchanged an interesting look with his stepfather that gave Lyall a heartbeat of hope. To Glenna, the earl said, "You might be better served with a husband to watch over you." He turned his thoughtful eyes on Lyall and studied him, then sat back in his chair. "Speaking of blood relations, my lady, you are very much like your sister."

"My sister?"

That had gotten Glenna's attention.

"Aye. Lady Caitrin has been my ward for all these years."

"Was she lied to also?" Glenna asked bitterly.

"Like you, she, too, recently discovered the truth, and she has made her thoughts known to me," the earl said calmly, refusing to give rise to Glenna's clear baiting. "Her new husband must deal with her opinions."

"New husband? So she was pawned off for the sake of the Crown? She might easily accept that fate, but I will not be so meek and biddable."

The earl choked on his wine and coughed and wheezed until one of his knights slapped him hard on the back, and he slowly recovered, his face going from bright red to a flush. He cleared his throat and said, "The choices your father made were difficult ones. I was there. I saw what he went through. His actions and orders were for your protection."

"What you call protection, I call lies, Earl Valan. Why could we have not known the truth and still been kept safe?"

"You are young. The truth could never be worth the risk. You do not know the extent to which your very existence could have fueled the struggle for the right to the Crown. Your father's enemies would see you married off to the kind of man who would control you and your father for their motives. I can assure you that would most unpleasant. Your father is also your king. Until you understand what he has faced, you cannot understand what he had to do. You have been raised in obscurity and what we believed was safety. You do not like that your identity was kept secret? Only someone who knows little of the world would want a life filled with only truths."

"As I see it, my lord, the king is not here. But if he were, I would argue to him what I have said to you. However, here or in exile, neither he nor you will dissolve my marriage. And trust, my lord earl, there are many secrets you do not know about me," she added.

Lyall understood what she was saying. Her brothers would never betray her or themselves and admit freely of their life of thievery. Earl Valan had not seen the plunder inside that cottage, and he was not privy to Glenna's skill at what had been her occasional profession. As Lyall watched his wife, he had the strong feeling that she deserved to keep her own secrets.

Long minutes passed in silence as earl Valan appeared to study the table, then his stepfather. No words were spoken and the air in the room began to vibrate, like before a great battle. Finally Earl Valan looked at Glenna and said, "I—"

The door rattled thunderously with someone pounding on it and one of Sutherland's knights opened the door. Alastair Gordon rushed inside, pushing past the knight and ignoring everyone and out of breath, waving a rolled parchment. "Glenna!" His face broke out into a wide grin. "I have it! We have brought your proof!"

THIRTY-FOUR

Alastair was here. He was here. Glenna took the parchment from him and threw her arms about him, whispering under her breath, "It took you long enough." She turned and approached the earl with the swagger of a conquering warrior. "You say a royal marriage must be witnessed. You claim if there is a witness, the marriage stands?"

She lay the parchment down on the rough hewn table, rolled it open and pressed down. "Here, my lord. Before you is the witnessed document, scribed at the abbey at Beauly, and sealed by the prior himself."

Lyall was right behind her and he laughed under his breath, telling her he was aware that they had just taken their opponent's queen. His arm slipped around her waist as she straightened and he gave her a quick wink. She smiled and placed her hand on his shoulder.

Together they could do anything, she thought.

There was another commotion at the door and El appeared, his face excited, his smile wide. "Glenna! Glenna look! Look what we have brought you!"

She heard a strangely familiar scampering sound, then a familiar bark and her heart leapt in her chest and something joyous swelled in her. Glenna's hand fell from Lyall's shoulder as he stood abruptly. Then she heard Lyall finally say her hound's name under his breath, whispered almost like a prayer. Next she heard him shout it, "Fergus!"

Her hound leapt toward them both, huge and shaggy, high in the air. Through a blur of fresh tears she had a glimpse of a silly shaggy grin and a tail wagging, awkward feet flying...

Fergus sailed right past them, landing awkwardly on the top of the table, skidding and sliding, pawing the air and the table.

"Oh, lud! Fergus...." she called out, her voice drifting off in horror, her hands to her mouth as she watched the goblets spill left and right, and the ewer wobble and tilt from Fergus's huge cumbersome paws. The wine spread out like blood on a battlefield, pouring over the table and right onto the earl, while the loud clank of pewter goblets hitting the stone floor and rolling sounded around her.

Lyall pulled Fergus off the table as she knelt down in front of her hound and let him lick the tears from her flushed cheeks. "Fergus."

She pulled back and caught the wet glint in Lyall's eyes, and she thought of Mairi's story, of Lyall at ten, the young lad who could not save his father, his brother, their home, and finally a beloved dog he called Atholl, the last animal he had ever named because he carried that regret and sorrow and guilt of his failure all those years since. His bright red eyes were staring at the remnant of the arrow wound, a scabby deep dark hole covered in some kind of dried poultice. Her hand touched her hound and scratched his floppy ears, and exchanged a look of deep love with her husband. Neither was lost to her, as she had thought. Her happiness was sudden, a live thing, golden as that knight she had watched dive into the sea. All of it warmed her blood and brought more tears to spill down her face. She felt her brothers move to her side.

She swiped at her eyes and turned back to the action at the table, where the baron stood at the opposite end of, looking dumbfounded at the earl, who had not moved amidst all that had happened.

But his squires had. They were rushing with cloths, sopping up spilt wine and scrambling to wipe the mess while the Lord Chancellor sat with his hands out in front of him, staring down at the wet red wine stains spreading over his tunic and earl's belt. One of the squires bent toward the floor, then straightened, holding up the sodden parchment in his fingers as wine mixed with dark bleeding ink and dripped from the edges of the now illegible document. Only the prior's circular seal was still visible, and it was slowly melting away, taking with it the most dangerous emotion to believe in—hope.

Glenna gasped, panicked. "You did read the document, my lord. You saw it was witnessed."

"Nay," the earl said, standing and frowning, "but—"

"It matters not because the witness is here." The prior was standing in the doorway, watching, a wry smile on his lips.

Alastair leaned closer and said under his breath, "He is why we took so long. The man travels on an ass that moves as quickly as a sloth."

There was hope again, still dangerous, but there all the same. She threaded her arm through his, gave him a grateful kiss on his rough cheek and said, "Thank you."

" 'Twas his idea, once he heard why we were there. An abbey like Beauly needs patronage. I imagine the opportunity to score the fat purses of Montrose and Sutherland was all too tempting."

Ramsey had joined the earl. "I am sorry for the chaos, Valan."

"I reek of wine." The earl shook his head and gave a wry laugh. "My own household makes this look calm, Donnald."

"I, too, am sorry, my lord. I had thought my hound lost to me. But we are here about my marriage. I would have your decision now," Glenna said to Earl Valan. "Surely you will not question the witness of the prior. To do so would question the validity of every marriage in the land. You cannot deny the Church. The only better witness would be my father."

"Or myself," the earl said and Glenna dared not hope he meant what she thought.

"You will wed here and now," he continued. "A ceremony with Montrose and myself as witnesses and standing for your father. I am certain the prior will be more than pleased to wed the two of you."

They had won. Glenna's face broke into a huge smile.

Lyall stood and glanced at his stepfather, who nodded, and then gave the earl a slight bow of respect. "Thank you, my lord. You will not regret your decision."

"Nay," the earl said and clasped Lyall's arm in friendship. "But if Lady Glenna is anything like her headstrong sister, my Cait, you might live to regret yours."

The candles on the wall prickets had long since burned down and the moon was bright silver and could be seen through the arched window of their bedchamber, dominating a dark, clear sky filled with enough stars to make one believe in things like redemption, love and God. The wind had started and awakened him. Even now he could hear the whistle of it across the battlements outside.

From the carpet near the bed came a slight canine snore. Fergus slept on his side, contented in contrast to the deep wound that was still visible and haunting. That the Gordons had come upon him in their search for Glenna and taken him to the abbey was what had saved him.

He lay back on the goosedown pillows with a sigh, crossing his arms behind his head, his bare hip still touching his wife's. Relaxed. The part of him that could never truly rest, that tenseness he'd carried deep inside of him for so long was gone. Love filled him like the swelling of the wind outside, and he took a deep breath of contentment. The scent of roses and woman filled his senses.

Mairi and his mother had placed wildflowers, ivy, and roses in vases and urns all over the room, and a hundred candles had lit the room when they'd finally escaped the celebration in the hall below and locked themselves away from the rest of the world. A pitcher of wine and bowls of dried fruit, nuts and apples were on that table. Next to the bed, the fattest candle, chapel candles that could burn for days, sat on the nearby table, next to a vase of deep, dark red roses, the last of them to bloom this year this mother had said.

His wife lay next to him in his bed, asleep, wearing only his wedding gift to her, a silver diadem he had made and set with stones he had won years back in a tourney in Normandy, and a drop in the center of a large and perfect pearl he had found in the River Tay, on a night when he had understood what love was.

This night, as she knelt before him, he had set it on her head in place of the flower bridal wreath she had worn when she came through the door to the chapel at Rossi, where earlier all had witnessed their vows and final bond. He stared up at the bed canopy, lost in thought. A sudden buzzing sounded and before he could move, a bee lit on the underside of his arm. He froze, watched it walk slowly across his skin and waited for the inevitable stung.

But nothing happened. The bee flew off, and crawled inside the center of one of the roses by the bed and disappeared.

"You look pleased and content," Glenna said sleepily, and she moved closer, comfortable enough with him to have flung one bare leg over his, settling her head against his shoulder, her breast heavy against his ribs.

He touched her, let her softness fill his hand, then he turned and covered her body with his, settling between her legs. "I am content, wife," he said. "And you look hungry."

"I am." She linked her arms around his neck and smiled, the kind of smile he could live inside and never want for another thing…his Glenna, his wife, the woman whose faith in him restored his trust and his belief in the good of the world. She was the thief who had stolen his horse, and his heart, and saved him from himself. He smiled. The light in her eyes said it all: she was looking up at him as if she expected something wonderful to happen.

But for Lyall, something wonderful already had.

AUTHOR'S NOTE

I'm a writer who researches meticulously, and I often find my story within the wonderful pages of history. But not this idea, which came to me many years ago. The idea did not exactly fit, so I set it aside. Eventually its call became too great for me to ignore.

For the sake of telling a work of fiction in my own way, I have played somewhat with history. William the Lion of Scotland did not have three daughters or a Norse wife who died in childbirth. However, there is history of multiple births, as many as live quintuplets, well before this time, and writings sited everything from a woman having seven birth chambers (and the possibility of birthing septuplets) to the cause of multiple births being tied to how much pleasure she engaged in during the sexual act.

As for William's long exile, he did rise up against Henry and lost that battle. There were hostages held for severe ransoms, including the sons of the rebellious Scots—a good reason to hide your children who would surely be pawns. Kings were the most valuable, and Henry Plantagenet needed money to secure his expansion. And there were warring factions for the crown throughout Scotland's history as well as in much of Europe, because the succession in those days was not always clear, as exampled in France, where the live king would announce his successor. A crown was not easily passed to sons or even eldest sons, as we saw in both earlier and later time periods.

Interestingly, at some points in history, the first born sons of the ruling king's daughters could be heir to the throne. A king's daughter was just that—a king's daughter. While there were royal princes, there were no princesses. The title did not exist until the 14th Century. Often the right to rule was passed down on strange whims and reasons only those at the time could probably justify, much of it having to with force, power, the Church, factions, blood, and allies.

I extended William's exile for the dramatic sake of my story, and I gave him a romantic history and three secret daughters. This story is set in Twelfth Century Scotland, which was Norman at the time. (The Scottish clan system as we know it in later periods did not come into play until the thirteenth century). It was a time of power struggles, a time of war, battles, treachery, and difficult compromises, a time when treaties were broken. To even hold onto power was extremely difficult with numerous enemy factions having royal ties to other parts of Europe.

Let's talk about pearls coming from mussels. Pearls from the River Tay have importance in history, too. Julius Caesar sited one of the reasons Rome invaded Britain was for the Scottish pearl trade. Pearls as well as gold were the basis for the Roman monetary system, and the size and quality of the pearls from the Scottish river mussels were exceptional. These fine, fresh-water pearls are still to this day displayed in the crown jewels of many countries, including Great Britain.

Writers often have to juggle the truth of history with what the average person believes is true. As time moves forward, and more and more historians, especially female historians, find new clues to life long ago, we will continue to make that history come alive on the pages. For thirty years I've always tried to be as accurate as possible in my books, even down to actual period character names. This is the first time I have felt the need to bend history for the best story I could tell, and I hope you feel it was worth the bending.

—Jill Barnett.

ACKNOWLEDGMENTS

No book is easy to write and it often takes a village to complete. I've been fortunate to have some wonderful village people. My friend Kristin Hannah, whose constant encouragement and belief in this story and in me is something I cherish. I'm so thankful for that cocktail party thirty years ago.

I've known Barbara Samuel for a long time. She is a brilliant artist with both words and brushes, and her discerning eye, writer's insight, and kind praise allowed me to make the final book the best it could be.

My sincerest thanks to Doris Cairns and Pat Riha, good friends whose sharp eyes caught those sneaky mistypes and missing words. Bless you both.

To my Jewels of Historical Romance sisters for sharing their knowledge and experiences in this unwieldy new age of publishing, Tanya Anne Crosby, Glynnis Campbell, Cynthia Wright, Kimberly Cates, Cheryl Bolen, Brenda Hiatt, Laurin Wittig, Colleen Gleason, Annette Blair, Lucinda Brant and Lauren Royal. You ladies are the best.

Lastly, I must thank my daughter Kasey and her husband Tom who made it easy for me to find the joy in writing again. I love you both.

ABOUT THE AUTHOR

New York Times Bestselling Author Jill Barnett is master storyteller known for her beautifully-written love stories rich with humor, emotion, and poignancy. In addition to the critical acclaim and numerous awards she has received, her books have been named Best of the Year, earned starred reviews, and have been published in 23 languages worldwide and appeared on numerous bestseller lists. She lives in the Pacific Northwest with her family.

Learn more at
www.jillbarnettbooks.com

Made in the USA
San Bernardino, CA
26 October 2017